Spectrum Guide to
NEPAL

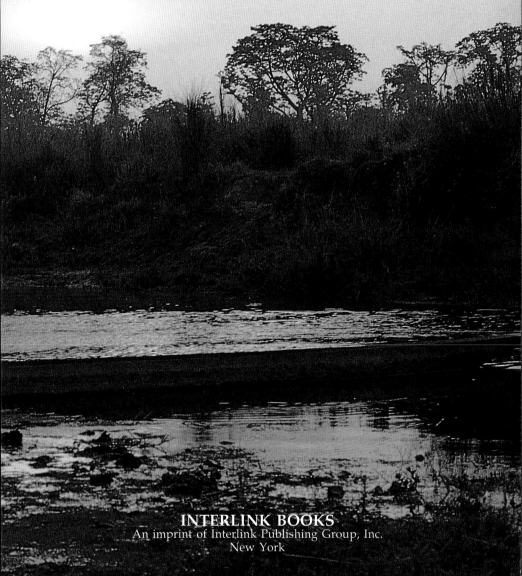

INTERLINK BOOKS
An imprint of Interlink Publishing Group, Inc.
New York

Spectrum Guide to Nepal

First American edition published
in 2000 by

INTERLINK BOOKS
An imprint of
Interlink Publishing Group, Inc.
99 Seventh Avenue
Brooklyn, New York 11215
and
46 Crosby Street
Northampton, Massachusetts 01060

This book was designed and produced by
Camerapix Publishers International,
PO Box 45048
Nairobi, Kenya.

To order or request a catalog, please call
Interlink Publishing at 1-800-238-LINK

Website: www.interlinkbooks.com

Library of Congress Cataloging-in-Publication Data

Spectrum guide to Nepal/compiled and
edited by Camerapix.
        p. cm. – (The Spectrum guides)
    Includes bibliographical references and
    index
    ISBN 1-56656-332-1 (pbk.)
    1. Nepal—Guidebooks. I. Camerapix
Publishers International.
    II. Title: Nepal. III. Series
    DS493.3.S64 1999   99-41838
    915.49604—dc21   CIP

Printed and bound in Singapore.

The **Spectrum Guide** series provides a
comprehensive and detailed description
of each country covered, together with all
the essential data that tourists, business
visitors, or potential investors are likely
to require.

Spectrum Guides in print:
African Wildlife Safaris
Ethiopia
India
Jordan
Kenya
Maldives
Mauritius
Namibia
Oman
Pakistan
Seychelles
South Africa
Sri Lanka
Tanzania
Uganda
United Arab Emirates
Zambia
Zimbabwe

Founding Publisher: The late Mohamed Amin
Editorial Director: Rukhsana Haq
Picture Editor: Duncan Willetts
Editor: Joy Ma
Production Editors: Jan Hemsing and
Roger Barnard
Graphic Designer: Rachel Musyimi and
Adam Nyakundi
Cartographer: Terry Brown
Photographic Research: Abdul Rahman

Editorial Board

Spectrum Guide to Nepal is the latest in the acclaimed series of high-quality, lavishly illustrated and immaculately researched international *Spectrum Guides* to exotic and exciting destinations, cultures, flora and fauna.

When it comes to the exotic, the unusual, the fascinating, the colourful, the exciting and the adventurous, nothing beats Nepal for the sheer variety of its attractions — from the world's highest mountains to the serene lowland beauty of the birthplace of The Buddha.

There are also many forbidden, virtually inaccessible corners of this land of the Sherpa and the Gurkha that only recently came out of the shadows of its centuries-old self-imposed isolation from the rest of the world

Few, if any, guidebooks but *Spectrum* — which with field trips and research has been 10 years in the making — take you to every far-flung, hidden corner of this awesomely beautifully, stunningly spectacular nation.

Most of the pictures are from the cameras of **Duncan Willets**, renowned among his peers for his superb photographic craftsmanship and the **late Mohamed Amin**, who was perhaps the world's most famous and respected photographer and news cameraman. They roamed far and wide capturing unforgettable images of Nepal.

But the text of *Spectrum Guide to Nepal* is largely the work of Editor **Joy J Ma**, an American-based Nepali, who contributed the most substantial part of the text and provided the insights only a Nepali can.

She also wedded together a formidable team of authorities on every aspect of Nepal — from its mountains to its teeming, colourful cultures, wildlife and botanical glories.

Editorial Director **Rukhsana Haq** organised the complex liaison and logistics involved in such a long-term project. Former Editorial Director the **late Brian Tetley**, who fell in love with Nepal during his first visit in the early 1980s when he wrote *Journey through Nepal*, worked in the early stages with Joy J Ma's meticulous copy, supplementing it — where needed — with his own contribution.

At the same time *Spectrum Guides'* team of Nepal-based experts stamped their knowledge across the rest of the guide's pages.

Foremost among these is Joy's brother, **William Ma**, who runs Lama Excursions and wildlife resorts in the Tera and has contributed much to the growth of the country's tourism industry.

Others whose extensive knowledge and love of Nepal enlightens these pages are **Dubby Bhagat**, **Rajendra Sharma** and **Arun Pokharel**.

London-based Editor **Roger Barnard** edited the finished text and Editor **Jan Hemsing** undertook responsibility for maintaining *Spectrum Guides'* in-house style.

Design was in the hands of Nairobi-based **Rachel Musyimi** and **Adam Nyakundi**. Through it all, veteran **Abdul Rahman** organised photographic research. Finally, Production Assistants **Maryann Muiruri** and **Azra Chaudhry** co-ordinated the preparation of manuscripts and listings.

TABLE OF CONTENTS

IN BRIEF

LISTINGS

MAPS

Half title: Bronze door with intricate design. Title Page: Sundown frames bombax trees over Royal Chitwan National Park. Following pages: 29,028-foot Everest, including jagged ridges of 27,890-foot Lhotse at right; Verdant rice field north of Pokhara, with the pyramid peak of sacred Machhapuchhare rising 22,944 feet above sea level; Array of umbrellas provides shelter from sun and shower for guards and workers in Royal Chitwan National Park.

TIBET

API

● Simikot

G R E A T

Seti

Khapted N.P.

Rara N.P.

Shey-Phoksundo
National Park

● Sanfebagar

● Jumla

● Lo Mar

● Siliguri Doti

Karnali

M
A
H
A
B
H
A
R
A
T
A

H
I
M
A
L

● Jomsom

●Mahendranagar

Royal
Suklaphanta
N.P.

● Dhangadi

● Surkhet

Dorpatan
Hunting
Reserve

▲ DHAULAGIRI

▲ ANNAPURNA

Royal
Bardia
N.P.

C
H
U
R
I
A

Baglung ●

SIDDHARTHA HIGHWAY

Sarda

◉ NEPALGUNJ

● Dang

MAHENDRA HIGHWAY

R
A
N
G
E

Tansen ●
Palpa ●

Kali G

N

G
E

◉ BUTWAL

● Tilaurakot

Lumbini ●

◉ BHAIRAHAWA

LUCKNOW ◉

◉ GORAKHPUR

Ghaghara

To Delhi

Nepal

Ganges

| 0 | 25 | 50 | 75 | 100 | 125 | 150 | 175 | 200 km |

| 0 | 20 | 40 | 60 | 80 | 100 | 120 miles |

I N D I A

Ganges

VARANASI ◉

14

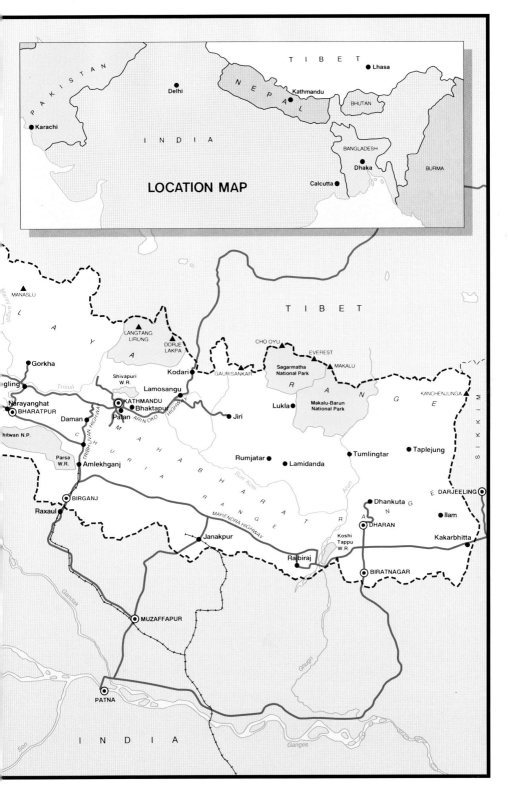

LOCATION MAP

The Nepal Experience

Sunburst over the Himalaya is unlike anything else on this earth. Suddenly the glittering diamonds of light on the ice-caps of Everest and its attendant cohorts, Lhotse and Makalu turn to a molten gold that bathes the world's highest glaciers with its warmth.

That sunny warmth is reflected in the smiling faces of its happy citizens everywhere you go in this riotously colourful country.

It is reflected, too, in the dazzling blooms of its temperate and semi-tropical flowers, in the joyful release of its many mighty rivers as they spring from their mountain birthplaces and in the chorus of birdsong that greets each new-born day.

This land of gods and goddesses is a daily celebration of life, a land where the reality of poverty is dismissed with a shrug of the shoulders — and concealed behind the words of greeting and the warmth of welcome shown to any peace-loving stranger.

No wonder Nepal — so often like a country still in the Middle Ages — is by its own calendar more than half a century ahead of the rest of the world. In 1999 the Nepalese were already embarked on the second half of the 21st century for in Kathmandu the year was already 2056.

And daily time is different from the rest of the world. Nepal's clocks are 15 minutes ahead of India, which counts its hours when the rest of the world counts the half-hour. If this sounds illogical, so be it, for Nepal is a classic demonstration of non-conformism and love of life.

From its ancient capital of Kathmandu, through the mountains and down to its sweltering lowland plains, it is one of the most compelling and awesomely beautiful countries in the world.

Catch the glimmer of the sun in the dappled shade of a rhododendron forest, or the smile on the face of a young beauty tending the family rice paddy, and enchantment is complete. A return to Nepal after a first visit is inevitable. It is a land whose people and magic constantly summon you back.

And always on the horizon, above your line of vision in this land of vertical perspectives, is the Roof of the World — mountains of such immensity and grandeur that no photograph can do them proper justice, for truly Nepal is a land that has to be seen to be believed.

A land where the extremes of polar ice and tropical sunshine are never far away for Nepal is all length and no breadth.

You can comfortably drive across it, from Indian to Tibetan border or vice-versa — through one of a few mountain passes with roads — in a single day.

But if you wish to traverse the length of Nepal above the Terai Plains be prepared for challenges that have never confronted you before. For great areas of the country are virtually inaccessible to all but the most intrepid mountaineer or trekker.

In some places only a single ledge carved out of a sheer cliff hundreds, sometimes thousands, of feet above a raging river — where one misstep means instant death — is the only way forward.

And yet, within the comparatively gentle folds of its midland mountains, undulating between 7,000 and 10,000 feet, are fairy-tale towns that seem to have been plucked from the Middle Ages.

While everywhere you go, among Nepal's Hindi-speaking lowlanders or the kindly but fearsome Gurkhas, Sherpas and Tibetans of the highlands, you will find the hand of friendship.

For the Nepalese have always believed that, invited or uninvited, 'a guest is a god in disguise'.

A belief symbolised, when the hands are clasped in gentle salute to the stranger, by the traditional greeting 'Namaste'.

Welcome.

Opposite: Sifting seed and grain in Khokana village near Kathmandu.

Travel Brief and Social Advisory

Some do's and don'ts to make your visit more enjoyable.

Getting There

By air

There are two ways to Nepal — by road or by air. The air journey is the more comfortable.

More than 90 per cent of Nepal's visitors arrive at Nepal's Tribhuvan International Airport, eight kilometres (five miles) from Kathmandu.

The modern terminal is a far cry from the chaotic old buildings of times gone by.

A number of international airlines operate scheduled services to Nepal including the national flag carrier, Royal Nepal Airlines Corporation (RNAC); Bangladesh Biman; Burma Airways Corporation (BAC); China Airlines (CAAC); Dragon Air; Indian Airlines; Lufthansa; Pakistan International Airlines; Royal Bhutan Airlines; Singapore Airlines; and Thai International Airlines.

The western route flies from Europe and the eastern United States with a stop-over in New Delhi or other Indian city. The eastern route, which originates on the west coast of the United States, or from Australia and other East Asian countries, has stopovers at Hong Kong, Singapore, and Bangkok.

By law all air fares purchased by foreigners must be paid for in foreign currency. You may need to use this for domestic fares instead of pre-booking because many special fares are available only in Kathmandu.

Since air fares change with the fluctuation of the exchange rate you should check with a travel agent before purchasing a ticket. Nepalese and Indian travellers can pay with rupees.

If the skies are clear there is no more exciting flight in the world. Left-seated passengers on west to east flights to Kathmandu see in succession Gurja Himal, 7,193 metres (23,600 ft); Dhaulagiri I, 8,167 metres (26,795 ft); the deep, dark, eight-kilometre (five-mile) gorge of the Kali Gandaki river leading north to Mustang; the six peaks of the Annapurna Range; Manaslu, 8,158 metres (26,766 ft); and the three lumps of Ganesh Himal, 7,406 metres (24,298 ft), that dominate the Kathmandu Valley.

Right-seated passengers on west to east flights to the Nepali capital see, in succession, Kanchenjunga, 8,598 metres (28,208 ft) on the border with Sikkim; Makalu, 8,481 metres (27,825 ft); Everest, 8,848 metres (29,028 ft); Cho Oyu, 8,153 metres (26,750 ft); Gaurisankar, 7,144 metres (23,438 ft); Dorje Lhakpa, 6,966 metres (22,855 ft); and, finally, standing above the Kathmandu Valley, Langtang Lirung, 7,245 metres (23,769 ft).

Regional flights operated by Indian Airlines also connect Kathmandu with Calcutta, Patna, and Varanasi; Bangladesh Biman has a flight to Dhaka; Burma Airways flies into Rangoon; Druk Air takes a weekly flight to Paro, and Southwest China Airlines operates a weekly flight to Lhasa.

There are two daily services to Delhi, and one to Varanasi (Benares); 10 weekly services to Dhaka; nine to Calcutta and Bangkok; four to Rangoon and Hong Kong; three to Karachi; two to Colombo, Singapore, and Patna; and one to Dubai. Between Nepal and India, Nepali and Indian nationals fly at reduced rates. International pasengers pay a departure tax.

By road

You can travel by land through the Indo-Gangetic Plain from Delhi, passing through a great chunk of rural northern India or from the north by trekking over the Tibetan plateau and then down through the Himalaya. Either way, it means tough travel. From India by utilitarian bus or jeep and from Tibet either by jeep and bus and foot. Both journeys will illustrate the way

Opposite: Four of the many faces of Nepal.

Above: The wide vistas from a bus window will often compensate for the crush inside.

most people in the subcontinent and its neighbours travel.

A popular overland route is from New Delhi through a combination of train and bus rides to Sanauli. You can take the Delhi-Lucknow-Gorakhpur train. From Gorakhpur it is a one-hour ride to the border.

There you will find buses leaving in the morning and evening — it is a 12-hour journey into Kathmandu. Most buses stop at Narayanghat on the Trisuli river and Mugling where drivers tuck into generous helpings of a Nepali staple, *dal-bhaat*.

From Darjeeling you need to reach Siliguri by rail or road, take a jeep ride to Kakarvita and from there to Birgunj. Other routes originate from the Indian cities of Gorakhpur and Patna.

If your journey takes you from Nepal to India you will need a visa to enter through any border post. Ask for a multiple entry visa if you plan to return to Nepal.

Four border posts exist along the India-Nepal border while one is along the China-Nepal boundary: Rani Sikiyahi south of

Biratnagar; Birgunj, near Raxaul, India (a popular entry point for overland travellers); Kodari, on the China border (travellers there need a Chinese visa with a road permit into Lhasa); Sanauli, on the road to Pokhara; and Kakarvita, a common entry point for travellers from Darjeeling, Siliguri and Kalimpong in India.

To enter Nepal by private car is often more trouble than it is worth. You need a *carnet de passage en douanes* for cars and motorbikes which will exempt you from customs for three months. To do this you may have to endure hours of the rubber-stamp red tape — if the British invented bureaucracy the Indians perfected it — that characterizes any formalities at an Indian border before you can enter Nepal.

An unexpired driver's licence is a must. And, as in India, cars are driven on the left side of the road.

By Rail

India runs frequent rail passenger services throughout India including trains to the Nepal border. But there are only two lines in Nepal. The 47-kilometre (30-mile) line between Raxaul, India, and Amlekhganj, built in 1925, is no longer used. The only line still working in Nepal, just for freight, built in 1940, runs for a brief 27 kilometres (17 miles) through Janakpur.

By Road and Rail

The combined rail–road route to Nepal from Delhi offers two real options — the others being far too time-consuming, boring and too much of a hassle for most. The quickest route is via Gorakhpur, while the other allows an interesting stopover in Varanasi.

From either city, buses make their way to Kathmandu or Pokhara via Sunauli. This route allows the option of visiting Lumbini, Buddha's birthplace, which is close to Sunauli.

If travelling on to Kathmandu, it means you can also stop over at Narayanghat and visit Royal Chitwan National Park, just two hours away by local transport. Similarly, the combined rail–road route to Nepal from Calcutta offers two interesting alternatives — via Muzaffapur or Patna — with bus connections to Kathmandu via Birganj.

The journey takes about 36 hours. By ferry from Muzaffapur, across the Ganges to Patna, takes approximately 90 minutes. Any other suggested routes to the Nepali border from India simply aren't worth the effort or aggravation.

If you insist on the hassle, however, then from Darjeeling there's a train to Siliguri, followed by a 60-minute taxi drive to Kakar Bhitta where you can catch a bus to Kathmandu.

Two advantages of this route are the ride on the miniature Darjeeling railway followed by a road journey through almost 400 kilometres (250 miles) of the Terai, including panoramic views of the Siwalik Hills.

You need a special permit to enter Darjeeling (including Commonwealth passport holders). And on your return from Nepal remember that you'll need an Indian visa to enter India through a border post.

Visas

All visitors except Indian and Bhutanese nationals require a visa and must carry a

Above: Welcome to Nepal.

valid passport and proof of inoculation against cholera and yellow fever. A single entry visa to Nepal — covering Kathmandu Valley, Pokhara and other major towns — costs UK£20 or US$35 for 30 days and should be obtained in advance from the nearest Nepalese Embassy.

If you don't have a visa, a 15-day one should be issued at Tribhuvan International airport for US$35 for all foreign nationals. These visas can be extended to the full 15-day period at no extra cost.

Trekking permits must be obtained for treks away from the main highways. You can get them from the Central Immigration Office of the Home and Panchayat Ministry at Kathmandu. After the first month visas may be extended for up to three months from the date of your initial arrival. The rates vary.

To stay longer you need approval from the Home Ministry. Visa extensions are available at the Department of Immigration Kathmandu. Office hours are 1000-1600, Monday–Saturday. The office is closed on Sundays and holidays. You will need to

Above: Locals will sit on top, or hang onto the back of an already overfull bus.
Opposite: Traditional way of carrying children, strapped to the mother's back.

take your passport and two passport-size photographs.

Extensions are normally granted on proof that you have exchanged the currency equivalent of US $10 a day for the length of the extension. You will need your currency card or Foreign Exchange Encashment Receipt.

It is best to get a multi-entry visa if you plan additional trips outside Nepal.

Visitors with trekking permits — 65 rupees a week — can extend their visa at no additional cost. Visitors wishing to cross the border at the Friendship Bridge to the Tibetan town of Khasa need a visa — a fairly easy process — from the Chinese Embassy, Kathmandu.

Getting Around

Getting around Kathmandu is generally a breeze. People are friendly when asked for directions or advice. If you speak English you will have no problem getting taxis, shopping or arranging for travel in the city.

Practically everyone connected with the tourist trade speaks English including the shopkeepers. You may also find the exceptional Japanese, German or French speaker in your travels.

It is not necessary to have an in-depth knowledge of Nepali, unless you plan to travel extensively in the rural areas. But knowing beyond the few working phrases of the language will open doors in your dealings with the Nepali people.

As a rule it is always better to travel with a companion, but if you decide to travel on your own Nepal is probably the safest place you could hope for. Women travelling on their own are not harassed. As a precaution, however, you should register with your consulate on your arrival.

Crime is almost non-existent. Petty crime is much less than you would find in any other city the same size as Kathmandu. However it is always recommended to stay alert when walking around and to keep your valuables safely locked in your hotel.

By air

Flying is the quickest way of travelling to different regions. The national flag carrier, Royal Nepal Airlines has a monopoly on domestic flights and runs an extensive network with a fleet of 44-seat Avro 748s, 44-seat Twin Otters, and five-seat Pilatus Porters. Timetables are often erratic — a combination of unpredictable mountain weather and Nepali *laissez faire*. From Kathmandu there are scheduled services to Dang, Dhangadi Jumla, Mahendranagar, Nepalgunj, Rukamkot, Safi Bazaar, Siliguri Doti, and Suikhet in the west; in the mid-lands to Baglung and Bhairahwa; and in the east to Bhadrapur, Biratnagar, Janakpur, Lukla, Lamidanda, Rajbiraj, Rumjatar Taplejung, Tumlinglar. Fares are reasonable, but lower still for Nepali and Indian

nationals. And Royal Nepal grants a 25 per cent discount on both domestic and international flights to cardholding students under 25 years. A daily 60-minute 'Mountain Flight' leaves Kathmandu early in the morning and flies along the Himalaya for a view of Mount Everest. The captain invites each passenger forward in turn to take photographs from the cockpit. The fare is reasonable.

On many domestic flights there is a 25-rupee airport tax and in contrast to Royal Nepal's splendid international service the in-flight service is minimal: sweets and — sometimes — tea.

Book well ahead, especially to destinations only served by the smaller aircraft. If you cancel 24 hours in advance, you pay a 10 per cent cancellation fee; 33 per cent if less than 24 hours in advance, and 100 per cent if you fail to show up. If the flight is cancelled the fare is refunded.

Occasionally, it's possible to charter one of the airline's small planes.

If you are flying to a restricted area you will need to produce your trekking permit before you board. And always carry your passport. Police frequently set up checkpoints on all roads, without warning.

Royal Nepal and Indian Airlines provide a bus service from Tribhuvan Airport to Kathmandu. Travellers on other airlines take taxis which accommodate three passengers. The driver often has an 'interpreter'. Travellers from Kathmandu to the airport can board the bus that leaves the RNAC building, New Road.

By road

Until the 1950s Nepal had no real roads. The different communities were linked by village trails and mountain paths. Any kind of business or trading was a long drawn-out affair, taking weeks, even months.

In the last four decades of the 20th century, however, development was swift and astonishing. Nepal's big power neighbours, India and China, were the catalysts for a major highway construction programme. By the dawn of the 1990s there were six main highways that constituted supreme feats of engineering, running as they do through some of the most precipitous and challenging gorges and mountains in the world.

The first of these, the Tribhuvan Raj Path, which links Kathmandu with Raxaul at the Indian border, 200 kilometres (124 miles) away, opened in 1956 and was built with Indian help. The 'Chinese Road' or Araniko Highway, 110 kilometres (68 miles) long, to the Tibetan border at Kodari, opened in the mid-1960s and was built by China.

Chinese engineers also helped to build the 200 kilometre (124 mile) Prithvi Raj Marg linking Kathmandu and Pokhara, which was opened in 1973. Since then there have been two major extensions: Dumre to Gorkha and Mugling to Narayanghat and a 188-kilometre (117-mile) extension from Pokhara to Sanauli on the Indian Border, known as the Siddhartha Raj Marg.

Nepal's most ambitious road project, however, came about through the co-operation of the former Soviet Union, United States, Britain and India. Running east-west through the southern lowlands for about 1,000 kilometres (620 miles), the Mahendra Raj Marg is part of the Pan-Asian Highway which eventually will link the Bosphorus with the Far East.

In September 1985 the 110-kilometre (30-mile) highway, from Lamosangu to Jiri east of Kathmandu was opened, built with Swiss help.

Despite all this you will find that whatever the road it will almost certainly be under repair. For, during the seasonal rains, water accumulates under the surface creating pockets of moisture that cause the ground to subside, thus forming large potholes.

Whether by bus or car, road travel in Nepal requires the patience and indifference of the stoic, or if you prefer, what you might call a Zen Buddhist outlook on life. The main benefit is that it is very cheap. Long distance bus fares are usually less than 100 rupees. But while a ticket will ensure you a seat — trespassers are usually evicted from any prepaid seat with great ostentation — you often have to fold yourself into an incredibly small space.

The aisles are occupied with baggage, livestock, and passengers. For tall people, the leg space is inadequate. That said, if

Above: An extensive domestic air network makes getting around Nepal fast and easy.

you have the right attitude, travelling in a Nepali bus provides a fascinating and microscopic insight into the lives of both Indians and Nepalese and gives you a vivid idea of who and what you will be dealing with for the rest of your visit. Indeed, for many, such a journey is often the memory of a lifetime.

When you take an overnight bus make sure that it does not screen video movies — unless you are prepared to watch blaring Hindi films all night long. Tourist buses, at double the price, are cleaner, more spacious and don't stop for passengers.

No matter what type of automobile you drive, the roads will be rough at best. All told, a road journey by bus or car will be a real adventure. Hire cars are also available from most travel agencies. Yeti Travels, near the Annapurna Hotel, run the Avis agency and Gorkha Travels, also on Durbar Marg, run the Hertz franchise.

By bus
Bus services operate on all the highways, with express coaches on the main routes.

Most services connect with Kathmandu. Minibuses, less crowded, faster, and more costly, also operate on the same routes. Book one day ahead.

By trolley bus
In Kathmandu Valley a fleet of trolley buses, a gift from China, ply the 18 kilometres (11 miles) between Tripureshwar and Bhaktapur and passengers pay virtually nothing for the journey.

Public scooters
Kathmandu's three-wheeled public scooters can carry up to six passengers. They always ply the same route, starting from Rani Pokhara. Black-and-yellow metered scooters are also available for private hire on payment of a surcharge of 10 per cent.

Rickshaws
Kathmandu's gaudy, honking rickshaws form part of the capital's vibrant street canvas. These large tricycles accommodate two passengers under cover in the back. Be sure that you agree on the fare before

you set off and that the driver knows your destination. They should not cost more than taxis.

Taxis
Taxis, with white on black registration plates, ply throughout Kathmandu Valley. Check that their meters are working and expect to pay an official surcharge of 10 per cent. You can negotiate special half- and full-day rates.

Cycling
Cycling is one of the most popular means of exploring the capital and the valley. Bicycles can be hired from many shops in old Kathmandu and near the main hotels. Check that the bell, brakes, and lights work. If there are no lights carry a flash-light as the law is enforced. For a few coins children will take care of the bicycle when you visit a popular tourist spot. Elsewhere, it is safe to leave it unattended — but locked — while you go sightseeing.

On foot
Above all, Nepal is a land best explored on foot. The most beautiful and the most interesting places can only be reached by walking. No Nepali counts distance by kilometres or miles, but by time. And a leisurely stroll through the rice and mustard fields, across villages, up, down, and around, is certainly the best way to 'absorb' Kathmandu Valley and the other regions, the people and their culture.

Trekking
Every trekker — or traveller for that matter — needs a permit to visit areas outside those included in your Nepalese visa. These are issued for one destination at a time on a set route. The charges are based on weekly rates and the permits can be obtained in Kathmandu and Pokhara.

Any reasonably fit person can trek but the fitter you are the more you will enjoy it. Do as much walking and exercise as possible to prepare yourself for Nepal's mountain trails.

The people
Few people in the world enjoy life as

Top: Crossing the shallow waters of Trisuli River. Above: Steel hawsered suspension foot bridge crosses the foaming waters born in the Everest region which feed the Dudh Kosi, one of Nepal's major rivers.

Above: Two passengers on a tricycle rickshaw trip around the town.

much as the Nepalese, perhaps inspired by the faiths that have sustained them for more than 2,000 years.

With such a shining faith — according to the Sanskrit Hindu epic *Mahabharata,* there are 33,333 Hindu deities. In other, later sources, that number is multiplied a thousand-fold — it's no wonder that Nepal is known as 'The Abode of the Gods'.

Devotion is still as great a part of Nepalese life as it ever was; perhaps more so, for whatever faith the people of this happy land follow — be it Hinduism, Buddhism, Tantric or animism — they remain true to their gods and to their joyous nature. Indeed, the line between all faiths in Nepal is so thin as to be indivisble.

'We may be poor,' says a typical young Nepali, 'but we're not miserable. When it comes to laughter we've got the highest Gross National Product (GNP) of any country — happiness.' The 20 million Nepalese people are as diverse and colour-ful as the serrated landscapes of their rectangularly shaped nation.

Each of Nepal's 35 different ethnic groups are characterized by their own dialect — any one of 22 major languages — locale, dress, and religion. Nepal society is a complex blend of two major religions, Hinduism and Buddhism.

For centuries, most of the people have worshipped each other's gods and displayed mutual respect for one another — from the day more than 2,500 years ago when Gautama, the Buddha, was born.

Hinduism in fact is an entire way of life. Cushioned against the travail of life's hard-ships by their philosophy, the seemingly happy-go-lucky outlook of the Nepalese is no matter of chance but a carefully evolved acceptance of destiny.

This sustains them so well that in most cases, in the midst of dire poverty, the poorest people — and there can be none poorer — display the most incredible cheerfulness. Hinduism seeks no converts nor does it attempt to impose its tenets on non-Hindus. Live and let live is the Hindu credo — all living things are sacred. By the same standard, paradoxical though it may seem, Hinduism abhors proselytism

— the act of seeking converts to another faith. Evangelism is a criminal offence in Nepal. But Christian, Jew, atheist, Muslim — whatever your religion — you can be sure of a warm welcome.

The Nepalese way of greeting one another is to clasp their hands together, bow their heads in deference, and murmur, 'Namaste' (pronounced Na-Ma-Stay) — 'welcome'.

They believe that, invited or uninvited, 'a guest is a god in disguise'.

And they mean it.

Language

The lingua franca, Nepali, is understood by virtually everyone but only spoken by about one-third of the population. It is derived from the North Indian vernacular, Pahori which is related to Hindi. Nepali uses the Hindi alphabet, Devagnagari, and has borrowed heavily from Sanskrit, the Hindu religious language.

There are almost as many local dialects as villages in Nepal, although, after

Above: School children outside Lord Shiva Temple, Kathmandu.

centuries of intermarriage, there is neither a pure tribe or race nor a pure language.

The Tibetan language — another traditional vehicle for religious teaching — remains widespread in northern Nepal, both in its pure, classical form and in the local dialects, such as Sherpa and Thakali that have evolved from it. The dialects of the various peoples of the Terai stem from Indo-Aryan dialects. The majority speak Maithili, which originated in the eastern Terai. English is widely spoken and understood in offices and hotels and most taxi drivers and shopkeepers in Kathmandu Valley have a basic knowledge of it, as do most Sherpas.

But English is little used or understood anywhere else and you may find difficulty in understanding — and being understood — though many younger people have acquired a smattering of English words. The idea that foreigners are wealthy is deeply ingrained in Nepali minds.

Palms extended, children in the streets chant 'Rupee! Paisa!' Ignore them and they usually smile and run away. And if they persist, adults normally send them away, for the idea of begging is abhorrent to the immensely friendly Nepalese people. Travellers, even lone women, can move almost everywhere with complete confidence. But bear in mind that the Nepalese have different values and standards from your own. For reasons that may be obscure to you, they may ask you not to enter a certain precinct or photograph a certain shrine. Many Hindu shrines are prohibited to non-Hindus.

Hinduism

The roots of Hinduism started in the great Indo-Gangetic plains of India 1,500 years before the birth of Christ. Pastoral nomads known as the Aryan tribes pushed their way over desert and mountains to settle in the fertile lowlands.

They brought with them the Vedas, sacred books that became the basis of the Hindu scriptures. The aboriginal Dravidians were significantly different from the Aryans: They lived in cities and practised animist beliefs with their own earth mother goddesses. Over a short time, the Aryans soon dominated over the Dravidians, but were still a minority. In order to preserve racial purity they forbade intermarriage.

This was perhaps the beginning of the caste system that became the backbone of society in north India. There is a written record of 30 million deities within the Hindu pantheon. This staggering number seems plausible because the deities are manifested in several different incarnations and forms.

They may be human, animal or have benevolent or terrible aspects. Most of the Hindus who begin their lives with the worship of several deities believe in this structure of the religion.

Others, often the more learned and academic, believe in a monotheism that manifests as the trinity: Brahma, Vishnu, and Shiva. Brahma is the creator of all life.

From his head came the Brahmans; his arms the warriors; his legs the merchants and businessmen; and his feet the labourers and serfs. Brahma is rarely given form in art and sculpture; his presence is so intellectual that it defies representation. Vishnu is the preserver of the universe. His followers are the Vaishnavites. It is said that in order to protect the universe, Vishnu has been reincarnated nine times, one of which was as the Buddha.

His tenth reincarnation as Kalki is yet to come. The Nepalese regard the king as an incarnation of Vishnu.

Shiva the destroyer is portrayed both as a sage always deep in meditation with little regard for his physical appearance or as the destroyer dancing the tandava that will destroy the world.

His body is covered with ashes, his hair matted, and a garland of snakes adorns his neck. There are stories of Shiva's wrath when roused from his reverie — he assumes terrible forms and destroys transgressors.

In Nepal he is symbolized as the Shiva lingam, a phallic stone pillar representing the erect male organ. Usually next to the Shiva lingam is the yoni representing his union with his consort Parvati. The fertility symbols are key to the beliefs of the Hindus who worship Shiva.

The ancient Tantric followers worship a form of Shiva. His consorts, also incarnations of Parvati, are Durga and Kali. Durga is often shown as riding a lion and destroying the demon Mahisasur; each of her 18 hands holds a terrible weapon. Kali is placated with blood sacrifices and libations of liquor.

The deities of Hinduism are sometimes depicted in sexual union. Erotic carvings festoon the beams that support the roofs of temples. Legends say that as the lightning goddess is poised to destroy the temple the sight of gods and humans in such intimate positions makes her blush and avert her eyes.

The survival of several temples to this day seems a coincidence. A more likely explanation is that the deities of the Hindu pantheon, like humans, have the same appetites. They love, quarrel and war against each other. The Nepalese take all aspects of their religion in their stride and are rarely aware of the prurient attitudes of western cultures. Both the Hindus and Buddhists believe in rebirth. The soul of

Above: Sculpture outside Durbar Square, Kathmandu.

Above: Fearsome mask of Bhairav displayed during the Indra Jartra Festival.

man is reborn into this world as a result of the sins or merits of his past life. If the sum of his sins is greater, he will return as an animal or lower form of life.

His merits will grant him life as a Brahman; in the course of many virtuous and pure cycles, he may attain freedom from being reborn into this world. The Buddhists know this as nirvana.

An accumulation of good deeds is essential to be reborn to a better life. This entails offerings and prayers to the gods on a daily basis and particularly during festivals.

A typical day consists of the woman of the house praying at the prayer house. Then she makes the rounds of the local shrines, offering grains of rice, vermillion, flowers, and fruits or vegetables. She takes back a gift from the temple in the form of a tika on the forehead or petals of flowers on the head. Hinduism has largely kept the main tenets of its faith intact. Although there are many different sects, the staying power of the religion has been its ability to adapt and absorb new elements in society. The religion has survived for almost three millennia and was interrupted only by Buddhism at its peak.

Buddhism

Gautama Buddha was born Siddhartha Gautama in Lumbini in 500 BC. He was born to a Hindu king and was sheltered from all the suffering in the world.

When he was 29, he witnessed four scenes that changed his life: a sick man, an old woman, a death and a sage in meditation. Siddhartha left the palace and roamed the land in search of answers.

He finally found them after meditating for years under a pipal tree. He was then known as Buddha or The Enlightened One.

The main teachings of Buddhism are the middle path — rules that are prescribed for living a righteous life. He taught that life is full of desires for the material world, but those who choose the middle path can overcome the suffering caused by these desires and ultimately achieve nirvana. (See also Part Three Special Features: The Enlightened One).

In the Beginning

In Nepal there is always a connection between the earthly and the divine. Every street has a shrine in the shape of the local temple or a rock bedecked with flowers and rice grains.

It is the belief of the Nepalese people that each peak is a goddess who protects the people who live close by. So it should come as no surprise that every day of the year there is a festival in some part of the country or other.

The two dominant religions, Hinduism and Buddhism, have been in peaceful co-existence for so long that each legend has both a Hindu and a Buddhist interpretation. And since most of the legends are part of the rich oral tradition, each rendition may differ from the last.

So by visiting a temple and listening to a friendly guide you may learn a little more about a certain legend than from the most detailed book.

Nowhere is the intertwining of these faiths so clear as in the legend of Kathmandu Valley. In Nepal, where there is always some connection between the earthly and the divine, legend has it that in ancient days when Kathmandu was a lake, it was called Naghrad, the home of the Nagas, the snake people.

The king of the Nagas, Krakotaka Raj, ruled the lake for centuries, and during his reign Naghrad was known as a place of great sanctity where saints and pilgrims came to worship.

As time went by, a lotus miraculously appeared above Swayambhunath Hill and a divine light shone from the lotus. When Manjushri, the Bodhisattva, came to the lake to worship he was enchanted by the lotus and wished to be near it.

He walked around the lake three times and finally with his sword cut a gorge in the mountain wall at Chovar and drained the waters of the lake. Deprived of the waters in which they lived, the Nagas left Kathmandu and Krakotaka Raj was granted a refuge by Chovar and is said to live in a pond by Taudaha. The lotus settled on a hill and sanctified it. Today some of the holiest temples and shrines in Nepal rest on Swayambhunath. Although many Tibeto-Burmese Nepalese were originally Buddhists, since the rise of the Gorkhas and in the centuries of coexisting which followed, many Newars have converted to Hinduism while retaining vestiges of their old beliefs.

The Hindus believe that Vishnu has 10 incarnations, one of whom is Buddha. Both faiths often worship in the same temple and celebrate the same festivals.

The remnants of early animist beliefs can also still be found. Shrines are abundant in the cities and villages of Nepal. It could be a rock, a tree, a hollow in a tree, at the corner of the road, temples or a fresh water spring. Telltale offerings of vermilion and rice indicate the presence of a shrine. The Buddha's birthplace in Lumbini is a pilgrimage shrine, holy to all sects of the Buddhist faith. Janakpur, the birthplace of Sita, Lord Rama's wife, is another popular pilgrimage place for the Hindus.

Clothing

Comfortable, casual clothing is recommended unless meetings with businessmen or government officials are planned.

During winter days in the Kathmandu Valley you'll be warm enough with light clothing but carry a warm sweater, padded anorak, or jacket for the evenings. Jeans, cord trousers, or long skirts, are fine and casual shoes essential, even if you don't intend to walk much. During the rainy season you can buy umbrellas locally for protection from both rain and sun.

The more trendy Nepali youths wear Levis, leather — and attitude.

Trekking gear, in standard sizes, can be bought or rented in Kathmandu and Pokhara together with sweaters, ponchos, caps and other woollen or down clothing.

During the hot season, between April and September, all you need is light summer clothing, preferably cotton. This is also true for most of the year in the Terai except in December and January when you need a sweater or jacket for evening wear.

Climate

Climates in Nepal range from the blisteringly hot in the Terai to Arctic temperatures in the far north, a result of the tremendous difference in altitude within a few kilometres. Kathmandu Valley knows three seasons. The winter — from October to March — is the best time to visit Nepal.

Night time temperatures drop close to freezing point, but by day these climb from 10°C to 25°C (50°F to 77°F) and the skies are generally clear. Mornings and evenings are invigorating.

There is often an early-morning mist. October and February are particularly pleasant. In Pokhara Valley, where temperatures rise to 30°C (86°F) at midday in the lower altitude, it is much warmer.

From April to early June the weather becomes hot and stuffy, with occasional evening thunderstorms. The land is frequently shrouded in heat mist. Temperatures in Kathmandu vary between 11°C and 28°C (52°F and 83°F) in April to between 19°C and 30°C (66°F and 86°F) in June, with maximum temperatures of 36°C (97°F).

Pre-monsoon rains usually start in May and the monsoon, which normally arrives at the end of June, lasts three months and for much of this time the Himalaya remain hidden.

The torrential downpours cause much flooding but it is still possible to tour Kathmandu Valley. With the rains come the leeches (jugas), however, and trekking stops and the lowlands are cut off by swollen rivers and landslides.

When the monsoon ends, around mid-September, the skies clear and the nights become cooler. The east-west span of the Himalaya protects the middle regions from the icy winds which sweep down from Central Asia. They also stop the monsoon winds, forcing them to rise along the mountain wall and precipitate their moisture on the southern slopes. The altitude and the amount of rainfall determine the vegetation of a region. The cool temperate zones have deciduous forests, and the hot subtropical Terai the dense evergreen tropical jungles. Thus Nepal enjoys an extreme variety of climates with altitude and exposure to sun and rain as the most influential factors.

Monsoons

The road shimmers in the heat, teasing the eye with shimmering images that vanish as you approach them. The birds rest in trees, quiet and exhausted by the unrelenting sun. The ground cracks and shrivels. This is no desert but the face of Nepal and North India before the monsoon.

There is a tangible air of expectancy as life in all its forms waits for the first hint of moisture in the air. Temperatures soar above 40°C in the Terai and, more recently, even in Kathmandu.

Meanwhile, far to the south, the sun has been beating down on the Bay of Bengal and the Indian Ocean, sucking the ocean waters remorselessly into the air, accumulating a tremendous build-up of moisture-laden air.

The South Asian landmass, heated by the same sun, causes hot air to rise creating a low pressure area that pulls the moist air inland. Unchecked, the air moves further inland until it strikes the Himalaya and begins its rise to cooler, higher altitudes.

The air then condenses into huge black clouds and a blaze of violent thunderstorms that bring to mind ancient Chinese legends of dragons writhing restlessly in the clouds. In Bhutan the thunderstorms are so spectacular that the country is known as Druk-Yul — The Land of the Thunder Dragons.

The southern slopes of the Himalaya that benefit most by the monsoon are covered with the lush forests of Nepal, Sikkim, and Bhutan. The effect of the monsoon is spectacular.

The dusty, parched land soaks up the moisture and plants thrive. Kathmandu is washed clean and the land, assured of another cycle of life, relaxes.

In the city the monsoon is characterized by frequent sharp downpours, but rarely to continuous rain as in Cherapunji in Assam, where the heaviest rainfall in the world is recorded. The greatest rainfall is from June to September. July is particularly wet. For those brave enough to trek during the monsoons this is a month to avoid as the rains may affect roads and trails. If you must trek in the monsoon it is better to go in August or September. There are many who swear by a fine trek in the rains. The air is cleansed of the dust, the flora is lush and the trails empty at the ebb of the tourist season.

Above: Crossing snow waters at Ghandruna and Chandrakat.

The whole outlook of life changes as the rains slow down the daily activities of the farmers while irrigating their fields for another fine harvest. Many employees use this down time to visit their families in their home towns and villages. This is also a popular time for weddings, celebrations and festivals.

The monsoon is a critical lifeline for the farmers of South Asia for whom it is the only means of irrigation. The late arrival of the rains can be truly devastating, for fragile agricultural systems rapidly spiral into famine and severe drought. Conversely, following a drought, the land may lose its ability to retain water especially in the event of a deluge.

This leads to heavy runoffs triggering landslides and floods. The felling of forests, intensive cultivation and the practice of leaving plots fallow causes topsoil to erode swiftly in the rains.

These silt-laden waters drain into the swift-flowing rivers which slow down as they approach the sea. The accumulation of silt chokes the deltas and prevents the water from draining to the sea and, as a result, floods the coastal plains.

The torrential downpours cause much flooding but it is still possible to tour Kathmandu Valley. When the monsoon ends, around mid-September, the skies clear, the nights become cooler, and the landscape is a symphony of autumn colours, brown and gold.

Health

Travellers are advised to take inoculations against typhoid, hepatitis, cholera, and tetanus. Never drink unboiled and unfiltered water. Avoid ice cubes and raw vegetables. Always wash and peel fruit and clean your hands often. Never walk barefoot. Stomach upsets are known locally as the 'Kathmandu Quickstep'. If trouble persists, it can develop into something more serious like amoebic or bacillary dysentery or giardiasis so get a stool test and seek medical help.

Malaria is on the increase, but most of Kathmandu is too high to support the malarial species.

For visits to the south, however, take a recognized prophylactic two weeks before you arrive in the Terai and continue to take this for six weeks after you leave. You should also carry a mosquito repellent during the warm months. Pharmacies in Kathmandu offer a wide range of Western drugs at low prices and some traditional Indian ayurvedic remedies. Most international hotels have a consultant doctor on call and hospitals in Kathmandu have English-speaking staff.

Power

Major towns in Nepal are on the 220-volt AC system, though this sometimes fluctuates. Hindus adore light and, during festivals, towns and villages are ablaze with light. Some international hotels maintain stand-by generators that cut in during the frequent power cuts.

Photography

Film stock is only available in Kathmandu and is extremely costly. Shops in New Road process black-and-white and colour film. Telephoto lenses are useful for wild-life and landscape photography.

Time

Nepal is 57 years ahead of the Western calendar and 15 minutes ahead of Indian Standard Time — and so five hours 45 minutes ahead of Greenwich Mean Time.

Government hours are from Sunday to Friday between 1000 and 1700. They close one hour earlier during the three winter months. Only embassies and international organizations enjoy a two-day weekend. Shops, some of which remain open on Saturdays and holidays, seldom open before 1000 but do not usually close until 1900 or 2000.

Remember that in this deeply religious country there are many holidays devoted to various deities, mythological events, astrological signs and traditional festivals, in addition to secular holidays marking phases of Nepal's modern history.

Money

On arrival, you must fill in a currency card with all relevant information except the amount of currency imported. When you exchange foreign currency, every instance should be recorded on the currency card and endorsed by the stamp of authorized dealers such as banks, hotels and currency stations.

You can change excess rupees at the end of your stay provided the amount does not exceed 10 per cent of the total amount exchanged. It is illegal to import or export Nepalese and Indian currency. Since the official rate of exchange fluctuates constantly you should check the rate in the daily newspaper, *The Rising Nepal.*

There is a flourishing black market for US dollars in Kathmandu. Keep in mind the currency card requirements and despite the attractive rates in the street, travellers should be careful.

Nepalese rupees are issued in denominations of 1,000, 500, 100, 50, 20, 10, 5, 2, 1; coins are available as paisa in denominations of 50, 25, 10 and 5, with 100 paisa equalling one rupee; half-a-rupee is 50 paisa. Basic units are mohars (nine paisa) and sukhas which are 25 paisa.

Accommodation

Travellers to Kathmandu have a wide range of choices — from five-star international hotels to basic board and lodging with shared toilets and bathrooms. Apart from the five-star game lodges in Royal Chitwan National Park the choice outside Kathmandu Valley is more homely and less expensive. During the high seasons — spring and autumn — Kathmandu's international hotels are almost always full so it is advisable to book well in advance. At the lower end of the price scale there are plenty of comfortable hotels. Most offer a choice of bed and breakfast, half-board — breakfast and one other meal — or full board. There are also a number of basic lodges with minimal amenities. Rates vary depending on facilities. Toilets and showers are generally communal, heating extra. Most are in old Kathmandu, around Durbar Square or in Thamel district. Tariffs are subject to a 12 to 15 per cent government tax.

Mountain lodges

In the mountains there are many basic

lodges, usually near airstrips, as well as the many traditional Nepali teahouses found in every village on the trekking routes.

National flower
The ubiquitous rhododendron, of which there are about 32 species, most with red and pink flowers, and rarely white, is the national flower.

National colour
Crimson-red, *simrik*, is Nepal's national colour. Regarded as both sacred and auspicious *simrik* is considered a symbol of progress, prosperity and action and is visible at all national and sacred occasions. Shiva is supposed to draw power from this vibrant hue.

   During Nepal's many Hindu festivals, red flowers are presented as votive offerings to the different gods and goddesses.

National bird
The Danphe Pheasant, a rare, brilliantly coloured pheasant, found between the 2,400 and 4,500-metre (7,800–15,000 foot) contours of the Himalaya, is the national bird of Nepal. It belongs to the same family as the peacock.

National dress
The national dress of the men is the *daura sural* and *topi*. Officials wear a coat jacket for their duties. Most of the men in urban areas dress in the western shirt and trousers. Virtually all Nepal women wear red during festivals and other sacred occasions. Usually red is the colour of the country's national dress, *labeda suruwal*, which is made of homespun cotton. On other occasions the colour is grey or light brown. It consists of a seamed, double-breasted tunic blouse that extends almost to the knees, fastened by two ribbons and trousers that are baggy around the thighs but tight at the ankles, similar to the *shalwa qamiz of* India.

   For some occasions sophisticated Nepali women wear the Indian sari.

National flag
The Nepal flag is formed by two adjoining red triangles, symbolizing morality, virtue and unity, bordered by blue. The top triangle contains a crescent moon emitting eight

THE COAT-OF-ARMS
OF
His Majesty's Government of Nepal

Top: The coat-of-arms of Nepal.
Above: The national flag.

ROYAL CREST

rays, the lower one, a sun emitting 12 rays.

These are symbolic representations of the many legendary solar and lunar dynasties to which the royal family belongs. The coat of arms includes leaf-shaped decorative pieces to symbolize the title of *Sri Panch* — five times glorified. For the crest, the heraldic device uses the plume of a bird of paradise which is believed to have been introduced to Nepal by former premier, Mathbar Singh Thapa. Below this are the footprints of Paduka, the guardian god of Gorkha, ancestral home of the ruling dynasty. Crossed *kukhuris* represent the national weapon, the traditional, curved sword of the famed Gurkha battalions. On either side are the sun and the moon, symbols of enlightenment and eternity.

The shield depicts Nepal, from the Himalaya to the Terai, and at the centre, hands clasped, sits Pashupatinah, creator as well as destroyer of the universe.

The Sanskrit motto avers that love of mother and motherland is superior even to love of heaven. The soldier recruit and veteran are also represented by a prayer exhorting them to defend their country, so long as the universe shall exist.

National anthem

Nepal's national anthem wishes for the continued prosperity of the 'excellent, illustrious, five times glorified King' and a similar fivefold increase in the number of his subjects.

Top: The Royal Crest.
Above: Rhododendron, the national flower.

PART ONE: HISTORY, GEOGRAPHY AND PEOPLE

Above: A small Sherpa village in the Phortse region.

Sun-Drenched Plains and Frozen Splendour

In Nepal, where eye-level is often 2,500 metres (8,000 feet) or more when you are deep in a rhododendron forest ablaze with colour and sheltered by snow-bound massifs, if you fix your eye on a peak and contemplate the height, you may feel the great tectonic forces that shaped the face of this land.

But if the earth doesn't quite move under your feet, the craggy mountains remain silent witness to the incredible upheavals millions of years ago when the Indian subcontinent broke away from the super continent of Godwanaland and ground into the Asiatic land mass, forcing massive folds in the surface of the earth.

So massive are they that they now rank as the highest point on the planet, literally, 'the roof of the world'. And there the earth moves still, under the pressure of the opposing continental plates, which continue to push against each other, racking up the mountains centimetre by centimetre each year.

Such pressures cause colossal earthquakes, some measuring the greatest magnitude in history, which since time immemorial have devastated large areas of Nepal and its neighbours.

With each wrack and warp, the Himalaya mountains grow higher. They and their western kin, the mighty peaks of the Karakoram and Hindu Kush, formed out of the same stupendous forces, boast the highest peaks in the world.

The beauty of such mountains at dawn is as mystical as it is awesome, a sight as no other.

As the sun flushes away the mists and shadows in the rills and ridges of the great peaks, to reveal unparalleled beauty wherever you look, a palette of all the colours of the spectrum rolls up and down across the valleys between you and the queen of the skies, Sagarmatha. Rich green fields stretch along a spur of a river, punctuated here and there by the dark verdure of a small forest.

The first spirals of smoke rise from the closely huddled houses of the villages where the far-distant sound of children at play melds into the tinkle of the streams, the roar of the rivers and the morning chorus of birdsong.

As you walk along a generations-old forest trail, footfalls echo off the trees, but whether of person or of beast the darkness of the forest never reveals.

To the outsider, this Kingdom of the Gods is often a bewildering glimpse of extreme contrasts between the ancient and the modern. But after the initial impact, the ease with which the Nepalese embrace the visitor and the constantly unfolding beauty of the country helps to separate reality from illusion. Yet illusion is never far away, for Nepal is truly different from any other land.

Discovering Nepal's heritage is a revelation of history and culture. Ancient temples, festivals and deep religious traditions are all part of Nepalese culture. Myth and legend manifest themselves in every aspect of life. Every peak is a goddess; in Kathmandu every street has a temple and every deity is capable of manifesting itself in a shrine, perhaps embodied in a tree or in a stately structure towering over modest roofs.

The culture of Nepal is a unique mix of Tibeto-Burman and Indo-Aryan cultures, and its diversity is so great that anthropologists have identified almost 50 groups, each with its own distinctive culture, dialect and costume.

The lack of natural boundaries between Nepal and India ties their histories together. Before the diaspora of the Aryan tribes into the subcontinent, native Dravidian civilizations based on animist beliefs had existed for centuries. When Mahmud of Ghazni and Muhammad Ghor began their invasions of north India, more people were brought into contact with the new settlers from northern India. The Hindu principalities that established themselves in western Nepal brought with them their religion and beliefs, which are based on the Vedas or scriptures.

The Vedas were brought by the Aryan tribes as they settled over centuries in the

Indus Valley. Hinduism is the outcome of Vedic beliefs and the animist belief of the indigenous Dravidian civilizations.

While Kathmandu Valley remained for the most part sheltered from the invasions of Muhammad bin Quasim, the invasions led to events that changed the destiny of the Newar kings.

A group of Brahmins (priest class) and Kshatriyas (warrior class) from Rajasthan fled before the invaders and settled in Gorkha. They were the ancestors of the Shahs who finally united the boundaries of Nepal under the rule of Prithvi Narayan Shah.

Another bond was formed between the two cultures when Buddhism, founded by Gautama Buddha, spread beyond India to Nepal and the Asian kingdoms. Since then, Nepal has been largely sheltered from the outside world and accessible only to a fortunate few.

When finally Nepal opened its doors to the world in the 1950s, visitors saw for the first time the indelible beauty of the country and its unique people and their warm hospitality. In the 1970s, Nepal became the Eldorado of the hippies, who made it their retreat at the end of long overland trips from Europe.

Now it remains as potently intriguing and mysterious and as profoundly beautiful as it ever was. From the fascinating, ancient capital of Kathmandu to the remote trails and villages, from flat Terai forests to the precipitous mountain torrents and windswept vistas, from the Hindi-speaking lowlanders to the proud and kindly Sherpas and Tibetans of its higher climes, Nepal is fascinating, complex, compelling and unforgettable.

Few people visit Nepal just once, for to do so is a promise to return. And many a tourist who comes to Nepal is content for hours, even days, to sit on a hotel balcony or on a quiet hillside in contemplation. But there is no need to sit still. Kathmandu has sights and sounds for every eye and ear, variations for every mind and culture.

Centuries lurk in its alleys and carved facades, its emblazoned temples and sharp roof-lines. Strange odours recall past lives and other ways. To come to Kathmandu is to reach back into yourself.

There are days, weeks, you could spend wandering this city and the paths that spread out from it across the nearby hills. But there is more wandering than this to be done: you can hike in every conceivable direction — up and down, to all the cardinal points and far beyond.

And if Kathmandu is one unique experience, rural Nepal is another. To walk through this calm, green and fertile hill land is to rediscover what has been lost in the 20th century.

Then although population growth and increasing competition for scarce natural resources has exterminated many species and reduced others, nonetheless, Nepal's scenery, history and sense of peace everywhere abound.

Above: Smiling images of Shiva and Parvati gaze out from an upper window of the Shiva Parvati temple in Kathmandu.

History: The Kingdom of the Gods

Written in the still-rising Cretaceous rocks of Nepal's mighty mountains and carved in its priceless treasury of ancient, religiously-inspired art and architecture is the story of a nation that has no like anywhere on earth.

The Kingdom of Nepal is a country whose history extends back to the very beginnings of humankind. Virtually unknown to the rest of the world until 1950, the prehistory and history of the region has only recently been seen by outsiders and translated. Much is still shrouded in legend.

As a modern country, Nepal has existed fewer than 200 years but Kathmandu has been its historical, social and political hub for at least 1,500 years.

From the earliest times this temperate and fertile valley has been cultivated intensively and has been self-sufficient in produce and some grain. It was also renowned as a conduit for traders from both India and Tibet.

Despite its sheltered location and the strong indigenous Newar culture, Kathmandu has at times been subjected to outside influences, chief among them the introduction of Buddhism and Hinduism.

In time, the extended influence of the Tibetan branch of Lamaist Buddhism fostered a unique coexistence of the two religions, which were a result of the migration of groups from the plains of India and the Terai, and from the northern lands of Tibet.

The range of features seen in modern Nepal can be classified loosely into three broad groups: Tibeto-Nepalese, Indo-Nepalese and indigenous.

Despite the changes in its history, Nepal has always remained independent. With the seat of power in Kathmandu, the earliest kingdom of the Lichhavis — fourth to eighth centuries — and the Mallas — 12th to 18th — was barely able to control the areas outside the valley. The monuments that remain today indicate the cultural prosperity of the kingdoms when the kings actively patronized the arts.

When the splintered grouping of principalities was finally united as one kingdom by Prithvi Narayan Shah — ruler of the small principality of Gorkha — Nepal became an imperialistic force. Its armies engaged the Chinese in Tibet and the English in India, but with small success. Eventually the might of Nepal's opponents stopped Nepalese ambitions and defined the boundaries of its borders to where they are now.

Ancient times

Little is known about prehistoric Nepal. Neolithic tools found in the valleys indicate that there were primitive settlements in the area.

A number of archaeologists believe that, even before the Himalaya reached their present grandeur, Orepithecus, one of humankind's early ancestors, inhabited the region.

About a million years ago tribes formed in the hills and made and used primitive tools. Not much is known about these early inhabitants, but legend suggests that relatively well-developed societies with oral traditions and an animistic religion settled there when a lake filled the Kathmandu Valley.

The first conquest

More recent legends tell of a people known as the Kirata, who ruled the valley after taking it from the Gopals or Abhiras, a cow-herding tribe. The Kirata are believed to be a Tibeto-Burmese people who lived in Nepal more than 2,500 years ago.

It was around 700 BC that the Kirata invaded from India. Their military exploits are described in the ancient Indian texts *Mahabharata* and *Ramayara*, but their influence probably only extended over a portion of

Previous pages: Buddhist monks at the Bodhanath stupa, throw handful of flour in the air during a religious festival.

Above: Brick temple, Maya Devi, marks the birthplace of Siddhartha Gautama Buddha at Lumbini.

the Terai and the midlands, where they established Patan as a stronghold, assimilating the earlier cultures. But for at least seven centuries, they controlled north-south trade and travel. There have been references in other Indian legends to the Kirata, and they were even mentioned by Ptolemy and other Greek writers. It was during their rule that Buddhism came to Nepal, where the Buddha himself was born.

It was the advance of the Arya, groups of tribes from Central Europe, into the subcontinent that shaped the more recent history of India and its neighbours.

Waves of these agrarian people swept into the heartland of the Indo-Gangetic plain and stamped their influence on the land and its people. As they established their own territories, these small principalities were constantly at war with each other

The great Mauryan Empire rose from the warring kingdoms and achieved glory under Ashoka the Great. He ruled an empire so vast that it covered the whole of South Asia to Afghanistan in the west.

Perhaps the most significant contribution of the Aryan invasion was the birth of Hinduism. The Arya brought with them the Vedas, sacred books, and the caste system, while the Dravidians, indigenous to the Indus Valley, supplied the animist beliefs in natural forces, fertility and mother earth figures. Many symbols of Hinduism hark back to its roots all those millennia ago.

The expansion of the Arya-dominated lands toward the Terai, which borders the Indo-Gangetic plain, gave rise to more principalities. At this time, the Khasa people, speaking Indo-Aryan languages, migrated into the western Terai. One small kingdom in the Terai was ruled by the Sakya clan, whose seat was at Kapilavastu, now on the border of Nepal and India.

The birth of Buddhism
Siddhartha Gautama was born into this clan c.563 BC in Lumbini, and into a life of luxury, but after he saw the squalor, despair and suffering of poverty, he renounced this life to go in search of

Top: The Royal Hotel, Kathmandu built in 1955. Above: The Royal Hotel's West Wing.

the meaning of existence. Through his teachings, he became known as the Buddha, The Enlightened One.

He spread his ultimate belief in the 'eightfold path' to enlightenment all across northern India and in the Kathmandu Valley. His remains were buried in huge stone mounds, called stupas.

In 250 BC, the most ruthless Indian Emperor, Ashoka, visited Nepal in peace. Nicknamed the 'Sorrowless One', Ashoka had converted to Buddhism after a bloody battle in southern India which was to haunt him for the rest of his life.

As a consequence, he renounced violence, became one of Buddha's most ardent disciples and made it his goal to spread the Buddhist philosophy across Asia. His trip to Nepal was one of rebirth. With his daughter Charumati, he is said to have visited Buddha's birthplace and constructed a memorial pillar.

From Lumbini, Ashoka went to the Kathmandu Valley to bathe in the Bagmati River. Charumati was married to a Kirata prince and remained in Patan. Memorials to the marriage and Ashoka's visit were erected in the city — four stupas rumoured to have been built under the patronage of Ashoka remain in Patan (Lalitpur).

Ashoka sponsored Buddhist missionaries throughout Nepal and the rest of Asia, and his son became a monk and took the Buddhist Sutrah to Ceylon.

Ashoka's descendant, Samudragupta, claimed the 'Lord of Nepal', paid him tribute and taxes. But there is no way to validate this: the only proof of intercourse between Nepal and the Mauryan Empire is from early Nepalese art.

In his own empire Ashoka supported religious tolerance, which perhaps he had learned on his trip to the Kathmandu Valley, where, even in the 3rd century BC, it appears that Buddhism coexisted with Hinduism. Another theory argues that it was during Ashoka's reign that the Hindus left India for Nepal. In any case, the Hindu shrine, Pashupatinath, and the surrounding settlement date from that time, and Hindu legends predate it.

During the next two centuries, until perhaps 50 BC, the Kirata influence waned

in the Valley. Other groups migrated there and mingled with existing populations to become the people referred to as Newaris. In the hills and mountains as well, tribal societies and kingdoms expanded and diversified. After the Kirata, the valley was ruled by the Somavashis, who also originally came from India.

Under the Somavashis, the Hindu religion flourished and a four-caste system was introduced. They renovated the holy shrine, Pashupatinah and, in the first century AD, constructed a temple on the site.

It was also during their rule that the roofs of the temples in Patan were gilded. Eventually, the Somavashis were conquered by the Lichhavi, who ruled the Valley between the 5th and 7th centuries.

These Hindu rulers, also from India, are credited with bringing an age of enlightenment with them. They fostered the study of Sanskrit and the production of carvings, many with elaborate inscriptions and dedications.

The Lichhavi dynasty
At the end of the 5th century, the written records of politics, society and the economy in ancient Nepal were kept by a ruling dynasty called the Lichhavis. They are said to have ruled from the time of Buddha, and the founder of the Gupta empire claimed to have married a Lichhavi princess. Despite an abundance of records of royal alliances, the Lichhavis were the first true kings of the Valley.

The earliest written record in the reign of Manadeva I dates from 464, and mentions three earlier rulers. The last Lichhavi inscription was written in AD 733.

All the Lichhavi inscriptions are documents reporting donations to religious foundations, particularly Hindu temples. They were written in Sanskrit, the language used in the north Indian courts. There was a strong cultural influence from India, possibly through the Mithila region, in the north of present-day Bihar.

To the north of Kathmandu, Tibet was a formidable military power throughout the 7th century. There are conflicting theories that Nepal was subordinate to Tibet but what is clear is that Nepal

Above: Eighth-century Lichhavi carving of Vishnu at Changu Narayan, a hilltop shrine near Kathmandu.

extended its contact both with India and Tibet and remained a trading centre.

The Lichhavis had a political system very similar to those in north India, where the king was at the apex of daily life. As the preserver of righteous order, the king had no limits to his domain. His borders were limited only by the might of his military power. This was the popular belief throughout South Asia, which was, as a result, kept in a constant state of war, as rulers tried to expand the boundaries of their kingdoms.

The Lichhavis are best remembered for spreading Buddhism to Tibet and central Asia, through merchants, pilgrims and missionaries. The trade routes in the Lichhavi period supported and strengthened the kingdom and as a bonus fostered the spread of Buddhism.

One notable Lichhavi ruler, Mana Deva, built the Changu Narayan temple in 388 Saka Sambat (AD 467), according to its inscriptions. A stela there praises Mana Deva's victories over the Malla tribes and the subjugation of the Thakuris.

Two centuries later, the last Lichhavi ruler, Shevadeva, gave his daughter in marriage to one of his strongest Thakuri vassals, Amsuvarman, who was well-educated and had written a Sanskrit grammar.

As Shevadeva preferred the monastic life to his royal role, Amsuvarman assumed many of his father-in-law's duties during the latter's lifetime.

On the death of Shevadeva in AD 605, Amsuvarman appointed himself king and expanded his influence beyond the valley by marrying his daughter Bhrikuti to the Tibetan King, Sron Tsan Gampo.

Bhrikuti is credited with converting the Tibetan king and his other wife, a Chinese princess, to Buddhism, thus beginning the eventual transmission of the religion to Tibet and China. The two brides have been canonized in the Buddhist tradition and are worshipped as the goddesses of compassion — Green Tara (Bhrikuti) and White Tara (the Chinese princess).

In AD 643 and 647 the Chinese sent the first diplomatic missions to Kathmandu Valley. The records of Wang Huen Tse, the leader of the second mission, show his mixed feelings about Ni-Po-Lo and its inhabitants:

'The kingdom of Ni-Po-Lo . . . is situated in the middle of snowy mountains and indeed presents an uninterrupted series of hills and valleys. Its soil is suited to the cultivation of grain and abounds in flora and fruits. . . . Coins of red copper are used for exchange. The climate is very cold.

'The national character is stamped with falseness and perfidy; the inhabitants are all of a hard and savage nature: to them neither good faith nor justice nor literature appear, but they are gifted with considerable skill in the art. Their bodies are ugly and their faces are mean.

'Among them are both true believers (Buddhists) and heretics (Hindus). Buddhist convents and the temples of the Hindu gods touch each other. It is reckoned that there are about two thousand religious who study both the Greater and Lesser Vehicle. The number of Brahmans and the nonconformists has never been ascertained exactly.'

Other members of the missions were more impressed with Nepali culture and art and, years later, Nepali architects were invited to China to build the first pagodas there.

This golden age of Nepal was followed by a dark age, during which tribes were at constant war with one another. Gone was art, learning and religious tolerance, and few records or relics of this period remain.

One significant event was the change from Sanskrit as court language to Newari, the language of the Newar people who were in a majority in the Valley.

Some historians believe that, during the reign of a Thakuri king, Guakanadeva around 950, the city of Kathmandu (then known as Kantipur) became the regional capital and the towns of Bhadgaon and Kirtipur were established. Commerce with India and Tibet increased and Tantric rites and ideals were introduced and integrated into the religions.

In the 11th century when the Muslims, under Muhammed Ghauri, began to take power in India and extended their empire into the northern kingdoms, Hindus and Buddhists fled north to Nepal and Tibet. It was from those refugees that the Malla dynasty that dominated the Valley until the 18th century arose.

The Malla dynasty

In the 12th century a group of leading families in Nepal took the name of *malla* — wrestler in Sanskrit — with its suggestion of strength and power. Arideva, the first ruler, emerged as a leader strong enough to bring peace to the Valley. He supposedly coined the name Malla for his descendants and thus the dynasty. According to popular legend, he was wrestling when news of the birth of his son was brought to him, and the king gave him the title 'Malla', 'wrestler' in Sanskrit.

The early Malla period was one of political upheaval in and outside Nepal. In India the Muslim Turks had conquered Delhi and established an empire, and they continued to conquer neighbouring kingdoms. The threat of invasion prompted the kingdoms to arm themselves, to the extent that a separate dynasty of Mallas reigned over Dullu in the Jumla Valley.

Above: The Ashoka Pillar in Lumbini, south-west Nepal, was erected by Indian Emperor Ashoka in 249 BC to mark the birthplace of Lord Buddha.

Repeated humiliation was dealt to the Mallas by rivals who claimed overlordship. The Khasa king, Ripumalla visited Lumbini and had an inscription carved on the Ashoka pillar to commemorate his visit. Then he entered Kathmandu Valley and worshipped at the Pashupatinath, Swayambhunath and Matsyendranath. In the 14th century, Sultan Shams-ud-din Ilyas of Bengal raided the Valley and destroyed most of the major shrines.

There were peaceful periods under the Mallas but these were interrupted by Muslim invasions from India. During a 14th-century attack, the Muslims sacked many temples and shrines in the Valley. Nonetheless, arts, architecture and learning advanced and there were three universities in the Valley.

Religious tolerance was so complete that Buddhists and Hindus worshipped in the same temples and celebrated each other's religious festivals.

The Valley remained divided during the

Above: Patan's 16th-century Durbar Square. Left is the white plastered profile of the Narasimha Temple dedicated to Narasimha, the fourth incarnation of Vishnu.

next 200 years but there were several rulers of note in Kathmandu, Patan and Bhadgaon.

Under the reign of Jaya Sthiti Malla, which began in 1382, a caste system was reintroduced after a Brahman priest convinced the king that the gods look with disfavour upon casteless societies.

The most aggressive of the Malla rulers, Jaksha Malla, extended the boundaries of his kingdom to include much of what is now Nepal. His territory extended north to Tibet and south to the Ganges River. He oversaw the construction of canals and water supply systems.

Unfortunately, shortly before his death, he divided the Valley amongst his children: Bhadgaon (also known as Bhaktapur), Banepa and Kathmandu went to his three sons, Patan to his daughter. The heirs, not content with their inheritances, were soon warring with each other.

Banepa became part of Bhadgaon and Patan eventually lost its independence to Kathmandu, but the period during which Kathmandu Valley was divided into the three kingdoms — Kathmandu, Patan and Bhadgaon — lasted from the 15th to the 18th centuries.

The development of the unique culture of the Valley is attributed to the reign of these Malla kings who fostered a society wealthy enough to indulge in the arts.

Kings were still regarded as the protectors of Dharma, and many built the temples and structures renowned today. Buddhism was still a powerful influence, with its centre in Patan. Newari became the literary language and was used in urban areas and in trading circles. Under King Siddhi Narasimha Malla (1618-1661), Patan grew considerably. King Siddhi Narasimha oversaw a major construction effort, which included 2,400 individual houses. But he was devoutly religious and left one day on a pilgrimage from which he never returned.

The life of one of his successors, King Bhupatindra Malla of Badgaon, reads much like a fairy tale. A wicked witch — his father's second wife — wanted her own son to inherit the throne. But Bhupatindra

Above: Statues of the 17th century Malla King, Bhupatindra, and his queen, in a gilded cage at Changu Narayan.

was the son of the first wife and therefore first in line, so the second wife decided to have the young prince killed.

Her conspirators took the boy from the palace into the forest to murder him. They did not have the courage to carry out the step-mother's wish, however, and abandoned the child instead. The prince was found by a carpenter who raised him as his own son.

Years later, the carpenter took his son with him to work in the Royal Palace. The king, the boy's real father, recognized him and welcomed him back as the rightful heir. Bhupatendra became king in 1696 when his father died, and his reign was marked by incessant construction. The finest remaining structures from this period are the Palace of Fifty-Five Windows and the Temple of Nayatapola. His rule was one of the most prosperous eras in the city.

But the end of Malla rule was hastened by the political situation in India, which led to events that were to change the history of Nepal. The Mughal dynasty had established its stronghold in Delhi.

Their repeated wars with the Rajput clans of North India caused a migration to the hills in the north, including Nepal.

Legends speak of exiled warriors who made their homes in western Nepal. The influence of the Mughals is reflected in the weapons and dress of the Malla kings at the time.

In the north, the Qing dynasty, taking advantage of the instability of Tibet, sent a force to install the sixth Dalai Lama as the political and religious leader. There were also the *amban*, the military governors who kept a watch on Tibet for the Qing dynasty. A delegation from the three kingdoms went to the Chinese emperor with greetings and presents.

Nepal's other contacts with foreigners were limited to the visit of John Cabral, a Portuguese missionary. The first Capuchin mission was founded in Kathmandu in 1715. Its influence was small and it never attained a significant number of converts.

In their religious fervour, these Christian missionaries are said to have burned more than 3,000 'pagan' books and manuscripts as 'works of the devil.' For this, they were expelled, leaving only a handful of converts. Meanwhile, the growth of the British East India Company in Bengal heralded the decline of the Mughal empire: the British, even as a private company, acquired the rights to govern Bengal. Although at this time the Mallas had no direct contact with Britain, except through trade, the presence of the British made a significant impact on the future of the kingdom.

Pratap Malla, King of Kathmandu from 1640 to 1674, was a man of letters who demonstrated his knowledge of 15 languages on a plaque in the Royal Palace. He also erected the statue of Hanuman, the monkey god, at the entrance to the palace which since then has been known as Hanuman Dhoka. He was also responsible for the construction of the steps and gold thunderbolt at Swayambunath.

At this time the Brahman priests placed themselves at the top of the caste, with 64 professional groups below, and shoemakers, butchers, blacksmiths and sweepers at the bottom, the 'untouchables'.

The second caste was the warriors, to which the royal families belonged. This caste was again subdivided into sub-castes, which led to suspicion and dissent among rulers and contributed substantially to the civil strife of the time.

Outside the Valley, meanwhile, other principalities were flourishing. Little is documented about life in these outlying kingdoms, but from one came the founder of modern Nepal — Prithvi Narayan Shah.

Forward the Gorkha

The Gorkha principality was established by Dravya Shah in 1559 in a hill area inhabited by the Magars. He was a descendant of the Rajput warrior kings, who had migrated from India in the 15th century. The first expansion of Gorkha was in the reign of Ram Shah and this continued with his successors until the early 18th century.

Depending on shifting alliances, Gorkha aligned itself with one of the three Malla kingdoms, gaining experience in the affairs of Kathmandu.

An apocryphal story of Prithvi Narayan Shah as a young boy in the land of the Gurkhas and fortified towns is still told. One day, when he was six years old, Prithvi Narayan went to the temple where he met an unhappy old man.

'I am hungry. Can you give me some curd?' begged the old man.

Prithvi Narayan fetched some curd. The old man ate his fill but kept a little in his mouth.

'Hold out your hand!' ordered the old man.

The boy obeyed and the old man spat what was left in his mouth into it.

'Eat!' he commanded.

But Prithvi Narayan did not obey and dropped the curdled milk to the ground.

'If you had eaten my spittle from your hand,' the old man said, 'you would have been able to conquer all the countries of your dreams. But since you have thrown it away, you will only be able to conquer those kingdoms into which you can walk.'

Then the ancient one suddenly disappeared.

When Prithvi Narayan ascended the throne in 1742 he aggressively made preparations for his conquest of the three kingdoms of Nepal. He visited the ruling family of Banaras to seek financial help and he purchased weapons.

On his return to Gorkha, he began to train his army in the use of modern armaments and, in a series of alliances and negotiations, he either bought or secured the neutrality of the kingdoms adjacent to Gorkha. Indeed, Prithvi Narayan spent 25 years expanding his territory and unifying a large part of Nepal. He was a great conqueror but, as the old man prophesied, he never realized his dreams.

Prithvi Narayan's plans were aided by the already simmering intrigues in the Valley kingdoms. In Kathmandu, King Jaya Prakash had been exiled by his wife, whom he eventually killed. Jaya's brother, the

Opposite: Intricate detail of the magnificent metal-work on the framed Golden Gate of Bhaktapur's Durbar Square.

King of Patan, was deposed by the Pradhans, a rival family, who spared his life but blinded him. Jaya came to his brother's aid, suppressed the Pradhan coup, forced them to beg in the streets and paraded their wives as witches.

The first big war began when the kings of Bhadgaon and Kathmandu quarrelled with each other. Seizing the opportunity, Prithvi Narayan Shah stormed the fortress of Nawakot, astride the main Tibetan trade route, and laid siege to Kirtipur, which was then under the control of the King of Patan.

The siege was broken when Prithvi Narayan Shah was almost killed. He withdrew his forces, isolated the Valley and sent in Brahman priests to stir up trouble.

With the trade routes secured, Prithvi Narayan Shah laid siege again to Kirtipur and was once again repelled. The Gorkhans then attacked Lamji and took it, after several bloody skirmishes. Armed with this victory the Gorkhans returned to besiege Kirtipur yet again. The siege lasted six months but Kirtipur was only delivered to the Gorkhans by a betrayer.

Prithvi Narayan Shah's rage at the stubborn resistance was great and he ordered the noses and lips of all males over 12 years of age cut off. Only those who played wind instruments were spared.

According to one account, Prithvi Narayan decided to weigh the accumulated collection of nostrils, which, it is said, came to a total of 86 lbs. Certainly, for generations Kirtipur was known as Naskatipur — 'The City of the Noseless Ones'.

Prithvi Narayan Shah then turned his attention to Patan but was stopped when a 2,400-strong British expedition appeared in defence of the three kingdoms. The British soldiers were so weakened by malaria, however, that the force soon retreated, and the Gorkhans took Kathmandu unopposed during the celebration of a festival.

Prithvi Narayan Shah was crowned king of Nepal and went on to annexe Patan and Bhadgaon virtually unopposed. With control of the Valley, Prithvi Narayan now held everything from Lamjung to Everest.

Making Kathmandu his capital, he set about excluding Europeans, particularly missionaries. 'First the Bible, then the trading stations, and then cannon,' he told his advisers.

Dreams of conquest

Prithvi Narayan Shah followed these early conquests by bringing eastern Nepal, under the Kirata, into his kingdom. Next in line was Sikkim but, by virtue of being subordinate to Tibet, and consequently China, it was protected from all-out assault. The king also planned to conquer Tibet, but died in 1774 before he could realize his goal.

Prithvi Narayan Shah's conquests, however, were only the first in a continuing expansion of territory by the Gorkha kingdom.

Following his death, the court was in turmoil as his descendants engaged in plots, conspiracies and assassinations in the struggle for power.

As a result of the constant upheavals, members of the court sought to appease the army's leaders and buy their neutrality. Prithvi Narayan was succeeded by Pratap Singh Shah, his son, who made little or no progress in building his father's grand empire because he died four years later, leaving a two-year-old son, Rana Bahadur Shah, on the throne.

Administration of the kingdom fell to a regent who followed in the footsteps of Prithvi Narayan. He sent armies into Kashmir, Sikkim and Tibet. The military was given practically free rein to continue its aggressive expansion which brought it into direct conflict with the Chinese and the British. The success of the army in taking lands to the east and west of Kathmandu encouraged it to engage Tibet directly.

There had been a long-standing complaint by the Nepalese government that its merchants in Lhasa and other towns were not treated fairly. And there was another dispute, regarding the control of the Kuti and Kairang passes, that affected trade.

Opposite: Patan's 16th-century terracotta Mahabauddha Temple built by the scholar, Abhayraj and his descendants.

When Tibet refused to comply with a Nepalese order to surrender the land around the passes, the Nepalese closed the trade routes to Tibet, and the Nepalese army advanced into Tibet as far as Shigatse, the seat of the Panchen Lama.

They withdrew after they were promised an annual tribute for the lands by local Tibetan and Chinese representatives. But when they failed to honour the promise, the Nepalese stormed Shigatse and sacked the monastery. When news of this reached Beijing, the Chinese emperor sent a large force into Tibet, a show of power which prompted the court at Kathmandu to sign a trade agreement with the British East India Company as protection against the Chinese. The British had no intention of confronting China, given the huge potential for profit through trade with the giant.

The Qing army reoccupied Tibet and advanced to within 35 kilometres (22 miles) of Kathmandu. Humiliated, the Nepalese were forced to sign a treaty relinquishing their trading privileges in Tibet and making them subordinate to the Qing Empire. Further, Kathmandu was required to pay substantial tribute to the Qing every five years. Thus the northward expansion of Nepal was checked for ever.

But to the east lay the hill state of Gharwal, in the gorgeous valley of Dhera Dun. From the 18th century, Gharwal had been the target of the Afghans, Sikhs and Marathas.

Thwarted by its Tibetan failure, the Nepalese army waited until Gharwal was destroyed by an earthquake before attacking, and then the army besieged the capital, Kangra.

In the years that followed, Nepal's General Amar — 'The Immortal' — Singh Thapa continued to quell uprisings in Gharwal and Kumaon which never truly became an integral part of the Nepalese state.

Nonetheless, by 1810, Nepal extended from the western borders of Kashmir to the eastern borders of Sikkim.

The British period

War between Britain and Nepal broke out after Nepalese troops attacked police outposts at Butwal and killed 18 police officers on 22 April 1814.

Top: Hooded cobra guards bronze statue of Yoganarendra, Patan's Durbar Square.
Above: Statue of King Bhupatindra Malla, hands folded, presides over Bhaktapur's Durbar Square.

Two fronts comprised the British campaign. To the east, two columns of l0,000 troops were to attack the Makwanpur-Palpa area. But the confusion of hill warfare made the campaign unsuccessful.

In the west, two columns were also to engage Amar Singh Thapa who, by his bravery, even though he was against conflict with the British, earned the additional title of 'The Living Lion'. Although one column failed to get through, the other, led by General Ochterlony, managed to defeat him.

The formidable power of the Nepalese army prompted the British to arm themselves with additional manpower and weapons in the second stage of the conflict the following year.

With more than 100 pieces of artillery, 35,000 men under Ochterlony marched to Makwanpur. The *chogyal* of Sikkim also marshalled troops against the Nepalese and the British-Sikkim alliance routed the Nepalese army.

Much of the territory they had taken was, of course, forfeited. Under the 1816 'Treaty of Friendship', Sikkim became a British protectorate; most of the richly fertile Terai was taken away, and the new western border drawn by the British removed Nepal not only from Kashmir but also from a good deal of the territory in between.

And by the time the British returned part of the land, some 40 years or more later, the royal family were rulers in name only.

The Treaty of Sagauli ceded the region west of the Kali River (Garhwal, Kumaon), and all the lands of the Terai, to the British. In return, Kathmandu was paid Rs 200,000 as compensation for lost revenue. As a final insult Kathmandu was forced to accept a British Resident.

The court was understandably nervous of the presence of the Resident, as most conquests in India had been preceded by such an installation. But, in the long run, the treaty was less damaging than initially perceived.

The Terai, it turned out, was too difficult to govern and the British returned it to the Nepalese and discontinued the annual payments. This was significant because Kathmandu depended on the fertile region

Top: Statue of King Tribuvan
Above: Statue of King Prithvi Narayan Shah the Great, creator of modern Nepal, looks out over central Kathmandu.

for land endowments which financed the government.

As for the Resident, the ruling families kept a close watch on his activities and the people he met, and shut him out of important meetings.

With an end to Nepalese imperialism the focus of the court turned inward. At the time of the British war, five main ruling families were scheming for power: the Shahs, Chautariyas, Thapas, Basnyats and Pandes. Advising them on matters of religion were the hill Brahmins. In the bureaucracy, administrative positions were held by the Newars. Bhimsen Thapa had become prime minister during Girvan Yuddha Shah's reign. As regent of the minor king, Bhimsen Thapa had unlimited power.

He gave appointments of state to his relatives and strengthened his position in court. He kept the king, Rajendra Bikram Shah, under virtual house-arrest. He was not allowed to leave without Bhimsen Thapa's permission.

But Thapa's power declined when the king came of age and fell under the influence of the Pandes. Spurred by the open favouritism of the British Resident, Brian Hodgson, for the Pandes, the king declared his independence from the prime minister. Thapa and his relatives were deprived of their power and members of the Pande family were promoted to prominent positions.

When the youngest son of the elder queen died, Bhimsen Thapa was charged with poisoning the prince. All the property of the Thapas was confiscated. A long trial ultimately acquitted Bhimsen Thapa of murder but it was the end of his power. Shortly afterwards, Rana Jang Pande became prime minister, and she reimprisoned Bhimsen Thapa, who committed suicide, bringing to an end the first stable government since the expansion of Gorkha.

The Rana era
The next important phase of Nepal's history begins with the rise to power of Jung Bahadur Kunwar. The first signs of instability within the court started when King Rajendra Bikram Shah delegated sovereign powers to his favourite junior queen, Lakshmidevi, who became very powerful.

The king issued a decree ordering his subjects to obey her over the heir apparent, Surendra. Queen Lakshmidevi had her own agenda — to put her son on the throne — and favoured Gagan Singh, who commanded seven regiments in the army. When Gagan Singh was found murdered, the queen ordered Abhiman Singh, a subordinate of Gagan Singh, to summon all military and administrative personnel to the courtyard of the palace armoury.

The Queen blamed the Pandes for the death of Gagan Singh and called on the prime minister to execute their leader. When Abhiman Singh hesitated, the situation exploded in a frenzy of bloodshed. Swords were unsheathed and used indiscriminately.

In the chaos, Jung Bahadur, the only one with his troops at hand, quickly took command and had many of his opponents killed. The most affected were the Pandes and Thapas, who lost almost all their leaders.

The Kot Massacre remains shrouded in controversy. Many issues remain unanswered, such as the absence of the king, and Jung Bahadur's convenient readiness for trouble.

The outcome of the complete devastation of the Nepalese aristocracy was that Jung Bahadur seized power as prime minister the next day. He immediately purged the court of all possible competitors, resulting in the mass exodus of the remaining aristocracy to exile in India. Jung Bahadur began what is known as the Rana dynasty, which, for the next century, held an unshakeable grip on the country's affairs.

One device Jung Bahadur used to consolidate his power structure was to maintain Nepal's closed-door society. The country's borders had remained virtually sealed — and visitors were rarely allowed to enter — since the treaty signed 30 years earlier. The British Resident and his heirs were the only perManint allies within Nepal for more than a century.

Soon afterwards, Jung Bahadur bestowed upon himself the title of Maharajah and vested himself with greater powers than those of the sovereign. At the same time he made his own line of succession hereditary — his office passing first to his brothers and then, later, to their sons.

Above: Statue of 18th-century King Prithvi Narayan Shah, outside the Singh Durbar (Lion Palace) Kathmandu.

It was a ruthless oligarchy. All power was bent to the sole benefit of the first incumbent and his successors. So great was their megalomania that the Ranas went down in history as the builders of the world's largest private palace.

With his competitors totally eliminated, Jung Bahadur concentrated on affairs of state. He travelled to Britain, where he tried, unsuccessfully, to talk to the British government. But after seeing the industrialization taking place in Britain, he saw that cooperation with the British was the best way to guarantee Nepal's independence.

He brought back European architecture, fashion and furnishings. He initiated other modernization efforts by having prominent administrators and interpreters revise and incorporate the legal system into one unifying law. The result, a 1,400-page document called the *Muluk'Ain*, was published in 1854. Among improvements was the abolition of corporal punishment, and of torture to obtain confessions.

During Jang Bahadur's reign, the king remained titular head but was kept under house arrest and all visitors had to have Jung Bahadur's permission to meet him. In effect, all powers of state and the military were transferred to the prime minister, and in all but name he assumed the powers of king.

In a series of matrimonial alliances, Jung Bahadur further cemented the bond between the royal family and himself by arranging for the heir-apparent to marry his two daughters. A son of this marriage ascended the throne in 1881.

On the international front, the situation with Tibet escalated into war when the Nepalese mission was mistreated by the local Tibetans during the five-year tribute mission.

The Nepalese protested at first and then sent troops to the Kuti and Ksirang regions. Finally, a treaty by the Chinese gave Nepalese merchants duty-free privileges in Tibet, made Tibet pay Rs 100,000 annually to Nepal and established a Nepalese Resident in Tibet.

Above: Rana Maharaja, royal guests and courtiers.

The Nepalese returned the territories they had taken and agreed to be a tributary of the Qing Empire. Later, when the Qing dynasty disintegrated, so did the fragile bond. In India, the Sepoy rebellion had broken out, and with it came the first real threat of expelling the British from India.

The British initially feared that Nepal would side with the Sepoys, but Jung Bahadur sent his troops in support of the British. He fought several battles with success and continued to persecute fugitives in the Terai region. In gratitude for the support, the British returned all the Terai lands to the Nepalese and remained a staunch ally of Jung Bahadur. Later, the British began to recruit infantry from Nepal, who came to be known as the Gurkhas.

In 1858, King Surendra bestowed on Jung Bahadur the title of Rana, derived from the old title used by the Rajputs, and for almost a century the Ranas remained the power behind the Nepalese throne.

Despite some of his improvements, Jung Bahadur is considered responsible for isolating Nepal from the world for a century and leaving the country in near primitive conditions. But his ability to rise above — and unite — the warring aristocracy and maintain stability makes him a unique historical figure.

Jung Bahadur's descendants maintained Nepal's isolation from the rest of the world throughout the next century. Although there were no major changes, small improvements were made, such as the abolition of *sati* — widow suicide by burning — and slavery, and some factories and mills signalled the country's entry into the industrial era. Trichandra College was founded in 1918, as were several high schools.

But for the most part, the population remained illiterate and lived medieval lives. Public health and economic growth were limited to Kathmandu and a few other towns. Despite the total suppression of any opposition, the lack of progress and development of the country did not go unnoticed. A great number of Nepalese soldiers aided the Allies during the First

World War and the soldiers saw the changes which were taking place in society in Europe and Asia.

Stage for revolution
During the reign of Chandra Shamsher, following the end of World War I, retired army officer Thakur Chandra Singh started two weekly newspapers in Kumaon — *Tarun Gorkha* (Young Gorkha) and *Gorkha Samsar* (Gorkha World). Another publication, *Gorkhali*, was started by Devi Prasad Sapkota after he retired from the Foreign Department.

These became forums in which exiled Nepalese were able to criticize the Rana government in relative safety. In the 1930s, a debating society called Nagrik Adhikar Samiti (Citizens' Rights Committee) was founded in Kathmandu to discuss religious issues. But when the debates criticized the Rana regime, the society was shut down.

Notably the first political party, the Praja Parshad (People's Party), was started by Nepalese exiles, who later opened chapters in the country.

In Bihar, the party published a periodical and encouraged a movement toward a multi-caste, democratic government with the overthrow of the Ranas.

The Rana police went undercover to infiltrate and expose the Kathmandu chapter and subsequently arrested 500 people. Four of the leaders were later executed. They were commemorated as martyrs in 1991.

The bulk of the leadership escaped to India, where they carried on their work in partnership with the Indian National Congress, headed by Mohandas K Gandhi and Jawarhalal Nehru. Gandhi advocated a non-violent civil disobedience movement to force the British to 'Quit India'.

The Indian people responded, leading to the paralysis of the majority of the labour force. Beset with other problems, the British found the Indian National Congress opposing participation in World War II when it was realized that there was no promise of independence.

When civil disobedience escalated after the party leaders were arrested, the British had no choice but to consider independence.

To the north, civil war between the Chinese Communists and the Nationalists had broken Nepal's tenuous link with the Qing dynasty. With the withdrawal of the British empire, complicated by the return of thousands of Gurkha soldiers from abroad, the Ranas were forced to make political changes.

Return to power
The Nepali Rashtriya Congress (Nepali National Congress) headed by Bishweswar Prasad (B P) Koirala, declared the party's goal to remove the Ranas from power peacefully and to establish democratic socialism. Support from India and the exiles put the Congress in a position to organize labour strikes.

The first strike, at the jute mills in Biratnagar in the Terai, disrupted traffic and brought out the army. In Kathmandu, supporters demonstrated but, despite the publicity, the strike was suppressed and the leaders, including B P Koirala, were arrested.

B P Koirala was the most prominent leader of the Nepali Rashtriya Congress. His father was a Brahmin businessman who travelled often to Bihar and Bengal. He was influenced by the political movement in India and the ideals of Gandhi in particular. B P Koirala grew up in a household full of progressive ideas, studied law in Calcutta and began work for the Congress Socialist Party. He was arrested for inciting Nepalese soldiers to rebel against the government. During that time, he advocated a rapid democratic decentralization and favoured developing industry through small cottage industry units, rather than huge factories. He stressed non-violence but did not rule out force if all else failed. His goal was a constitutional monarchy as the first step to democracy.

Then Prime Minister Juddha Shamsher resigned the post and gave it to Padma Shamsher, who promised to improve the Rana regime. Following the suppression of the Biratnagar strike, he issued reforms for government that included establishing a separate judiciary.

In the light of these promised reforms, the Nepali National Congress called off the strikes. In January 1948, the first constitution of Nepal was established, instituting a

Above: Mohan Shamsher and J B Rana.

the Communists, who secured Tibet once again in 1950. The Indian government was too concerned with the security of the north to involve itself deeply in the affairs of Nepal. The king was assured protection and the insurgents were allowed to operate along the India-Nepal border.

Fighting continued, with the rebels taking Pokhara and Palpa. Finally, some of the 'C' class Rana officers resigned their commissions and sections of the army began to surrender to the rebels. Negotiations for peace were moderated by the Indian government. Mohan Shamsher promised an amnesty to all political fugitives, and elections by 1952. The king agreed.

An interim government was formed under Mohan Shamsher, with five Ranas and five Nepali Congress Party members. The king returned to Kathmandu in February 1951.

The system of government that followed divided power between two factions, with the king and the army on one side and the political parties on the other.

The king managed to control most executive powers, including foreign affairs; he was able even to dismiss the prime minister. The political parties, on the other hand, saw the rise of two other prominent parties: the Communist Party of Nepal and the Praja Parishad.

The infighting among the parties hindered the progress of democracy. The king frequently replaced ministers with people from weaker parties and successfully kept the membership of the Nepali Congress Party at bay.

When King Mahendra Bir Bikram Shah ascended the throne he continued in his father's footsteps, experimenting with different ministries and councils. But a spate of civil disobedience forced him to announce elections for a representative body for 18 February 1959, almost seven years after they had been promised.

While the political parties prepared for elections, the king had a commission draw up a new constitution, which he gave the nation a week before the elections. By that constitution, the king retained powers of state, commanded the army and still had control over the legislation. The winner

two-chamber parliament, a separate high court, and a prime minister assisted by five council ministers. But there were too many problems for the prime minister and he resigned his post. Events came to a head when Mohan Shamsher took over as prime minister. He outlawed the Nepali National Congress and arrested the leaders after a series of coups. B P Koirala was released at the insistence of the Indian government.

When the Nepali National Congress absorbed the fledgling Nepal Democratic Congress, the party evolved into the Nepali Congress Party, ready to wage war with the Ranas.

On 6 November 1950, King Tribhuvan Bir Bikram Shah, who was opposed to the Ranas, escaped to the Indian embassy in Kathmandu. Skirmishes erupted in the volatile Terai region. Without backing from Britain or India, Mohan Shamsher found himself alone in this war.

Although guerrilla warfare continued in areas outside Kathmandu up to Gorkha, the fighting never reached the city.

To the north, China was controlled by

of the national elections was the Nepali Congress Party, and B P Koirala finally became prime minister.

In the short time the Nepali Congress Party was in power it accomplish some significant changes. The autonomy of the principalities of the western hills was abolished, thus centralizing power in Kathmandu.

A Trade and Transit Treaty was established with India, as was an agreement on the Gandak River Project which ensured free provision of water to Nepal. Koirala established diplomatic ties with China, the Soviet Union, France and Pakistan. On the economic front, the government initiated a second Plan after the first Five-Year Plan failed.

These changes made the king and the aristocracy uncomfortable. Despite the majority of the Nepali Congress Party in the legislature, factional rivalries were vicious, resulting in constant unrest in the country, particularly in the Terai.

Using this as the reason, the king dismissed the cabinet and arrested all the leaders for their inability to maintain rule of law. Political parties were banned. Koirala remained in prison for eight years and in exile another eight.

The Panchayat System

The gravity of the political situation prompted the king to consider a new system of government based on the traditional panchayat system, whose members reported directly to the king. The panchayat system was instituted on 16 December 1962, with the new constitution.

The system consisted of a four-tier structure, starting at the local village, district and zonal assemblies. The zones acted as the electoral colleges that elected the National Panchayat. Its power was restricted. Members could not criticize the king, introduce bills without the king's approval or discuss the issues of a non-party democracy. The stage was set for the first elections to the National Panchayat in March-April of 1963.

The disbanding of political parties did not go unopposed. A series of skirmishes involving Nepali Congress supporters erupted along the India-Nepal border.

Indian backing for the Nepali Congress disappeared, however, in the face of a much bigger problem: war between India and China broke out on 20 October 1962. China was swift to occupy disputed territory, spurring India to focus on the strategic stability of the Himalayan region. In an unexpected move, India aligned itself with the king. With the loss of the support of its strongest ally, the Nepali Congress called off the armed struggle and poised itself for elections. Although, theoretically, there were no political parties, a third of the legislature was associated with the Nepali Congress. The panchayat was unable to oppose the king in any significant way, since he had the support of the army.

An informal truce was declared by the Nepali Congress, to the extent that the king released all the leaders. The party went on to split into three factions. B P Koirala's group was popular with the youth, Subarna Shamsher's party upheld loyalty to the king outside the panchayat, and the last wing attempted to work within the restraints of the panchayat system. The disunity among the political parties allowed King Mahendra to make some reforms. Land reforms confiscated large Rana estates, and privileges to the western Nepal aristocracy were curtailed.

A third, and then a fourth, Five-Year Plan was initiated. Eradication of malaria, the construction of the Mahendra east-west highway and resettlement of the Terai led to a huge migration into the region.

A New King

In 1972, King Birendra Bir Bikram Shah ascended the throne. The panchayat system endured without much change. Although there were continuing disturbances in the foothills, orchestrated by the Nepali Congress, it was evident that the situation was going to remain the same.

B P Koirala returned to Nepal with his associate, Ganeshman Singh, to reconcile relations with the king. He was arrested for anti-national activities but released soon afterwards due to his poor health. After a short meeting with the king, he went to the United States for medical attention. On his return, he was arrested again, submitted to

Above: King Birendra Bir Bikram Shah and the Queen on the Palace balcony.

five trials and finally acquitted. Following his trials, Koirala accepted the king's power and did as the other political parties — proclaimed loyalty to the king but opposed his government. The king is still regarded as the incarnation of Vishnu by the majority of rural Nepal.

A referendum in 1980 decided in favour of the panchayat system, but only by a slim margin. The seriousness of the situation saw the king allow freedom of speech and political activity and the formation of an 11-member Constitution Reforms Commission.

In December 1980, the Third Amendment of the 1962 Constitution came into effect. It resulted in the election of representatives directly into the National Panchayat, which would elect one member prime minister, to be approved by the king. The elections were boycotted by the Nepali Congress who rejected the amendments to the constitution and refused to participate in the elections. Surya Bahadur Thapa became prime minister.

Koirala died in 1982, at a time when the turmoil in Nepalese politics was at its peak. Notably, in the elections, 70 per cent of the candidates favoured by the king lost. The Communist Party was gaining ground on college campuses. The early 1980s saw a rapid succession of prime ministers and their governments. All the while, the Nepali Congress boycotted the elections, until they finally allowed their members to participate at the local level. The embarrassingly poor results revealed the party's alienation from the rural electorate.

In 1989, a trade dispute with India led to economic collapse. On 23 March, all the border entry points were closed, except for two. Student anti-Indian demonstrations escalated into anti-government protests. All campuses were shut down for two months. This brought to the forefront Nepal's tenuous position as a landlocked minnow sandwiched between two giants.

Nature's paradise
Despite all these changes and unrest, international interest in Nepal has exploded since the opening of its borders to foreigners.

In the beginning, there was only one Western-style hotel and virtually no tourist amenities. Nonetheless, visitors found that the warm, welcoming nature of the Nepali people made visits a pleasure. The word spread and soon it was evident that tourism would become a major foreign exchange-earner.

Since 1960, the number of visitors has risen from fewer than 5,000 a year to around 400,000 today. Most come to trek the high country and stay between two and six weeks. Others make Kathmandu a short stop on a round-the-world voyage.

Kathmandu now offers a full range of tourist services, while the high-country remains an adventure for those seeking distance from the distractions of modern civilization.

Regardless of how long they stay, few travellers are disappointed. A visit to Nepal often changes your vision of the world. As Stephen Bezruchka wrote:

'Nepal is there to change you, not for you to change it. Lose yourself in its essence. Nepal is not only a place on the map, but an experience, a way of life from which we all can learn.'

Top: His Majesty King Birendra Bir Bikram Dev Shah.
Above: Her Majesty Queen Aishwarya Rajya Laxmi Devi Shah.

The Land: High and Mighty, Sweet and Lush

Landlocked Nepal lies in the embrace of the Himalaya, the 'Abode of the Snows', between India and China. Although many people think that most of Nepal is above the snowline and freezing throughout the year, there are in fact three distinct and diverse climatic zones, with large tracts of agricultural land.

In the south, subtropical jungles form the low-lying Terai; in the middle, the central mountains break into valleys, the largest of which is Kathmandu; and finally, such peaks as Mount Everest, Kanchenjunga and Annapurna dominate the north.

Again, at first glance, Nepal seems totally covered by mountains, but in fact only 75 per cent of the country lies in the Himalaya, a name that derives from two words in Sanskrit, the language on which Nepali is based, *him*, meaning snow, and *alaya*, abode.

Yet, above all, the beauty of Nepal is in its vertical perspectives, for it contains eight of the world's 10 highest peaks, all of them above 8,000 metres (26,250 feet).

With the restoration of the Royal Prerogative in 1951, Nepal's borders were at last open to the many climbers who wish to tackle the greatest mountains in the world. After more than a century of isolation, these were shrouded as much in myth as in the raging mists which, driven by the jet stream, frequently plume from their lofty summits, like the royal standards of their divine residents.

Notable among the first explorer-climbers was the team of H W Tilman and Eric Shipton, who first climbed together in Kenya in the 1920s, and who opened up much of central Nepal and the Everest region for those who were to follow.

Two of their contemporaries were the Frenchmen Maurice Herzog and Louis Lachenal, who surmounted countless problems in dealing with the inflexible bureaucracy left behind by the Ranas to become the first men ever to stand above a height of 8,000 metres (26,250 feet) when they stood on the 8,092-metre (26,545-foot) summit of Annapurna, the world's 10th highest mountain, on 3 March 1950. Looking down the precipitous south face, the two judged it unclimbable, yet only 20 years later, Don Whilans and Dougal Halston, two British climbers in an expedition led by Chris Bonnington, succeeded in achieving the 'impossible'.

The Frenchmen's achievement paled, of course, against that of Edmund Hillary of New Zealand and Sherpa Norgay Tenzing of Nepal, who reached the apex of the world, to stand on the 8,848-metre (29,028-foot) summit of Mount Everest on 29 May 1953. Sagarmatha, as Everest is called in Nepali, was named after the surveyor-general of India in the first half of the 19th century, Sir George Everest, who ordered the first survey of the mountain.

The first map to mark the mountain, using the name Chang-Mo-Langma, meaning 'Mother Goddess of the Universe', was a German one, drawn in 1717.

Besides having eight of the world's 10 highest mountains, Nepal also boasts almost 150 peaks above 6,000 metres (19,700 feet) of which 49 are above 7,000 metres (23,000 feet).

These mountains form a stupendous pedestal which lifts at least a quarter of Nepal's land area more than 3,125 metres (10,000 feet) above sea level. Before the northern wall of the Himalaya, a daunting massif or rock which, at an average height of 6,250 metres (20,000 feet) is 'The Roof of The World', lie the foothills of the Mahab-harat, which rise between 1,560 and 2,815 metres (5,000 and 9,000 feet).

Although, by virtue of this, Nepal is the highest nation in the world, it is also one of the smallest, little larger than the state of Florida in the USA, or than England and Wales combined. Yet it is surrounded by India and China, the world's two most

---

Opposite: Sunrise over Terai Plains. Following pages: Buddhist temple at Kyangjin, Langtang.

Above: Cattle crossing at River Trisuli.
Opposite: Man carries bhar across the stone bridge in Suikhet Valley.

populous nations, and within its 141,414 square kilometres (54,586 square miles) are more contrasts of cultures and landscapes than in countries three or four times larger.

The country's four discernible geographical zones begin with the southernmost Terai, followed by the Churia foothills, the mid-mountain region, and finally the Himalaya.

The Terai, is a narrow strip of land, only 34 kilometres (20 miles) at its widest, that marks the northernmost reaches of the fertile alluvial Indo-Gangetic plain. It is heavily cultivated.

The word *terai* is derived from the Persian for 'damp', an apt description of its hot and humid climate. Three major river systems irrigate the plains — the Kosi, Narayani and Karnali. In the past, the malaria-infested forests proved a natural barrier against British expansion, and even when the British did occupy the Terai, the population proved too volatile to govern. The revenue-generating capacity of the Terai lands and its wealthy landowners

made it a hotbed of political activity in the first half of the century. There were frequent protests and armed insurgency as political parties were formed and the country inched towards a democratic government.

In some areas, subtropical forests and savannah vegetation have been cleared for cultivation. The average annual rainfall is 1,500 millimetres (60 inches), resulting in a dense canopy of tall trees competing for sunlight. 'Sal' (*Shorea robusta*), 'simal' (*Bombax ceiba*) and 'khair' (*Acacia catechu*) trees dominate the land.

The northern section of the Terai, close to the Churia range of hills, is a marshy stretch of land interspersed with riverine tracts and tall grasslands with abundant wildlife. The rich forests are home to sambhar deer, wild boar, tiger, leopard, rhino, pheasants and a host of other birds. Most of the natural habitat is protected by the government within the boundaries of national reserves such as the Royal Chitwan National Park, the Royal Bardia National

Above: Golden Gate and the fifty-five window Palace at Bhaktapur Durbar Square.

Park, the Royal Suklaphanta Wildlife Reserve, and the Parsa Wildlife Reserve.

The fight for survival continues, as the rapidly growing population around the parks turns to the forests for fuel and a livelihood.

The Churia range of hills, which dominates the second zone, rises sharply to heights of 1,250 metres (4,000 feet). Large basins between the Churia and the Mahabharat range in the north are known as the Inner Terai. Frequently there are no distinct demarcations and each zone makes inroads into the next.

Before the land was cultivated, the hills were covered with forests and savannah vegetation. There are only patches of vegetation left that still have natural flora. The largest population density is concentrated in the mid-mountain region, which starts at the Mahabharat range and ends at the Himalaya. Kathmandu, the largest valley in the subcontinent, and the valley of Pokhara arose from ancient lakes that filled with glacial and riverine deposits.

Despite the virtual isolation of the Kathmandu Valley, it has always been Nepal's cultural and political centre, with Kathmandu city the administrative centre.

Over the centuries, migrations from Tibet and India have made the hills a densely populated area. The sides of the mountains are sculpted into an intricate lattice of terraces and fields. The short growing season has reduced the land's productivity, forcing many households to rely on work as seasonal migrant labourers to supplement their meagre income. One of the most popular part-time jobs has been portering for trekking agencies.

Finally, far north, perpetually bound in snow, the Himalaya mountains rise from 4,375 to 8,848 metres (14,000 to 29,028 feet); among them are Everest, Kanchenjunga, Cho Oyu, Dhaulagiri I, and Annapurna I. These lie at the centre of the Himalayan range that has its origins in the windswept Pamirs of Central Asia.

The craggy slopes and extreme temperatures are not conducive to life or settlement. The only cultivated region is the upper Kali Gandaki Valley where the sparse population

Above: Lake Gokyo facing Tibet.

survives by trading and pastoralism. Herdsmen, by the nature of their employment, migrate to different areas with the season; traders also migrate seasonally between the highlands and the lowlands, where ample supplies in the high reaches are necessary for the snowbound months.

Finally, the Great Himalaya Range borders the plateau of Tibet. Nepal's location in the subtropics and its wide altitude range — from 67 to 8,848 metres (220 to 29,028 feet) — provide conditions under which most types of vegetation, from rainforest to arctic montane, can grow. This has resulted in a vast variety of animals, birds, reptiles, insects and plants.

Evolution

The Himalaya, which curves more than 3,000 kilometres (1,800 miles) across the subcontinent, from northern Pakistan in the west to Burma in the east, forms the scimitar-like backbone of Nepal. The average height of northern Nepal is above 6,000 metres (19,686 feet), yet all this was once the bed of an ancient sea. The 8,848-metre

(29,028-foot) summit of Everest — 'Goddess of the Universe', Sagarmatha — is made of marine rock dating from the Cretaceous Age. Eighty to 60 million years ago, it formed the bed of the Tethys·Sea, which then separated Asia from India.

At the end of the Mesozoic era, the Asian continent and the island of India began to jostle with each other. The sea between them receded and, as they rubbed shoulders, the soft sea bed — a mixture of sand and mud dumped into it by rivers from both land masses — rose up into a series of folds.

Thus was Sagarmatha, 'Goddess of the Universe', created; it is now hardened into steely granite by the weathering of the ages but still rising centimetre by centimetre as the relentless forces beneath the continental plates exert their tremendous pressure. The new range cut off the more humid air from the oceans to the south and caused increased precipitation on the newly-formed, steep southern slopes, which in turn created new rivers — of such volume and force that they carved through the bedrock almost as soon as it was raised.

71

It was not until some 600,000 years ago, during the Pleistocene period, that the Himalaya peaks rose to their current heights, when another collision between India and Asia forced the mountains so high the rivers could no longer cut through them. The Mahabharat and Siwalik hills in southern Nepal were also formed at that time, damming some of the rivers flowing south and forming a large prehistoric lake in Kathmandu Valley, which dried up about 200,000 years ago.

The Himalaya mountains, which run along Nepal's entire 885-kilometre (550-mile) northern border with Tibet, are regarded as the world's youngest mountains.

Seen from the air, it seems impossible that anyone, or anything, can live within their frozen embrace. But locked in scores of secret valleys, accessible only by narrow footpaths carved or worn into the rock, often thousands of feet above a narrow gorge, are tiny towns and hamlets.

In most of Nepal, travel is by trail, footpath and suspension bridge over some of the earth's toughest terrain.

All length and little breadth, Nepal at its widest measures only 240 kilometres (150 miles), and at its narrowest 150 kilometres (93 miles). Within that short distance, it climbs from the narrow strip of flat, fertile checker-board, that which lies at 67 metres (220 feet) along the Indian border to more than 8,000 metres (25,600 feet). No more than 160 kilometres (100 miles) separate the highest point on earth — the summit of Everest — from the tropical plains where its melting snows swell the floodwaters of the major tributaries of the sacred Ganges.

Nepal's rivers, which all begin as a trickle of ice-melt, swiftly become raging torrents as they are joined and swollen by countless tributaries. Through the millennia, they have cut some of the world's deepest gorges, plunging in a matter of kilometres from heights of more than 6,000 metres to just above sea level.

From Arctic ice to tropical jungle, in spate, these rivers complete such a journey within 12 hours. There, on the Terai plains, which account for just over 20 per cent of Nepal's land mass, they slow down and span out to endow the fertile fields with their bounty of silt and water.

With one of the world's highest populations, Nepal is hard-pressed to achieve self-sufficiency in food. Over-cultivation of the precipitous valley slopes above the river gorges has turned the landscape into a textbook case of deforestation and soil erosion. Unprotected by deep-rooted tree systems and perennial vegetation, each year the monsoons ravage what little soil cover is left, flushing it away and causing hundreds of landslides.

Yet Nepal remains virtually indestructible. Its sheer scale and form, even of the eroded valley walls, is of such magnificence that it will take away the breath of even the most jaded traveller.

Left: Wheat is sown in the higher terraced fields of Kathmandu Valley. Opposite: Sherpa country ice water, Dhoja Peak and Loza Peak.

The People: From Stone Age to Jet Age

Nepal's many diverse cultures have been shaped over thousands of years by the weather and the environment — and there is a direct living link between groups still in the Stone Age and the metropolitan elite of Kathmandu who are in the Jet Age.

The country's Stone Age groups, where people still make fire with flint and iron and use stone axes, are found in Bajhang and the high, hidden valleys of the west.

As is evident from a quick glance at the population of the country, the culture of Nepal is a unique mix of Tibeto-Burman and Indo-Aryan cultures. Although the national census has an official count of 17 groups, the diversity within the country is so great that anthropologists have identified almost 50 groups, each with its own distinct culture, dialect and dress.

The Indo-Aryan branch of the Nepalese people originally came from Gorkha, whose people in turn were descendants of warrior-castes who migrated from Rajasthan in India.

The Tibeto-Burman groups include the Tamang, Rai, Limbu, Sherpa and Sunwar.

Take a walk in the streets of the capital and see how many different ethnic groups you can spot by their features and dress. Even in a city that leans more and more to Western ways, you will see the subtleties of Nepal's ethnic diversity. The reason for such a plethora of ethnic groups in so small an area stems from centuries of migration from the south and the north.

The migration from the north of the Mongoloid races from Tibet dates back to the early nomads who preceded the migration of the Indo-Aryans. Integration with indigenous groups has given rise to the Tibeto–Nepalese group. The Indo-Aryans, who came from the Indian plains, after the northern migrants, were the Brahmin and Kshatriya Rajputs, who fled before the advance of the Mughals (descendants of the Mongols). They settled in the middle hills and grew over time to be a strong political force in the shaping of modern Nepal. The royal family comes from this group. Another important migration is the continuous influx of Indians from Bihar to the Terai in search of work and a livelihood. Since democracy, more and more have settled in Kathmandu.

The Indo-Aryans brought with them their religion and culture, based on the ancient Vedas. They were bound by a rigid caste structure that took hold and perpetuated itself in some indigenous Nepalese ethnic groups, such as the Newars and Kirants. The caste system was initially divided into the Brahmins or the religious caste; the *kshatriyas*, warriors; the *vaishyas*, the merchants; and the *shudras*, the untouchables. The caste system in Nepal was modified to accommodate the other ethnic groups who adopted Hinduism.

Life in Nepal is still rural. Fewer than 10 per cent of the population lives in the rapidly growing urban areas. Much of the rural population receives a basic primary education in local schools, though many children often have to juggle classes with their duties in the fields.

Occasionally, some rural youngsters are able to get higher education but most stay in their homes and live off the family's ancestral lands.

In spite of the many travel agencies which might lead you to believe that tourism is a huge industry, the mainstay of the economy is still agriculture.

You can see this by just stepping out of Kathmandu to the fields around the outskirts that supply the capital with produce. Farming is still the main occupation — for some it is the only livelihood. In highland areas, where the land and short growing season do not yield much, the men and sometimes women often supplement their

Opposite: Child helping family stack maize which is a significant subsistence and cash crop, Annapurna route.

Above: Sherpa mother with child at Namche Bazaar.

income by working as porters or as migrant workers.

The family (*paribar*) is the basis on which Nepali society is formed. Usually it is a patriarchal unit with an extended family. Nepalese people cherish children and have an average of six in their lifetime. But even in the best of times, one child out of six does not survive to the age of five. A son ensures that *shraddha* rites will be performed at the death of the father, and sons traditionally support the parents in their old age.

A large family provides the labour required to work the land but strains the resources of the family. The older woman of the household normally keeps control of the family finances.

However, the extended family does not always work, as happens when the sons are all married and compete among their siblings for family lands. Sometimes, land is divided among the children to resolve quarrels or is divided when the father of the family dies. The resulting fragmentation of the land has led to small plots that are insufficient to support families.

The village is the social centre of rural Nepal. Some are large collections of houses with specialized services provided by tailors and blacksmiths. There are also villages that have only a few homes.

Although each household is an individual unit, villagers often practice *parmar* — trading labour during times of planting or harvest. A popular trend has been to supplement household incomes by sending a child to work in the homes of the military, civil servants or other urban occupations. This buffers the family in times of hardship, especially if the year's crops fail.

Life is basic. Unless the household includes a lodge or rents beds to trekkers, it probably does not have electricity, running water or heat.

Women spend the day tending the fields, walking miles for firewood and preparing the meals. Often mothers strap babies on their backs while in the fields. Men, free from the day-to-day chores, help with farm work and take care of family business.

The Brahmins still occupy the topmost

rung of the caste làdder, followed by the Thakuris and the Chhetris, who form the warrior class. The perceived superiority of the other groups in relation to one another is often not shared by the 'lower' caste. There is no place in such a hierarchy for Sherpas and Mananges, who are Buddhists.

The two main racial groups are Indo-Aryan and Mongoloid. The southern communities, Brahmins and Chhetris, are of Aryan stock. The Sherpas and Tamangs of the north are pure Mongoloid. In between come such groups as the Newars of Kathmandu, the Kirantis of the midlands, the Gurungs and the Magars, who are a mixture of both.

The main ethnic groups of the midlands are the Kirantis — Rais and Limbus — Tamangs, Gurungs, Thakalis and the Newar. Those of the Himalaya mountains are the Sherpas, Lopas and the Dolpos, the latter numbering just a few hundred.

In the lowlands, the main groups are

Above: Young Tamang girl. Living in the eastern and central hills around Kathmandu, the Tamang community – also known as Murmi – is one of the largest of the country's 35 ethnic groups.

the Tharus, Satars, Dhangars, Rajbansis, Danwars, Majhis and Darais. Among the minorities are the Muslims, who number around two per cent of the population, and about 6,000 Tibetan refugees who have settled in Nepal and obtained citizenship.

The Gurkhas

Perhaps the best-known of all these communities are the Gurkhas and the Sherpas. In fact, the Gurkhas are not an ethnic but a warrior grouping, with more than 300 years of tradition in the armies of Nepal and as mercenaries in the pay of the Indian and British armies.

Gurungs

Among the ethnic groups that provide recruits are the Gurungs, whose villages are found in the foothills of the Lamjung and Annapurna ranges.

In the Dhaulagiri region, slashes of brilliant orange or white mark the farms of the Brahmins, Chhetris, Gurungs and Magars. Their gardens are filled with the colours of poinsettias, marigolds, and other flowers, and shady banyan trees. Barley, wheat, millet, rice and maize are grown in the valleys that lie between the mountains.

The people of the Manang Valley, however, are famous for their trading. Tibetan in culture, they travel to many parts of the Orient — Singapore, Hong Kong and Bangkok — to do business.

The land is a maze of terraces and farms. They have an oral-only language with three main dialects, also Tibeto-Burmese. A general pattern indicates that Tamangs living in higher regions are Buddhists while the ones living lower down are Hindus.

Magars

The Magars live in the same region as the Gurungs and also serve as Gurkhas. Their unique culture is also Tibeto-Burmese. They have their own dialects which are further classified into several sub-dialects.

After tourism, military service in foreign armies is the country's second-largest source of foreign exchange. Salaries, pen-

sions and related services bring between US$15 and $20 million a year. The bravery of Gurkha soldiers, who form the elite force of the Royal Nepali Army, is legendary. Short and stocky hillsmen, they have fought and distinguished themselves in some of the greatest battles in military history. During the last two centuries their daring feats have earned them endless awards, notably 13 Victoria Crosses, Britain's highest award for valour. Most recently, in the 1982 Falklands War between Argentina and Britain, their bravery was acknowledged yet again.

The name Gurkha denotes their status as the bravest of the brave. It originated from the Gorkha community of central Nepal which raised the first two Gurkha battalions in 1763 to serve the founder of the present royal dynasty.

Calling themselves the Sri Nath and the Purano Gorakh, these battalions first saw action against the British in 1768. They also took part in campaigns against Tibet.

By 1814 this force, made up mainly of Thakuri, Magar and Gurung tribesmen, had slashed their way through the central Himalaya with the khukri — the fearsome, long, curved blade that, by the end of the 19th century, had become the most celebrated weapon in the arsenal of hand-to-hand combat.

Their derring-do during the two-year Anglo-Nepal War (1814-1816) impressed Western observers, and the British East India Company began recruiting Gurkhas on an informal basis. These casual contracts continued for another 70 years. When the Gurkhas were formally acknowledged, eight units were already in continuous service in India.

Most units were made up of Magar and Gurung tribesmen, but officers had already begun to draw other recruits from the Rais, Limbu and Sunwar tribes of the east and from the Khasas in the west.

During the 1857 Indian Mutiny they demonstrated not only tenacity and bravery but also loyalty that would become equally as legendary. As Bishop Stortford, in a 1930 introduction to Ralph Lilley Turner's *Nepali Dictionary*, remembered:

' . . . my thoughts return to you . . . my

Top: Gurkha soldier. The name Gurkha denotes their status, as the bravest of the brave. Above: Woman from Annapurna region.

comrades . . . Once more I hear the laughter with which you greeted hardship . . . I see you in your bivouacs . . . on forced marches or in the trenches, now shivering with wet and cold, now scorched by a pitiless and burning sun. Uncomplaining you endure hunger and thirst and wounds; and at last your unwavering lines disappear into the smoke and wrath of battle. Bravest of the brave, most generous of the generous, never had country more faithful friends than you.'

In the last half of the 19th century, these warriors fought all across south Asia, from Malaya to Afghanistan — even in Africa, in Somaliland — displaying remarkable endurance as well as courage.

Several Gurkhas have also stood out as mountain climbers. In 1894, Amar Singh Thapa and Karbir Burathoki climbed 21 major peaks and walked over 39 passes in the European Alps in an epic 86-day trek during which they covered more than 1,600 kilometres (1000 miles).

Thirteen years later, Karbir Burathoki, with Englishman Tom Longstaff, completed the first major ascent of any Himalayan peak, 7,119-metre (23,357-foot) Trisul. Between 1921 and 1937, Gurkha porters helped to mount five assaults on the then-unclimbed Everest.

By the end of World War I, more than 300,000 Gurkhas had seen service across Europe, Africa and in the Indian Army. In a battle in Flanders in 1915, Kulbir Thapa won the first of the 13 Victoria Crosses; Karna Bahadur Rana won the second in Palestine in 1918.

Certainly, without these doughty stalwarts, Britain would have been even more hard-pressed to defend itself and its colonies in World War II. Expanded to 45 battalions, Gurkha troops distinguished themselves in action across the Middle East, the Mediterranean and in Burma, Malaya and Indonesia.

Two battalions were formed into crack paratrooper outfits. By war's end, the Gurkhas had accumulated another 10 Victoria Crosses. In 1947, Britain began to dismantle its empire and the Gurkha regiments were divided. Six became the Indian Gurkha Rifles and four the British Brigade of Gurkhas.

Top: Clad in an elegant sari a bride during a Nepalese wedding.
Above: Young women enhance their beauty with silver jewellery.

Above: Clad in rich scarlet, reds and gold, women feast and pray during the Teej Festival at Pashupatinath Temple.

Subsequently, the Gurkha regiments of the Indian Army fought against China in 1962 and Pakistan in 1965 and 1971. The British sector served with distinction in Malaya, Indonesia, Brunei and Cyprus. In 1965, in action in Sarawak, Lance-Corporal Rambahadur Limbu won the Gurkhas their 13th Victoria Cross, for 'heroism in the face of overwhelming odds'.

Today, the descendants of these brave men sign up for service in faraway British outposts — Singapore, Brunei and Belize in Honduras, Central America. It was from there that the Gurkhas were rushed into action when war broke out in the Falklands in 1982 between Argentina and Britain.

Described by the Argentinian press as a cross between dwarfs and mountain goats, they presented such a ferocious mien as they advanced on the Argentinian positions that the Latin Americans dropped their weapons and fled — not wishing to discover the Gurkhas' legendary skill at disembowelling the enemy with their wicked-looking khukri blades.

The Kiranti hillsmen from eastern Nepal are now among the principal recruits to the Gurkha regiments. Of Mongoloid and Tibetan stock, they are said to have won the battle of Mahabharat. Their religion is a blend of animism, Buddhism and Hindu Shivaism.

Numbering more than half a million, they speak a language that derives from Tibet. Most Kirantis, military mercenaries or farmers, carry the Gurkha khukri tucked beneath the folds of their robes. Tradition says that once this is drawn it cannot be put back in its scabbard until it has drawn blood.

Until recently, Kiranti honour could only be satisfied by the slaughter of a chicken or duck. Now they settle for another compromise; it is cheaper by far and less complicated simply to nick a finger and spill their own blood to satisfy this centuries-old belief.

Above: Sherpa mother in the hills around Lukla prepares the family supper: potato pancakes.

The Sherpas

The Sherpas of Solu-Khumbu have long earned fame as the world's most skilful high-altitude mountain porters and climbers. Today they control many trekking agencies in Nepal and are actively involved in any mountaineering activities.

Bhote
This term generally describes all the groups in the Himalaya who resemble Tibetans in culture and characteristics. Among them are the Indian Bhutias and the Sherpas and Manangis of Nepal.

Generally, they have similar languages and traditions, and belong to the Tibetan branch of Buddhism. These groups live in the higher regions of Nepal.

In the past, these people have survived through a combination of trading and farming. Some migratory practices were necessary to ensure sufficient food for their livestock. The Sherpas, a Nepali ethnic group

Above: Young Sherpa children learning how to write.

of Mongoloid stock who number between 25,000 and 30,000, migrated centuries ago over the Himalaya from Minyak in eastern Tibet.

It was Sherpa Norgay Tenzing who, with Sir Edmund Hillary, conquered Everest and it is the Sherpas who accompany every major mountain-climbing expedition. For endurance, few equal them. They are Buddhists and most earn a living by trading, farming, and herding yaks.

Alpine mountaineer A M Kellas first used Sherpas in a mountain assault in 1907 in Sikkim. But renown came with the opening of the Nepal Himalaya in the 1950s. So courageous and skilful were the Sherpas that the Alpine Club gave them the title 'Tigers of the Snow'.

Sherpa Tenzing earned immortality from his ascent with Hillary, but he died penniless in exile in Delhi, India, in 1986. Others of his kin have since followed him to the top of the world. One, Pertemba Sherpa, has been there twice.

The high altitude of the Sherpas' environment prepares them physically and mentally for the challenges of climbing 8,800 metres (29,000 feet) into the sky.

Since the Mongol invasions 700 or 800 years ago, the Sherpas have maintained much of their nomadic lifestyle; in summer they move up to the sparse pastures above 5,800 metres (19,000 feet). In the past, they migrated to Tibet in summer, returning in winter to the Khumbu region. Slowly, they settled in more permanent communities, tilling the fields, growing vegetables and root crops.

Made up of 18 clans, each speaking its own dialect, Sherpas follow tribal laws that prohibit intermarriage not only between members of the same clan but also between members of specific clans. Gifts of the Sherpa home-brewed beer, *chhang*, are exchanged between heads of families when their offspring become engaged. Weddings are elaborate and lavish affairs with great feasting and drinking.

Traders and moneylenders are prominent in society. Usury is big business, with loans at 25 to 30 per cent interest not uncommon.

Yaks provide butter for the lamps which burn in the monasteries and private homes, and for the rancid Tibetan tea served in these parts. Arts and handicrafts are limited but images, scrolls, murals and rock-carving provide lucrative rewards for those Sherpa priests, or lamas, who have become skilled artists. They belong to the oldest Buddhist sect in Tibet, still largely unreformed. The priests borrow freely from the arts of sorcery and witchcraft to sustain their authority, and sacrifice is a ritual tool to deal with the mythological demons and gods who inhabit every peak and recess of the region, and whose presence is confirmed in the Buddhist scriptures.

Thakali

The Thak Kola region in central Nepal is home to the Thakalis, who are renowned as able traders and shrewd business people. In the days of the salt trade with Tibet, when salt was a much sought-after commodity, Thakalis served as the middle men. Their colourful trade caravans of mules, loaded with sugar, kerosene, and rice, travelled through the low-lying Kali Gandaki gorge, the deepest in the world and for centuries one of the most important trade routes linking Tibet with Nepal and India. Like the Manang community, their settlements are distinguished by the flat roofs of their houses.

Their original Tibetan Buddhist beliefs have given way to gradual conversion to Hinduism. Many Thakalis now live in Kathmandu and the Terai.

The Dolpos

Of Nepal's many diverse communities perhaps the smallest is that of the Dolpos, a few hundred people who herd their yaks and goats in the sterile, stony moors of Nepal's western Himalaya. They also grow wheat, barley and potatoes.

Lamaist Buddhists who speak a Tibetan dialect, they are mainly traders who use pack beasts to move their goods in caravans from Tibet to the more populous areas of Nepal. They ride tough highland ponies and are adept horsemen.

Opposite: Sherpa woman carrying load from Nala village.

Above: Bright-eyed smiling Newari girls from Kathmandu Valley.

The Tharus

The Tharus are the indigenous inhabitants of the most fertile part of Nepal, the southern corn and rice belt of the Terai. They number close to a million. Over the centuries, they have been joined by many migrants from the midland valleys and the mountain highlands — the Terai is also host to the majority of Nepal's 300,000 Muslims — lured to the plains by the fertile soil and climate.

The Tharus, especially those of high-caste birth, are much more conservative and rigid in their values than the rest of their countrymen. In the south they live together with non-caste communities such as the Danuwar, the Majhi and the Darai, along the Terai's northern edge and in the west with the Rajbansi, the Satar, the Dhimal, and the Bodo people, and in the east the Morang.

The Tharus have lived there longest, building up a resistance to malaria and living in cool, spacious, airy houses with latticework brick walls to allow in any breeze. Besides farming, they hunt, breed livestock and fish. Their bejewelled women are noted for their stern demeanour. They marry early, but if the groom cannot afford the dowry he must work for the bride's family — for up to five years — to be eligible.

They worship tigers, crocodiles, and scorpions in a form of Hinduism tinged with animism.

Newars

In Kathmandu Valley, the oldest community is that of the Newars. Descended from the Mongols, they practise a form of the Hindu caste system, ranking hereditary occupations such as carpentry, sculpture, stonework, goldsmithing and others, according to ritual purity. Their crafts adorn almost every corner of the valley and its cities.

To the Newars, every day is a celebration of life and death. Together with their extended families, they observe a constant round of rituals worshipping and placating the many deities whose blessings rule their daily lives. Once a year, they honour one of the family cows, usually a calf, which personifies Lakshmi, the goddess of wealth, treating it to grain and fruit. Windows

Above: Rai woman and child.

are lit throughout the night to please the divinity, who circles the earth at midnight, and to bring her blessings on cash boxes and grain stores.

Each stage of a Newar's life is marked by colourful ceremonies. In a land where few people live more than 50 years, the old are venerated. When a man reaches the golden age of 77 years, seven months and seven days, there is a re-enactment of the rice-feeding ceremony, *pasni*, which marks the seventh month of every male child. He is hoisted on to a caparisoned palanquin and paraded through the town, his wife following behind on a second palanquin. He is given a symbolic gold earring which marks him out as a wise one for the rest of his life.

Death is marked by cremation at any one of the many burning places near the holy Hindu bathing places, or ghats, which, in Kathmandu in particular, line the banks of the Bagmati River. Mourners walk around the body three times before setting the funeral pyre alight, while relatives shave their heads and ritually purify themselves with the slimy scum-laden waters of the river. After this, the ashes are scattered in the Bagmati and the wind-borne smoke carries the soul to the abode of Yama, the god of death, where it will merge with the divine.

Young Newar girls are symbolically married to Vishnu. Thus, 'married for life', they escape any stigma if widowed or divorced from their earthly husband. These little sisters also pay homage to their brothers — often their only source of support in old age — during the Tihar Bhaitika festival. The boys, seated behind decorative symbols of the universe, the mandala, receive the mark of the *tika* and the blessing, 'I plant a thorn at the door of death; may my brother be immortal.'

Rai and Limbu

Descendants of the Kirata who were referred to in the *Mahabharata*, the Rai and Limbu, are reputed to have once ruled Kathmandu. They still retain the name Kirata to indicate their origins.

PART TWO: PLACES AND TRAVEL

Above: Suikhet Valley woman carrying firewood to the village of Dhampus.
Opposite: Bhaktapur's Nyatapola Temple, one of Nepal's five-storeyed pagoda temples, clings like a fretted pyramid rising more than a hundred feet into the skies. This is dedicated to the Goddess Lakshmi, Queen of Water and its doors were bolted, never to be opened again.

Where Fact and Fable Become One

There is something about Nepal's mountain regions that make the far-fetched and fanciful believable. But perhaps, too, given the millennia in which the Hindu faith has flourished in these parts, this is part of the national ethos — nowhere more so than in fabled Kathmandu Valley, seat of the Malla kings and repository of all Nepali art and culture.

Over the centuries, despite its isolation deep in the mountains, Kathmandu has been the historical hub of Nepal. The original inhabitants of the Valley, the Newars, have written records dating back 2,000 years. There are no records of the earliest settlements.

The Newars' skills as artisans are apparent in the fine craftsmanship of the ancient buildings found in Bhaktapur, Patan and Kathmandu. Also remarkably intact are the traditions, rituals and festivals of the Newari people.

There are several theories about the origins of the Newars. Some believe that they are descendants of the Mongol people; others that they are related to the Dravidians who were the original people of the Indian subcontinent. Yet others believe that they migrated from eastern India, or perhaps their ancestors were the cowherd kings mentioned in the Hindu scriptures.

The range of facial features among the Newar points to the likelihood that they are a mixed group from Indo-Mongolian ancestors.

The apex of the valley's prosperity came in the 1600s, when the Hindu Malla kings ruled the dominions of the Valley. The three sister cities were Kathmandu, Bhaktapur and Patan. Most of the ancient buildings that have survived to this day were built during the reign of the Mallas.

Around that time, a group of Brahmans and Kshatriyas, the highest castes of the Hindus, fled Rajasthan in north-west India before the invasions of the Mughals. They settled in Gorkha and eventually began expanding their territories. By the 1700s,

during the reign of King Prithvi Narayan Shah, the borders of the Gorkha kingdom reached the outskirts of the valley. The Mallas were feuding at the time and were split into three factions in Kathmandu, Patan and Bhaktapur. The first two attacks were repelled by the villagers of Kirtipur.

Enraged, Prithvi Narayan Shah returned with a large army and conquered the town. He ordered that the noses of all males, except those playing wind instruments, be cut off.

Meanwhile, despite the threat of invasion, the people in Kathmandu prepared for the festival of the Living Goddess. When the Shah forces attacked, the king of Kathmandu fled to Patan, and Prithvi Narayan Shah presided over the celebration of the festival. The blessing of the Living Goddess sanctified the powers of the new king.

Set 1,365 metres (4,478 feet) above sea level, at roughly the same latitude as Florida, Kathmandu Valley boasts one of the most perfect climates in the world — neither too hot nor too cold. Summer maximums touch around 30°C and the mean winter temperature is 10°C.

Such munificence in matters of weather must have been ordained by the gods and Nepal justifiably celebrates its divine fortune by reaping at least three harvests a year, of grains such as rice and wheat. Ringed by gentle, tree-clad, evergreen hills, verdant with stands of oak, alder, rhododendron and jacaranda, touching about 2,370 metres (7,736 feet), slate-blue in the misty haze of spring and summer, the Valley's eternal backdrop is the Himalaya. From the top of 2,200-metre (7,218-foot) Nagarkot, you can see the Annapurna massif and Dhaulagiri in the west, and Everest in the east. This is a vista of such purity that for the artist it represents a daunting challenge. Perspectives are so foreshortened by these mighty pinnacles that few, if any, can capture them in pencil or on canvas. As if the mountains and natural beauty were not enough, down in

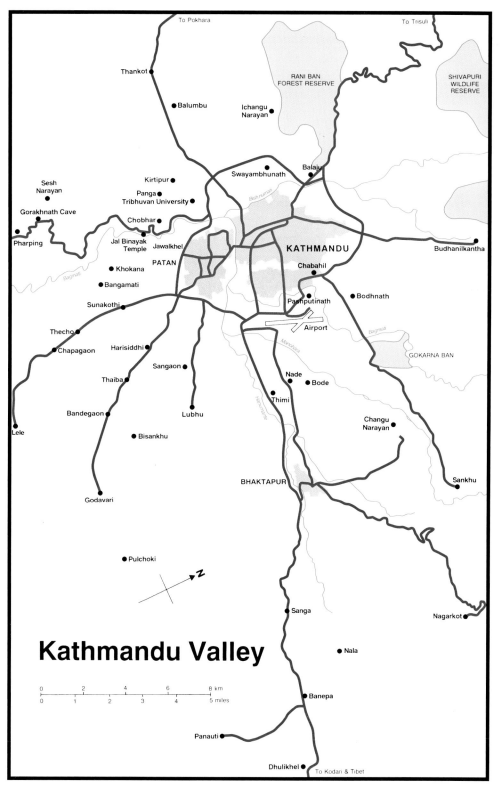

To Pokhara

To Trisuli

Thankot

RANI BAN
FOREST RESERVE

SHIVAPURI
WILDLIFE
RESERVE

Balumbu

Ichangu
Narayan

Balaju

Sesh
Narayan

Kirtipur

Swayambhunath

Panga

Bish numati

Gorakhnath Cave

Tribhuvan University

Chobhar

KATHMANDU

Pharping

Jal Binayak
Temple

Jawalkhel

Budhanilkantha

Khokana

PATAN

Chabahil

Bangamati

Bagmati

Sunakothi

Pashputinath

Bodhnath

Thecho

Airport

Bagmati

Chapagaon

Harisiddhi

GOKARNA BAN

Sangaon

Nade

Thaiba

Bode

Thimi

Bandegaon

Lubhu

Manohara

Changu
Narayan

Lele

Bisankhu

Sankhu

BHAKTAPUR

Godavari

Pulchoki

N

Sanga

Nagarkot

Kathmandu Valley

Nala

| 0 | 2 | 4 | 6 | 8 km |

| 0 | 1 | 2 | 3 | 4 | 5 miles |

Banepa

Panauti

Dhulikhel

To Kodari & Tibet

Above: The serene countryside and dramatic mountain views from Nagarkot village.

the Valley and on the crests of the surrounding hills stands what must rank as the greatest single collection of religious architecture in any one place on earth, from the giant mounds of the Buddhist holy places, *chaitaya* and stupas, to the sublimely beautiful pagoda Hindu temples, with their multi-tiered rooftops.

Many say there are more temples than houses in Kathmandu and it is true that you find them everywhere. Since in Nepal the two faiths are virtually indivisible, these shrines are sacred to almost all worshippers. Many of the most beautiful date from the Malla dynasty which ruled the Valley and the three ancient cities there — Kathmandu, Patan and Bhaktapur — until the 17th century. In those three cities each assembly of temples, sculpture and art is concentrated in a central area or square, living repositories of the most vibrant age of the valley. Much of this heritage, and that of other eras, was wiped out in the great earthquake of 1934, yet so much remains that students of religion, art or architecture would need as many months to take in the wonders of Kathmandu as

the trekker or climber to approach the many mighty peaks above.

Yet all around is evidence of Nepal's dramatic progress. Though it came to the Western world's 20th century — and its own 21st century — in the last half century, it has adapted gracefully.

The Valley floor is lined with a network of broad malls and well-maintained highways, built with overseas aid, many shaded by glorious avenues of trees. China provided the city's 27-kilometre ring road and supplied the quiet, pollution-free trolley buses which ply the 18 kilometres between Tripureshwar and Bhaktapur, charging a pittance. Technology's graft on the ancient in Nepal, however, is only skin deep. Indeed, in the 1990s, a walk down some of the narrow, cobblestone streets of the ancient cities of the Valley, with their overhanging 'Juliet' balconies and delicately carved windows, was like taking a stroll back through time — into the Middle Ages of medieval Europe.

Aeons ago, the floor of Kathmandu Valley was a lake which, perhaps in one of the cataclysmic earthquakes which

Above: Lions guard the Hara Gauri Temple. Following pages: Panoramic view of Kathmandu's gilded pagoda temples and the residential houses which adorn the centre of the city.

occasionally shake the region, suddenly drained itself. Legend says it happened when the sage Manjushri used his sword to slash a gorge — now bridged by a Scottish-built suspension bridge — at Chobar, about eight kilometres (five miles) south-west of the modern capital, where the Bagmati, one of the Valley's major rivers, begins its plunge to the Ganges. There is a temple, of course, right by the gorge — Jal Binayak — which pays homage to the myth. Whatever the cause, the waters left behind a loam so rich that Kathmandu farmers count themselves blessed. Abundant rains and sunshine combine with the loam to ensure that everything grows with profligate ease in the Valley. No land goes fallow. The ox-plough keeps dominion still over the grain and paddy-fields, there among the brown-brick houses scattered across the fields without any perceptible form of planning — except in the built-up metropolitan area. Most of Kathmandu's 300,000 people seem to have a small patch of ground to till.

Kathmandu is the largest Valley in the Himalaya and has enjoyed a virtually unbroken history because of its location. This made it one of the best-kept secrets in the world until the mid-1960s, when the country was officially opened to tourists. The preservation of the culture and traditions of the Nepali people are nowhere more evident than in this fertile Valley. Indeed, from a distance, the richly fertile basin must look much the same as it did when it was first farmed.

Before that time, the only communities lived near the shrines and pilgrimage sites that lay on the slopes of the encircling hills.

The earliest settlements in the valley go back beyond 2,500 years, their beginnings shrouded in ancient legends and myths. Those that remain, such as the Buddhist stupas, evoke reminders of eras long before Kathmandu came into existence.

Kathmandu Valley is peppered with these stupas, of which Swayambhunath and Bodhnath are the two most visible. The flight into Kathmandu is one of the most dramatic experiences you can enjoy. As you cruise north, over the great Indo-

Above: One of many ancient Buddhist chaitaya found in Kathmandu and the Valley; and in other areas of Nepal.

Gangetic plain, the crisp line of snow peaks signals the approach into the Himalaya.

It seems as if you are flying into an impenetrable mountain wall until the heights suddenly open. To the east is Bhaktapur and to the west Patan, the two ancient sister cities of Kathmandu — and then down below is the city itself.

Kathmandu

The best place to start your travels in Nepal is Kathmandu. The city and its neighbouring areas are the strongholds of Newari culture, which has stamped its influence all over this fertile valley. One of the best ways to enjoy the city is to wake up with it in the morning.

Because of the temperature changes, the

Opposite: Farmland south of Kathmandu.
Right: Refreshing coconut slices, spiced with onion rings, carried aloft by a street vendor in ancient Bhaktapur.

Valley floor is often covered by a thick fog, which usually burns away by mid-morning. In winter, flights may be delayed for hours until the sky clears briefly and, in a hectic flurry of activity, planes make a series of rapid take-offs. Down below, the streets are almost completely shrouded in thick cloud, which obscures familiar sights and hides well-known landmarks.

The densely packed houses on the Valley floor are in sharp contrast with the rich green terraced fields cut into the sides of the surrounding mountains.

The bustling streets draw vendors and hawkers from all parts of the country to sell their goods — from the colourful wares from the depths of Nepali rural communities to the shovelware imported from south-east Asia.

As you explore the city, you will notice the deep-seated religious beliefs of the Nepali people, represented by the many shrines and temples on almost every street. The importance of religion in the daily lives of Nepalis is so deeply ingrained that deities manifest themselves in every aspect of the culture.

One of the first daily duties of the women is to pray at the altar in their households. Later, they go to the local *mandir* to make their offerings to the deities.

They carry with them plates heaped with rice, vermilion powder, blossoms and coins. After prayers, they take home *prashad* (gifts) in the form of a paste made of vermilion and rice, and apply *tika* to their foreheads. In tiny tea shops, men and women sip glasses of tea, while produce vendors walk past carrying their goods on poles. Shopkeepers open their shops, dust their wares and settle in for the day.

Although most people in Nepal still live a simple life, development has recently become a buzz word in Kathmandu. Not so many years ago, the urban portion of the city was contained entirely within the Ring Road. Today, the road is but one of many spearheading the expansion of the city.

Looking out to the sides of the Valley, which are transformed into green and yellow murals of rice and mustard fields in the harvest season, you can see the pressure of urbanization as the fields slowly recede.

The heavy influx of migrant workers from India and rural areas has prompted a lively growth of buildings and urban development.

Getting there

Kathmandu is well-served by international airlines and has daily flights from various points in India. It is 200 kilometres (124 miles) by winding precipitous road from the nearest Indian border post at Birganj and takes about eight hours by bus. There are also entry points at Bhairawa and Nepalganj to the West Bengal.

When to go

Kathmandu and Kathmandu Valley are pleasant at any time of the year, though for many perhaps too hot and humid in July and August and a shade too cool in December-January.

Where to stay

In Kathmandu City, the accommodation ranges from splendid five-star hotels, such as the Annapurna, the Everest Hotel, the Soaltee Holiday Inn and the Yak and Yeti, through four-star establishments such as the Malla, the Narayani, the Sanker, the Woodland and the Shangrila, to the many three- two- and one-star lodgings and comfortable and economic guest houses. (See listings under 'Hotels'.)

Sightseeing

Kathmandu itself is neatly divided into two separate districts, distinguished by their different architecture. In the west, there is the Old City, and at its easternmost periphery Tundikhel, Kathmandu's Hyde Park. The division between the two districts is marked by the Kanti Path — King's Way — which runs from north to south, skirting the Royal Palace and cutting across the diplomatic precinct of Lazimpat to continue as far north as the reclining Vishnu of Buddhanilkanth.

The centre of the city begins at the old quarter with the Durbar Square while Durbar Marg is the main street where most of the big travel agencies are located. The palace is situated at the top of this street.

Three of the five-star hotels of the country

Above: Durbar Square, Kathmandu.

line Durbar Marg, and there are plenty of good restaurants to choose from. Most central areas are within walking distance. The streets tend to be crowded so take a small backpack or keep your wallet in a money-belt when walking.

Old City
The three settlements on the floor of the Valley were originally designed in specific shapes. Patan's streets radiate out like the spokes of a wheel; Bhaktapur spirals out as a conch shell and Kathmandu is built in the image of Lord Majushri's sword, the hilt of which is at the confluence of the Bagmati and Bishnumati rivers, where the old city was built on a bluff. It was an ideal site with fertile soil and plentiful water and could be easily defended. The north or upper city was separated from the south or lower portion of the city by Makhan Tole and led to great rivalry between the residents of the two areas. In fact, the rivalry manifested itself in an annual and rather vicious stone fight between contestants from each side. The losers were sacrificed at local temples.

The bloody game was banned by Prime Minister Jung Bahadur Rana after the British Resident was wounded by a stone.

New Road (Juddha Sadak)
Old Kathmandu has remained virtually unchanged throughout the centuries except for **New Road** — Juddha Sadak — built over the devastation of the 1934 earthquake.

Running west from **Tundikhel**, it ends at **Basantapur** and **Durbar Square**, in front of the old royal palace. New Road is the pulsating mainstream of this fascinating city, where you can find everything from the latest electronic appliances, cosmetics, expensive imported food and drugs to jewels and priceless antiques.

Running off the thoroughfare between traditional terraced houses is a series of paved alleys, each with their squares with corner *pati,* central *chaitya,* and occasional temples. The medieval ambience is an authentic time warp, save for the gossiping crowds and the whine of transistor radios.

In a small **square,** halfway along, intellectuals meet under a **pipal tree** to philosophize and debate. Facing the

97

Above: Through the centuries Hindu artists carved many works on the struts and woodwork of the countless pagoda temples that dot the countryside.

Crystal Hotel at the end of New Road is a small, isolated **shrine**.

Where New Road ends near Basantapur Square, Prime Minister Juddha Shamsher Rana's **statue** stands vigil. He masterminded the building of New Road. There is also a supermarket complex filled with foreign goods. Continue walking past the end of New Road until the flagstones begin.

Basantapur

Basantapur takes its name from a large tower looming over the massive **Hanuman Dhoka Palace**, and is a large open space where the royal elephants were once kept. But when New Road was completed, the square turned into a market place, to be replaced by a brick platform built for King Birendra's 1975 coronation celebrations.

Touts sell an assortment of cheap bric-a-brac — local trinkets, bracelets, bangles, religious images, swords and knives — all over the square. The area is overrun with souvenir stalls selling items ranging from the deadly khukris — the Gurkha short sword — to sonorous singing bowls. It is

also the beat of hustlers who sell practically anything you want — or don't want. They are very persistent.

But nowhere in Nepal is there such a vibrant cultural centre where centuries of trade and everyday life is compressed into one small area. In the morning you jostle with vendors, hawkers and office-workers. Women make their rounds to the local temples as a part of their morning duties. In the evening, people stop on their way home to buy produce or drop in for a cup of tea at a friend's shop, the last bustle of the day before the streets clear for the night.

Red bricks of the old Royal Palace mark the limits of old Kathmandu. This comprises the nine-storeyed **Basantapur Tower,** the most prominent part of the palace.

The tower has great significance because Malla kings were born on the first floor, held court on the second floor, watched the girls from the third floor, and climbed to the fourth floor to view the rooftops of their city to ensure that smoke emerged from every house, and that their subjects were well-fed.

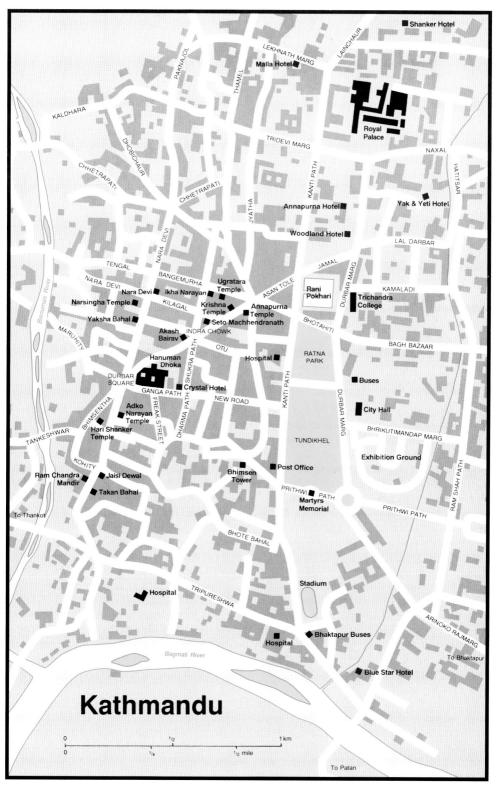

Kathmandu

This is probably pure legend, since the tower was much shorter in those times. The tower itself has been worked on over the years, as the many different tones of the bricks indicate. Some of the finest wood-carvings in the Valley can be found there, in the shapes of serene gods and erotic scenes.

Kumari Bahal

To the west of Basantapur is the ornate residence of the Kumari known as the **Kumari Bahal**. This structure, believed to have been built in the 18th century, has a white stuccoed facade with intricately carved windows depicting images of deities and birds.

Two **stone lions** guard the **steps** into the inner **courtyard**. The craftsmanship of the woodwork surrounding the court-yard is among the best in Kathmandu. The attendants of the Kumari accept donations, after which the Kumari, the living goddess, appears briefly for an audience at one of the windows above. Photographing the person of the Kumari is prohibited, but you can photograph her residence without fear.

The Kumari is believed to be the living incarnation of a goddess, but as to which one depends on the religion of the person telling the story. The most popular belief is that she is the incarnation of either Kanya Kumari or Durga, both manifestations of Shiva's chaste consort Parvati.

Yet others hold her as one of the Ashta Matrikas or eight mother goddesses. The current Kumari is referred to as the Royal Kumari, to identify her from the other Kumaris who still live in the Valley.

The legend of the Kumari, as with other legends, has two stories. One tells of a Malla king who played dice with a human form of the goddess Taleju. One night, he had lustful thoughts of the goddess, who perceived his motives and left in a great rage, vowing never to return to the kingdom. Terrified by the prospect of the kingdom without patronage from the goddess, the king implored her to return. At length, Taleju promised to return as a young virgin.

The other story is about a Sakya girl in the 8th century who claimed to be the living goddess. She was exiled by the king for her claims but, under great pressure from his queen, he reinstated the girl and confined her to a temple.

The process of choosing the Kumari is a long and often terrifying ordeal for the young girls. The Kumari can only come from the Sakya group, who are commonly goldsmiths and silversmiths. She is usually four or five years old when initiated. Among the many requirements, the Kumari's physical body must be unmarked and without flaw, and she must possess the 32 virtues.

Finally, after the initial selection process she must spend a night in the hall of the temple with severed heads of animals and endure the antics of men dressed as demons to scare her. The successful candidate is the one who shows no fear in the face of such terror. Additionally, she has to select the clothes and ornaments of the previous Kumari to show that she is indeed the chosen one.

When astrologers have confirmed that the horoscope of the intended Kumari is compatible with that of the king's, she is named Kumari and housed in the Kumari Bahal. She lives there with attendants until puberty or until she sheds blood as from a wound. She leaves the Bahal only during festivals and is carried through the streets so that her feet do not touch the ground.

The most spectacular procession of the Kumari is during Indra Jatra when, over three days, men carry her flower-adorned chariot through the city.

When the Kumari reaches puberty, she is given a considerable sum of money and items to furnish her new life as a commoner. Kumaris have few suitors however, for fear of an early death and bringing bad luck to the household. Others feel a young pampered girl may not be suitable as a homemaker and mother.

Teeming Temples

Walking away from the Kumari Bahal, you

Opposite: A virgin living Goddess, Kumari at Indra Jatra Festival.

Top: Statue of Bhairav Shiva at Durbar Square Kathmandu.
Above: Reading newspapers on the streets is a common sight in Kathmandu.

enter the Durbar Square, which sprawls across a wide area with more than 50 temples and palaces, most of which were built over a long period of time.

It is a sweep of incredible instant images: shuttered, carved, leaded windows and timbered gables, metal and stone statues of people, beasts and gods and goddesses in every material, including gold and silver, and buildings, both oriental and baroque and in many other styles — all quite unlike anything anywhere else in the world. In fact, the only places to equal it are just a few kilometres down the road in **Patan and Bhaktapur** — and nowhere else.

There is scholarly dispute about some of the historical detail of each of these pristine works of art and architecture, but that should be of no concern to the visitor.

The old square at **Hanuman Dhoka** is the linchpin of the Valley. Trade and commerce converged there during the reign of the Mallas. Unlike similar squares in Patan and Bhaktapur, the **Durbar Square** in Kathmandu is still an area of active commerce.

Vendors and curio-sellers throng the lower steps of the Narayan temple with their wares spread out on sheets. It is also a popular throughway for porters and village folk who bring their produce to the city. And, as in any other street in Kathmandu, cycles and motor cars compete with pedestrians for dominance on the road.

The difference in architectural styles and the apparent lack of planning is testimony to the dynamic changes that were made to the Durbar Square. The most prominent of the ancient buildings is the three-tiered **Taleju temple**. Many of the structures that remain are evidence of the Malla kings' patronage of the arts. Immediately you enter the square there is a **Narayan temple,** with a raised 17th-century grey-stone **statue** of Vishnu's personal mount, Garuda, in a kneeling position outside. What is inside nobody is quite sure, since the inner sanctum has long been closed.

Facing it is the **Gaddi Baithak,** an ornate annexe of the old royal palace built early in the 20th century by a Rana premier, Chandra Shamsher, during the reign of King Tribhuvan Bir Bikram Shah Dev.

It is there that Nepal's top brass gathers with the Royal Family to celebrate Indra Jatra and other festivals and state occasions. There is a **throne** for King Birendra in the main room, which is lined with **portraits** of his ancestors.

On the other side of the square, behind the Narayan Mandir, is a temple dedicated to **Kamdeva,** God of Love and Lust, built by King Bhupatindra's mother, Riddhi Laxmi, and adorned with an immaculate sculpture of Vishnu with Lakshmi. Close by, on a flank of Vishnumati Bridge, is the **Kasthamandap**, which derives its name from the Sanskrit *kastha,* wood, and *mandap,* pavilion.

Renovated in the 17th century, it is from this structure also that Kathmandu takes its name. Built in the pagoda-style, with balconies and raised platforms, it was for many years a place for Tantric worship but it is now a **shrine** with an **image** of Gorakhnath, a deified yoga disciple of Shiva, as its centrepiece. The image of the god, set in the middle of the temple, is protected by a wooden structure.

The solid two-storeyed temple is believed to be built around a central wooden beam, remnants of a marker on the ancient crossroads between India and Tibet.

Centuries have added new structures but the symbol of old trade routes remains in this fascinating older section of Kathmandu.

Kasthamandap — or the House of Wood — originally served, when it was built in the 12th century, as an informal gathering place for people during festivals and other events. Two bronze **lions** stand sentinel at the gate. Various other deities are worshipped in the temple. The **carvings** on the first tier depict scenes from the Hindu epic. On the corner of Chikan Mugal, opposite this inspiring fountainhead of the capital, is the lion house, **Singha Satal.** It

Overleaf: During the eight-day Indra Jatra Festival in Kathmandu's Durbar Square a team of supporters hauls one of the chariots escorting the living Goddess, Kumari.

Above: Vendors and curio-sellers throng the lower steps of the Narayan temple with their artefacts spread out on sheets. Opposite: Entrance to Taleju temple, Kathmandu Square.

was built from the lumber left over from the construction of the Kasthamandap, and has a second-storey balcony and several small shops on the ground floor.

The tiny **Ashok Binayak shrine** stands in the shadow of the Kasthamandap. It houses the **Kathmandu Ganesh**, which is also known as the Maru Ganesh. This popular shrine is visited by would-be travellers, who pray for safety during their journey.

North of the Kasthamandap and the Temple of Narayan is a **Shiva temple** identifiable by the three roofs set on nine giant steps.

Standing in the shadows of the Laxmi Narayan is a small 19th-century **temple** built by King Surendra Bir Bikram Shah Dev, who dedicated it to the elephant-headed God, **Ganesh**; it is where the kings of Nepal worship before their coronation.

Near the temple is **Nava Yogini**, an 18th-century **temple** dedicated to Shiva and Parvati, guarded by **lion statues**. The wooden **statue** of the divine couple is set on the centre window of the upper balcony.

Opposite Nava Yogini is another **temple** dedicated to the **Goddess Bhagvati**. The **statue,** set on a pillar by the Nava Yogini, is that of King Pratap Malla who was patron of most of the structures around him. **Statues** of the king and his consorts are placed on a platform on the third floor of the **Degu Taleju Temple** next to the pillar.

Krishna Mandir stands at the outer edges of the courtyard next to the pillar of King Pratap Malla. Its octagonal shape distinguishes it from the surrounding temples. At one end of the temple the huge gilded **mask** of **Seto Bhairav** — white Bhairav — is sheltered from the outside by a lattice screen. The grinning mask was carved in the 18th century by Rana Bahadur Shah to ward off evil. It is still there, offering benedictions.

Each Indra Jatra festival, sanctified rice beer, *jand*, flows through its grinning orifice from a tank above to the men below who struggle for a gulp of this holy liquor. They will be particularly blessed, it is believed, even if cursed with a hangover next day.

Nearer the centre of Durbar Square, past the **Big Bell**, and a stone **temple** to Vishnu, is the famous **Hanuman Dhoka**. It is the old royal palace, the Durbar Square's inner treasury, which derives its name from a large statue of Hanuman, the monkey-god, and the Nepali word for gate, *dhoka*.

All this is something of a royal mall. The old palace — some parts of it have withstood the ravages of six centuries — is difficult to miss. For 300 years or more, the kings of Nepal have been enthroned there. The first most noticeable feature is the **house** on the corner overlooking Durbar Square, which has three distinctive **carved windows** on one side, where the Malla kings used to watch processions and festivals. Two are carved from ivory, a discovery made in 1975 during preparations for King Birendra's coronation.

A **statue** of **Hanuman** stands to the left of the entrance under a small *chatri*, or umbrella. Just by its right-hand side, a low fence guards an inscribed 17th-century **dedication** to the Goddess Kalika on a **plaque** set into the wall. The inscription, in

Top: Sacred metal image in Kathmandu.
Above: Puppets on sale in Kathmandu.

at least 15 different languages — among them English, French, Persian, Arabic, Hindi, Kashmiri and, of course, Nepali — was written by King Pratap Malla, a gifted linguist and poet.

The statue is covered by a red cloth and its face is smeared with *sindur*, a paste of vermilion powder and mustard oil. As told in the *Ramayana*, Hanuman is famous for his part in helping Lord Rama rescue his wife Sita from the clutches of the demon king Ravana. Hanuman locates Sita and carries her back from Lanka to Ayodhya. His legendary antics and quick wit are popular with both adults and children.

The brightly painted **gates** of the palace are protected by two **stone lions**; the figure on the right lion is **Shiva** while the female on the left is his consort, **Parvati**. Inset into the top of the gate are elaborate **carvings** of the Tantric Krishna, another more benign Krishna with two *gopi*, and King Pratap Malla and his queen. The massive entrance, elaborately decorated with intricate motifs and emblems, is a fitting gateway for kings-to-be.

Inside the gate is **Nasal Chowk,** a large interior courtyard where the royal coronations take place. Nasal, which means 'the dancer', takes its name from the figure of Shiva dancing to the **east** of the courtyard. It was there, on 24 February 1975, that King Birendra was crowned King of Nepal.

The **museum** in Hanuman Dhokha is dedicated to King Tribhuvan.

Although the original Royal Palace was built during the Lichhavi reign, most of what still remains was built by the Malla dynasty. Among the older additions are **Mohan Chowk** and **Sundari Chowk**, two smaller courtyards. The eastern section of Nasal Chowk was built by Prithvi Narayan Shah.

Coloured **towers**, each representing one of Kathmandu's four cities stand around Lohan Chowk. The largest and most prominent is **Basantapur Tower**, and smaller towers — **Kirtipur**, **Lalitpur** and **Bhaktapur** — stand at each corner of the chowk. Parts of Durbar Square were restored by the Ranas and restorations continue.

To the left of the gate as you enter the chowk is **Narsingh**, the lion manifestation of Vishnu, frozen in perpetual conflict with his arch-enemy, the evil Hiranya-Kashipu. The portraits are those of the present Shah dynasty kings.

A little further on stands the pentagon-shaped **Pancha Mukhi Hanuman**, the five-faced Hanuman. The only other five-sided shrine is in Pashupatinath.

The two-tiered temple outside Hanuman Dhokha is **Jaganath temple**, outstanding for the **erotic carvings** on its struts. The oldest surviving part of the structure dates from the 17th century. The small shrine to the right is **Gopinath Mandir**.

Continuing north, you see a huge **Kal Bhairav** — Black Bhairav, the aspect of Shiva the Destroyer. Bhairav is an awe-inspiring figure with a fearsome visage and terrible powers. This manifestation is strikingly adorned with brilliant red and gold **ornaments**, **diadem** and a **garland** of **skulls**. Its piercing eyes and bared fangs, and three pairs of arms holding **weapons** and **severed heads**, are enough to make you shiver, even in the bright sunshine of a Kathmandu summer. The statue stands on a human corpse and extends a bowl fashioned from a skull, into which worshippers place their offerings.

All these are trifles compared with the **Taleju temple,** which rises from a mound to the **right** of the palace, and dominates Durbar Square. Considered Kathmandu's most beautiful temple, it is dedicated to Taleju Bhavani, the tutelary goddess of the Malla dynasty who was a consort of Shiva's. The three-story temple rises about 36 metres (120 feet), and each of the three pagoda roofs is gilded with copper and embellished with hanging bells. The three huge tiers tower over the lesser temples.

Taleju was originally a goddess from South India brought to Nepal in the 14th century. She quickly became the ruling family's deity and eventually a symbol for the king and his powers. There are other Taleju shrines in Patan and Bhaktapur.

The present structure was revered by King Mahendra Malla. Human sacrifices were made in the temple's precincts but these were discontinued after King Prithvi Narayan Shah came to make a customary sacrifice and displeased the goddess.

Top: Mask of Bhairav depicting Shiva.
Above: Vishnu Temple at Durbar Square, Reincarnation of Vishnu as Narsimha.

Above: Taleju Temple at Durbar Square, Kathmandu. Following pages: New Year's Eve in Bhaktapur as revellers prepare for the fall of the wooden lingam and straining supporters hustle to win the battle of chariots.

The ornately carved and painted **white facade** of the entrance is guarded by two painted **stone lions**. Only open to the public once a year, nobody but members of the Royal Family are allowed to enter the main **sanctum**.

To the north-west is an open **courtyard** called the **Kot**, meaning armoury. Surrounding it are police and army offices and quarters. This was the site of the infamous Kot massacre in 1846, when Jung Bahadur Rana, the founder of the Rana dynasty, eliminated all other noblemen who posed a threat to his power.

During Dasain, the Kot is drenched in the blood of sacrificial animals as soldiers sacrifice many buffaloes and goats in the head of the animal.

Finally, at the entrance of Makhan Tole, a **statue** of **Garuda** is partially buried in the ground. To the **right** stands **Tarana** carved doorways and **carvings** of the Asta Matrika goddesses.

For anything to equal all this, you will have to move on to Bhaktapur or Patan and, unless you want a surfeit of erotica on temples and statues, by the time you have walked around both, you will have enough memories of Kathmandu's man-made treasures to last you a lifetime.

Durbar Square environs

Nearby, to the **south** of Durbar Square, is legendary **Freak Street**, the end of the rainbow for the dropouts and the hippies of the 1960s, with the guitars strumming Beatles and Beach Boys numbers. The famous hash and pie shops have disappeared; the hash shops no longer exist and the pie shops have a new home in Thamel. The vestiges of the Woodstock era are a few dingy shops festooned with brocade and trinkets.

Some distance south of Durbar Square, faced in ceramic, the three-storeyed temple to **Adko Narayan,** one of the four main Vishnu temples in Kathmandu, is guarded by an image of Garuda and lions, with erotic carvings on the struts that support the second storey. Nearby there is a small temple dedicated to Shiva, **Hari Shanker.**

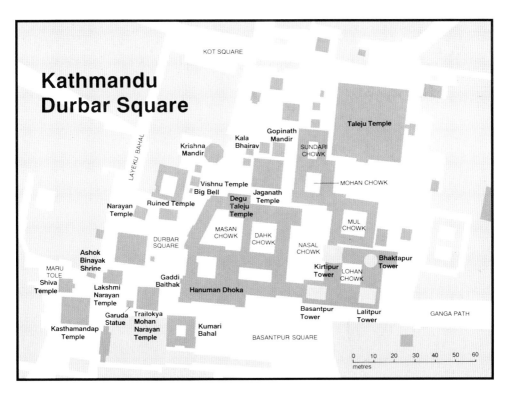

Kathmandu Durbar Square

KOT SQUARE

Taleju Temple

Gopinath Mandir

Kala Bhairav

Krishna Mandir

SUNDARI CHOWK

LAYEKU BAHAL

MOHAN CHOWK

Vishnu Temple
Big Bell

Jaganath Temple

Narayan Temple

Ruined Temple

Degu Taleju Temple

MUL CHOWK

MASAN CHOWK

DAHK CHOWK

NASAL CHOWK

DURBAR SQUARE

Ashok Binayak Shrine

Bhaktapur Tower

MARU TOLE

Kirtipur Tower

LOHAN CHOWK

Shiva Temple

Gaddi Baithak

Lakshmi Narayan Temple

Hanuman Dhoka

Garuda Statue

Trailokya Mohan Narayan Temple

Basantpur Tower

Lalitpur Tower

GANGA PATH

Kasthamandap Temple

Kumari Bahal

BASANTPUR SQUARE

0 10 20 30 40 50 60
metres

Walk on to a crossroads, where the struts of the three-storeyed 17th-century Shiva temple, **Laisi Dewal,** on top of a seven-stepped pyramid, has very finely carved erotica. Set in a **yoni,** behind it is a massive, free-shaped **lingam** — a truly erect stone. It is thought the lingam may date back to the Lichhavi era.

Not far away, on the struts of the **Ram Chandra Mandir** is more classic erotica — tiny, delicately but explicitly detailed carvings. Next you come to a **stupa** ruined in the 14th century, the **Takan Bahal,** a round stucco mound covered by a brick building.

From there you can wander around the narrow streets and alleys of the southern end of the **Old Town,** discovering ancient houses and more ancient religious shrines.

Also, south-west of Durbar Square, near the **Vishnumati Bridge,** stands a **shrine** dedicated to Bhimsen, the god of traders and artisans, whose shops occupy its ground floor. Another manifestation of Shiva, Bhimsen has been worshipped in the Valley since the 17th century. There are some Buddhist **stupas** next to the temple.

Indra Chowk

Close by, north of Durbar Square, a busy intersection of streets from Thamel, Asan Tole, New Road and the Durbar Square merge and one of them leads to **Makhan Tole** and the city's famous **Indra Chowk,** an area noted for its silk bazaar with many fine blankets and textiles, including woollen shawls. It is approached through the **Makhan Tole,** flanked by a many-hued facade with wooden balconies and columns.

Between Makhan Tole and the chowk, a temple situated in a three-storeyed **house** to the south, with white, purple, and green ceramic tiles, yellow windows and two balconies, from one of which hang four gilded griffins, is the **Akash Bhairav temple.** The shrine is popular during festivals, especially the Indrajatra celebrations, when the image of Bhairav is displayed to the public to worship. A long lingam pole is placed in the centre of the square in lieu of the symbolic phallic stones that used to stand there.

Nearby, in the **Mahadev Mandir,** a solid stone building set above a four-stepped plinth where carpet sellers lay out their

Above: Crowd during Kot Puja. Opposite: Carved wooden strut in Basantapur, Kathmandu.

wares, sits a small brass **Ganesh image**. Women vendors display their wares on the **stone plinths**, selling ornaments and vermilion-coloured threads.

The *pashmina* sellers are everywhere, from street vendors with piles of gaudily coloured shawls to small, neat shops selling the best, earth-coloured wraps. Some shops also sell the traditional Newari cover, made from a brightly coloured cloth sandwiched between thin muslin.

Indra Chowk is usually crowded in the evening as office staff leave work, and porters hurry home. Motor cars are forbidden but cycles and motor bikes compete with pedestrian traffic. The chowk is noted for its important shrines and buildings.

As you go on towards Asan Tole, the pashmina shops give way to bolts of brightly coloured fabrics, obscuring fabric store fronts. Next come the shops full of shining stainless steel utensils, then the food shops, with all manner of spices, grains and household staples.

Seto Machhendranath

At one end of the chowk, to the east, past a small shrine smeared with blood, is one of Nepal's most revered temples. The Seto — 'White' — Machhendranath is at the centre of a monastic **courtyard**, but distinguishable from residential buildings by two splendid **brass lions** which guard the entrance. Built at an unknown date, it was restored early in the 17th century.

Each evening, beneath the **porch** that leads to the courtyard, musicians gather and chant sacred verses, gazing at the temple as it rises behind a foreground of stelae, *chaitya* and carved pillars, its gilt-copper roof glowing in the evening sun. The finely carved pillars and *chaitya* sport images of deities. Mythical guardian beasts protect the entrance to the inner shrine which guards an image of Padmapani Avalokiteshwara. There are also **carvings** of Avalokiteshwara in his many forms. To Buddhists, Padmapani Avalokiteshwara is the most revered deity in the Valley because of his immeasurable compassion. Hindus know him as Machhendranath.

Once a year, around March and April, the image is taken out in a chariot during the Seto Machhendranath festival. It is driven three times around the temple as part of the final ceremony, after which the chariot is dismantled and the image returned in a colourful palanquin to its principal temple near Asan Tole. Around the inside courtyard are many shops selling a variety of goods — wool, paper prints, cloth, string, ribbons, beads, curios, Nepali caps and pottery. As with most structures in Nepal, the courtyard is also shared by small shops selling local and tourist articles.

The small three-roofed Tantric temple on the left of the Seto Machhendranath is the **Luchun Lunbun Ajima**. Erotic carvings festoon the interior and, on the inner altar, lie portraits of the king and the queen.

Continuing north, you see a multi-sided three-roofed temple sandwiched between residential buildings, most of them quite old. The first tier of the **Krishna Temple** is elevated and occupied by vegetable sellers. Six streets radiate out of Indra Chowk. Various peddlers wander among the cloth- and flower-sellers, past a dried-fish market into the bead bazaar, where the colours of tawdry bangles and necklaces dazzle the eye.

Beyond Indra Chowk, the open space of Khel Tole is a fast and furious Nepali bazaar area, a never-ending hubbub, with a constant stream of shoppers and peddlers, sightseers and cars, forging through the narrow street, watched by families from the balconies of their houses. It is the oldest trading sector in the area, only quietening down during the night.

The rest of the walk toward Asan Tole is a fascinating look at the many facets of everyday life in the city. You will come across some notable temples, but the most interesting aspect of the road is the liveli-hoods that thrive there.

In some sections, where four- or five-storeyed buildings are stacked next to each other, the road becomes almost a tunnel. The textile shops give way to shops selling everyday goods from shiny stainless steel utensils to plastic buckets or dried fruit.

These neighbourhood stores are virtually community centres where people stop on their way home for a quick visit. Produce and grains are easily available to the city residents and housemaids make their rounds of the market shopping for the day.

Asan Tole, the capital's rice bazaar, is where mountain porters gather seeking employment. This venerable bazaar is still quite pristine, as far as Newari architecture goes, and untouched by tourism.

Small, family-owned stores sell groceries, hardware, utensils, clothing and grain. Wonder never ceases when you enter a shop and see how many shoes can be packed into a room 10 by 10 by 10!

The centre of Asan was previously an area for produce vendors, who hiked from the outskirts of the city to sell their vegetables. Then the vendors moved. What remains are shops that sell clothes, grain and oil, the flute sellers — their canes bristling with flutes, stalls selling vermilion-coloured strings for the hair, and street food-vendors.

Asan Tole has three temples, including the **Annapurna temple**, a three-storeyed building notable for the upturned corners of its gilded roofs and a bell rung by devotees. Many come to pay homage at its **shrine**, which contains a pot. There is also a mini-**Narayan shrine** near the centre of the square and a smaller **Ganesh temple**. The shops near the temple also sell oil, measured in every conceivable unit.

To the left, take a lane with shops run by the Manang people, who sell imported clothes and shoes from Hong Kong and Thailand. They were the first traders allowed to import goods. The lane to the right also has shops selling shoes and clothes produced locally.

The **Nara Devi,** a popular three-storeyed temple guarded by red and white lions, to the west of Asan Tole, is dedicated to one of the Ashta Matrikas. Inside, women prostrate themselves, surrounded by dazzling ceramic tiles and paintings.

Nearby is the three-tiered **Narsingha temple,** with its **image** of Vishnu with a lion's head. Along the same road is an open **courtyard** with a Swayambhunath-like stupa, **Yaksha Bahal,** and four sensual 14th-century **carvings** of the female form.

It faces a painted metal **door** with two **figures**, one with four eyes, while above,

Above: Washed clothes are hung over the balconies to dry.

an attractive woman's face appears out of a carved window frame, entrance to the house of the deity Kanga Ajima.

If you head north-west from Asan Tole through the city's vegetable and fruit market, the street becomes narrower and narrower until you reach a door that opens into the **Haku Bahal** courtyard. This has a notable carved window **balcony**, supported by small carved struts, and an exquisitely carved doorframe, all of the 17th century.

Nearby is the three-storeyed **Ugratara temple,** dedicated to the relief of eye infections and ailments. The temple wall is adorned with reading spectacles donated to the Hindu deity who cares for the gift of sight.

Walk on now until you see the two-storeyed **Ikha Narayan temple,** with its magnificent four-armed **Sridhara Vishnu**, dating from the 10th to 11th centuries, flanked by Lakshmi and Garuda.

There is another **monument** to a healing deity, Vlasha Dev, the God of Toothache, opposite this shrine. The idea is that you hammer a nail into a large piece of wood and thus nail down the evil spirits causing the pain. If this fails, there is a street of friendly, neighbourhood dentists, complete with off-the-peg molars of all shapes and smiles, in the nearby lane.

If you continue north, past a 16th-century **Narayan temple**, you will find one of the capital's oldest and most remarkable antiquities — a carved, black-stone, fifth-century **image** of **Buddha**, and beyond that a bas-relief **Shiva-Parvati** as Uma Maheshwar, set in a brick case.

On now to a passage guarded by **lions** which leads into a monastery **courtyard** containing the **shrine** of **Srigha Chaitya,** a likeness of the Swayambhunath stupa. It is believed that those too old or too sick to climb the hill to Swayambhunath can earn the same merit by making pilgrimage there.

Eventually, you emerge at **Kanti Path**, one of the city's main thoroughfares, with a notable *ghat* (pond) — on one side of it, the **Rani Pokhari**. In the 16th century, the wife of the Malla King Pratap built a temple in the centre to honour her young son after his death, but it later collapsed. Since then, a new **shrine** has been built.

On the lakeside stands **Trichandra**

117

Above: Women enhance their looks with nose jewellery.

College, built by the Ranas, with its **clock tower** and, to the south, **Ratna Park** and the wide expanse of the Tundikhel, used for military training. The column of the **Bhimsen Tower**, a 70-metre (200-foot) edifice, and Kathmandu city's most visible landmark, rises over this area of the city.

Built as a watch station, it was damaged by the earthquake that rumbled through Kathmandu in 1934 and was later rebuilt. For safety reasons, however, it is now closed to the public — thus denying them what was a popular and spectacular 360° panoramic view of the city. Described as Kathmandu's 'tallest erection' by a guidebook of yore, Bhimsen Tower is reputed to have had someone leap off it astride a horse.

Northwards, the Kanti Path runs within view of the imposing **Narainhiti Royal Palace** — built during the reign of King Rana Bahadur Shah and extended in 1970 to mark the wedding of Crown Prince Birendra, later king, while southwards Kanti Path runs along the open space of Tundikhel.

Tundikhel

Tundikhel, with its **royal pavilion**, is where the nation celebrates state occasions and festivals with colourful parades, horse races and acrobatic shows. It is decorated with **statues** of the six Gurkha VCs of the two world wars and around the park are **equestrian statues**. The park, says local lore, was the home of a giant, Guru Mapa, and each year, during the Ghode Jatra festival, a buffalo and mounds of rice are laid out in supplication to Guru Mapa, to keep the peace.

South from the Tundikhel across the broad mall of the **Prithwi Path** is the **Martyrs' Memorial**, an impressive modern archway honouring those who gave their lives to overthrow the Ranas.

There are also four black marble **busts** of rebel leaders — Shukra Raj Shastri, Dharma Bhakta, Dasharath Chand and Gangalal — executed in 1940, either by hanging or firing squad, when Juddha Shumsher was premier.

Singha Durbar

Kathmandu's most impressive modern architectural work, the **Singha Durbar** —

built by the Ranas and once the world's largest private palace — was put to use as government offices with the restoration of royal power in 1951.

Built in 1901, the palace is one of the greatest monuments to mankind's conceit ever conceived. It was raised to symbolise the power of the Rana dynasty. Although it contained **1,700 rooms**, with **17 courtyards** set in 31 hectares (77 acres) of ground, it was completed within 11 months. Sadly, much of it was burnt down in 1973.

The palace's most impressive feature, the mirrored **Durbar hall**, furnished with a **throne**, **statues**, **portrait**s of dead rulers and a line of **stuffed tigers**, still survives.

Today, Nepal's Parliament meets in the Singha Durbar, which is also the head-quarters of the national broadcasting system. Radio Nepal has been on the air for some years but television came late, the first transmissions being made in May 1986.

Beyond the City

Exploring the towns and hills surrounding Kathmandu City is a perfect way to spend a day away from the crowds. Life in most villages is a throwback to the last century or even further. Women wash clothes in a nearby stream. Mothers thresh stalks of rice while keeping an eye on their babies. Men sit and smoke *bidi* over cups of tea. And shopkeepers work out of the homes their ancestors built.

Holy sites abound, too, in the scenic hills outside the Valley. As you visit the different shrines and temples, certain aspects of religious culture are seen in their proper context and become clearer.

Although Nepal is a Hindu kingdom, Buddhists have always been free to practice their religion. It is common to find a Buddhist avatar manifested as a Hindu deity or to learn of legends that combine the beliefs of both religions.

Some holy sites are giant monuments, keeping vigil through their cosmic eyes; others a muddy pool where women wash clothes. At each site, temples, shrines and stat-ues sanctify the abodes of gods and god-desses or commemorate important events.

Getting to these places is easy. Depending on where you are based, if you are fit, you can cycle to many of them. But you will need a good map and comfortable shoes.

Another option is to rent a car and driver or take a taxi. It is not a good idea to drive yourself in Nepal, where traffic has its own 'peculiarities' and everyone claims right of way.

The all-seeing eyes

North-east of the city, the stupa known as Bodhnath is the largest in the country. Its most prominent features are the huge all-seeing eyes with the symbol of unity — *ek*, or 'one' — painted on all sides. Wide concentric steps at the base lead to a perfectly symmetrical half dome; from an aerial view you can see that the steps are designed to represent a mandala. The base has 108 images of the Buddha. Dedicated to Bodhnath, the god of wisdom, the stupa, surrounded by a self-contained Tibetan township, is ringed by the inevitable prayer wheels, each given a twirl as

Above: Traditional Nepalese hat, the Dacca, is so named because the type of cloth used was first woven in the Bangladesh capital.

Above: Bhimsen Tower, Kathmandu Valley.

devotees circle the shrine clockwise.

Most worshippers there are from Tibet. The Bodhnath lama is said to be a reincarnation of the original Dalai Lama, for the stupa's obscure origins are tenuously linked to Lhasa, ancestral home of the now exiled spiritual leader.

A relic of the Buddha is said to lie within the solid dome, which symbolizes water and is reached by 13 steps, again symbolizing the 13 stages of enlightenment from which the monument derives its name, *hodh* meaning enlightenment, and *nath* meaning God.

Saffron and magenta-robed Tibetan monks celebrate their colourful rituals as worshippers chant prayer verses and mantras and clap their hands, while travellers, especially those heading for the Himalaya, seek blessings for the journey.

Although the identity of the stupa's builder remains a mystery, a touching legend identifies Kangma as the original builder of the monument. Kangma was born to a swineherd's family in punishment for stealing flowers from Indra's garden.

She worked as a goose girl and managed to save a fortune. Later, when she was widowed with four children, she requested the king to give her as much ground as the hide of a buffalo would cover to build a temple for Lord Buddha. The king readily granted her wish and she cut the hide into thin strips and joined them. It gave her the square on which to build Bodhnath, a popular place for festivals. Indeed, at the beginning of the Tibetan New Year — February or March — people come from all over to witness the ceremonies performed by the lamas.

The devout are usually dressed in ceremonial garb made of thick, colourful hand-woven fabric, and wear their heirloom *kho*, which are studded with priceless turquoise and cowrie shells. During Gai Jatra, the festival of cow worship, after the morning worship of the sacred cows the courtyard around the stupa becomes a sea of spectators watching and heckling a procession making its way around.

Men dressed garishly as women or politicians, or personifying a current ill in society, strut around. No issue is sacred and all can be criticized without fear of reprisal.

The Mardi Gras-like atmosphere makes this one of the best-loved holidays in Nepal. King Pratap Malla is considered the founder of this tradition in the 18th century. After a desperate attempt to console his grieving wife, who had just lost her son, he declared a reward for anyone who could make the queen laugh, and promised immunity to all participants. The result was a huge procession of people dressed outlandishly; some mimed well-known figures, others lampooned various aspects of social ills. The queen could not help laughing when she saw this unusual turnout. Ribbons of colourful pennants now flutter from the gilt-copper pyramid which surmounts the stupa as the monks blow their long copper horns and, in the crescendo of the climax, everyone hurls fistfuls of ground wheat into the air.

The centrepiece of these festivities is usually a large portrait of the Dalai Lama held high and shielded under a large canopy.

Many try to touch it, sometimes falling flat on their faces as they stumble and trip over the line of lamas, who later, wearing masks, dance for hours in a nearby field.

Tibetan folk dancers often turn up to dance well into the night, invigorated by liquor and merriment, and sometimes by hashish or marijuana.

So distinctive is the shrine — with its striking colourful eyes — that seen from afar, it was perhaps the inspiration for *Mad Carew*, the 19th-century ballad by an unknown British author which goes as follows:

There's a one-eyed yellow idol
    To the north of Kathmandu;
There's a little marble cross below the town,
    Where a broken-hearted woman
Tends the grave of Mad Carew,
    And the yellow god forever gazes down.

He was known as Mad Carew
    By the subs at Kathmandu;
He was hotter than they felt inclined to tell.
    But for all his pranks,
He was worshipped in the ranks,
    And the colonel's daughter smiled on him as well.

He had loved her along
    With the passion of the strong,
And that she returned his love was plain to all.
    She was nearly 21
And arrangements had begun
    To celebrate her birthday with a ball.

He wrote to ask what present
    She would like from Mad Carew.
They met next day as he dismissed the squad.
    And jestingly she replied
That nothing else would do
    But the green eye of the little yellow god.

On the night before the dance,
    Mad Carew sat in a trance,
And they chaffed him as they puffed on their cigars.
    But for once he didn't smile,
He just sat alone awhile,
    Then went out into the night beneath the stars.

He returned next day at dawn
    With his shirt and tunic torn,

And a gash across his temple, dripping red.
    He was patched up right away
And he slept throughout the day,
    While the colonel's daughter watched beside his bed.

He awoke at last and asked her
    To send his tunic through.
She fetched it and he thanked her with a nod.
    Then he bade her search the pockets,
Saying 'That's from Mad Carew':
    It was the green eye of the little yellow god.

When the ball was at its height
    On that dark and tropic night,
She thought of him and hastened to his room.
    As she crossed the barrack square,
She could hear the dreamy air
    Of a waltz tune stealing softly through the gloom.

His door was open wide,
    Silvery moonbeams streaming through;
The floor was wet and slippery where she trod.
    A cold knife lay buried
in the heart of Mad Carew:
    It was the vengeance of the little yellow god.

There's a one-eyed yellow idol
    To the north of Kathmandu;
There's a little marble cross below the town,
    Where a broken-hearted woman
Tends the grave of Mad Carew,
    And the yellow god forever gazes down.

Ancient Chabali

Just one-and-a-half kilometres (one-mile) west of Bodhnath is the stupa at Chabali which, during the Lichhavi era, was an important town at the crossroads leading to Patan across the Bagmati River and the road from Kasthamandap between India and Tibet. Little defines the boundaries of the old village now as it merges with the outlying areas.

The stupa itself is similar to that of Bodhnath but on a much smaller scale and built to an older tradition. Around the main stupa are small Lichhavi *chaitya*. An impressive **statue** of a freestanding *bodhisattva* in black stone is one of the few images left intact. The stupa is believed to

Following pages: Monkey Temple at Swayambunath, Kathmandu.

Above: Horn-blowing Buddhist monks at the Bodhnath stupa, near Kathmandu.
Opposite: Buddhist monks inside the temple.

have been built by King Ashoka's daughter, Charumati.

With about 5,000 exiles living in the Valley, Kathmandu has a distinctly Tibetan ambience with a number of recent monasteries around Bodhnath and one, in the form of a castle, on the wooded slopes beside **Gorakhnath cave**. This guards the footprints of a 14th-century sage who lived in the cave as a hermit.

Not far from this cave, Tibetans built another **monastery** — one that commemorates Guru Padma Rimpoche Sambhava, a saint who rode down to Kathmandu from Tibet to conquer a horde of demons.

But Tibetans are just one of the many colourful communities who have made their home among the original inhabitants of Kathmandu Valley, the Newars.

These hardy folk and their extended families observe a constant round of rituals, worshipping the many deities whose blessings and curses rule their daily lives, in a complicated mix of Hinduism, Buddhism and animism.

Swayambhunath

The Tibetan connection is strong, too, at another of the Valley's holy shrines, clearly visible on top of a 100-metre (350-foot) hill in the west. The Buddhist stupa of Swayambhunath floats above a sea of early-morning mist, the rising sun setting fire to its burnished **copper spire**.

On the four sides of the base of the spire, Buddha's all-seeing eyes, in vivid hues, keep constant watch over the capital. Many believe this sacred ground protects the divine light of Swayambhunath, the Self Existent One who, when the waters drained from the Valley, emerged as a flame from a lotus blossom atop this hill. People worshipped there long before the advent of Buddhism, perhaps at a projecting stone which now forms the central core of the stupa. There, it is said, Manjushri discovered the Kathmandu lotus which floated in its ancient lake.

Whatever the legends say, there is evidence that this site existed before the advent of Buddhism. An inscription, dated around AD 460, recorded that King

Manadeva I had commissioned work at the existing shrine, some 600 years after Emperor Ashoka is reputed to have paid homage there.

By the 13th century the area represented an established centre of Buddhist learning and had close ties with Lhasa. Destroyed in 1346 by the Bengali troops of Sultan Shams ud-din Ilyas, it was rebuilt by the 17th-century Malla monarch, King Pratap, who added a long stairway leading to it, two adjoining **temples** and a symbolic **thunderbolt** at the top.

The stupa is shaped like a lotus flower and, in the past 2,000 years, saints, monks, kings and others have built monasteries, idols, temples and statues which now encircle the original stupa and the entire hilltop. At the base of the hill three enormous stone **Buddhas,** painted in vibrant colours, sit in meditation and 300 flagstone **steps**, adorned by stone **statues** of animals, lead up to the main shrines.

Even if you have no sense of religion or history, you will find the antics of the monkeys, which inhabit the temples and the shops, fascinating — they use the **handrails** of the steps as a slide — and the views over Kathmandu on a clear day as breathtaking as the stiff climb.

Legend says the monkeys came from the lice in Manjushri's hair; after the lice dropped to the ground as he had his hair cut, they sprang up as monkeys. It is also said that each strand of his hair which fell also sprang up again — as a tree.

On the stupa, only Buddha's all-seeing **eyes** are depicted; disdaining the sounds of praise, ears are omitted, and abhorring the need for speech, so is the mouth. There is no nose, only the Nepali letter which is a symbol of both oneness and virtue, *dharma.* Mounted on a **brass pedestal** before the stupa is the thunderbolt, or *vajra* — so powerful that it can destroy anything — and representing the divine strength of Lord Indra, King of the Heavens, in contrast to Buddha's all-pervading knowledge. Beneath the pedestal stand **12 animals** of the Tibetan zodiac: rat, bull, tiger, hare, dragon, serpent, horse, sheep, pig, monkey, rooster and jackal.

The stupa, more elaborate than the one at Bodhnath, was built to the rules that governed the construction of most older stupas. The white **hemisphere** represents the four elements — earth, fire, air and water. The thirteen **tiers** at the top of the shrine symbolize the degrees of knowledge on the path to nirvana, represented by the umbrella at the top. Four **Buddhas** face each compass point in different postures of meditation. And around the stupa, **prayer wheels** are kept in constant motion by the faithful. Remember to turn them clockwise.

A *gompa* (monastery) faces the stupa and holds a regular service at 1600. It is easily distinguishable from the Hindu services that take place in the mornings by the sound of booming trumpets and sonorous chants. Other shrines around the main stupa are dedicated to various deities. A temple consecrated to Saraswati, goddess of learning, is besieged by students during Basant Panchami, the festival of learning. There are also **images** of goddesses Ganga and Jamuna by the stupa, whose eternal flame is enshrined in a cage behind the stupa, where a priest makes regular offerings.

Swayambhunath is patronized by countless Buddhists, who rise before dawn to make their pilgrimage up the holy hill. If you go early enough, you will see figures prostrating themselves every four steps and climbing slowly up the hill. The elderly often think nothing of a four-mile walk. Opposite, on a neighbouring hill, the serene image of Saraswati, Goddess of Learning, gazes down on the often frantic throng around Swayambhunath, perhaps in benign — and divine — astonishment.

Changu Narayan temple

On another hilltop 11.5 kilometres (seven miles) east of Kathmandu, the Valley's oldest **temple, Changu Narayan**, stands in almost derelict splendour, its struts and surroundings covered with hundreds of finely detailed, delicately carved erotic depictions.

Opposite: Palanchok carving of Bhagawati expressing power, Kathmandu Valley.

Above: A worshipper circles the giant Bodhnath stupa ritually turning each prayer wheel – as in the foreground – as she walks, seeking blessings and benedictions for the future.
Opposite: Tibetan woman with a prayer drum.

It is one of the best examples of the temples dedicated to Vishnu. Founded around the 4th century AD, it represents the very best in Nepali art and architecture, and it is difficult to imagine a more stunning example of what Kathmandu Valley is all about. Woodwork, metalwork and stonework combine in dazzling harmony — nowhere to more effect than in the **sculptures** of Bhupatindra, the 17th-century Malla king, and his queen. The most popular route to the temple is from the **Sankhu road** across the **Manohara River**. After a walk uphill, you come to a pair of **stone elephants**. A few small **temples** flank the two-tiered **main shrine**, and a twin-roofed **pagoda**. On the right, a temple houses two **sculptures**. Vishnu, in the form of Avatar Narsingh, a lion-headed figure, is depicted destroying the king of demons. The other **statue** is of Vishnu Virkantha, a dwarf with six arms.

Further back on a terrace, an upright, flat **black stone** bears an **image,** created between the 5th and 6th centuries, of Narayan reclining on Ananta at the bottom, and Vishnu — with 10 heads and 10 arms — going through the different layers of the universe. It is surrounded by later sculptures from the 9th century.

A man-sized **image** of Garuda, with a coiled snake around his neck, graces the front of the main temple and also dates back to the 5th or 6th century. One of the oldest and most prominent Lichhavi **inscriptions**, which stands beside it, records the military feats of King Mana Deva, who ruled for 27 years from AD 464 to 491. Though fire and earthquake have often damaged Changu Narayan and its environs, this link with its ancient past remains. Life's rhythms there in the cobble-stone square remain unchanged, too, with pilgrims' platforms and lodges surrounding it and the central temple.

Cows, chickens, pye-dogs and snot-nosed youngsters wander around while women hang their saris to dry in the evening sunlight which, like some pastoral idyll of old, bathes the red brick in glowing orange.

Above: Bode women gain a vantage point to witness Dilip Kumar Shrestra's New Year act of penitence. Opposite: Monkey temple, Kathmandu.

Besides the spectacular views from the hilltop, the area around Changu Narayan offers many good opportunities to walk and explore. Along the ridge to the east, a two-hour walk takes you to the road to Nagarkot.

Pashupatinath

From the highest point of the hill on which the temple stands, the majestic panorama of Kathmandu Valley unfolds in a 360° sweep — and down there, at **Deopatan,** is **Pashupatinath**, holiest and most famous of all Nepal's Hindu shrines. Set on the banks of the Bagmati, where it leaves a once-forested gorge, it is reserved exclusively for Hindu worshippers.

For a better perspective, there is a series of terraces on the opposite bank — thickly populated with hundreds of rhesus monkeys, regarded by Hindu believers as kin of the gods, sun and stars — where you can study the classic proportions of the pagoda's gilded **copper roof**, surrounded by tatty, corroded tin roofs and despoiled by higgledy-piggledy power lines.

Pashupatinath is always crowded with pilgrims from the rest of Nepal and India. Although non-Hindus are not allowed into the temple, by following the ancient route taken by the pilgrims you will enjoy a fine experience.

In the age of mythology, Lord Shiva and his consort lived there by this tributary of the holy Ganges and today it is reckoned a more sacred place of pilgrimage than even Varanasi on the Ganges. Shiva is the most human of the gods in the Hindu trinity. Although the destroyer of the universe, he is also the god of fertility. It is more logical to see Shiva as both creator and destroyer; the many names he is known by reflect the manner in which his believers perceive him. In his benign form, he is Mahadeva, the king of gods — or Pashupati, Lord of the Beasts. In his terrible aspect, he is the terrifying visage of Bhairava.

Shiva is best known as the ascetic deep in meditation in the mountains. In his reverie, he is covered in ashes and has for his sacred brahman thread three coiled snakes. His neck is blue since the time he swallowed the poison from the cosmic ocean when Ananta the snake disgorged

Above: Monkey at Pashupatinath Temple near Kathmandu. Opposite: Golden conical canopy of the Golden Temple atop the 2000 years old Swayambhunath Stupa, west of Kathmandu.

shabbiness. It is best to bear in mind that, after centuries of use, these are still not monuments or museums but living places of worship, in many cases sadly in need of immediate work to preserve their glories. Pashupatinath is no exception. Much of the exterior is close to collapse, stained with the patina of centuries and with litter lying everywhere. Its most precious treasure is its **carved Shivalingam,** or Shiva's phallus, stepped in a representation of the female sex organ, the **yoni** of Parvati, Shiva's consort.

Vishnu

Vishnu is another of the trinity of Hindu gods, with Brahma and Shiva. His role as the preserver of the universe ensures his presence in many parts of the Valley. The worship of Vishnu dates far back to the days of King Hari Datta, who built several Vishnu shrines.

For centuries, however, the worship of Shiva overshadowed the cult. In the 14th century, King Jayasthiti Malla patronized the worship of Vishnu and established himself as an incarnate of Vishnu.

The King of Nepal is still regarded as an incarnation to this day. Vishnu, in the form of Narayan, is often portrayed as lying in the primeval ocean sheltered by the giant snake, Ananta. The most impressive **statue** of this pose is found in **Budhanilkantha**, a township eight kilometres (five miles) from Kathmandu. There, a five-metre (16-foot) stone image — Vishnu, nestled within Ananta's 11 hoods, and bearing four powerful symbols in his four arms — lies in a shallow pool. The discus in the upper right hand symbolizes the mind, while the mace in the upper left hand represents knowledge, a conch in the lower left hand the five elements, and a lotus seed in the lower right hand the universe.

Sculpted at least 1,400 years ago, the stone was probably brought in from outside the Valley. From certain angles, the entire statue is reflected on the water of the pool, which gives the illusion of two identical statues joined at the back.

The temple is popular with worshippers, who adorn the statue with flowers, vermilion, coins and rice. Each morning the face of the god is washed by a priest.

his venom. Comic books portray Shiva as blue, in much the same way as Krishna is portrayed. Shiva's consort is the chaste Parvati, who manifests herself as Durga and the fearsome Kali.

Everywhere outside Pashupatinath temple, Hindu holy men, *sadhu* — dressed in loin cloths and marked with cinder ash, looking immensely wise and benign but still wanting cash to have their picture taken — sit, cross-legged deep in meditation, surrounded by the temple's delicate gold and silver filigree work.

All year round, families bring their dead to cremate them on funeral pyres on the bank and scatter their ashes in the river. Even on winter mornings, Hindus brave the cold to bathe in the holy waters. There was a temple there as early as the first century AD, and long before then — in the 3rd century BC — there was what may well have been the Valley's first settlement.

To the visitor, the most astonishing thing about almost any Hindu shrine is its

Above: Statue of reclining Vishnu at Buddhanilkantha. Opposite: Erotic carvings on Vishnu temple at Changu Narayan. Following pages: Famous shrine – Pashupatinath at Deopatan.

A similar statue is located in Balaju, and another was brought to Kathmandu during the reign of King Pratap Malla and installed in the palace grounds. The last reclining image was found within the confines of Pashupatinath. It is said that the Kings of Nepal may not look upon the image in Budhanilkantha, as they would be looking upon their own image.

Royal Game Sanctuary

Pashupatinath is not far from the forested slopes of Gorakhnath, close to the open glades and myriad birds of the Royal Game Sanctuary that is now a safari park for citizens' recreation. For those who fancy a touch of Maharajah-style travel, a lone elephant plods across the nine-hole **golf course** among herds of grazing **chital,** rare **black-buck** and other **deer, rabbits, monkeys** and **pheasants**.

There is also a Royal Bengal **tiger** in a well-planned but strongly fenced natural sanctuary. The tiger, a notorious man-eater, once terrorized villagers on the Terai.

Sekh Narayan

At the bottom of the Gorakhnath Hill stands the **temple** of **Sekh Narayan**. Four pools at two different levels give this shrine a character of its own. You may find women bathing and washing clothes in the lower pools.

Submerged in an algae-green **pond**, the **image** of Surya, the sun god, also associated with Vishnu, stands as it has for centuries. The gods represented in the **carving** along the footpath are Shiva and Parvati.

Two **stairways** lead to the temple of Sekh Narayan at the top. This has been a popular pilgrimage since the 15th century. Nestled against an overhanging cliff, the single-storeyed temple is adorned with a slew of erotic **carvings** on the struts. An image of Vishnu is held within.

Bishankhu Narayan commands another wonderful view of the Valley. A dirt road off the Godavari road leads to this site, beyond the village of Bandegaon. Despite its significance, the **shrine** is represented by a natural twisting **rock cave**. A precarious and narrow rock-cut **stairway** leads to a

wood platform, from where you can see the tiny opening.

The story goes that Shiva was forced to hide in the cave to escape from the demon Bhasmasur, to whom he had given the power to turn all living things to ashes and dust just by the touch of his hand. Vishnu thwarted the demon by making him touch his own head and destroy himself. The hill next to the cave is believed to be the heaped ashes of Bhasmasur.

A popular route for pilgrims during the month of *Kartik* — October–November — is to begin at Ichangu Narayan and walk to Changu Narayan, Bishankhu Narayan and Sekh Narayan. Ichangu Narayan is situated north-west of Swayambhunath; the two-storeyed structure was built in the 18th century by legendary King Hari Datta.

Godavari Royal Botanical Gardens
Natural wealth also blossoms in this fecund spot, which is like a second Eden. Nepal's flora enchanted early European visitors, who exported it lock, stock and root to their own climes. In the words of Nobel laureate Rudyard Kipling:

> *Still the world is wondrous large —*
> *Seven seas from marge to marge —*
> *And it holds a vast of various kinds of man;*
> *And the wildest dreams of Kew*
> *Are the facts of Kathmandu.*

Though sadly deforested during the past half century, perhaps the easiest place to see much of Nepal's unique flora is at the foot of the Valley's highest point, 2,750-metre (9,000-foot) **Pulchoki Hill**.

There, the sacred waters of the River Godavari spring from a natural cave, and **Godavari Royal Botanical Gardens** bloom with some 66 different species of fern, 115 orchids, 77 cacti and succulents, and about

200 trees and shrubs, as well as many ornamentals — and these are only a small proportion of the country's 6,500 botanical species.

It also has orchid and cacti houses, and fern, Japanese, physic and water gardens. Throughout, by lily ponds and on grassy slopes, the visitor can find rest and shade in thatched shelters.

Every 12 years, thousands of pilgrims journey from all over Nepal and India to bathe in the Godavari's divine waters.

Patan
Patan nestles in a crook of the Bagmati River south of Kathmandu. Gleaming in the sun, its gilded roofs give it the semblance of a sea of gold. To its residents, Patan is also known as Lalitpur — the beautiful city.

It was in Patan that the Malla kings ruled, lived and worshipped, and that is why its Durbar Square is surrounded on all four sides by awe-inspiring temples and shrines built specifically in relation to the palace. The square itself is a study of the various styles of architecture that have made their homes in this courtyard.

If there is any truth in the story that the four stupas next to the palace were

Opposite: Wives pray for the loyalty and long life of their husbands during the Teej Festival at Kathmandu's ancient Pashupatinath temple. Right: Hindu holy man, sadhu, at a Kathmandu temple. These spiritual ascetics travel hundreds of miles by foot and their lives are devoted to meditation.

Above: Inside the courtyard of the old Palace, Sunaari Chowk, Patan.

erected by King Ashoka, it would make Patan the oldest existing Buddhist city. Until recently, Patan was its own entity, and travelling from Kathmandu city to Patan was like crossing from one town to the other.

There is little demarcation, with the traffic flowing from the streets of Kathmandu across the Bagmati Bridge into the industrial areas of Patan. But once you step into Durbar Square, you move into another world.

Sightseeing

Right at the entrance to Patan's Durbar Square, another royal mall, is an octagonal **Krishna temple** near an immense copper bell cast in the 18th century by Vishnu Malla and his queen, Chandra Lakshmi.

Traditionally, the bell's deep sonorous clanging summoned worshippers, but it was also used as an early warning system in the event of emergencies: fires, earthquakes and raiding armies. How the people of Patan distinguished the difference is not explained.

The Royal Palace is made up of three *chowk* (courtyards). The gate to the oldest, **Mul Chowk**, is guarded by two **stone lions**.

Another smaller courtyard enclosing the **Bidya Mandir** stands within the quarters of the old Patan royal family.

To the south of Mul Chowk lies the smaller **Sundari Chowk**, whose prize, a recessed **bath** called **Tusha Hiti**, is contained by two stone **Nagas**. The delicately carved **figures** that adorn the side of the bath are stunning in their detail and in quality of their craftsmanship. Originally, eight miniature **statues** of the Ashta Matrikas — earth mother goddesses — Bhairava and Nagas were carved; some are missing today. Finally, a gilded stone **spout** feeds water into the bath.

On the other side of Mul Chowk, beyond the **Taleju Bhawani Temple,** is the **shrine** to Degu Talle, patron god of the Mallas. Patan's most imposing monument is the sculpture of **King Yoganarendra Malla** seated on a lotus atop a six-metre (20-foot) pillar in front of the Dega Tule Taleju temple. He ruled at the beginning of the 17th century and it is still popularly believed among Patan folk that one day he will return to take up his rule again. For this reason, one door and one window in the palace always remain open to welcome him.

The three-tiered building was built by King Siddhi Narsingh Malla in 1640, and reconstructed after it was destroyed in a fire in 1662. The temple was used by kings for special ceremonies. It is open only 10 days each year, during the September to October Chaitra Dasain festival.

Its smaller **Taleju Bhawani Temple,** though not as impressive, is held more sacred. Two **statues** of Ganga and Jamuna, each on their mounts, lead the way into it. The temple is easily recognizable by its three-tiered octagonal **tower.** An unmistakable **Golden Gate** leads to a third courtyard, **Mani Keshab Narayan Chowk,** next to the **temple** of Degu Talle. The two **figures** at the top of the **gate** are Shiva and Parvati.

Hidden in the shadow of the chowk to the north is **Manga Hiti,** spouting water through three carved **crocodile heads.** People still line up to refresh themselves in the cool water.

The temple that faces Manga Hiti, the **Bishwa Nath Mandir,** suffered severe damage during a storm in 1989. It has since been reconstructed. The **temple** next to it, the three-storeyed **Bhimsen Mandi,** is well-maintained for the simple reason that it is the patron god of the traders and so is supported and kept up by its devotees. Parts of the temple are painted in silver, the rest gilded.

The **Krishna Mandir,** facing the Mani Keshab Narayan Chowk, has conspicuously different architecture from the other Newar temples. It resembles the Hindu temples of south India and borrows heavily from the Mughal era. Intricate black stone **pavilions** form the first and second levels. The elegant central *shikara* (tower) is gilded at the top. The focus of thousands of devotees each year celebrating Krishna's birthday around August to September is a narrative carving on the frieze, depicting stories in Newari from the Hindu epics.

One of the most beautiful temples in the country, and generally regarded as a masterpiece of architecture, the Krishna Mandir is built entirely of limestone and is the legacy of King Siddhi Narsimha Malla, who reigned for 41 years in the 17th century.

In 1682, the king's son, Shri Nivasa

Malla, restored the undated Bhimsen temple after it was damaged by fire. Since then it has been restored once more, following the 1934 earthquake. The gods make Kathmandu tremble frequently.

Not only the gods. When King Prithvi Narayan Shah swept into the Valley in 1768 to oust the Mallas, the 14th-century Royal Palace was badly damaged. However, its ornate gates, delicately-carved struts, statues, open courtyards and many rooms — conference halls, sleeping chambers, kitchens and so forth — recall the glory of Malla architectural splendour.

A **statue** of a gilded **Garuda** at the top of a column faces the **Krishna Mandir** in prayer. Another figure, shaded by a Naga meditating atop a pillar is King Siddhi Narsingh Malla. Behind him, the oldest **temple** in the square, dedicated to **Char Narayan,** is a two-storey brick structure, dating to 1565, which celebrates four of Vishnu's 10 avatars.

The next temple is **Hari Shankar,** followed by an eight-sided Krishna Temple — not to be mistaken for the Krishna Mandir. Its stairway is guarded by two stone **lions.** Further back, the **Bhai Dega** houses a Shivalingam with a huge **bell** hanging from two pillars.

Set next to the Krishna temple is a three-storeyed **Vishnu temple** notable for its tympanums, the ornate triangular recesses set between the cornices of its low gables. One of Patan's oldest temples, **Charanarayan,** is believed to have been built around 1566 by King Purendra, although lately, architectural historians suspect it belongs to the 17th century. The struts of this two-storeyed pagoda building are embellished with lively and acrobatic erotica — either inspiring, or inspired by, the *Kama Sutra* — and enough to give any gymnast food for thought.

Patan's treasures are not confined to the immediate precincts of its Durbar Square. Five minutes, walk away there is a **Golden Buddhist temple**; another Buddha shrine, Mahabuddha, lies two kilometres (1.2 miles) distant. There is also **Kumbheshwar,** one of two five-storeyed temples in Kathmandu Valley where Shiva is believed to stay for six months each year during the winter,

Above: Temple in Patan.

before leaving to spend summer with his consort Parvati on the crest of Gaurisankar.

Around Patan

At the south-western edge of Patan is **Jawlakhel,** location of the valley's largest Tibetan camp and a centre for **Tibetan handicrafts.** There, men and women are always busy carding wool and weaving carpets. In the first building, rows of women in traditional costume sit on the floor, one to three on a carpet, weaving traditional patterns, chatting and singing. In the next building, old women and men comb the wool before it is spun into threads. Shops display these handicrafts for sale. Portraits of the king and queen of Nepal and the Dalai Lama look down from the walls on to a maze of carpets, blankets, woven bags and small coats.

Jawlakhel Zoo, near the craft shops in the industrial area, has a selection of exotic south Asian animals, especially Himalayan species, and is open daily.

South of Patan

Various trails and tracks line the settlements and sacred sites of the one-time capital to the south of Patan. West of the Bagmati River are **Kirtipur**, with its satellite hamlets of **Panga** and **Nagaon**, while the twin settlements of **Bungamati** and **Khokana** lie either side of the sacred Karma Binayak site. There, a road leads to the **Lele Valley,** and a trail to Godavari and Phulchoki passes through **Harisiddhi, Thaibo** and **Bandegaon.** An eastern lane takes travellers to **Sanagaon** and **Lubhu.** All these villages have close links with Patan.

Bhaktapur

About 16 kilometres (10 miles) from the heart of Kathmandu city lies Bhaktapur, eastern gateway to the Valley. It is probably the most visited of the three historic cities, nicely compact and only a brief walk from Nyatapola, the tallest and most popular of Nepal's pagoda temples.

Like Kirtipur, Bhaktapur is a medieval town locked in centuries-old beliefs and traditions. But, unlike Kirtipur, the town is economically robust; walking its streets you find artisans at work, craftsmen producing their wares and modern facilities.

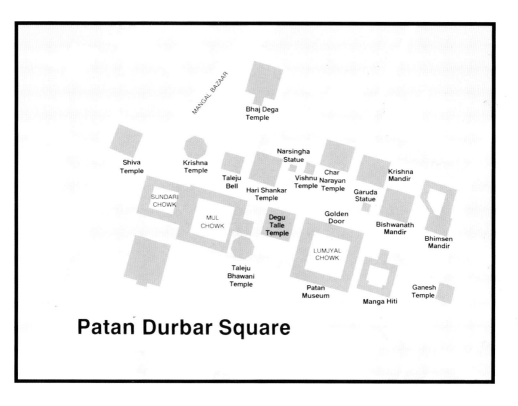

Patan Durbar Square

Also known as Bhadgaon — city of devotees — the name of the ancient city indicates its religious antecedents. King Ananda Malla is reputed to have founded the town — although it is more likely that a group of villages involved in trade with Tibet slowly came together to shape it. Bhadgaon reached the pinnacle of its glory during the Malla era and Bhaktapur has maintained its individuality mainly by virtue of its self-sufficiency and isolation from Kathmandu.

Fields still encircle the town, cultivated by Bhaktapur's farmers for centuries. The town grows its own crops and its traders even manage to service the population. The women wear the distinctive black *patasi* bordered with a bright red strip.

The town's Durbar Square is usually overrun with tourists, who sometimes stand there stunned, not only by the incredible dimensions of the Nyatapola Temple but also by the nonstop hurly-burly of hawkers, pedestrians and children who occupy the place by day and seemingly by night. Most seek sanctuary in a tea room, where a good hour can be spent sipping the piquant local tea and studying the erotica on the tea room struts.

Getting there

Journeying from Kathmandu, you pass a big open field, Tundikhel, and the Siddha Pokhari, a water tank, before entering the city. The pokhari is four centuries old and has a group of temples dedicated to Shiva and Vishnu and a stupa nearby. Local residents believe it to be the home of a large snake and balk at the idea of draining its none-too-clean waters.

If you continue along the road through Bhaktapur you can go left to the Durbar Square to see the town's fine monuments. The right-hand fork takes you into a residential area with many traditional houses.

Sightseeing

Durbar Square was badly damaged by the earthquake of 1934 and lost its largest temples. However, the 1989 earthquake spared the temples and levelled instead about 200 traditional houses. Now the Durbar Square does seem much emptier than those at Kathmandu and Patan.

After the **main entrance**, the two **statues** flanking the small gate in front of the **police station** are of Ugrachandi Durga, depicted with 18 arms, and Bhairav, with 12 arms. The **arch** of the **gate**, built of lime-plastered brick in the 18th century by Bhupatindra, is a depiction of the face of glory. It looks out on three remarkable **temples** of different styles, whose divine proportions are concealed by all being huddled together. One, the single-storeyed **Jaganath**, houses an **image** of **Harishankara**; the second, a two-storeyed **Krishna temple** standing in front of it, contains **images** of Krishna, Radha and Rukmani; and the third, the **Shiva Mandir**, is built in the shikhara style, four **porticoes** each with a **niche** above it for plated **images** of gods.

The temple opens its doors only once a year, during the Vijaya Dashami festival celebrations, between September and October, when Taleju's golden statue is placed on the back of the horse, stabled in the courtyard, and led around the town in a procession. During the festival the goddess is believed to take up residence in the south wing of the building.

The adjacent palace is renowned mainly for its **55-windowed Hall of Audience**, an elaborately carved balcony and its collection of **wood-carvings**, some damaged in the 1934 earthquake but still considered priceless. It is a prime example of the artwork of Kathmandu Valley, regarded by many as its finest.

One of the carved windows is believed to be the handicraft of Bhupatindra. His statue — with him sitting, hands folded reverently before Taleju — faces the famous **Golden Gate,** or Sun Dhoka, which is the most priceless artefact in the country, commissioned in 1754 by King Jaya Ranjit Malla to adorn the outer entrance to the Taleju temple.

The body of the gate is copper, overlaid in gold. As with many Newar structures it has both Hindu and Buddhist influences. At the top of the frame is a **carving** of Garuda. Stand there as the evening sun falls, as does the morning sun, on the gate. When the gate catches the sun's rays it glitters and sparkles like the precious metal itself.

On the left, before going through the gate, a restored portion of the **old palace** is used as the **National Art Gallery**. The gallery **gate** is guarded by Hanuman and Narsingh. A fine collection of *thangka* are on display in the Gallery.

Beyond the Golden Gate a **courtyard** leads to other courtyards. The sides of the chowk are festooned with delicate and beautiful **carvings**. Two sacred chowks definitely worth mentioning, but out of bounds to non-Hindus, are the **Taleju** and **Kumari chowks**. The entrance of Taleju chowk is on the **left**, the gate to Kumari chowk on the **right**.

Sundari Chowk was the ritual bathing place of the king. The large **tank** is decorated with many **statues** of deities. In the centre, an impressive **naga** rises from the bottom of the tank, facing another almost identical **carving**. The tank, which is now dry, used to be filled with water from the nearby hills.

The **Chaysilin Mandap**, destroyed during the earthquake in 1934, was reconstructed as a gift to the Nepali people by the former German Chancellor Helmut Kohl. It took three years' work to restore it from sketches. The **woodcarving** was carried out by the Valley's artisans.

The next most prominent part of the square is the awesome **Nyatapola Temple**, Nepal's tallest ancient structure, built by King Bhupatindra Malla. It stands in five tiers and is balanced by the five foundation **platforms** that stand at the base.

From as far back as you can stand, it looks like a fretted pyramid climbing up to the clouds, reaching a height of more than 30 metres (100 feet). Its inspiration is said to have been a form of appeasement to the terrifying menace of Bhairav, who stands in another temple. There seems to be more than just fancy to this tale.

Certainly, no menace terrifies those who swarm over its plinth and up its **steps**, which are guarded on each side by legendary sentinels. Jaya Mal and Patta, two wrestlers said to have the strength of 10 men, are at

Above: Birdlike sculpture in front of the Vishnu temple in Patan. Opposite: Newari man, Bhaktapur.

the bottom. Next come two huge elephants, each 10 times stronger than the wrestlers, then two lions, each as strong as 10 elephants, two griffins, each as strong as 10 lions and, finally, on the uppermost plinth, two demi-goddesses, Baghini in the form of a tigress, and Singhini, as a lioness, each 10 times stronger than a griffin.

Siddhi Lakshmi, to whom the temple is dedicated, is consequently the most powerful of all these figures. She is depicted with other deities on the struts. Even the caretaker priests can only see the image of the goddess inside the temple at night.

It is a pattern of guardian sentinels found nowhere else in Nepali temple architecture and is considered significant evidence of the measure of appeasement required to placate Bhairav.

Again, this Durbar Square also boasts a **large bell** that was used both to summon worshippers and to sound alarms, particularly if there was a night curfew, when it was rung to send citizens scurrying home.

There are other temples in the Durbar Square — to **Kumari, Vatsala, Durga, Narayan, Shiva** and **Pashupatinath.** The last is the oldest in the city, built around the end of the 15th century by the widow and sons of King Yaksha Malla in his memory, though some argue it was built much later, in 1682, by Jita Malla, father of Bhupatindra. Bhaktapur legend says Lord Pashupatinath appeared before him in a dream and ordered him to build the temple.

Another legend has it that the king wanted to visit the temple at Deopatan but was unable to cross the Bagmati in full flood, and so he ordered another temple to Pashupatinath to be built in Bhaktapur.

Bhaktapur's famous **peacock window** is tucked away in a side road near the **Pujari Math**. The **pottery bazaar** is a good example of the robust cottage industries that thrive in the town. All around, you will see women going about their daily duties. At harvest time they work the fields or tend to rice drying in the sun. Sometimes rafts of fiery red chillies are seen drying on the roofs of homes. Bhaktapur is famous for its delicious *juju dhou* — the king's curd. Flat earthen containers full of yoghurt can be found in some stores. Take care to spoon off the top of the yoghurt before you eat.

Thimi

Just three kilometres (1.9 miles) west of Bhaktapur is Thimi — the Valley's fourth-largest settlement. Founded by the Malla dynasty, it takes its name from the Nepali word for 'competent' — *chhemi*. This is an honour bestowed upon Thimi's residents by the Bhaktapur monarchs for their skill in fighting off the rival kingdoms.

It is a town of potters, where families, using skills handed down from generation to generation, turn out handsome china-ware fashioned from the red clay of the Valley fields — vessels for domestic use and art works such as peacock flower vases and elephant representations.

The colourful 16th-century **Balkumari temple** is the town's main **shrine** and nearby, in a much smaller dome-shaped **shrine,** is a brass **image** of **Bhairav.**

But Thimi is more renowned as the location, along with two other adjacent villages — **Nade** and **Bode** — of the most riotous of Nepal's New Year (*Bisket Jatra*) celebrations. Nade is noted for its multi-coloured, three-storeyed **Ganesh temple** while, across the **dykes** that meander through the rice paddies, Bode boasts a **Mahalakshmi temple**, a two-storeyed 17th-century building on the site of an early temple built according to local legend in 1512, after Mahalakshmi appeared in a dream to the king of Bhaktapur.

Every year on New Year's Day, the **square** around the **Bal Kumari temple** in Thimi witnesses a spectacular gathering of 32 deities carried in elaborate multi-roofed palanquins under ceremonial umbrellas. Later, the crowds move across the field to Bode to witness another New Year ritual (see Festivals).

Kirtipur

About five kilometres (three miles) south-west of Kathmandu, perched on a twin hillock, 12th-century **Kirtipur** was to become an independent kingdom and ultimately the last stronghold of the Mallas when, in 1769-70, Prithvi Narayan Shah marched in to conquer the Valley. It withstood a prolonged siege, during which the Malla army taunted Prithvi's Gorkha forces as they hurled them back down the fortress-like hill.

The insults were a mistake for, when Kirtipur finally fell, the vengeful Gorkha ruler ordered his men to amputate the noses and lips of all Kirtipur men — the only exception being those musicians who played wind instruments.

Now only the **ruined walls** remain to remind Kirtipur's 8,000 residents of this epic battle and Kirtipur is a place of trade and cloistered learning.

Part of nearby Tribhuvan University's **campus** sprawls across the former farmlands. The traditional occupations, apart from farming, are spinning and weaving. At Kirtipur's **Cottage Industry Centre,** 900 hand looms spin fine cloth for sale in Kathmandu.

Although it has withstood the earthquakes that have caused so much damage elsewhere in the valley, Kirtipur has been unable to withstand the ravages of time. Yet, decayed and neglected as it is, a walk beneath the exquisitely-carved windows of the town's multi-storeyed houses, laid out on terraces at different levels, all linked by ramps and sloping paths, reveals an ambience that seems to belong to the Middle Ages.

The main approach is by a long flight of **steps** that enter the town, which is settled on the saddle between the two hills, beside a small lake.

On top of the hill to the south, a huge stupa, the **Chilanchu Vihar,** is encircled by eight **shrines** decorated by stone **images.** There are many Buddhist monasteries around the stupa. On the hill to the north, which is higher, some Hindus have settled around a restored temple dedicated to **Uma Maheshwar.** The three-storeyed **Bagh Bhairav temple** stands at the high point of the saddle between the two hills, a place of worship for both Hindus and Buddhists.

It is decorated with **swords** and **shields** taken from Newar troops after Prithvi Narayan Shah's 18th-century victory. It contains an image of Bhairav, manifested

Opposite: Siddhi Lakshmi Mandir in Bhaktapur.

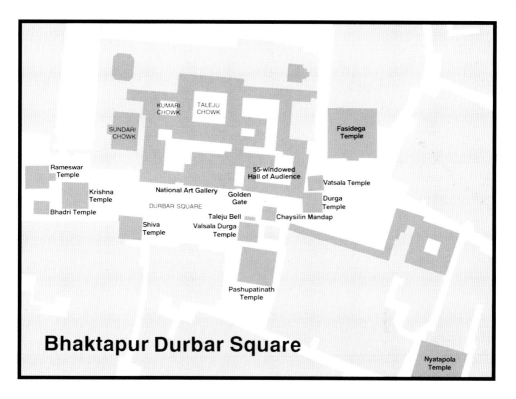

KUMARI CHOWK
TALEJU CHOWK
SUNDARI CHOWK
Fasidega Temple
Rameswar Temple
55-windowed Hall of Audience
Vatsala Temple
Krishna Temple
National Art Gallery
Golden Gate
DURBAR SQUARE
Durga Temple
Bhadri Temple
Taleju Bell
Chaysilin Mandap
Shiva Temple
Valsala Durga Temple
Pashupatinath Temple

Bhaktapur Durbar Square

Nyatapola Temple

as a tiger, and the *torana* above the main sanctum shows Vishnu riding Garuda, and Bhairav attended on either side by Ganesh and Kumar.

From the temple there are striking views of the valley and the brightly coloured patch-work of farm fields below, with the villages of **Panga** and **Nagaon** in the south-east.

You can take a **path** through the rice fields from Kirtipur to Panga, which was established by the Mallas as a fortress town to stall invaders from the north. None of its six or so **temples** dates beyond the 19th century. The path continues from Panga to Nagaon, a name that means 'new village'.

The 16th-century Malla king who ruled Kathmandu from Patan, concerned that his subjects might move too far from the city to serve its defence, established two settlements — **Bungamati** and **Khokana** — near the **Karma Binayak shrine**, amid fertile fields. During a major drought, the king sought the blessings of the rain god, Machhendra, at a temple in India, inviting the deity to come and settle in the Valley. He built a **shrine** at Bungamati where, some time in the last decade of the 16th century, it became the custom to keep the image of the Rato Machhendra during winter, moving it back to Patan by palanquin in summer.

Many small votive *chaitya* line the processional way from Patan to Bungamati which, surrounded by terraced rice paddies and small copses of trees, nestles against a hillside.

The village is noted for its strongly stated, shikara-style **Rato Machhendranath temple.** The adjacent **Lokeshwar shrine** contains an **image** of Bhairav's massive **head** in full, demoniac fury. Yet another **shrine, Karma Binayak,** stands on a tree-clad hill and beyond that, 10 minutes walk away, is a brick-paved **village** famous for the manufacture of mustard-oil, **Khokana.** It has a **temple** dedicated to the nature

Opposite: Bhaktapur's Durbar Square holds matchless treasure of medieval architecture and art.

Above: Dhatta Traya women cleaning grain at Bhaktapur Square. Previous pages: Royal Palace renowned mainly for its 55–windowed Hall of Audience, an elaborately carved balcony and collection of wood-carvings at Bhaktapur Durbar Square.

goddess, Shukla Mai, or Rudrayani. Rebuilt after the 1934 earthquake, its main street is noticeably wider than in similar villages.

To the west
Many interesting rural communities, with fascinating temples and shrines, are close to the capital, Kathmandu. In the west, on the old 'Silk Road' to Tibet, stand the villages of **Satungal, Balambu, Kisipidi** and **Thankot.** The first three cluster together within walking distance, no more than six kilometres (3.7 miles) from the city.

Satungal, Balambu, Kisipidi
The first, Satungal, was built in the 16th century as a fortress to thwart invaders from the north. Many of its 1,000 residents work in Kathmandu. Its **main square** is notable for the two-metre (6.5-foot) stone **image** of a seated **Buddha** on a freestanding platform. Nearby, to the north of the

square, steps lead through an embellished **gate** to a **Vishnu Devi temple.**

Several inscriptions testify to the antiquity of the second village, **Balambu,** built more than 1,000 years ago at the time of the Lichhavi dynasty, but it was fortified later. Its main feature is a two-storeyed **Mahalakshmi temple,** set in the central **square**, and some smaller **temples**.

Among the three-storeyed houses which line the square is one that is dedicated as the god house of Ajima Devi. The third village, **Kisipidi** with its lush green trees and small, stone-walled gardens, is renowned for the two-storeyed **Kalika Mai temple** in its centre.

Thankot
Travel on along the main highway, the Raj Path, and after two kilometres (1.2 miles) you come to the fourth village, **Thankot,** built by the Mallas, and later made a fortress by Prithvi Narayan Shah — its name, in fact, translates as 'military base'.

On a hill above the village stands an impressive two-storeyed **Mahalakshmi temple,** much admired for its carved **tympanum** and **columns**, **erotic carvings**, open **shrine**, and **images** of kneeling devotees.

Four kilometres (2.5 miles) south-west stands the 2,423-metre (7,950-foot) peak of **Chandragadhi,** 'Mountain of the Moon', reached by a **trail** through a dense **forest** of bamboo, pine and sal trees.

At the crest, there is a small Buddhist *chaitya* and splendid views of Kathmandu Valley.

Back on the Raj Path, look for a **monument** to **King Tribhuvan,** built to commemorate the restoration of the monarchy after the Rana regime. It has a raised hand.

There is another **monument** along the road which honours the men who built it between 1953 and 1956 — Indian engineers and Nepali labourers. Before then goods were moved laboriously from India to Nepal by railway, and then from the Terai by ropeway to Daman, and by porters to Kathmandu.

The Lele Valley Road
Two of the Valley's most ancient villages, **Chapagann and Lele,** date from Lichhavi times. The road to them cuts through a green and yellow quilt of mustard fields

Above: Famed peacock window in Bhaktapur, carved almost six centuries ago.

and rice paddies stretched out beneath the hazy grey-blue foothills of the Himalaya. Standing on a high plateau at the edge of another valley, 16th-century **Sunaguthi** has a **shrine** to **Bringareshwar Manadeva**, which houses one of the most sacred **lingams** in Kathmandu Valley. Next to the shrine is a two-storeyed **Jaganath temple.**

Now the path climbs gently upward through the emerald, terraced fields to **Thecho**, with its brightly-decorated **Balkumari temple.**

There is another **temple**, to **Brahmayani,** in the north of the village, guarded by the deity's vehicle — a duck — atop a column, with the usual lion on the steps of the two-storeyed temple.

Two kilometres (1.2 miles) from Thecho, guarded by a metal **Ganesh shrine** and a **statue** of Brahma beside a huge **yoni**, the road enters **Chapagaon** where, goes a famous Valley legend, one of the Malla kings sent his son into exile for founding a caste of his own. The central **square** contains two **temples**, both two-storeyed, dedicated to **Narayan and Krishna.** The struts carry incredibly-detailed **erotic carvings**.

Close by, in a single-storeyed building, is an image of **Bhairav,** the village's major deity. South of Chapagaon are the two small hamlets of **Bulu** and **Pyangaon**.

King Anand Malla, the founder of the Bhaktapur dynasty, is said to have built seven new villages in the east of Kathmandu Valley, but of these, three were already in existence — Banepa, Nala and Dhulikhel. The four that he did build are Panauti, Khadpu, Chaukot and Sanga, although some lie outside the Valley.

Nonetheless, King Anand Malla's vision gave Banepa and Dhulikhel, situated as they were on the main Silk Road from Kathmandu to Tibet, much greater status and strategic value.

Above: For centuries, potters have practised their delicate skills in Bhaktapur's famous Pottery Market.

Sanga and the Araniko Highway

The road climbs out of the Valley over a **pass**, five kilometres (three miles) east of Bhaktapur. There is a small **lane** to the **north**, off the Araniko Highway, that takes you into **Sanga**, where a **vantage point** offers an amazing panorama of the entire Valley.

Despite its antiquity, the historical merit is a small **Bhimsen shrine** to commemorate a Kathmandu legend that, when the valley was a lake, Bhimsen crossed it by boat, rowing from Tankot in the west to Sanga.

From there, the Araniko Highway zig-zags steeply down into the lush **Banepa Valley** and the **village** from which the valley takes its name.

Standing at the foot of a forested hill, much of the village was razed by fire in the early 1960s, but it remains the main centre of commerce for the surrounding hill areas. Banepa's **Chandeshwari shrine** overlooks the valley from the top of a hill to the north-east of the town.

North-west, a rough trail leads to **Nala**, seat of a Buddhist meditation site, and **Lokeshwar**, about 100 metres (330 feet) west of Nala, by the old Bhaktapur road. **Pilgrim shelters** surround the **temple** which has a **water tank** in front of it.

A steep alley in the village centre takes you to the four-storeyed **Bhagvati temple** in the centre of a **square** — the locale for many colourful processions during the village's annual festivals.

Dhulikhel

Back on the highway at Banepa, you now drive on to Dhulikhel, which commands a prominent location on top of a high hill. There are several sights worth seeing in Dhulikhel.

Dhulikhel's main square contains a **Narayan shrine** and a **Hansiddhi temple**. The village houses are renowned for their beautiful, **carved woodwork**. In the north on a hill above the village stands a magnificent three-storeyed Bhagvati **temple**, famous for its ceramic-tiled **facade**. It is also a good vantage point for views of the major peaks of the Himalaya. The mud-and-thatch houses in the sweltering valley below are home for a community of low-caste Nepali.

Dhulikhel remains one of the trade gateways between the Kathmandu Valley, eastern Nepal and Tibet.

Panauti

One of the most fascinating Newar towns in the area, Panauti stands at the confluence of two rivers south of Banepa, in a small valley surrounded by mountains.

There used to be a king's palace in the main village **square** and the town is noted for two fine examples of Malla temple architecture — a three-storeyed 16th-century **Indreshwar Mahadev temple** and a **Narayan shrine,** both of which have been restored.

Architecturally and historically, the Indreshwar Mahadev temple is regarded as one of the most important of all the Newar shrines in Kathmandu Valley. It is thought to have replaced an earlier one built in the 11th to 12th centuries. The **carving** on its struts conveys the profound serenity of Shiva, in his many incarnations.

Two **shrines** guard the **courtyard** — one to Bhairav, another to an original nature goddess. This is simply a symbolic **stone**. There is another **Krishna temple** on a peninsula at the confluence of the two rivers, with several **Shivalingams** nearby and a sacred cremation **ghat**.

On the other side of the Bungamati River, a famous 17th-century **temple** has also been restored and a chariot festival is held there each year. It is dedicated to **Brahmayani**, chief goddess of Panauti after Indreshwar Mahadev.

Top: Women use mud to wash their hair as soap contains animal fat.
Above: Black statue of Bhairav, Shiva in his most terryfying incarnation.

Trekking in Nepal: The Road to Tibet

Just for the fact that it lies no more than 50 kilometres (30 miles) from the crest of the great peak of 8,013-metre (26,291-foot) Shisha Pangma, or Gosainthan, in the west, and much the same distance from 8,848-metre (29,028-foot) Everest, in the east, **Kodari** would be remarkable.

But this tiny settlement is still more extraordinary because it is only 1,768 metres (5,800 feet) above sea level, yet only 100 kilometres (60 miles) from Kathmandu.

Though this short distance takes between four and five hours to cover by car, the time passes swiftly, for the road cuts through a wonderland of raging rivers, valley towns and forested slopes.

Araniko Highway (Rajmarg)

You set out along the valley highway in the early morning sun. Diffused by the soft spring haze of April, it casts a golden halo over the surrounding hills. Casual brickworks dot the fields and the buildings display the earthy colour of the material. Suddenly, you are over the hills and the road plunges several hundred metres in a series of hairpin bends.

Like most roads in midland Nepal, the Araniko Highway was built by the Chinese. It is frequently damaged by landslides and wash-aways that send whole sections — and sometimes the vehicles on them — plunging to the swollen torrents below. Though it winds through the foothills of the greatest mountain range in the world, the hills themselves are so high and sheer that views of the snowcapped peaks above them are rare.

The exception is at **Dhulikhel**, at the top of a narrow ridge just below the pass out of the valley — a thin ribbon of road with steep drops on either side — which offers a stunning vista of the Himalaya, including Everest. Drive on, and after a few kilometres, at **Dolalghat**, a long low bridge crosses the wide bed of the **Sun Kosi**, just below its confluence with the **Indrawati River**. The bridge is almost half-a-kilometre long and the crystal-clear waters are inviting in the spring sunshine. The bridge, built in 1966, is a reminder of Nepal's progress in the years since it reopened its borders.

From there, the road winds on to **Lamosangu,** where trekkers into the little-visited reaches of one of central Nepal's more remote and haunting valleys alight from the Kathmandu bus.

Rowaling Himal

The Rolwaling Valley — *rolwaling* is a Sherpa word that means 'the furrow' — has been shaped by the floodwaters that burst out of a nine-metre (30-foot) opening in a sheer rock wall on the east bank of the Bhote Kosi River, fascinating those who visit it.

Many pilgrims believe that this is the spot where Shiva thrust his trident into the mountainside to let the waters cascade down to the holy Ganges.

It is also there in the upper reaches of the Rolwaling Valley that members of the Sherpa and Tamang communities talk about the yeti — that elusive Abominable Snowman which has been seen so often by Sherpa guides who live in the valley.

Perched at around 2,000 metres (6,500 feet), just a few hours drive from Kathmandu, the small pleasant village of **Charikot,** with hotels and shops, is gateway to this region.

But progress through Rolwaling Valley from there onwards is solely on foot. Three dining chairs stand outside the tea house in the tiny 10-house hamlet of **Piguti,** its quietness broken only by the scurry of pye-dogs chasing a lone trekker through its one street. There, too, trekkers are few, leaving Rolwaling's many splendours — including the amphitheatre of Gaurisankar — to delight only the rare

Opposite: Stone elephants guard the Uma Maheshwar Temple, Kirtipur Village, Kathmandu.

visitor. Higher up, one-, two-, and three-storeyed houses cling to the edge of the precipitous paddy fields, now brown, awaiting the monsoons, as cotton wool clouds dab the little knolls and grassy shoulders with a chill-like balm to ease the sting of the sun.

The paths that climb up the mountain slopes veer left and then right, across perilous-looking rope or steel-hawsered suspension bridges, many run on a toll basis.

Slowly, the trail winds through the forests to the highest settlement — a small close-knit Sherpa community. The 200 families of Beding live in small but striking stone houses with elegantly painted and carved exteriors.

There is also a monastery. Among the many holy places of the Himalaya, Beding is remembered as the refuge of Guru Padma Sambhava, the mystic Tantric recluse who chose the small cave in the cliff, about 150 metres (500 feet) above the monastery, as his place of meditation 1,200 years ago. Above the Rolwaling Himal, the greatest mountain in the world looks down in all its serene majesty.

At the far end of the Bhote Kosi gorge, 7,180-metre (23,557-foot) Menlungtse and the slightly lower 7,144-metre (23,438-foot) mass of Gaurisankar stand sentinel, like Lhotse and Nuptse, guarding Everest.

Getting there

The actual starting-point of the trek is the small village of **Charikot** which you reach by van from Lamosangu.

Where to stay

You need full equipment, including durable tents and Sherpa guides.

Trekking (First day)

From Charikot, **Rolwaling Himal** is clearly visible in the far distance. The **trail** out of town leads down a wide, gentle gradient through many hamlets to the village of **Dolakha** with its striking three-storeyed houses.

Turn **right** in the **village square** to a steep ridge that descends to the right bank of the **Tamba Kosi** and there cross the **suspension bridge** to the **left**, on to an easy trail along the river bank. The trail leads to **Piguti** where it crosses the **Gumbu Khola**.

There, a lovely **meadow** makes a pleasant **campsite**. Depending on your age and fitness, the weather and the season, the trek can take anything from six to nine hours.

Second day

Leave camp, bypassing the **suspension bridge** over the main stream, and follow the **path** along the **right bank** where, at the far end of the valley, you get your first glimpse of the splendour of 7,144-metre (23,438-foot) **Gaurisankar**. Not long afterwards you reach a checkpost at **Shigati**, where **Shigati Khola**, a large tributary of the **Bhote Kosi**, enters the river from the left. Once across the **suspension bridge** over the Shigati Khola, the valley narrows into sheer cliffs, leading to another **suspension bridge** that takes the trail back to the **left bank** along an up-and-down path to the village of **Suri Dhoban.** From there, the trail crosses the **Khare Khola** over another **suspension bridge** and on through the steep **Bhote Kosi Valley**, where occasional landslides may mean a detour down to the riverbed — or up over the hills.

Straight on, or up or down, you finally arrive among the **terraced hills** and **cultivated fields** of **Manthale**, set at around 1,070 metres (3,500 feet), where you camp. Allow anything between five-and-a-half and eight hours to complete this leg.

Third day

Take the **path** out of the village through the fields across a **bridge** to the **right** bank and a walled path that climbs gently to **Congar**, where it crosses a **stream**. Beyond Congar the valley closes in with steep walls where the trail traverses an area of tumbled rocks and boulders to a **waterfall** on the opposite bank. There, you reach a **crossroads** on the old Silk Road to Tibet and take the **path** on the **right** to a **bridge** and **river** below. From there you face a

Opposite: Friendship Bridge at the border of Tibet and Nepal.

steep zigzag climb through breaks in the valley walls.

When you reach the top, the path, lined with *mani* stones and *chorten*, cuts through terraced fields to Simgaon, set at 1,920 metres (6,300 feet). Far below, the Bhote Kosi cuts deep through the valley gorge, its waters diverted to the fields spread over the hills on either side. You should complete this section within six or seven hours.

Fourth day
Follow the path, through terraced fields, to the crest of a ridge — with splendid views of Gaurisankar — and zigzag up the mountain through a dense and beautiful rhododendron forest to the crest of another ridge. Walk along the ridge, through more rhododendron, to emerge in the fields and meadows around Shakpa. From there you start to climb the mountains on the Rolwaling side of the valley into more thick forest. When you leave the forest the path drops steeply. Take care — it is dangerous and tricky. On the valley floor you cross a stream and skirt beneath a ridge to Cyalche, set at 1,698 metres (5,570 feet). There you can camp on the grass.

Fifth day
The path descends steeply and diagonally from the campsite to the Rolwaling Chhu, where it follows the riverbed, before eventually veering on to the left bank through a narrow valley to a covered wooden bridge that crosses over to the right bank.

The path continues across a stream by the bridge and, climbing gently, follows an undulating path to Nyimare, then Ramding and Gyabrug, where the roofs of the stone-walled houses are weighted down with stones.

It then crosses another stream before climbing, briefly, to the last permanent village in this region, Beding, set at 3,690 metres (12,100 feet), which boasts 32 houses and a monastery.

You can camp near the river, with views of Rolwaling Himal's major peak, 7,180-metre (23,557 feet) Menlungtse. From this base you can make a three-day diversion to Manlung La by taking the trail along

the mountain flank on the right bank, just after the village. The first day it climbs to a 4,877-metre (16,000-foot) campsite, via Taten Kharka. The second day takes you to Manlung La, set at 5,486 metres (18,000 feet), and back. The trail is crevassed and you will need ropes, picks, and ice axes.

Sixth day
Leave the village, past the Manlung La diversion on your left, and follow the right bank of the Rolwaling Chhu on a gradual climb through the valley to Na Gaon, a village with terraced and walled potato fields.

Leaving the village, the trail crosses a wooden bridge and mountains come into view — 6,698-metre (21,976-foot) Chobutse and 6,269-metre (20,569-foot) Chugimago — before the snouts of the Ripimo Shar and Tram Bau glaciers push in ahead to block the valley and the view. The trail crosses a wooden bridge, shortly thereafter leaving the main path and turning left to Omai Tsho up a ridge that offers a vista of 6,735-metre (22,097-foot) Kang Nachungo and the mountains surrounding Ripimo Glacier.

The path to Tsho Rolpa skirts the base of the Ripimo glacier and passes between Ripimo and Tram Bau glaciers on to the right bank of Tram Bau Glacier. It becomes narrower and narrower as the valley becomes shallower.

Rising up at the far end of the valley are 6,730-metre (22,081-foot) Pigphera-Go Shar and 6,666-metre (21,871-foot) Pigphera-Go Nup. Soon you arrive at the last camp, Rolpa Chobu, set at 4,572 metres (15,000 feet). It takes five days to return to Charikot from this point.

On to Kodari
Back on the Araniko Highway, not far beyond Lamosangu, on the Sun Kosi, stands one of the country's first hydroelectric schemes built in 1972 with Chinese aid.

Nepal's first hydroelectric station was built in 1911. Despite occupying only a tiny fraction of the world's land surface Nepal's hydroelectric potential totals an impressive 2.27 per cent of world capacity.

The power station lies some 900 metres (3,000 feet) above sea level between

Above: Shops selling souvenirs in Kathmandu.

Lamosangu and **Barabise**, and it is **north** of bustling Barabise that the road begins to climb upwards. All along the road the sparse winter and spring waters are tapped for irrigation and domestic use through ancient but well-kept **aqueducts**, models of traditional engineering dug out above the side of the streams and lined with stone, with the fast-flowing water taken off the main body, which soon descends below the level of the aqueduct.

Many visitors stop at **Tatopani,** where **hot springs** from the raging cauldron beneath the Himalaya have been tapped, pouring forth day and night in an ever-lasting supply of running hot water.

At occasional intervals there is the inevitable **temple** — and at **Chakhu**, only 15 kilometres (nine miles) from Tibet, there is an improbable **circus** pitched on a river bank just below the edge of the road. Eight kilometres (five miles) beyond, at **Khokurn**, a **temple** occupies a **tall rock** in the middle of the gorge — with no indication of how worshippers climb up its sheer rock faces on all sides — and a sparkling **waterfall** leaps and jumps hundreds of metres down

the sheer, lush-green wall of the mountain. The perpendicular rock walls of the gorge press inexorably closer and closer. They seem to lean over the narrow ribbon of road that clings so precariously to the hillside.

Where the road cuts beneath a cliff, you may ask yourself what sustains such faith in the power of the rock to suspend itself indefinitely with such a mass of weight pushing down on it — and, perhaps more importantly, what sustains the faith of those who pass beneath it?

On the hillsides above, seemingly also suspended by faith alone, peasants carve little terraced **smallholdings** and till them with an agility similar to that of the sure-footed native goats. In the raging white waters below, equally nimble-footed villagers plant primitive — but effective — fish traps made of withies and bamboo. Then the gorge closes in and, round one more bend, there is an **immigration post** and beyond that a **police post.**

Finally, you reach the **border** which is spanned by the **Friendship Bridge**, the source of a thriving tourist trade. Day

Above: Trekkers take a break after climbing the trail from Lukla going towards Dudh Kosi Canyon.
Opposite: Thousands flock to the temple during the Indra Jatra Festival.

trippers disgorge themselves from their coach to be photographed with the Tibetan town of **Khasa,** 600 metres (2,000 feet) higher up the gorge, and the **snows** of 6,000-metre (19,550-foot) **Choba-Bahamare** in the background.

To the east, in line with Kodari, mighty Gaurisankar, only 35 kilometres (21 miles) distant, remains invisible beyond the rise of the gorge wall.

A **yellow line** across the middle of the bridge marks the **border** between Tibet and Nepal. Nepalis can cross unhindered but visitors must have obtained a visa — a fairly easy process — back in Kathmandu. Khasa's **Zhangmu Hotel** runs an enviable occupancy rate on European and American guests eager to stay overnight on a two-day visa that marks the magic China immigration entry into their passport.

Where the border actually crosses — and which side of the hill is Tibet or Nepal — is anybody's guess. On the other side, the road winds back into what, hypothetically anyway, must be Nepal.

In between the two, the waters of the

Bhote Kosi rage down the gorge with a thunderous roar, even though it is the dry season. It is awesome to think of the Bhote in spate during the monsoons and thaw. The thickness of the strong walls that buttress the bridge foundations suggest the power they deflect.

Above: Royal Nepal AIrlines Twin Otter prepares to launch itself from the cliff runway at Lukla.

The Road to the Apex of the World

At the far end of the Bhotey Kosi Gorge, 7,180-metre (23,557-foot) Menlungtse and the slightly lower 7,144-metre (23,438-foot) mass of Gaurisankar stand sentinel guarding 'The Goddess of the Universe', Sagarmatha, hiding her massive pyramid from prying, curious eyes.

Though almost 1,830 metres (6,000 feet) lower than Everest, Gaurisankar is truly majestic. In the form of an amphitheatre, its back faces north-west and, where the evening sun casts its glow over the curve of the shoulders, it paints its sheer ice cliff in soft gold.

Surely, it is easy to believe that Shiva and his consort still live there, where the wind plays ancient anthems in the crevasses and cracks, singing songs of praise to faiths older than humankind's. Spindrift raises a plume of white that plays across the mountain's brow.

The twin citadels of Gaurisankar and Menlungtse are the westernmost bastions of the Everest massif.

Peak to peak, a distance of about 70 kilometres (44 miles) separates Shiva's abode from that of Sagarmatha. In between, and around and about, dozens of lesser ramparts ascend to the central pinnacle, most rising above 6,100 metres (20,000 feet).

Thirty kilometres (19 miles) north-west from Everest, 8,153-metre (26,750-foot) Cho Oyu guards the approach while, fewer than eight kilometres (five miles) from the pinnacle of the world, 8,500-metre (27,890-foot) Lhotse guards the eastern flank and 7,879-metre (25,850-foot) Nuptse the south-western flank.

Sixteen kilometres (10 miles) beyond Lhotse, 8,481-metre (27,825-foot) Makalu and its four other peaks barricade the approach from the south-east.

Thus well-guarded from ground or air, Everest hides, almost demurely, behind a cluster of courtier peaks, with Nuptse and Lhotse serving as ladies-in-waiting. Yet the mountain's perfect apex, befitting the

Rolwaling and Everest

MAKALU

MT. EVEREST

GYACHUNG KANG   PUMORI   LHOTSE

NUPTSE   ▲ BARUNTSE

Everest Base Camp

PYRAMID PEAK

CHO OYU   Nuptse Gl.   CHAMLANG

Khumbu Glacier   Hongu Glacier

Lungsampa Glacier

Ngozumba Glacier   AMA DABLAM

Nangpa Gl.

T I B E T

Renzo Pass   Thyangboche

Lunag Gl.   KHUMBILA ▲

Bhote Kosi   Khumjung   Namche Bazaar

Drolambo Gl.   Kunde   Jorsale

Ripimo Shah Glacier   Thami

TENGI   Lukla

MELUNGTSE

CHOBUTSE   PIPHERA GO SHAR   KARYOLAUG

Manlung La   KANG NACHUGO   NUMBUR

GAURISHANKER   Beding   Nagaon   Rolpa Chobu   Trakarding Glacier

Ramding   Rolwaling Chhu   CHUGIMAGO

CHOBA BAHAMARE

Bhote Kosi   Shakpa   Phaphlu

Simigaon

Khare Khola

Gongar

Khasa   Manthale

Sangawa Khola   Suri Dhoban

Kodari   Shigati

Gumbu Khola   Piguti   Jiri   Rumjatar

Okhaldhunga

KALINCHOK

Dolakha

Barabise   Charikot

Tamba Kosi   Likhu Khola

Lamosangu   Nigale   Sun Kosi

Ramecchap

Indrawati   Dolalghat

Sun Kosi

Dhulikhel

Nala   Banepa

Sanga

To Kathmandu   Panauti

| 0 | 10 | 20 | 30 | 40 km |
| 0 | 5 | 10 | 15 | 20 | 25 miles |

highest point on earth, was surely designed to be seen. In the foreground, the attendant spires form jagged needles in the sea of cloud which covers the outer slopes. The jet stream keeps a constant plume of spindrift flowing eastwards off the 8,848-metre (29,028-foot) peak.

Getting there
Royal Nepal Airlines flies — often in some of the worst-possible weather in the world — to perhaps the most inaccessible airfields in the world.

In a roadless land, they are often the only link between one small community and another, flying an assortment of single-engined, high-winged 10-seater capacity planes, twin-engined planes and Fokker-Friendships, through narrow mountain defiles often wreathed in cloud, to landing strips that stand as high as 4,250 metres (14,000 feet).

People prefer to travel by air, no matter the peril. It is easy to understand why. On foot, from the nearest road, it takes anything from 12 to 15 days to reach Namche Bazaar, for instance — the launching-point for assaults on Everest or treks along the narrow valleys beneath it.

By plane, however, it is only 40 minutes from Kathmandu to Lukla, just over 2,750 metres (9,000 feet) above sea level, where the landing strip is on an uphill gradient with one side dropping precipitously hundreds of metres to the floor of the Dudh Kosi Valley.

Where to stay
Namche Bazaar is well above Lukla. But there is also a 4,000-metre (13,000-foot) airfield nearby — at Shangboche, where guests of the Everest View Hotel, with oxygen in all the bedrooms, alight.

Trekking (First day)
Almost every visitor to Nepal dreams of standing at the foot of the world's greatest mountain but it is an achievement only for the fittest. Most of the **trail** takes you above 4,000 metres (13,000 feet) in, freezing raw air — chest pounding, lungs gasping — to 6,076-metre (20,000-foot) **Everest base camp**, higher than any point in Africa or Europe.

Yet it is not just the mountain and its huddle of neighbouring peaks, three of the world's seven highest, which is the sole attraction, for this is also a land of fable and monastery, remote meadows and wildlife, and home to the hardy Sherpa folk and their colourful culture.

The trail from **Lukla** climbs up the **Dudh Kosi Canyon**, zigzagging through stone-walled **fields**, rustic **villages** and hardy **forests**.

The Buddhist prayer — *Om mani padme hum*, Hail to the jewel in the Lotus — is carved everywhere, on stone walls and the huge **boulders** which stand by the side of the trail. Before **Namche Bazaar**, at the **village** of Josare, stand the **headquarters** of **Sagarmatha National Park** where rangers and wardens, used to high-altitude living at 4,000 metres (13,000 feet), relax with games such as volleyball.

More than 5,000 trekkers a year climb this trail to enter the National Park's 1,243 square kilometres (480 square miles) of mountain wilderness: the rumpled brown-green buttresses of **Everest** ascending ever higher as you climb upward.

Namche Bazaar, **capital** of the Sherpa community, is set on a small **plateau** at the foot of sacred 5,762-metre (18,901-foot) **Khumbila**, which staunches the long run of the **Ngozumba Glacier** where it slides down from the base of **Cho Oyu**. It is the focal point of everything that occurs in the Everest region.

Every Saturday morning there is a colourful **market**, when hundreds trek in from the surrounding villages and towns to haggle and argue, buy and sell. Namche's **streets** step up the barren, rocky slopes of Khumbila, lined with pleasant white-washed two-storeyed **homes** with shingle and tin roofs.

Of Mongolian stock, the Sherpa people migrated over the Himalaya centuries ago from Minyak in eastern Tibet. Numbering between 25,000 and 30,000, they are known the world over because it was Sherpa Norgay Tenzing, with Sir Edmund Hillary, who conquered Everest — and it is Sherpas who accompany every major expedition.

For hardiness, courage and endurance there are few to equal these stocky, ever-

Above: Village at Namche Bazaar. Following pages: Sir Edmund Hillary, conqueror of Everest in May 1953, joyously accepts the gift of a white shawl, *khada*, from young Sherpa novice monks at Tyangboche Monastery during a 1986 visit.

cheerful, uncomplaining folk.

Sherpa **monasteries**, reflecting their Tibetan heritage, are the most striking in Nepal. You will find them in the towns of **Kunde** and **Khumjung**, which stand above Namche Bazaar — and are well worth visiting if you can make the climb — on the slopes of Khumbila.

West of Namche, at the foot of the **Bhote Kosi Valley** which is fed by the **Jasamba Glacier**, there is a particularly striking monastery in the **village** of **Thami**.

You can use Namche to approach Cho Oyu, either west up the Bhote Kosi Valley or north of Khumbila up the Dudh Kosi Valley.

If you take the westward route you will climb the **Renjo Pass**, coming down to **Dudh Pokari**, a beautiful **glacial lake** in the Ngozumba Glacier.

There is a passable chance en route of seeing some of the **Sagarmatha National Park's** wildlife: **wolf**, **bear**, **musk deer**, feral **goats** and maybe the brilliant **crimson-horned** or **Impeyan pheasants** of this region.

On the trail to Everest, a hard four-hour slog, or a full day's strenuous effort from Namche, you will come to the best-known of Khumbu's monasteries, **Thyangboche**, known the world over from photographs with stupendous views of Everest, or maybe Lhotse, or with the unmistakable **obelisk** of 6,858-metre (22,494-foot) **Ama Dablam**, in the background. After his successful ascent of Everest on 29 May 1953, Sir Edmund Hillary became New Zealand's Ambassador to India and Nepal, and devoted much of his diplomatic career and personal life to improving life for the Sherpa community he had come to love.

He is a frequent visitor to the monastery and the lama who presides there. It was his initiative which led to the establishment in 1975 of Sagarmatha National Park, which was run by New Zealand experts until 1981, when Nepal took over its management.

Hillary returns frequently, helping to build schools and community centres. Forces of change — not all for the better — have come apace to the once-isolated

Sherpas, whose festivals add colour and fantasy to life in this barren but beautiful region.

Trisuli Valley

Kathmandu is also the base from which to plan treks or visits to Trisuli Valley through Trisuli Bazaar — which is also the starting point for treks to neighbouring Langtang Himal.

When Nepal first opened its doors to foreigners in 1950, the first to venture into its hidden mountain sanctuaries were British climbers Eric Shipton and H W Tilman, who 'discovered' the Langtang Himal's many marvels —just 75 kilometres (47 miles) north of Kathmandu — which were then unknown even to many Nepalese.

Virtually at the capital's back door, no city in the world can claim a more delightful backdrop. Tilman called it 'one of the most beautiful valleys in the world' — still considered an understatement by many.

Getting there
Trisuli Bazaar is the base for both the Trisuli Valley and Langtang Himal and is served by road and regular bus services. You board a bus at **Sorkhuti** on the northern side of Kathmandu. Reserve your seat in advance. The journey takes four hours

Sightseeing
When you visit Trisuli Valley you walk through **hills** clad with evergreen **forests**, thundering **waterfalls**, and alpine plants — **oaks**, **alders**, **firs** and **rhododendrons**.

Villages are built of sturdy, two-storeyed gabled brick-and-thatch houses. Among the many large **monasteries** are some which are strikingly small: one with pagoda-style roofs and circular top is like a cross between a lighthouse and a Suffolk grain store.

A 14-day trek leaves **Ganesh Himal** in the **east** and takes you around the north face of **Himal Chuli** and **Manaslu** — almost into China's back yard — through bleak and

Opposite: Thyangboche Monastery.
Right: Sherpa porter.

windswept **passes**, skirting **glaciers** and frozen **lakes** up to a height of more than 4,573 metres (15,000 feet). It also takes you to **Samdo**, Nepal's most remote perManint settlement, a village of 200 souls — about 40 families — whose fields and paddies are covered in snow until late in the year.

There are also the twin **villages** of **Lhi** and **Lho** to delight lovers of tongue twisters. Inevitably, all along the way the **trails** are lined with the **prayer stones**, *mani*, of the staunch Buddhists who occupy the region.

Manaslu

The outward trek takes you from **Trisuli Bazaar** to the **Burhi Gandaki**, through huge and steep valleys and over snow-clad passes and foaming rivers to the three peaks of Manaslu, known as 'the Japanese peaks'.

Excellent equipment and Sherpa guides are essential and, because of its duration, so are adequate food supplies and physical fitness. Plan on extra rest days to help you recover during the course of the trek.

First day

Camp in the **meadow** in front of the **military post**, a short climb up from Trisuli Bazaar town. Take the **path** along the **riverbed** and up the **right-hand plateau** to **Raxun Bazaar**. It is a wide, smooth path that cuts through the paddies to **Gote Thab,** by **suspension bridge** over the **Somrie Khola** along its **right bank**, and on through the villages of **Ghorakki, Shiraune Bash**, and **Kaple Bash.** Before long, signs of cultivation vanish and the river is dry. Now the path climbs a **ridge** to **Somrie Bhanjyang,** set at 1,280 metres (4,200 feet), over a **pass** lined with **tea houses** to the valley floor and the **hamlet** of **Kinu Chautara** with its many **tea houses**.

The path continues through **farm fields** and then crosses to the **right bank** of the **Thofal Khola,** down a gradual incline to the **hamlet** of **Jor Chautara**. Soon after this it reaches **Baran Gurun** where you can camp in the **compounds** of people's homes or in the **fields**. It is close to six hours walking in all.

Second day

Leaving camp, the trail crosses a small **stream** and then climbs up some steep **stone steps** to **Baran** through a small **hamlet** and along a winding mountain path to the Tamang village of **Tharpu**. Shortly afterwards it reaches **Tharpu Bhanjyang**, with its one **general store**, and descends to **Boktani**. Not long after reaching there, it begins to climb a ridge to **Col Bhanjyang**, where it joins the mountain trail along the side of the Thofal Khola. All this is gentle, pastoral countryside — small foothills rolling away to distant horizons, sheltering gentle valleys — and eventually the trail takes you through **Katunje**, which boasts a **bank** and **post office**, on to the trail to **Charanki Pauwa** and **Charanki Phedi,** where you can camp in the **fields** outside the village.

Third day

Leaving the village, the narrow path crosses a small **stream** — over **Achani Bhanjyang Pass** — and then descends to the **left bank** of the **Ankhu Khola** before it crosses a **suspension bridge** to **Kale Sundhara bazaar**.

At this point, the landscape is sweltering and subtropical all the way to **Gaili**

Above: Tea house along River Langtang Khola.

Chautara where, just beyond the village, you leave the main path and take the **trail** to the **left**, much of it along the side of the river, through **Hansi Bazaar,** with its **tea houses** and **shops**, and between **paddy fields** in the **riverbed**. Where the Ankhu Khola bends to the left, the **path** veers **right** to **Arughat bazaar**, through a small, narrow valley and over a sprawling terraced hill that stands between the Ankhu Khola and Burhi Gandaki. When it reaches the village of **Soliental,** and the Burhi Gandaki, you can see **Arughat bazaar** below. Take the **path** along the **left bank** of the Burhi Gandaki for Arughat Bazaar, a small, bustling **town** on either side of the river.

Its central shopping area, with **bank**, is on the right bank of the river across a **suspension bridge**.

You can camp in the **grove** near the **school**, just outside the town. The entire walk should take from four-and-a-half to five hours.

Fourth day

Out of Arughat Bazaar, the trail follows the **right bank** of the Burhi Gandaki to its

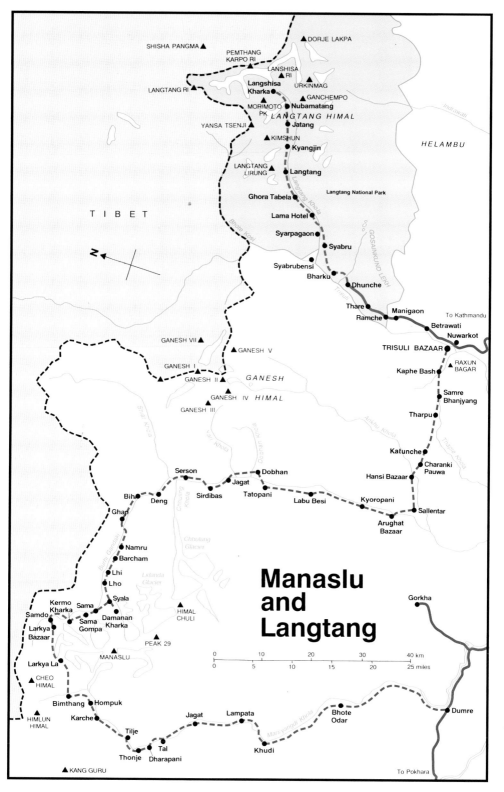

Manaslu and Langtang

Above: Tamang woman at Trisuli market.

source, along a path through farm **fields** and **Mordar**. When you reach **Simre**, the dry season trail follows the **riverbed** to **Arket**. During the monsoon, it climbs over the hills. You cross the Arket Khola at **Arket**, through the **village** and its **tea houses**, and across more **farmland** to the **Asma Khola**, which you cross to climb up to **Kyoropani**.

From this hamlet, the path is straight and level for a short distance and descends to the river bank and on through another hamlet to its **confluence** with the Soti Khola, where you can camp in the **fields** on the right bank. Total walking time is between four-and-a-half and five hours.

Fifth day

Follow the trail along the riverbed for about 10 minutes and then take the winding path up the forested hill to **Almara, Riden** and **Riden Gaon.**

Soon, the Burhi Gandaki Valley becomes a precipitous gorge, until it reaches another valley that cuts into the opposite bank and opens up. Now the trail crosses **farmlands** to **Labubesi** and then down to the

white bed of the **Burhi Gandaki**. Another **path** follows the mountain contours, rejoining the trail from the riverbed near the hamlet of **Kani Gaon**.

Continue along an undulating path above the river to **Machha Khola,** with its **tea house**, where you can **camp** in the **fields** outside the village. It should take no longer than six hours.

Sixth day

Leave across the Machha Khola and follow the **path** along the river bank into a precipitous valley and across the abundant flow of the **Tado Khola** to **Kholabensi,** a hamlet of eight houses.

The trail now continues along the bank of the **Burhi Gandaki**, between two walls of sheer cliff, to the **hot springs** of **Tatopani**. Soon afterwards it crosses a **suspension bridge** to the **left bank** into **forest** and then along a **gravel path** by the river to **Dobhan**, where there is a **tea house**. There the trail crosses the Dobhan Khola and some **rocks** to the point where the Burhi Gandaki bends right into raging **rapids**. It climbs the hill above the rapids,

Above: Tamang woman carrying building stones.
Following pages: Yak in front of a stupa at Thyangboche.

which suddenly broaden out into a sluggish, meandering stream between white beaches.

Now cross the **Yaru Khola**, climb into the forested hillside to **Lauri** and the **suspension bridge** to the **right bank**, where the trail climbs again, along a winding path that dips down once more to the riverbed and an easy walk through the fields to the checkpost at **Jagat**, set at 1,355 metres (4,400 feet).

This is the last village with a **shop**. You can camp in the fields outside the village. Total walking time is between six-and-a-half and seven hours.

Seventh day

You leave Jagat down some **stone steps** to the river, crossing the **tributary** flowing in from the left, and then walk along the **right bank** before climbing a terraced hill to **Salleri**, where you can suddenly see 7,177-metre (23,540-foot) **Sringi Himal** rising up at the end of the valley. Follow the undulating path along the **right bank** to **Sirdibas** and on to the next village, **Ghatte Khola**, where you cross the **suspension**

bridge to the **left bank**. This is where the **trekking trail** to **Ganesh Himal** diverges to the **right**. You continue along the river bank to **Serson Gaon**.

There the valley walls close in, trapping the Burhi Gandaki between sheer cliffs. Not much later you reach the **Chhulung Khola tributary,** flowing in through the **opposite bank**, and cross the **bridge** to the **right bank**. The trail climbs for about 100 metres (90 yards) before turning **right**, along a winding path through a **pine forest** above the **Shar Khola**.

The trail follows the **river** through the centre of the valley before crossing over to the **left bank**. Walk for about another 30 minutes and it returns once more to the **right bank**.

Soon you come to the junction of the Nyak trail that climbs up to the left, the main trail continuing along the river's **right bank** until you climb up to traverse its gorge. Finally, you cross the **Deng Khola** into the tiny **hamlet** of **Deng**, with **four houses**. You can camp in the fields outside. The total time for this stretch is between seven and eight hours.

Eighth day

Leave the village along the high, winding path that soon leads down to the river bank, where it crosses a **suspension bridge** to the **left bank** and climbs steeply to **Rana**, where you begin a gradual climb through **Unbae**, with its **stone gate** and *mani* **stones**, before the trail dips down once more to the river, past a **waterfall** on the right.

Now it climbs up again across a terraced hill, past the village of **Bih** and across the **Bihiam Khola,** on a twisting path lined by **mani stones**, to a tiny **hamlet** near the Burhi Gandaki.

Soon it reaches **farm fields** and a **stone gate** — entrance to the Tibetan village of **Ghap**, at 2,076 metres (6,800 feet) — where there is a **suspension bridge** across the Burhi Gandaki. You camp in the **meadow** on the left bank, near the entrance to the village. In all, this walk takes about four hours.

Ninth day

Follow the path along the **right bank**, past a long *mani* **stone wall**, into forest and then through **Lumachik** — a lone house — and across the **wooden bridge** over the Burhi Gandaki Gorge.

The trail climbs upward through **forest** to a **wooden bridge** that takes it across to the **right bank** and on through the forest to the **checkpost** at **Namru**. Leave Namru by crossing a **stream** to a grassy **field** with a **waterfall** and stone **cliff** to the left, over the pastures to **Bengsam**, where the trail climbs out of the village through a **stone gate** and on to **Li**. There it crosses the **Hinan Khola**, streaming down from the **Lidanda Glacier**, to climb up to **Sho**, guarded by its stone gate.

Soon afterwards, the trail rounds a bend to reveal views of **Naike Peak**, 7,163-metre (23,500-foot) **Manaslu North** and, finally, 8,158-metre (26,766-foot) **Manaslu**. Climbing gradually, the path passes between **houses**, farm **fields** and a bubbling **spring** to **Lo**, set at 3,140 metres (10,300 feet) in its stone-walled fields. Behind you, at the head of the valley below, stands 7,406-metre (24,298-foot) **Ganesh Himal**. You can **camp** by the spring at the entrance to the village. Total walking time is around six hours.

Tenth day

Cut through the village, lined by a long *mani* **stone wall**, then down across the **Damonan Khola** and the climb along the river. Ahead, the horizon is dominated by the snowcap of 7,830-metre (25,690-foot) **Peak 29**, while the Shara Khola flows in from the right.

After a short distance, the trail comes to a **left fork** — the main path ascends the ridge to **Sama** — that climbs to **Pungen Glacier**, via **Honsansho Gompa** and, despite the effort, the diversion is worthwhile, simply for the views of Peak 29 and Manaslu. The narrow path climbs through thick forest to **Honsansho Gompa** and over a gentle ridge, and cuts diagonally across a rocky **riverbed** to another small **ridge**. Not long after this it reaches **seven stone huts** at **Kyubun**, then climbs over a small **ridge** formed by the moraine of Pungen Glacier where you can see the battlements of Peak 29 and Manaslu. The moraine leads on to **Ramanan Kharka**, but to reach Sama, climb down the glacier and,

Above: Old Tamang woman.

from the small **ridge**, cut across its **snout** to the rock-strewn riverbed and a *chorten*.

From this point, it is just a short climb down to the **main path** and the **potato fields** and houses of Sama, set at 3,500 metres (11,500 feet).

Another 20 minutes' walk brings you to the **meadow** at **Sama Gompa**, where you can camp before a panoramic view of Manaslu. The walk takes about six hours.

11th day

Leave the meadows, skirting a ridge of lateral moraine, to the **banks** of the Burhi Gandaki, after crossing a stream born in the ice-melt of **Manaslu Glacier**. If you **turn left**, you can make a 60 to 70 minute excursion to a **glacial lake**.

Meanwhile, the **main trail** leaves the grasslands down to the riverbed and on to **Kermo Kharka**, with stupendous views of Manaslu. From there, it passes a long **stone** *mani* **wall**, at **Kermo Manan,** where the valley begins to close in and the trail climbs above the trickle of the newly spawned Burhi Gandaki before climbing down to the riverbed.

Cross the river, up a **terraced hill** on the opposite bank, and through a **stone gate** to the remote village of **Samdo** where around 40 families share life's alpine travail. There is no more wood for fuel after this, so take what you need with you.

The path goes down the mountain from the village, through a **stone gate**, and across the Gyala Khola, before climbing gradually upwards. Below you, to the left, you may see the **ruins** of **Larkya bazaar**.

Larkya Glacier soon appears on the opposite side of the valley after the trail crosses **two streams** and skirts around **Sarka Khola**. Then it climbs to a strong **shelter**, at 4,450 metres (14,600 feet) where you can spend the night. This leg takes from six to seven hours.

12th day

From the guesthouse, a short climb takes the trekker up to a glacial valley, with views of **Cho Dhanda**. As the gradual climb continues, the unmistakable image of Larkya Peak comes into sight opposite a **small glacier** on the other side of the valley.

Soon the trail leads into a **level glacier** and gradually upwards until a final short, steep climb brings it to **Larkya La**, set at 5,135 metres (16,850 feet) — and a breath-taking view to the **west** of 7,126-metre (23,380-foot) Himlung Himal, Cheo Himal, Gyaji Kang, 7,010-metre (23,000-foot) Kang Guru, and finally 7,937-metre (26,041-foot) Annapurna II. Climbing down the steep, snow-covered **west face** of the pass, unlike the east face, is a tricky business, so be careful. Now down to **Larcia,** opposite a hill on the other side, called **Pangal**, which also offers stupendous mountain views. From Larcia, the trail climbs down some moraine to the roofless **stone hut** of **Tanbuche,** set at around 3,900 metres (12,800 feet). All in all, this part of the trek runs to around six hours.

13th day

As you leave Tanbuche and head for **Bimthang** you can study the west face of Manaslu and 6,126-metre (20,100-foot)

Above: Weaving trathor cloth, Langtang.

Above: Ploughing and planting potatoes, Langtang.
Opposite: Heavy loads of fodder are carried by women.

Phungi. From the ghost town of Bimthang, with its *mani* stones and **deserted houses**, the trail climbs a **lateral moraine** and then leads down to a **riverbed** where it enters the Burdin Khola to lead to the **Manaslu base camp**.

If you climb a 4,145-metre (13,600-foot) **ridge** thereabouts, you will be rewarded by fine views of the **west face** of 7,162-metre (23,500-foot) Manaslu North peak, Annapurna ll and 6,893-metre (22,609-foot) Lamjung Himal.

Now follow the riverbed, over the **wooden bridge** above the headwaters of the **Dudh Khola** and up a lateral moraine, before descending through a magnificent **rhododendron forest** to Hampuk.

Finally, before entering the forest again, draw breath for your last look at the west face of Manaslu, then continue through the forest along the **right bank** of the Dudh Khola to **Sangure Kharka** and its **single hut**.

Manaslu North Peak and Larkya Peak are now behind as the trail continues down the **right bank** of the narrow valley, crossing the **Surki Khola** where it enters from the

right, to the **fields** of **Karche**, set at 2,785 metres (9,130 feet), on the opposite bank. The total time taken on this stretch is likely to be from four-and-a-half to five hours.

14th day
The trail leads up to the **paddy fields** on top of a **terraced hill** and over **Karche La Pass**, then down through the **fields** to **Goa** and along the **right bank** of the Dudh Khola to **Tilje**. There the trail crosses a **wooden bridge** to continue down along the left bank to the **Marsyangdi Khola** where it returns, across a **wooden bridge**, to the **right bank** and the **checkpost** at **Thonje**. Leave the village and follow the trail on the **left bank** of the Marsyangdi Khola, returning to the **right bank** across a covered **wooden bridge**. Now there is a short climb to the trekking trail around Annapurna.

From there, the path leads gradually down to the **checkpost** at **Dharapani** and on to **Bhote Odar** and **Dumre**, where you can take a bus to Kathmandu.

Langtang Himal

Trisuli Bazaar is also the base for treks into one of Nepal's most enchanted regions — fabled Langtang Himal with its monasteries, stupas, prayer walls and places made sacred by the Hindu scriptures.

This is the most popular of all Nepal's wilderness areas — a wonderland of hardy mountain people, animals, birds, forests and mountains, much of it preserved as the nation's second-largest national park, spread across 1,243 square kilometres (479 square miles).

Ancient bo-trees, their gnarled limbs like rheumatic fingers, spread a canopy of shade over Langtang's version of the patio, old stone terraces with seats stepped into the stone work, outside the rustic tea houses which refresh the traveller. Outside the 20 or so alpine villages roam 30 different species of wildlife, while more than 150 different kinds of bird have made their home among the region's 1,000 botanical species.

Mud-and-thatch houses serve as police posts. As much concern for trekkers' welfare as good government housekeeping, everybody needs a permit to visit these remote highlands, issued for one destination at a time along prescribed routes.

Dominating the valley at its north end is 7,245-metre (23,769-foot) Langtang Lirung, a few kilometres beyond which, on the Tibetan border, rises its sister peak, 7,239-metre (23,750-foot) Langtang Ri. Both overshadowed by Shisha Pangma — sacred 8,048-metre (26,398-foot) Gosainthan of Hindu mythology — which lies a few kilometres inside Tibet, the legendary abodes of Shiva.

You get sudden and unexpected views of some of these peaks as you take the spectacular trail hacked out of the wall of the gorge above the Trisuli River. In the more level areas, it cuts through thickets of juniper and rhododendron, blue pine and cushion plants. For centuries it has been a trade route between Kathmandu and Rasuwa Garhi in Tibet.

During July and August the rocky track becomes a mass of humanity as devout Hindu pilgrims, worshippers of Shiva, head for Langtang's Gosainkund lakeland, half-a-dozen small gems sparkling in the midday sunshine, said to have been formed when Shiva thrust his trident into the mountainside.

From Gosainkund it is possible to walk on over the pass into the remote but ever-beautiful reaches of Upper Helambu, best in spring when the rhododendrons bloom.

There, too, the headwaters of Nepal's major river, the Sun Kosi, mingle from scores of tumbling waterfalls, roaring rivers and laughing streams.

Swiss explorer, geologist and adventurer, Tony Hagen, shared Tilman's passion for Langtang Himal and ignited the same feelings in another Swiss national — a UN farm adviser who built a Swiss cheese factory close to Kyangjin Monastery at around 4,268 metres (14,000 feet), which, whatever the quality of the cheese, provides some of the most spectacular mountain views to be found anywhere.

The people are of Tibetan stock from Kyirong, who intermarried with Tamangs from Helambu and use a dialect similar to that spoken by the Tibetan community in India's Sikkim area. They cultivate small-holdings for grain and vegetables but are mainly pastoral, herding sheep and yaks.

To western eyes, the yak is one of the oddest-looking species of cattle, but it is well-equipped for its primary role as a high-altitude beef and dairy animal. It thrives in the frosty reaches of the Himalaya but fares disastrously if translocated to lower regions. It never descends much lower than 4,200 metres (14,000 feet) and in summer often reaches as high as 6,000 metres (20,000 feet). Long and low, its massive body, which weighs more than 500 kilos (1,100lbs), is entirely black, with long hair that falls at the sides in sweeping fringes and a tasselled tail.

Found still in feral communities, many of the domesticated breed are used as pack beasts, others as meat and dairy stock. The domestic hybrid species found at lower altitudes — a cross between a cow and a yak — is smaller.

Where to stay

In what is regarded as the most perfect alpine landscape in the world, a 9-10 day trek allows you to enjoy it in full. With many hotels and eating places, it is also one for the casual and not-so-hardy trekker.

Above: Tamang woman, Trisuli bazaar.

Trekking (First day)

Leave the bazaar and climb the terraced hills, past the **reservoir** on the left, where the road ends and a **level path** follows some **water pipes** to the foot of the **iron bridge** that carries them across the **Trisuli River**.

After crossing the bridge, take the **road left**. You can travel along this by jeep, past the village of **Bainshi** and along the river with its picturesque **hamlets**, to **Betrawati** with many **inns** and **hotels**. On foot, the journey takes about two-and-a-half hours.

Second day

Cross the **Phalongu Khola**, passing the **checkpost** through the village to an **old path** that climbs **left** to **Bhotal**, where you can take the path to **Banwa** with its **tea house restaurant**. Now cross some terraced **fields** to a **mountain path** which leads to the **crest** of a **ridge** with views of **Mani Gaon** ahead. Follow the gradual decline to the stream on the right, before climbing up to Mani Gaon. The trail runs through **fields** and **houses** for some distance and then up a gentle slope across another ridge, where

it circles a stream on the right, before a steep hairpin climb to **Handebre**. There it eases into a more gradual incline to **Ramche,** set at 1,829 metres (6,000 feet), with one hotel and some restaurants.

You can stay at the hotel or camp in the garden of the restaurant. Pay your park fees at the national park office at the entrance to the village. This walk takes about five hours.

Third day

The road leads out of Ramche, round to a **subsidiary ridge**, along a **level path** high above the **Trisuli River**, to the stone-walled, broad-roofed houses of **Garang**. From the top of the ridge, out of Garang, you get your first glimpse of snowcapped 7,245-metre (23,769-foot) **Langtang Lirung**. Now the path undulates along the hillside to **Thare,** across a **stream** and rock-strewn area, skirting a ridge, to **Bokajundo** with excellent views of Langtang Lirung. You take the road through the **village**, marked by *chorten*, and into mountain **forest** that leads into a gorge, where you cross two streams and the path becomes a **gravel road**.

Now it passes a **rock path** leading into a side valley before reaching the **checkpost** at the right of the entrance to **Dhunche,** set at 2,042 metres (6,700 feet) and focal point of the district, with hotels, shops and government offices. There, you can enter the **valley** of the **Trisuli River** to travel to **Gosainkund,** the sacred Shiva lake. The journey to Dhunche takes six hours.

Fourth day

The road leaves Dhunche across some **fields**, down the forested banks of the **Trisuli Khola**, across a **suspension bridge**, and up a **steep hill** along a small stream. After some 20 minutes walk, the trail leaves the stream and travels up the hillside on the **left** to a **tea house** atop a ridge. There is a fork in the trail there — straight on to Gosainkund and left to Syabru, a rather narrow path past the tea house. It skirts the ridge, with Dhunche in view on the opposite bank, and carries along the mountainside on the **left bank** of the Trisuli River to some **fields**, where the path to Syabrubensi branches left, near **Bharkhu.**

From Bharkhu, cross the **fields** and climb the steep mountain pass, an exercise rewarded to your rear, where the path levels out and leads left through forest, by a view of Ganesh Himal. Then it passes another **village**, to the left below, and through more **forest** to a **rest area** at the crest of a ridge.

From there it dips down gradually to **Syabru,** set at 2,230 metres (7,316 feet), where you can camp in the **monastery grounds** or hotel garden. This leg takes approximately five-and-a-half to six hours.

Fifth day

Walk down the ridge, between the **houses,** turn **right** past some **fields**, then through **forest**, across a **stream** and a flat mountain trail on the left which leads to the crest of a ridge. The other side leads down a steep slope through thick forest to the **Langtang Khola**, where it follows the **left bank.** Soon it crosses a stream and continues the

Right: Rhododendron tree, Langtang trek.
Opposite: Cattle passing through struts, Langtang Village.

climb up the valley to a **wooden bridge** across the Langtang Khola to the **right bank.** There the path climbs high, leaving the river far below, and then it drops down around the flank of the mountain, to join the **path** from **Syarpa Gaon.**

Not far from this junction, the trail veers back to the river bank and later climbs up to the **Lama Hotel** surrounded by other **tea houses** and **hotels.** When it cuts into forest, through breaks in the tree cover you see majestic **Langtang Lirung**.

The path climbs past **Gumnachok**, and its **lone hotel**, to a short steep **hill** where it leaves the river bank and the valley broadens. Not long after this it reaches the **checkpost** at **Ghora Tabela**, set at 3,017 metres (9,900 feet). Time taken on this leg is around six hours.

Sixth day

The trail leaves Ghora Tabela through the farm **fields** on the valley floor and after a short distance crosses a steep grassy knoll, above a **monastery**, to **Langtang** where **gardens** are enclosed by **stone walls**. Some little distance from the village there is a

Above: Fishermen have to make a trap for their daily catch on the Trisuli River. Placid waters provide a bounteous yield of fish for the local community.

chorten followed by one of the longest *mani* **walls** in Nepal.

The trail leads along the top of green and lovely hillsides, past **two villages**, after which the valley broadens out and the path enters a level, dry **riverbed**. Where it crosses the flow from **Lirung Glacier**, 6,477-metre (21,250-foot) **Kimshun** and 6,543-metre (21,467-foot) **Yansa-Tsenji** can be seen to the left.

Now the trail cuts across moraine covered with loose stones to **Kyangjin Gompa**, set at 3,810 metres (12,500 feet), where there is a cheese factory. To the **north** of the village, on a 4,000-metre (13,000-foot) **crest**, there are magnificent views of Langtang Lirung's north face and the surrounding mountains. You can stay in the **town hotel** or camp in one of the stonewalled **fields**. Beyond this point, you will need tents and supplies, and must beware of mountain sickness. The walking time is between five and six hours.

Seventh day
The trail from Kyangjin Gompa crosses a wide alluvial **delta**, across a **stream**, to an

airstrip with vistas of Langtang Lirung's full profile.

From the airstrip, the trail follows the river and 6,280-metre (20,600-foot) **Langshisa Ri** comes into view at the far end of the narrow valley, with **Ganchempo** visible on the opposite side. From the river, the trail climbs through the rocky hills to the **seven stone huts** of **Jatang**. Just beyond, it descends once more to the dry **riverbed**, then up some more hills, with views of **Shalbachum Glacier** pushing its snout into the valley.

Nearby is **Nubamatang,** with **five stone huts**. Now the trail cuts across the grassy fields and climbs the glacial moraine, with views of the far end of the valley, which is dominated by the 6,830-metre (22,400-foot) **Pemthang Karpo Ri**, **Triangle**, and 6,855-metre (22,490-foot) **Ri**; to the **right** is **Langshisa Ri**. Now the trail descends to **Langshisa Kharka**, at 4,120 metres (13,500 feet) for views of 7,078-metre (23,221-foot) **Kanshurum** and 6,151-metre (20,180-foot) **Urkinmang** at the far of the Langshisa glacier. The journey time is around four

Above: White-water expedition speeds through rapids on the Trisuli River.

hours. You can camp in the **stone huts** at Langshisa Kharka or in the grassy **fields**. The return to **Trisuli Bazaar** from this point takes five days.

Eighth day

To trek from Langshisa Kharka to the Langtang and Langshisa glaciers, you have to be exceptionally fit and well equipped.

The trail from Langshisa follows the top of a **level hill** and down a winding **path** to the **riverbed**. There it begins to climb, past a small **stone hut** and through thorny scrub, to a **second hut**. From there the trail is faint and difficult to follow, as it is not often used. Some distance after this, a valley leads to the **Morimoto Peak base camp**, on a wide plain, with views of 6,874-metre (22,550-foot) **Gur Karpo Ri** and 6,750-metre (22,150-foot) Morimoto Peak.

The trail crosses the **plain** and enters the valley again. Around the corner, where the valley ends, it begins to climb to the glacier.

This is the extreme for most trekkers, with an excellent camp and outstanding views. The total time taken is around five hours.

It is possible to visit **Langshisa Glacier**, if you follow the trail a short distance upstream from **Langshisa Kharka** to a **log bridge**. It is sometimes wrecked by landslides, so check if it is there before you start.

Then the trail climbs through **scrub** before descending to one of the streams running off the glacier, which you enter at the **snout**. Then the trail slowly climbs until 6,966-metre (22,855-foot) **Dorje Lakpa** comes into view — magnificent even from Kathmandu, unbelievable when so close. The glacier veers right and when you round the corner, you get a breathtaking view of 7,083-metre (23,240-foot) **Lenpo Gang**, the highest of the Jugal Himal's peaks. You can camp at a site set at 4,800 metres (15,750 feet) often used as a base camp by climbing expeditions. The climb takes about five hours.

There is an abundance of wildlife in the median altitude range of the Langtang National Park, including the yak.

Indeed, Langtang's principal purpose is as a wildlife — and botanical — reservoir for the endangered **snow leopard, leopard, Himalayan black bear, red panda** and **wild dog**.

The canines are different from domestic species. They have fewer teeth and their colour varies, according to locality. Bigger than jackals but smaller than wolves, they are found throughout the Himalaya and eastern Tibet. They are Nepal's most efficient and ruthless killers, running down large deer and sometimes even taking on other predators — there have been recorded instances in the Terai where a pack has taken a tiger. Packs vary from six to 60 animals, and they usually hunt around dawn and dusk. They kill on the run, ripping out the victim's entrails while it tries to escape.

In Nepal, wild dogs are found in remote high regions like Langtang, as well as on the tropical plains.

The park's **avifauna** is also precious. One hundred and sixty species of birds have been recorded, including **crested grebes**, **coots**, **snow cocks**, **tufted pochard**, **teal** and the **bar-headed goose**, as well as game birds such as the **blood pheasant**.

Top: Red Panda.
Above: Himalayan Snow Cock.
Opposite: Glacier from Langtang.

Western Nepal: Wild and Wonderful

Nepal's remote and sparsely populated western provinces include the Gorkha Province and the breathtaking Valley of Pokhara. If you travel by road you can make a stopover at Gorkha on your way to Pokhara. It makes a pleasant break, as well as providing an opportunity to study an important place in Nepal history.

Getting there

Gorkha is five hours from Kathmandu and four hours from Pokhara. Since direct buses are almost non-existent, change buses at Abu Khaireni and wait for a local bus or minibus to the town.

South-west of Kathmandu, the Trisuli Gorge meets that of the Mahesh Khola River. From the capital to the confluence of the two rivers you take another major road, the Prithvi-Tribhuvan highways, as scenic as they are dramatic. A memorial to those who died building both highways stands at the top of the pass close to a Hindu shrine.

The pass out of the valley leads down the almost sheer escarpment in a series of tortuous and terrifying hairpin bends to the Prithvi Highway, which starts at the town of Naubise, where it leaves the older Tribhuvan Highway heading southward to Hetauda. The building of the Prithvi Highway — in 1973, with Chinese aid — is marked at Naubise by a stone tablet set in the side of the rock wall.

Hamlets and villages — the main highway being their one street — abound along the road. On the level sections on either side are emerald-green rice paddies. Cultivating rice is a family affair — the men bullying the oxen teams, the women and children planting the young green shoots with astonishing speed and dexterity.

The paddies cling to the mountain hundreds of metres above, protected from sliding away only by a fragile buttress of precious topsoil. Fields end abruptly at the edge of a gully or cliff. Many disappear in the monsoons, leaving only a void where once stood half-an-acre.

Charoudi, the most popular 'put-in'

place for shooting the Trisuli's rapids, is a small, one-street hamlet, after which the road drops quickly to **Mugling,** veering westward over the elegant suspension bridge.

Not long after Mugling, take a turn north off the highway to Gorkha which is nestled in the mountains some 18 kilometres (11 miles) from the Kathmandu-Pokhara Highway and is the ancestral seat of the Shah dynasty, rulers of Nepal since the 18th century. Gorkha is just a small town. The facilities, adequate and unpretentious, are not aimed at tourists.

Where to stay

Lodgings in Gorkha are simple. Most of them are clustered around the bus stop and are basic. Since Gorkha is off the beaten path for most tourists, rates are relatively cheap. Try Hotel Thakali if you plan to stay near the bus stop. In town, look for Hotel Gorkha Bisauni, which also offers the only Western food in town. Stay with dal-bhaat.

Sightseeing

King Prithvi Narayan Shah's **old palace** still stands on a mountain **ridge** overlooking this **ancient capital**, from which the Gurkha soldiers derive their name.

From the bus stop, the road passes by the town's **Tundikhel** and an **army camp**. A group of **temples** stands by the pond-like **Rani Pokhari** and a **stone statue** of Prithvi Pati Shah honours Prithvi Narayan Shah's ancestor. He travelled to Kathmandu and returned with Newar craftsmen, who were responsible for most of Gorkha's ancient buildings, which are conspicuously Newari in style.

The small-town air is more apparent when you come to the **main street**, which is practically a car-free zone. There, **shops** selling local goods jostle with ubiquitous **tea shops**. Men meet in their favourite **tea stalls** to discuss the day's events, and women gather at **Tin Dhara**, the public water source.

Tallo Durbar, a structure built in the

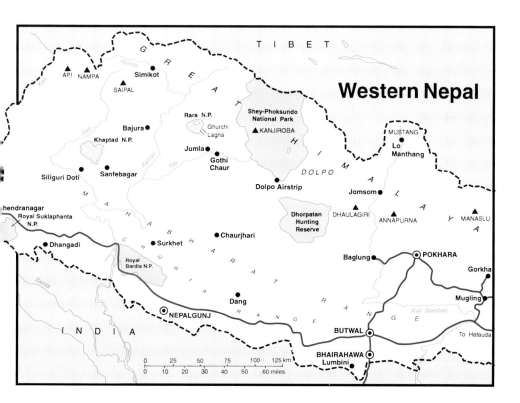

18th century, stands close to the town centre. It is believed to be the original site of the Gorkha palace, before the Shahs came to rule there. In 1996 there were plans to convert it into a **museum**.

The **palace** on the ridge above the town is **Upalo Durbar**, the home of the Shah kings. Its unmistakable prominence was both strategic and a sign of dominance.

To reach Upalo Durbar, climb a long flight of **stone stairs** leading off the main road. The climb takes about 30 minutes but it is well worth the effort. Directly ahead, magnificent mountains stand out in the centre of an east-west span — **Dhaulagiri**, **Annapurna**, **Manaslu and Ganesh Himal**, while behind you in the south are the **Mahabharat Hills**. Ram Shah built the first palace in the 1600s. It has since been renovated and much has been added to its sprawling intersections.

Many areas are restricted and, in those open to the public, you must remove any articles made of leather.

Because of its associations with Prithvi Narayan Shah, the Durbar is regarded as a sacred monument. In the areas open to tourists, you can see Newari crafts. The Durbar is remarkably well maintained, perhaps because of the dedication of the residents of Gorkha.

Kalika Durbar and **Raj Durbar** comprise the palace. A **Kali temple** was built into the **western section** of the palace, served only by a special sub-caste of Brahmins. Only the kings and these priests may look upon the **statue**, since it is believed common folk might die if they behold the goddess herself. The **entrance** to the shrine is a popular site for animal sacrifices and during the harvest festival, Dasain, the entrance is bathed in blood.

The **east section**, which housed the actual living quarters of the king, is called Dhuni Pati. Since this was the birthplace of Prithvi Narayan Shah, the area has the status of a shrine.

No photographs are allowed. Neither are any articles made of leather — shoes, bags, belts. These rules are eagerly enforced by the stone-faced guards.

The palace is off-limits, but you can explore the lower area level which houses a **feast hall** and **pilgrims' rest-house**.

193

Above: The Royal Nepal Army, considered the bravest in the region, was once awarded the most distinguished of all awards of bravery.

The **staircase** leads to the mouth of a **trail** that links Gorkha to the surrounding area.

Further up the ridge is **Upalokot**, with fine views over the surrounding countryside.

Tallokot is all the way over on the **west end**, where a **helipad** was built for royal visits.

Below the **south end** of the palace is the sacred **Gorakhnath cave**, carved out of a rock face. Gorakhnath was an actual 12th-century sage who became the patron saint of the Gorkha kings and was eventually deified as an incarnation of Shiva. He reputedly blessed Prithvi Narayan Shah's conquests, which eventually led to his victory. It is believed that he made a promise to appear wherever Gurkha soldiers were in battle.

The **entrance** is within the palace and **stone steps** lead to the **main shrine** and a host of other **images**.

During the clear season there are stunning views of Annapurna and its sister mountains from Gorkha, but nothing beats the panorama that awaits you in the trekking and climbing capital of Pokhara,

Above: Gurkha of the Royal Nepal Army.

Above: Gorkha Palace, the ancient seat of the Shah dynasty.

where the mirrored reflection of sacred Machhapuchhare shines in the still waters of Phewa Lake.

Pokhara Valley

Like Kathmandu, the Pokhara Valley is blessed with fertile soil and an average of more than 420 millimetres (165 inches) of rain a year. The land burgeons with lush vegetation: banana and citrus trees, cacti, rice and mustard fields, bounded by hedges of thorny spurge spiked with red blossoms, and walls studded with *ficus*. The patchwork terraces are cut through by gorges channelled by the Seti River and studded with lakes that glitter like diamonds in the spring sunshine.

The ochre mud-and-thatch homes of the Hindu migrants from the Terai are in contrast with the white-walled, slate-roofed homes of the Lamaist tribes from the flanks of the mountains.

Several years ago, Pokhara town was the antithesis of all things urban. Almost tropical in comparison with Kathmandu.

The first motor vehicle, a Jeep, arrived in 1958 — by plane. Progress since then, encouraged by tourists and climbers, the advent of hydroelectric power in 1967, and the Prithvi Highway in 1973, has been swift. Within a decade Pokhara's population doubled to 50,000. There is even a movie house and fun fair.

Pokhara Valley is blessed with beauty seldom seen in one place in the Himalaya. The weather is temperate but heavy rainfall makes it a lush subtropical refuge.

Small shops and restaurants are truly small family concerns. Tiny entrances open to large lakeside gardens where tourists sip rum and coke in the sun and watch the ferry go back and forth.

The chilli chicken found on the menu is a modification of kung pao chicken. Meatballs are no large tomato sauce-drenched entrée but a fried delicacy that make it worth the mistake.

Pokhara lies at the heart of traditional Gurung territory. But, as with the rest of the country, over the centuries the town has been affected by migration from the lowlands. The struggle for dominance

Above: Crossing the river to go to Pokhara.

between the outsider caste groups and the indigenous Gurungs continued until the 17th century, when the Kasi kingdom, a part of the Chaubise Rajayas, or 24 kingdoms, gained the upper hand. The Chaubise Rajyas are thought of as a sub-branch of the current Shah family. Pokhara was absorbed into the larger Nepali kingdom when Prithvi Narayan Shah annexed the kingdom during his reign.

All through the strife, Pokhara continued to be an important trading station between the highlands and the surrounding area. Mule trains bore wool and salt which were exchanged for food from the lowlands. Even today you still see mule trains, colourfully adorned, walking on the sides of the tar roads.

Getting there
Pokhara is 198 kilometres (124 miles) from Kathmandu. There are virtually no direct bus services and, with only two flights a day, airport activities are more entertaining than disturbing.

Where to stay
While not as sophisticated as Kathmandu, full-board accommodation in Pokhara covers the whole spectrum. You can find cheap lodgings behind the hotels that dominate the main street and lakeside. The prices vary depending on whether or not there is an attached bathroom.

Rooms are basic and clean, with hot water. Some of the better hotels have gardens for relaxation. If your hotel has no garden, it may have a terrace from which there are good views.

The most popular area for tourists is east of Phewa Tal by the lakeside or up by the dam (*pardi*). With the exception of Fish Tail Lodge, the expensive hotels are near the airport. Other inexpensive hotels near the bus station are usually frequented by Indian and Nepali businessmen.

By the lake
The hotels and lodges by the lake are off the main street. Sometimes you find a lodge nestled between houses and run by a family — bed-and-breakfast without the breakfast. But in the 1990s, hotels were

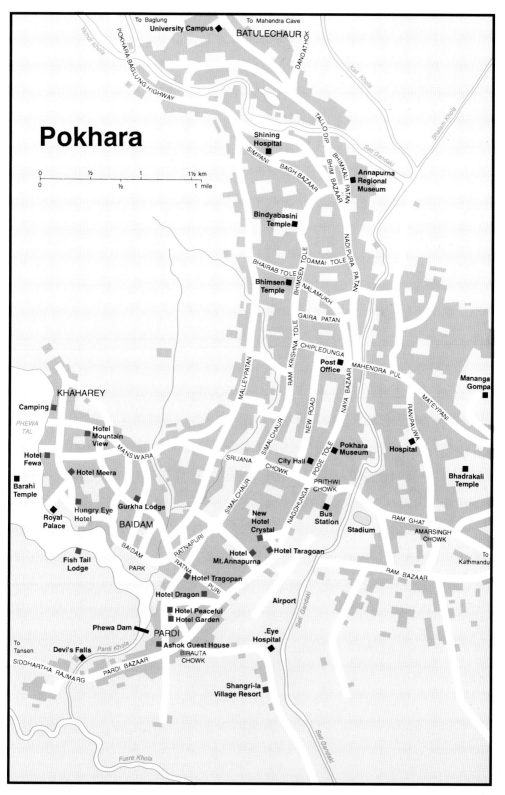

Pokhara

To Baglung
To Mahendra Cave
University Campus
BATULECHAUR

POKHARA-BAGLUNG HIGHWAY

Yamdi Khola
Kali Khola
Seti Gandaki
Bhalam Khola

0   ½   1   1½ km
0   ½   1 mile

Shining Hospital

DANDATHOK

TALLO DIP

BHIMKALI PATAN
BHIM BAZAAR

SIMPANI
BAGH BAZAAR

Annapurna Regional Museum

Bindyabasini Temple

BHAIRAB TOLE
BHIMSEN TOLE
ODAMAI TOLE
NADIPURA PATAN

Bhimsen Temple
NALAMUKH

GAIRA PATAN

RAM KRISHNA TOLE
CHIPLEDUNGA

MAHENDRA PUL

Mananga Gompa

KHAHAREY

Camping

PHEWA TAL

Hotel Mountain View

Hotel Fewa

Hotel Meera

Barahi Temple

Royal Palace

Hungry Eye Hotel

Gurkha Lodge

BAIDAM

Fish Tail Lodge

BAIDAM PARK

MANSWARA

MALLEYPATAN

SIMALCHAUR

SRIJANA CHOWK

SIMALCHAUR

NAGDHUNGA

POST OFFICE

NAYA BAZAAR
NEW ROAD

MATEYPANI
RANIPAUWA

Hospital

Bhadrakali Temple

Pokhara Museum

PODE TOLE
PRITHWI CHOWK

New Hotel Crystal

City Hall

Bus Station

Stadium

RAM GHAT

AMARSINGH CHOWK

To Kathmandu

RAM BAZAAR

RATNAPURI
RATNA PURI

Hotel Mt. Annapurna

Hotel Taragoan

Hotel Tragopan

Hotel Dragon

Airport

Hotel Peaceful
Hotel Garden

Phewa Dam

PARDI

To Tansen

Devi's Falls

SIDDHARTHA RAJMARG

PARDI BAZAAR

Pardi Khola

Ashok Guest House

BIRAUTA CHOWK

.Eye Hospital

Shangri-la Village Resort

Seti Gandaki

Fusre Khola

Seti Gandaki

changing at a rapid pace. Some were here today, gone tomorrow. The Gurkha Lodge, with only three rooms and a tranquil garden, is an antidote to stress. It is situated by the Baba restaurant.

The popular Hotel Hungry Eye has the most central location, and is behind the restaurant of the same name. Further north, the Hotel Fewa is the only hotel by the lake. It has a nice garden and the rates are reasonable. Pokhara also has a camping ground north of Hotel Fewa, an open area devoid of shade and patrolled by police to prevent theft. You would probably be better off in a lodge, but if you do camp, keep your valuables in a safe place.

Lodges in Khahare

At the south end of the lake, near the dam, some guest houses offer an option to the tourist-trap lakeside. There you find better views, a trade-off for the distance you have to cover. The rural charm of the surrounding area is also a big plus.

Some of the better-known lodges are Hotel Garden, Hotel Peaceful, Hotel Mountain View and the large Ashok Guest House.

The big tourist hotels are New Hotel Crystal, complete with air-conditioning, tennis court and swimming pool; non-air-conditioned rooms are cheaper. Hotel Taragoan, run by the government, offers cheaper rooms and is less flashy than its neighbour.

Two other fine places, Hotel Himal and Hotel Mount Annapurna, both have a Tibetan flavour. The restaurant at Hotel Himal serves up fine *momos* and *thugpa*. Hotel Meera, rooms only, is spotless, with big rooms and a restaurant.

At Pardi, two good hotels vie with each other. Hotel Dragon sports air-conditioning, a fine garden and good Thakali food. Hotel Tragopan has fans in its rooms and serves good Indian food.

The Fish Tail Lodge is built on land in the lake reached by a hand-drawn ferry. Resort-like, Hotel d'le Annapurna caters for the leisurely traveller. The mountain views are unsurpassed, while the panoramic-view restaurant is nice on a cold winter night.

Sightseeing

There is plenty to do in and around Pokhara, which is the main centre for expeditions to the great mountains nearby The **Annapurna** and **Dhaulagiri** massifs form the natural world's greatest amphitheatres. From Annapurna's 8,092-metre (26,545-foot) peak in the **west**, in an anti-clockwise direction the climber can look south to **Fang,** 7,650-metres (25,089 feet); **Moditse Peak,** 7,220 metres (23,683 feet); **Hiunchuli,** 6,442 metres (21,133 feet); **south-east** to **Machhapuchare,** 6,964 metres (22,842 feet); **east** to **Annapurna III,** 7,557 metres (24,787 feet); **north-east** to **Gangapurna,** 7,456 metres (24,457 feet) and **Glacier Dome,** 7,070 metres (23,191 feet), and **north** to **Roc Noir,** 7,485 metres (24,556 feet).

As if this were not enough, in the middle of this stupendous amphitheatre, truly an arena of the gods and goddesses, stand **Tent Peak,** 5,663 metres (18,580 feet) and **Fluted Peak,** 6,501 metres (21,330 feet).

All this lies within an inner radius of no more than 40 kilometres (25 miles). Its

Above: Womenfolk harvesting in Pokhara.

only equal — in scale, form and drama — lies directly opposite, across the Kali Gandaki Valley, where Dhaulagiri's six peaks and those around them form another breathtaking amphitheatre.

One pleasant way to go sightseeing around Pokhara is to hire a **bicycle**, **pony** or *conga* (long, dugout canoe). Bicycles are cheap, and ponies cost just over 100 rupees for half a day, from Pokhara Pony Trekking.

For those who would like to cruise the lake, *conga* are for hire at 25 rupees an hour — a bit more if one of the boat-boys does the paddling. Modern boats are also available.

On **Phewa Lake**, you may be drawn to a small pagoda-style **temple** situated on a tiny **island** and dedicated to the goddess **Barahi**. It is a famous place of pilgrimage and animal sacrifice. You can also swim and fish in the lake. Native and imported **plants** grace the many **gardens**, with a mix of **orchids**, **papaya**, **banana**, **rhododendron** and **jasmine**. Although the town is now growing rapidly, rural sights still linger and you will see cowherds driving **water**

Above: Children playing ball above Tolkha Valley.

buffalo through back roads, and friends gossiping by the roadside, oblivious to the tourists who stream by.

The charm of Pokhara is that it has something special for everyone. Even though the pastoral quality of the town is on the decline, the dominating presence of the sacred 6,964-metre (22,842-foot) Fish Tail — **Machhapuchhare** — and its reflection on Lake Phewa is unique.

No one has ever conquered the mountain. After an Englishman came to within 150 metres (500 feet) of the summit in the 1950s, the Nepalese decided that it should never be desecrated by human footsteps, and closed Machhapuchare, perhaps the most beautiful of all Nepal's mountains, from any intrusion for all time.

Shops and **restaurants** line the **east shore** of the lake, serving up all manner of products, from fruit shakes and shepherd's pie to rare books. Non-trekkers come to Pokhara for a break from the bustle of Kathmandu.

Pokhara is the starting point for many important treks, notably the **Jomosom** and **Annapurna circuits**. Recently, die-hard or second-time trekkers have completely bypassed Kathmandu, choosing to start their journey in Pokhara.

The **centre** of the town by the lake is unmistakable for its dense cluster of **shops** and **restaurants**. Most of the hotels are also lined up at this end.

The lake itself, **Phewa Tal**, can be explored in rather garishly painted rowing boats. The lake, an ancient glacial ribbon lake, has a few **islands** and there is a **Royal Winter Palace** for winters on the lake shore. Local legend says the lake covers an ancient city engulfed during a cataclysmic earthquake millennia ago.

Today local fishermen ply their *conga* on the placid waters, ferrying pilgrims to the **shrine** of **Barahi**. If you take a boat trip on a Saturday you will see many Nepali worshippers on their way to the temple, with offerings and probably a picnic lunch. The **shores** opposite are **forested** and quite secluded, a good place to stop if you can find a suitable landing place. Although the water may seem inviting, you are better off admiring its beauty rather than indulging in it, as it is rather polluted.

Above: Placid waters of Lake Phewa at Pokhara in the shadow of Annapurna.

To the south, **Phewa Fant**, a flat area of reclaimed land, is occupied by rice fields. On the **northern reaches**, a **dam**, built with Indian aid, supplies the valley and neighbouring areas with power. Pokhara is not immune to the continuing problems of over-population and defor-estation. Other lakes are silting up and even Phewa Tal may disappear in 50 years if the situation remains unchanged.

There are two **museums**. The **Pokhara Museum**, located between the **bus station** and **Mahendra Pul**, features **jewellery**, **costumes**, **musical instruments** and infor-mation about various ethnic groups. It closes on Tuesdays. The **Annapurna Regional Museum** boasts a wide **butterfly collection** but little else. The museum is closed on Saturdays.

Around Pokhara

The origins of Pokhara can be traced to the small trading post of **Pokhara Bazaar** which lies seven kilometres (4.2 miles) away between the villages of **Sarankot** and **Khanu Oanra**. Off the tourist path, the town is near the **Seti River**. You can get there with a mountain-bike. Take plenty of water because the ride is mostly uphill.

The town itself is a quiet rural cluster of modest houses and roads lined with trees. The essentially Newari culture is seen in the architecture and the **temples** left by the early traders. The most important **temple** is **Bindyabasini Mandir** on a **hillock** in the **centre** of town. A devastating fire in 1949 razed most of the original houses of Pokhara Bazaar, including the old temple. The deity is the goddess **Bhagwati** and her **image** is housed in the white **main structure**.

Two **figures** of the king and queen sit atop the Malla-style **pillar** in front of the temple. The rest of town is typical of rural Nepal. Most houses are styled in the more modern idiom since the fire of 1949. The

Above: Divine 'fish-tail' peaks of sacred Machhapuchare rise above a halo of cloud north west of Pokhara.

main street has a mix of food, utensil and produce **shops**.

You can take a side trip to the **south** to the **Mahendra Pul** which crosses the sliver-like gorge cut by the Seti River. To get there, drive to the **middle** of the **first bridge** along the Kathmandu Highway. Look below and you see the 4.5-metre-wide (15-foot) gorge, more than 14 metres (45 feet) deep, carved by the flow of the Seti. There are also many natural sites of interest in the Pokhara area.

Devi's Falls is located **south-west** of the **airport**, along the Siddhartha Highway.

This dramatic but seasonal **waterfall**, known locally as *Patle Chhango*, is created where a small stream flows out of the lake and surges down the rocks into a steep gorge, impressively so during the season of ice-melt and monsoons. Another interesting site is the **Mahendra cave, north** of **Shining Hospital** and the **University campus** near **Batulechaur** village. It is one of the few **stalagmite** and **stalactite caves** in Nepal, known locally as a 'holy' place. Carry a flashlight.

Some villages in the mountains around Pokhara, en route for longer treks, also make fine day excursions and offer the nicest views of Machhapuchare and other mountains, depending on where you go.

Ram Bazaar, east of Pokhara, is a small but picturesque **village**, with shops, a school and artisans. The most interesting **Tibetan village**, just **north** of the town in **Lower Hyangja**, is **Tashi Phalkhel**. **South-west** of the airport, beyond Devi's Falls, is **Tashiling**.

Batulechaur

Some miles **north** of Pokhara, **Batulechaur** is famous for its gaine singers, who tell of the rich history of Nepal in rhapsodic songs. They play small four-string, violin-like instruments (*sarangi*) with horsehair bows, to accompany their voices.

Sarangkot

At the **peak** of the 1,600-metre (5,250-foot) **Sarangkot** are the **remains** of a **fortress** used by King Prithvi Narayan Shah in the 18th century. Go **west** of Pokhara, past **Kaskidanda ridge**, to **Gyarajati village**, where you climb to the **summit**.

Baglung

Some distance **west** of Pokhara lies **Baglung** — approachable only on foot or by dubious road from the Terai — gateway to the **Royal Dhorpotan Hunting Reserve**. **Handmade paper** for packing and **bamboo crafts** are its most famous products. It is the home of the Thakalis, a group of 20,000 people of Tibetan-Mongoloid stock who speak a Tibetan-Burmese vernacular and whose faith is a mixture of Buddhism, Hinduism and Bonpo, the pre-Buddhist religion of Tibet. Baglung also earns praise, from the impotent and those on the wane, for the power of a local aphrodisiac — *silajit*. Locals travel far **north** along the Kali Gandaki Gorge to exploit deposits of this tar-like substance which oozes from the rocks and fetches high prices in India.

Tastefully produced crafts include woollen **blankets**, **vests**, **rugs** and other sewn or woven products.

Muktinath

One of many places of pilgrimage in the hills that line the **Kali Gandaki basin** is **Muktinath**. At 3,800 metres (12,460 feet), its **eternal flame** draws Hindu and Buddhist alike.

Black ammonite **fossils**, thought of as the embodiment of Vishnu, are found in profusion, and pilgrims travel long distances over rugged trails to collect these.

Kali Gandaki Gorge

The deepest gorge in the world, **Kali Gandaki Gorge**, is flanked on one side by the daunting massif of **Annapurna** and on the other, only 35 kilometres (22 miles) away, by the 8,167-metre (26,795-foot) summit of **Dhaulagiri I**.

In between, almost eight kilometres (five miles) below and at just 1,188 metres (3,900 feet), sits the village of **Tatopani**.

With Dhaulagiri and Annapurna, you are at the frontier of the highest land in the world — and ready to open the gateway to some wonderful trekking experiences.

Opposite: Paddy fields around Annapurna.

Annapurna

A 12-day trek along the **Marsyangdi Khola,** down into the Manang basin and over Thorong pass and then down into the **Kali Gandaki gorge** gives the trekker a roundabout tour of the Annapurna massif. It is also one of the most varied and comfortable.

Getting there

Take the bus from Pokhara to Sisuwa, where you begin the trek. The trail leads up from the bus stop through the neighbouring villages to a wide mountain path that climbs a ridge path where there are excellent views of both the Manaslu and Annapurna ranges above and the blue waters of Begnas Tal to the left below.

Where to stay

There are many hotels and tea houses en route, so you do not have to carry camping equipment.

Trekking (First day)

The ridge trail leads **right** to **Rupa Tal** where it dips down into the valley on the right. It travels upstream, through paddy fields, to Tarbensi with its **tea house**.

There the trail enters a small valley and travels upstream between two rivers which eventually dry up, just before **Sakkara Bhanjyang,** a village with many **tea houses**, set at the top of a **pass**.

When you go down into the valley the trail veers **left** to **Achari Bhanjyang**, with **three tea houses**, and continues into the valley, where it becomes rocky and difficult.

Soon, the valley broadens out into fertile **grain fields** and **rice paddies**, and when it reaches the **ridge** on which **Bagwa bazaar** stands, you will see the **snowcap** of 7,937-metre (26,041-foot) **Annapurna II**.

Walk through the paddy fields and take the **right bank** of the **Madi Khola** until the trail reaches a **suspension bridge** across the river to **Karputar**, where there are **shops**, **tea houses** and **health clinic**. You

Above: Basket-making at Chandrakot village.

come into view. **Nalma** is a Gurung village with several scattered settlements. You can camp in the **central village**, the one with a **school**. Total time taken is between four-and-a-half and five hours.

Third day
A **stone path** leads out of Nalma up an undulating ridge with excellent views from its summit of 8,158-metre (26,766-foot) Manaslu to the right and Annapurna to the left — standing up incredibly high, their snows glittering in the morning sun.

The trail passes through a **rest area** into a **forest** on the **left**, and then down and up past a **spring** to **Baglunpani**, set at 1,615 metres (5,300 feet). The two great mountain massifs are still visible, Manaslu in particular filling the horizon with its majestic pinnacles. Now the trail descends through **forest** to a **rest area**, where the valley broadens and cuts through **terraced fields** to **Samrong**. Turn **left**, down toward the **Bhoran Khola** and **Lama Gaon**, across a **suspension bridge** and down to the riverbed.

As you approach Marsyangdi Valley, the trail leaves the riverbed and crosses **farm fields** at the **left** of the valley to **Sera**, which is on the **right bank** of the **Marsyangdi Khola**. Leave the village along the **river bank** about 100 metres (320 feet) above the foaming waters, past a **hamlet**, where the valley bends to the right. Manaslu and Peak 29 rear up above the far end of the valley as the trail reaches **Khudi**, at the base of a **suspension bridge** across the Khudi Khola.

You can camp in the **meadows** on the **left bank** or stay at one of the village's **two hotels**. Total time taken on this walk is between five-and-a-half and six hours.

Fourth day
Walk through the village, past a **school** on the **lower right**, to the path on the **right bank**. Just after the school it crosses a **stream** to **two hamlets**, then crosses a **suspension bridge** to the **left bank** and **Bhul Bhule** which has **hotels** and **tea houses**.

The path begins to climb but, in the dry season, you can follow the **riverbed** and

can camp in the **meadows** on the **left bank** of the Madi Khola or stay at one of the tea houses. Total walking time is from five to six hours.

Second day
The trail leads along the **right bank** of the Madi Khola, some distance from the river, across the **paddy fields** and along a mountain path to **Laxmi Bazaar**.

After this it follows an irrigation canal through the fields, moving nearer and nearer the river as the valley narrows, and finally reaches **Shyauli bazaar** which boasts several **tea houses**. There is little shade.

Now the trail becomes undulating, climbing up the hills from the riverbed into a well-shaded area, through a **hamlet** and across a **suspension bridge** to a **tea house** on the **left bank**.

From there in the dry season the trail follows the **riverbed**, but in the monsoon, it winds up the hills to a final steep climb to the top, where it levels off. Turn **right**, into the hills, through terraced fields to **Nalma**, atop a ridge where **Manaslu's three peaks** and the **Annapurna range**

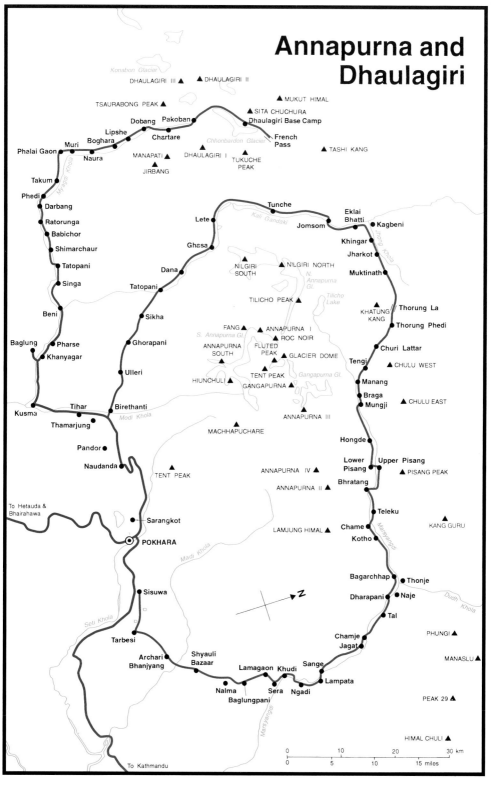

Annapurna and Dhaulagiri

Above: Village houses and maize storage barns in Suikhet Valley.

take a gradual incline to the Manang village of **Ngadi,** lined with **hotels** and **teahouses.**

The trail out of the village crosses a **stream** to the **left bank** of the **Ngadi Khola,** a **tributary** that has its source in the snows of 7,893-metre (25,895-foot) **Himal Chuli,** where a long **suspension bridge** leads to the **right bank.**

Soon it leaves the bank and climbs to the **crest** of the **ridge** which divides the **Marsyangdi** and Ngadi. By the **tea house** at the **summit** is a well-shaded **rest area.**

The path from there follows the **left bank** of the Marsyangdi, climbing gradually all the way, through the **village** of **Lampata,** to the **Bahundanda Pass** at 1,250 metres (4,100 feet) where there is a **checkpost.** There is a village on the **hill** overlooking the pass, with **tea houses, shops** and **hotels.** You can stay overnight in one of the hotels or camp in the **fields** around the pass. It takes roughly four hours to complete this leg.

Fifth day

Follow a **small ridge,** branching out from the pass, down to flat and fertile **farm fields,** then through a **forest,** across a **stream** and up again to a **tea house,** then on to a **stone path** that takes about 10 minutes to traverse before it crosses the **rice paddies** and **grain fields** into **Kani Gaon.**

Ahead, the Marsyangdi Valley begins to narrow into a steep, precipitous valley, along a winding **mountain path.** On the **opposite bank** of the river a **waterfall** heralds the approach to **Syanje,** over a **suspension bridge** to the **right bank,** past **hotels, tea houses** and **houses,** and down to the **riverbed** where the trail almost at once begins to climb upwards, past a **single house,** to a **flat plateau.**

Not long after this, the rocky trail dips some 200 to 300 metres (650–1,000 feet), past a spring, to the riverbed, and then into **Jagat,** set at 1,280 metres (4,200 feet), where there are **hotels** and **tea houses.** Or you can camp in the **fields** near the village. Total walking time is just three-and-a-half hours.

Sixth day

From Jagat, the path leads down almost to the **riverbed** and then climbs an ex-

Above: Living in the mountain area near Annapurna Trek.
Following pages: Verdant rice fields above Suikhet Valley near Pokhara.

tremely **precipitous trail** opposite a sheer cliff. When the climb ends, the trail levels out all the way to **Chamje**, which is notable for the splendid **waterfall** on the **opposite bank**.

Soon afterwards, it dips down to cross a **suspension bridge** to a hair-raising trail on the **left bank** — precarious and narrow along the edge of the gorge's sheer wall. One slip could be fatal. It is not for anyone prone to vertigo.

Now the path undulates until it reaches a **tributary** that flows in from the **other bank**. The main river is littered with massive **boulders**, some as big as office blocks, and in the dry season it's hard to see the river water at all. Not long after this, the trail leaves the river bank and takes a zigzag course to the **top** of a hill overlooking the **Tal River**, enclosed by precipitous walls of rock. The path is level, extremely soothing after the perilous journey that has preceded it. It goes down to the **river bank** and into **Tal**, which has **hotels** and **tea houses**.

Soon after this village, the valley narrows

and the riverbed becomes much narrower, while the trail cuts through **rock walls** high above before descending to **Karte**. Take the **stone steps** behind the village, past **Naje**, to climb to **Kurumche Kharka**, with a clear view of the **south-west face** of **Manaslu**. This diversion takes a day-and-a-half.

From Karte, the path continues down to the **river bank** and across a **suspension bridge** to the **right bank**, close to **Dharapani** and its **checkpost**, set at 1,830 metres (6,000 feet). You can sleep in one of many **hotels** or camp in the **fields** behind the checkpost. This leg takes five hours, possibly longer if you exercise extreme care on the dangerous sections.

Seventh day
Follow the trail through a **narrow field** when you leave the village and come to the **confluence** with the **Dudh Khola**, spawned in the ice-melt of Manaslu's south face, on the opposite bank.

Below, to the **right** as you climb the path through **pine forest**, you will make

207

Above: Mountain trail through Suikhet Valley near Pokhara.

out the roofs and streets of the village of **Thonje**. Now the Marsyangdi bends **left**, and when you see Annapurna II ahead, you are at the **entrance** to the **Bhote village** of **Bagarchap**, prayer flags fluttering in the breeze.

The path continues its climb, past the **tea houses** at **Dhanakyu**, across a **stream** and by a cascading **waterfall** on the **left**, to where the Marsyangdi Khola Valley becomes a gorge traversed by steep **stone steps**. Look back there for splendid views of Manaslu and Phungi, then continue the lung-sapping climb to a **level path** through a colourful **rhododendron forest** and **two houses** at **Ratamron**, then on up and across a **stream** to the **lone house** at **Tanzo Phedi**.

There the trail cuts through **pine forest**, over an area of crumbling rocks, to the **checkpost** of **Kotho**, dominated by the mighty mass of Annapurna II and Peak 29, towering, it seems, almost directly over the hamlet.

The trail cuts through the village and up through more **pine forest** to **Chame**, set at 2,670 metres (8,750 feet), with government **offices**, **shops** and **hotels**. It is a good place to replenish your food rations. You can stay in one of the hotels or camp near the **school**, or by the **hot springs** across the **bridge** on the **left bank**. Total walking time is roughly six hours.

Eighth day
Cross a **wooden bridge** as you leave the village to the **left bank** and, with wonderful views of the shimmering snows of 6,893-metre (22,609-foot) **Lamjung Himal**, pass through Chame.

As the trail climbs up the valley, past **Teleku,** the mountain is hidden by the **foothills** and then the trail cuts deep into **pine forest** and up a winding **rocky face**. On the other side, the valley wall is a sheer cliff, evidence of the change of terrain.

The valley is extremely steep and the path leaps back and forth across the river, following the easiest route available until it crosses a **wooden bridge** to the former military **fortress** of **Bhratang** on the **right bank**. Now only the **ruins** remain.

From there, the trail climbs a **rocky path** to first one **wooden bridge**, and then up again to another **timber bridge** leading into **thick forest** on the **right bank**.

Where the forest ends, the valley broadens out into more gentle terrain, and the **east peak** of Annapurna II dominates the horizon as the track leads gradually down, past a *mani* **stone**, to a level field with a pond. It leads to another **timber bridge** over the river and through a **terraced field** with scattered clumps of trees. There are good views of Annapurna II's **north face**. Finally, it skirts the lower level of the village of **Upper Pisang** and crosses the Marsyangdi to **Lower Pisang**, set at 3,200 metres (10,500 feet). You can stay in one of the village's **two hotels** or camp in the **meadow** next to the **spring**. Total walking time is five hours.

Ninth day

Take the **timber bridge** across the **Tseram Tsang Changu**, past a *mani* **stone** and some *chorten*, to the **right bank** and through **thick forest** up to the mountain pass marked by a *chorten*. From there you can see **Manang airfield** straight ahead.

The trail dips down to a level section, past **Ongre**, where the **north-east face** of Annapurna III is visible, to the **airstrip** at **Omdu**, and then across a broad **plain** and the **Sabje Khola**. There, the massive **peak** of 7,525-metre (24,688-foot) Annapurna IV appears on the horizon.

The trail then crosses another **bridge**, over the newborn **Marsyangdi Khola** to the **left bank** and **Mungji,** encircled by verdant **farm fields**. To the **right**, beneath a small mountain, stands **Braga** with its magnificent **monastery**.

There are many large *chorten* and *mani* **stones**, and soon you come to **Manang,** set at 3,505 metres (11,500 feet) beneath a panoramic vista surely made in heaven: from a terraced hill above the town spread out before you are Annapurna II, Annapurna IV, Annapurna III, 7,456-metre (24,457 feet) Gangapurna and, behind, 7,134-metre (23,406 feet) Tilicho peak.

Manang's streets and houses are lined with many fluttering **prayer flags** and there are **five hotels**. You can stay in one

of these or camp on their **rooftops**. Total walking time is about four hours.

10th day

Now begins the toughest part of the trek, through Manang and up to the village of **Tinge.** All along this route you will see Annapurna Himal on the horizon, with Peak 29 and Himal Chuli in the distance behind it.

Tinge is the last perManint settlement in the Marsyangdi Khola Valley but the path winds up through the summer village of **Kutsuan** and, soon after a **deserted village**, levels out and crosses a **bridge** over the Gundon Khola. In the mountains ahead you can see the walls of the **Thorong pass** — your destination.

The trail now becomes a gentle switchback before crossing a **delta** with many yak **meadows** and then crossing the **Kenzan Khola** to **Churi Latter**, with its **lone hotel**. From there, the trail climbs a gradual incline to the snout of a **ridge**.

Then it dips down to cross the **bridge** over the Marsyangdi Khola and goes up the mountain path on the **right bank**, then down a rocky section to the **riverbed**, which it follows for between 10 and 15 minutes' walk. Finally, it climbs a rocky path to the **plateau** and **Thorung Phedi,** set at 4,495 metres (14,750 feet), which has one combined **hotel-tea house**, serving very basic Tibetan fare. You can bed down on its **earth floor** or camp nearby. Total walking time is from six to seven hours.

11th day

Leave early, prepared for extreme cold and severe gale-force winds as you climb the most testing section of this trek — **Thorong pass.** The zigzag trail leads up a steep hill in front of the hotel, through a rocky area to the top of the ridge. There it crosses a **stream**, some lateral moraine, and continues over a **lake** to the **glacier** above.

It then traverses **left**, between small hill-like **ridges** above 5,000 metres (16,500

Following pages: Mountain trail winds through the verdant rice fields above Suikhet Valley near Pokhara.

feet), and soon Annapurna II, in the rear, passes out of sight. Now the angle eases as you begin the **ascent** to Thorong pass at 5,416 metres (17,770 feet), its **crest** marked only by **cairns.**

This is one of the entrances to the eight-kilometre-deep (five-mile) **Kali Gandaki Gorge**, and ahead, as you enter an old lateral moraine for the descent, Dhaulagiri II and III and Tashi Kang rise up over the valley. The **final leg** is down an extremely **steep cliff.** Finally, you reach **Chabarbu** and its **one hotel.**

From there, the path levels out through the valley to cross the **Khatung Kang**, which flows in from the left, to the lunar landscape of the **Jhong Khola Valley**, which you descend with magnificent views of 8,167-metre (26,795-foot) **Dhaulagiri I** and 6,920-metre (22,704-foot) **Tukuche Peak.**

Once through the valley, you are close to the **checkpost** at **Muktinath**, at 3,798 metres (12,500 feet), where there are **three hotels.**

12th day
With Dhaulagiri I, Tukuche Peak and Dhaulagiri II and III still in view, the trail leads down from Muktinath to **Jharkot**, where there are the **ruins** of an **ancient fortress**. Now the path passes through **two stone walls** to a gradual descent down the mountains and along a wide level trail to **Khingar,** after which it dips gradually to a **crossroads**. The **right turn** leads to **Kagbeni**, famous for the **ruins** of its **medieval castle.**

The **path** on the **left** leads down the mountain flank to the **left bank** of the **Kali Gandaki River** and **Eklai Bhatti** and then on to **Jomsom** in the afternoon.

The path follows the river bank to a **wooden bridge** that takes it on to the **right bank**, which it follows briefly before returning to the **riverbed.**

Continue thereafter along the river path, with Dhaulagiri I in view. The trek from Jomsom to Pokhara takes from five to six days.

Dhaulagiri

Starting in Pokhara, this takes you through some of the finest pastoral and mountain landscapes in Nepal — providing the savour of simple lifestyles in and around the **Myagdi Khola basin.** You need full camping equipment, rations and Sherpa guides.

Trekking (First day)
Trek from Pokhara to **Naudanda** along the **Jomsom route**, turning to the **left** when leaving **Naudanda**, down a gradual slope through **forest**, past **Pandor** and across a **stream** to **Daudari Dhara.**

Leaving the village, take the **left fork** past the **school**, and follow the trail down the mountain through **Bane Kharka** to **Sallyan.**

There you climb a **ridge** and on through **forest** to **Thamarjung** — a walk of about six hours. You can camp in the **compounds** of some of the houses.

Second day
Leave the village, down a gradual decline to **Tihar** and a level trail to **Gijan**, with splendid views of the **sacred peak** of 6,964-metre (22,842-foot) **Machhapuchhare, Gangapurna** and **Annapurna South.**

From the ridge, take the **steep trail** down to the **confluence** of the **Dobila Khola** and **Modi Khola**. There, the trail crosses a **suspension bridge** and climbs the mountain on the **right bank** of the Modi Khola to **Chuwa,** winding its way over several **small ridges** and through **farm fields** to the **shops** and **tea houses** of Kusma.

From there, cut through **forest** and down a **steep hill** from **Chamurkang** to the **Kali Gandaki River,** where the trail follows the **left bank**, past **Marmati**, with its tea house, to **Nayapur.** This walk takes about six to six-and-a-half hours. You can camp near the village.

Third day
Continue along the **left bank**, past the **suspension bridge**, through **Saus Dhara** with

its row of **tea houses** where, soon after from the **high path**, you get splendid views of Dhaulagiri I before the trail dips down to the riverbed. Soon, it climbs back to the **left bank** and into **Khanyagar**, with its **hotels** and **tea houses**. The trail leaves the village, continuing up a gradual incline, past the **suspension bridge** to Baglung on the **opposite bank**, and continues to **Pharse**, where there are more **tea houses** and **hotels**.

Still on the **left bank**, the path crosses a **stream** into **Diranbhora**, then goes up a gentle incline to **Beni**, on the **opposite bank** of the Myagdi Khola, where there is a **checkpost**.

It is a bustling town and administrative centre and you can camp in **fields** outside the village. The walk takes anything from five-and-a-half to six hours.

Fourth day

The trail from Beni cuts through **Beni Mangalghat's** single street of **shops** and into desolate mountain country, past the **lone tea house** at **Jyanmara**, and goes on a wide, level path to **Singa,** with many **shops** and **tea houses**. Beyond this village, the trail follows the **left bank** of the Myagdi Khola above the riverbed, past a **hot spring** to the left below, and through the **farm fields** that herald the approach to Tatopani.

Soon after leaving the village, it crosses a **suspension bridge** to the **right bank**, through the **hamlet** of **Bholamza** and more fields, before swinging back to the **left bank** via another **suspension bridge** to **Simalchaur**.

Some distance beyond the village, there is a **suspension bridge** across the **Newale Khola**, which flows in from the right. The trail continues along the **left bank** of the Myagdi Khola, past the villages of **Shiman** and **Talkot**, and then climbs to **shops** and **tea houses** of **Babichor**. You can camp on the grass next to the **village granary**. The walk takes approximately five hours.

Fifth day

From Babichor, the high, winding trail crosses the mountainside into a broad and fertile valley, across **paddy** and **grain fields** and through the **cobblestone street**

of **Shahasharadhara**, where you cross the **Duk Khola**. Continue through the paddy fields to the hamlet of **Ratodunga**, where the valley ends.

Now the undulating trail follows the **river bank** on the **left**, past **Bodeni** to **Chachare**. The valley narrows at the town of **Darbang,** its **main street** lined with many **shops**.

There the trail crosses to the **right bank**, via a **suspension bridge**, past the **Ritum Khola tributary** at **left**, and through the **hamlet** of **Darbang**.

The trail then skirts a gaunt cliff face to **Phedi**, set at 1,100 metres (3,500 feet), where there are **two tea houses**. It is not a pretty place but it is the only camping site for several kilometres around. The walk takes about four hours.

Sixth day

When you leave Phedi, you face a long climb to **Phalai Gaon** and should make an early start. Soon after leaving the village, the trail crosses the **Dang Khola,** where it flows in from the **left**, and climbs a ridge on the **opposite bank** in a series of hair-pins, above the Myagdi Khola. Soon the gradual climb leads into **Dharapani** and steeply out again, before descending to the farm **fields** beyond **Takum**.

After **Sibang**, it cuts through **forest**, past **Mattim** to the **crest** of a **ridge** which provides a magnificent view of **Dhaulagiri Himal**, dipping down to the **Gatti Khola** to skirt the base of the ridge and enter **Phalai Gaon**, set at 1,830 metres (6,000 feet). You can camp in the **school grounds** outside the village. The walk takes between six and seven hours.

Seventh day

For **Mur**, follow the **stone-walled path** from Phalai Gaon over the **terraced fields** to the **right**, and cross the **suspension bridge** over the Dhara Khola. During the dry season the trail goes down the valley next to the school, across to the **opposite bank**, and up a steep hill.

But the main path from the suspension bridge climbs up the mountain, above the village of Dhara, and through a **hamlet** to an undulating walk that links up with the

Above: Chillies and grain drying in Bhaktapur Square.

short-cut. After skirting a **ridge** it emerges once more on the **right bank**.

Now it climbs again, in a series of hairpins, and then skirts another **ridge**, to reveal stupendous views of **Dhaulagiri I** and 7,193-metre (23,600ft) **Gurja Himal**. Soon it reaches the **Magar village** of **Muri**, which you leave down a gentle slope, across a rocky **stream**.

Continue down to the farm **fields** along the Dhara Khola, cross the river and then climb up the mountain on the **right** to **Ghorban Dhara pass**, with its fine views — including your first glimpse of 6,465-metre (21,211-foot) **Ghustung South**.

From the pass, the trail leads down to the **right bank** of the **Myagdi Khola**, and a **lone house**, where you can camp in the surrounding fields — beneath the **village** of **Jugapani,** perched on the mountainside above. Total walking time is around five hours.

Eighth day

Leave along the **right bank**, past **Naura**, and climb the mountain for a short while to a **path** which traverses a steep, grass-covered hill. Where the traverse ends, the Myagdi Khola Valley becomes a precipitous gorge. Even though the path along the steep, grassy edge of the gorge is well-constructed, with many **stone steps**, take care — at the top of the climb, the trail traverses **right** and you risk falling into the gorge.

Eventually, the trail dips down through forest, across a **ridge** and some **terraced fields** to **Boghara,** set at 2,073 metres (6,800ft). You can camp in the **compounds** of the houses or the **terraced fields**. It takes around four-and-a-half to five hours to complete this stretch.

Ninth Day

Leave the village as the trail descends through the fields, crossing a **small ridge** to the **left**, and go on through thin forest to **Jyardan**, the region's most remote village.

From the village, the trail is high and winding, then it cuts across a boulder-strewn stretch of landscape to a grass-covered traverse, before dropping down some steep **stone steps** to the **river bank**. It follows upstream some distance, then

217

Above Himalayan peaks are an ever-present backdrop on the trekking trails.
Opposite: Ozumpa Glacier.

starts climbing again, crossing a **stream** beneath a beautiful high **waterfall**, where it eases into a gradual incline to **Lipsiba.**

Now the trail continues its undulating course through the forest-lined **walls** of the steep **Myagdi Khola Gorge**, before emerging at a little **glade, Lapche Kharka,** where you camp overnight. All in all, this leg takes no more than five hours.

10th day

When you leave camp, the trail continues to climb through **forest** to a level area at **Dobang**. Soon after this, it crosses a **timber bridge** over the **Konabon Khola**, flowing down from the **Konabon Glacier**. There, the trail continues through **thick forest**, with occasional glimpses, through breaks in the trees, of the **west face** of majestic Dhaulagiri I. Some distance beyond, the trail dips down and the Myagdi Khola comes into view.

You cross to the **left bank** by a **wooden bridge** with a **handrail**. Once again, the path cuts through forest as it climbs the course of the **Pakite Khola,** never too far

from the river. The **crest** of 6,062-metre (19,889ft) **Jirbang** dominates the end of the valley and then you cross a **stream** to the plateau at **Chartare**, set at 2,820 metres (9,250ft).

There is a crystal-clear **stream** flowing through the middle of the **meadow**, making it excellent for camping. Total walking time is no more than five hours.

11th day

From Chartare, return to the forest trail until it passes two **small caves**. There it leaves the forest and cuts across some rocks up the mountainside, across a small **stream**, to the **Choriban Khola** which it skirts for some distance before finally crossing it to climb the **bank** on the other side.

Look behind at this point and you will get a splendid view of the ice-white silhouette of 6,380-metre (20,932-foot) **Manapati**. Soon after climbing the **steep hill**, the path narrows into a gentle gradient, through the forest to a **grassy clearing** at **Puchhar**.

It now crosses a **small glacier**, down to **another glacier** born on the **west face** of

Dhaulagiri, and then climbs the **opposite wall** to another **grassy area, Pakabon,** set at 3,581 metres (11,750 feet), where you can camp. Ahead stand the massive **western ramparts** of Dhaulagiri I.

To the right is Manapati — and behind, the granite walls of **Tsaurabong Peak** shadow the sky as if about to fall over the camp. Total walking time is around five hours.

12th day

From Pakabon, follow a lateral moraine to a **rocky ridge** which you descend to the **right**, into a valley deep in snow and glacial detritus. Approaching the **headwaters** of the **Myagdi Khola** you are closed in by daunting rock walls.

The steep path follows its course high above the **right bank** before descending to the valley floor and on, by intermittent footpath through the gorge, to the terminal moraine of **Chhonbarban Glacier.**

The trail enters the area from the **right bank**, crossing the undulating surface of the glacier where the valley bends right through a large gorge.

At this point, 6,920-metre (22,704-foot) **Tukuche Peak West** stands brooding over the far end of the glacier.

Soon the trail levels out into easy walking up a gradual gradient, then the glacier veers **left** and the trail moves onto the right bank.

It terminates at **Dhaulagiri base camp,** set at 4,725 metres (15,500 feet), with a stunning perspective of Dhaulagiri 1's **north face** and, to the **west**, 7,751-metre (25,429 feet) **Dhaulagiri II**, 7,703-metre (25,271 feet) **Dhaulagiri III**, and 7,661-metre (25,133-foot) **Dhaulagiri IV** — a sheer ice fall streaming from the **north-east col**.

13th day

At this stage there is a real risk of mountain sickness as the trail climbs out of the camp up the **right bank** of the glacier, and then up another mountainside to cut across the flank and cross the moraine on the side of 6,611-metre (21,690-foot) **Sita Chuchura** to an easy snow-covered **incline** on the right

that leads to **French pass** at 5,364 metres (17,600 feet).

From there, you can see Sita Chuchura, the mountains of **Mukut Himal**, and the 6,400-metre (21,000-foot) **Tashi Kang**. To the right is Tukuche Peak West and to the rear stands Dhaulagiri I. It takes 11 to 12 days to return to Pokhara.

Lost Horizons

For centuries, the **Kali Gandaki Gorge** has been one of the passes to the mysterious and untouched mountain fastnesses of western Nepal.

North-west of the gorge stand the little-known Kanjiroba Himal, a cluster of mountains that takes its name from the highest peak. Eleven peaks rise above 6,000 metres (20,000 feet), including 6676-metre (21,902-foot) Kanjiroba Himal.

These mountains encircle the ancient Kingdom of Dolpo and the sacred Crystal Mountain to form the natural boundary of the 3,540-square-kilometre (1,367-square-mile) Shey-Phoksondo National Park.

Dolpo came into the kingdom in the 18th century as a result of King Bahadur Shah's conquests. Dolpo's neighbouring kingdom, where myth and fantasy seem stronger than reality, is **Mustang.** It lies on a barren valley floor at around 4,572 metres (15,000 feet), snug against the Tibetan border on three sides and guarded by formidable 7,375-metre (24,000-foot) mountains pierced only by narrow passes.

In Nepal, massive Dhaulagiri, at 8,167 metres (26,795 feet) the world's seventh-highest mountain, provides the defence which has sealed Lo, as the locals call it, from the outside world for centuries.

Getting there

Mustang is reached by a long trek through the Kali Gandaki Gorge. From there you cross — over the one, desperately high, south-east-facing pass — into Dolpo.

Permits are needed for travel to these areas. With one, you can take the scheduled

Opposite:Tickling a snow leopard, known as *hiun chituwa* in Nepali.

Above: Log bridges in Mustang are the usual way across the rivers of trekking trails.

domestic flight either to Jomosom, the nearest airstrip for Mustang, or to Likhu, the nearest airstrip for Dolpo — or go on foot with guide and porters from Pokhara.

Sightseeing

Mantang, the capital of Mustang, is dominated by **fortress walls** and its central feature is the massive white-walled **Royal Palace** in which lives the world's least-known monarch. Schools are bringing change, but while the youngsters come home filled with stories of space flights which they have heard on the classroom wireless, their grandparents still believe the world is flat and shaped like a half-moon.

Lo Mantang, in fact, is the full name of the 2,000-square-kilometre (772-square-mile) kingdom of King Jigme Parwal Bista, founded in the 14th century by the Tibetan warlord Ama Pal.

Fabled Mustang, as it is now known on the maps, is only an 'honorary' kingdom these days, but each night, King Jigme, the 25th monarch since the 1480s, orders the only **gate** of the mud-walled capital shut and barred.

Twelve dukes, 60 monks, 152 families and eight witches occupy the capital. King Jigme still owns serfs who plough his stony fields for grain crops.

But Lo's treasures are many and priceless: a wealth of **Tibetan art**, **monasteries** and **forts** set in **23 villages** and **two** other **towns**. Many of Mustang's monasteries — the name derives from the Tibetan phrase meaning 'plain of prayer', *'mon than'* — are carved into cliff faces. You climb ladders to reach them. Other wealth lies in the rocky hills — **turquoise** and rich deposits of **alluvial gold** in the beds of the **rivers** that course through the land. But Lo's citizens consider the task of panning for this metal beneath their dignity.

The King's subjects — Lopas, who are Lamaist Buddhists — number around 8,000 and speak their own dialect of the Tibetan language.

The women practise polyandry — often marrying two or three brothers. The king keeps his authority as a ruler by virtue of a 160-year-old treaty with King Birendra Shah's dynasty and payment to Nepal of 886 rupees a year and one horse.

In return, he holds the rank of colonel in the Nepali Army. So archaic is the kingdom, matches were unknown until a few years ago and superstition is rampant.

The whole land goes to bed in terror of Lo's 416 demons of land, sky, fire, and water, and life is dedicated to warding off the evil spirits which can cause Lo's 1,080 known diseases, as well as five forms of violent death. Thus, for three days each year, King Jigme's subjects celebrate New Year by 'chasing the demons': with the noise of cymbals, drums, and notes made by playing on human skulls, filling the air.

Not a single tree grows in this arid and withered land. To supplement their monotonous diet of yak milk and sour cheese, they nurture **fragile gardens**. For trade, the Lopas deal in salt from Tibet. The trail they follow winds for 240 kilometres (150 miles) along the Kali Gandaki Gorge.

Dolpo

South-west from Mustang, across the forbidding perils of the 6,502-metre (21,331-foot) barrier of Hanging Glacier Peak, lies the equally remote kingdom of Dolpo. It will never be a tourist retreat. It is so far from the nearest road that it takes three weeks of tough walking to reach it. Dolpo and its monasteries straggle up a pitch of long, tortuous ridges, above an expanse of rumpled, brown and barren mountains. The creed of the Shaman — spirit-possessed holy men — still rules there, as it has for 15 centuries. In the rarefied air of these 3,000 to 5,000 metres (10,000–16,000 feet) heights, perceptions and sensations are acute.

Sitting atop a mountain ridge in the dark night in a yak-hair tent, wind howling, rain lashing down, watching the Shaman as he is taken hold of by 'Fierce Red Spirit with the gift of the life force of seven black wolves' is enough to convince even the most cynical witness from western civilization of the power of the supernatural.

Sightseeing
The population of a few hundred in Dolpo

has been swollen by Tibetan refugees. All make votive offerings, some of **clay tablets** carved with a pantheon of Buddhist deities.

At a height of more than 4,000 metres (13,000 feet), Dolpo's **grain fields** are among the highest cultivated land in the world.

The **paths** and **trails** that lead through this tiny principality of old are often no more than fragile, crumbling shale strata sticking out of a cliff face. With a sheer drop centimetres away on one side as you stoop low under an overhang, it is only for the brave and agile.

Nepal's wildlife — free from molestation or pressure for land from swift-growing populations — flourishes in these remote highlands. **Musk deer**, **bears** and other species roam freely there, along with the delightful **red panda**. But this diminutive creature, also known as the red cat bear, a relic of a long-gone era from the age of the rhino, which walks like a bear and spits like a cat, is threatened with extinction.

Not much more than 60 centimetres (23 inches) from claw to shoulder with a 40-centimetre (16-inch) tail, coloured with bright chestnut rings, its glossy fur glows

Above: Smiling Sherpa children.

with a rich rufous sheen. The face is catlike and, although it has claws similar to a bear, like a cat it can partially retract them.

The red panda lives in temperate forests up to the 3,650-metre (12,000-foot) contour. It is mainly arboreal. The animals, hunted for their pelts which fetch high prices in India, make delightful pets.

Undisturbed, the **Shey-Phoksondo National Park's** 3,540 square kilometres (1,367 square miles) of **alpine forests** and **meadows** and cloud-wreathed **ice peaks**, are notable for **blue sheep**, **yak**, **wild dog**, **brown bear**, **muntjac**, **musk deer**, **goral**, **thar** and elusive **snow leopard**.

Bird life is rich, too, with the **snow partridge**, **snow cock**, the **yellow-billed chough**, **blood pheasant** and **Tibetan twite** among the endemic species. Nepal's wild sheep, like the **Great Tibetan sheep**, and the **blue sheep**, are prized trophies — thus their numbers are diminishing, despite the strict controls imposed by the wildlife authorities, difficult to enforce in such isolated and rugged places.

The blue sheep has particularly impressive horns. Rams have a black face and chest but the general body of both male and female blends well with the slate-blue shale of Dolpo, where they favour open grassy slopes between the 3,650- and 4,880-metre (12,000- and 16,000-foot) contours.

The largest of all Nepal's wild sheep, the Great Tibetan sheep is diminishing fast through poaching, hunting and encroachment on its normal environment.

Its broad, corrugated horns are dramatically curved in the male. Generally a shaggy-looking grey, it lives above 4,880 metres (16,000 feet) in summer, descending to more sheltered slopes in winter.

The Himalayan thar, a superb species of mountain goat, clings to precipitous cliff faces. Reddish-brown in colour, the long, lean head with erect ears forms a lovely profile. The November to January rutting season is spectacular for the fights between rival males, which send many crashing down the cliff face to their doom. Only the strongest and most sure-footed will mate.

Strangely, the goral — described as a goat antelope by Himalayan wildlife authority Dr Tej Kumar Shrestha — is common and remains unmolested. Or perhaps not so strangely, since it offers little for the trophy hunter.

If any wildlife survives anywhere in Nepal, it will be these alpine species in such places as the magic valley of Dolpo.

Walking through one of the thick forests, along the lower slopes of a **river gorge**, it is sometimes possible to see a rare flash of another threatened species: the muntjac — or barking deer. Or, even rarer, perhaps frozen in the dappled sunlight of a glade in the thickets, the startled look of the musk deer.

Its numbers have dropped steeply in the past decade, for it is hunted ruthlessly for its musk pod, despite its place in Hindu religious scriptures. Well adapted to its mountain environment, sure-footed, agile and able to leap and run over the most precipitous slopes, it is renowned for its lithe grace and beauty. Its hooves have evolved to enable it to keep up a swift pace, even on ledges along a narrow cliff, but it has no antlers. Reaching a metre (just over three feet) at the shoulder, the hindquarter is slightly higher, which enables it to run more swiftly and jump more powerfully. As it ages, the deer's dappled coat changes to yellowish-brown. Its musk is highly prized for perfumes and medicines.

The elusive and threatened snow leopard has made Dolpo a recent centre of study. The least known of all the big cats is still shrouded in mystery and legend. Wildlife writer and zoologist George B Schaller described the 'imperilled Phantom of the Asian Peaks' from observations in Pakistan in the late 1960s and Peter Mathiesen wrote a fascinating book about it, *The Snow Leopard*.

The snow leopard's range stretches more than 3,000 kilometres (1,864 miles) — the length of the Himalaya — from the far east end of the range to the borders of Afghanistan in the west. Zoological specimens are rare — fewer than 100, and, as Schaller says, the cat's 'luxurious smoky-grey coat, sprinkled with black, both protects and imperils the snow leopard. It permits it to fade into rocky backgrounds, but its magnificence arouses man's greed.'

The snow leopard's main prey is the blue sheep and for this reason Shey-

Above: Pine forest at Kakani near the Himalayas.

Phoksondo National Park is one of the few places where they can be studied in the wild.

The leopards' range of territory extends to great heights but they normally live in rock and forest between the 3,050 and 4,267-metre (10,000 and 14,000-foot) contours.

Snow leopards, known as *hiun chituwa* in Nepali, are smaller than the common leopard, just over a metre (four feet) from muzzle to rump, with a long and slender tail of about equal length. They breed in the winter and spring, between January and May, often living close to one another and following common trails, but tending nonetheless to remain solitary. In Dolpo they have come perilously close to extinction, hunted by poachers armed with poisoned spears planted in traps along rivers and rocky passes known to be used by the animals. Even a superficial wound from one of these spears is lethal.

Although the leopards have an extensive territorial range — often occupying 160 square kilometres (60 square miles) — they return frequently to their preferred area.

Dolpo is also a land of **holy peaks**, of which the most revered is the valley's sacred **Crystal Mountain**. According to local legend, a thousand years ago, a Tibetan ascetic, Drutob Senge Yeshe, flew to the top of the harsh slab of rock, a massif that rises out of the shale around it, aboard a magic snow lion, and challenged the god who lived there. When he defeated him, the rock turned to crystal.

Now Dolpo people circle the 16-kilometre (10-mile) circumference of the mountain's base in an annual pilgrimage known as *kora*. Its many **strata** — layers of rock — also draw pilgrims of a different faith: geologists hunting fossils.

Jumla and Lake Rara

South-west of Dolpo you are deep into Nepal's mystical west — almost as closed and little-known as Dolpo. Yet it once nurtured a great kingdom of the Mallas.

The Mallas kept a winter capital in the south of the Mahabharat Hills, at Dullu, and maintained a territory that stretched from the humid Terai to the Taklahar in Western Tibet — over trails that few tackle.

Getting there

Jumla, the capital of this ancient kingdom, set almost 2,400 metres (8,000 feet) above sea level, can only be reached by plane — unless you are an untiring trekker prepared to walk for weeks. Consequently, though there is a scheduled Royal Nepal Airlines service to Jumla — subject, of course, to weather and other vagaries — there are few visitors.

Sightseeing

Ringed by magnificent peaks, Jumla is truly a natural paradise, a quaint rural town with a **bazaar**, lined by the **flat-roofed houses** of the region and boasting no more than **50 shops**, a **bank**, **police station**, and the inevitable **tea houses**.

The Mallas left a magnificent legacy in Jumla: sculptured **temples**, **stone pillars**, and the still-living folk songs of the region. But this beauty is well-guarded. Few disturb its tranquillity and population is sparse. The **Karnali Zone** — one of 14 in Nepal — has a total population of around 300,000, no more than 12 people to every square kilometre.

There is an old highway along the **Tila Nadi Valley** where you measure your pace by the distance between the **ancient milestones** placed there as long ago as the 15th century.

Two days' hard slog brings its reward — a refreshing dip in the **hot springs** at **Seraduska.** Walk east for three days and you will reach **Gothichaur,** an alpine valley set more than 2,900 metres (9,500 feet) above sea level and flanked by pine forests with a **stone shrine** and a **water spout**, a reminder of the Malla dynasty, together with stupendous views of two little-known peaks, **Chyakure Lekh** and **Patrasi Himal.**

Best of all, make the four-day trek over high passes like **Padmora, Bumra,** and the 3,456-metre (11,341-foot) **Ghurchi pass,** and finally **Pina**, to **Lake Rara,** Nepal's most enchanting **National Park**.

The lake is the Kingdom of Nepal's largest sheet of water, covering 10 square kilometres (four square miles) almost 3,000 metres (10,000 feet) above sea level.

Snow lingers there as late as May and June but its crystal-blue waters are haven to a treasury of hardy avian visitors, particularly **mallards**, **pochards**, **grebes**, **teals** and other species from the north.

The park itself covers 104 square kilometres (41 square miles). Alpine **meadows** line the lake shores and fields of millet and wheat are flanked by **pine forests**.

There are **apple orchards**, and the lake waters are rich with fish. Several **villages** stand on its shores, their houses, terraced like the land, backed on to steep hillsides. Wildlife includes hordes of impudent **monkeys** who raid farms and grain stores with seeming impunity.

Set like a sapphire in its Himalaya amphitheatre, Lake Rara is both a botanical and a faunal treasury.

Another national park, **Khaptad** — several days distant, south-west of Rara — stands at much the same height, covering 187 square kilometres (73 square miles): it is a floral repository of high-altitude **conifers**, **oak** and **rhododendron forests**, and its open **meadows** are reserved for royalty.

Jumla is also the stepping-off point for a long, hard trek to the Shangri-la valley of **Humla.** To the west lie more little-known valleys reached only on foot, for there the Himalaya mountains curve southward, enfolding the country and dividing it physically from the northernmost reaches of India. Though smaller by comparison with its sister peaks in central and eastern Nepal, the highest of these western peaks is **Api.** Yet outside Asia few mountains in the world rise as high as Api's 7,131 metres (23,396 feet). With its neighbours, it forms a formidable massif in the far west. Peak to peak, directly in line with Api, only 60 kilometres (37 miles) away is its easterly neighbour, **Saipal,** just 97 metres (318 feet) lower. The actual border is marked by the **Kali River**, which flows beneath Api.

Api dominates a range of magnificent but rarely seen and little-known peaks, including **Jetibohurani**, at 6,848 metres (22,468 feet); **Bobaye**, 6,807 metres (22,333 feet); **Nampa**, 6,755 metres (22,163 feet); and also **Rokapi**, 6,466 metres (21,214 feet).

Close to Saipal stands the jagged peak of **Firnkopf West**, at 6,683 metres (21,926 feet); to the north the lonely **Takpu Himal** gazes down on the lovely **Humla Valley**

Above: Nepal is home to Little Egrets.

and its remote capital of **Simikot** from 6,634 metres (21,766 feet).

Although relative minnows compared with the peaks of central and eastern Nepal, these mountains remain virtually untouched by climbers. Japanese teams conquered Api in 1960, Saipal in 1963, and Nampa in 1972.

A major trade route to the plains — a long trek through tough country — winds between these two massifs, cresting a saddle more than 5,500 metres (18,000 feet) high between Nampa and Firnkopf West, after leaving Tibet over the Urai pass.

Nepal's wildlife, free from molestation or pressures of a swift-growing human population, flourishes in these remote highland areas. Musk deer, bears and other species roam there and there's the delightful red panda. This diminutive creature, also known as the red cat bear, which walks like a bear and spits like a cat, is threatened with extinction.

Not much more than two feet from claw to shoulder with a 40-centimetre-long tail, coloured with bright chestnut rings, its glossy fur glows with a rich rufous sheen.

The face is cat-like and although it has claws similar to a bear, like a cat it can partially retract them.

It lives in temperate forests up to a height of 12,000 feet and is mainly arboreal, doing little on the ground. Red pandas, hunted for their pelts which fetch high prices in India, make delightful pets.

Undisturbed, the park's 3,540 square kilometres of alpine forests and meadows and cloud-wreathed ice peaks, are notable for blue sheep, yak, wild dog, brown bear, muntjac, musk deer, goral, thar and elusive snow leopard.

Birdlife is rich, too, with snow partridge, snow cock, yellow-billed chough, Blood pheasant and Tibetan twite among the endemic species.

The trade caravans — even goats and sheep are used as pack animals — must travel daunting distances over forbidding terrain before reaching the temperate and fertile lands of the Mahabharat and the tropical fields of the Terai.

Eastern and Central Valleys

In the narrow neck of land that connects north-east India with the rest of that vast country — and also divides Nepal from Bhutan, another tiny Himalayan kingdom — lie West Bengal and Sikkim. From Siliguri the road crosses the Mechi River, a tributary of the Ganges, to Kakar Bhitta in Nepal. You can also take an alternative hill road from Darjeeling through the Mani pass and down to the rolling tea fields of Ilam.

Set at around 1,300 metres (4,265 feet), the tea fields are particularly lovely, rolling away from either side of the road in every direction — a carpet of vivid green laid out at the feet of Nepal's north-eastern mountains among dramatic views of Kanchenjunga, the world's third-highest mountain, astride the Sikkim-Nepal border.

With its weathered brick houses, Ilam is a gracious town, by Nepali standards, of about 12,000 people. Its principle industry is tea and you can visit the factory where the leaf is cured before it is shipped to Kathmandu and the rest of Nepal. Villagers also run cottage industries, turning out a wide and attractive range of handmade cloth, blankets, sweaters, and carpets.

Getting there
By bus from Biratnagar or Dharan to Birtamodh and then by another bus from Birtamodh to Ilam. Also one hour by bus from Bhadrapur (Chandragadhi).

Dharan Bazaar

The focal point of this region, lying at the base of the evergreen Vijaypur Hills, is **Dharan bazaar**. An unusual feature of town life is the **Union Jack** that flies over one of the squat single-storeyed buildings.

This is one of the British Army Gurkha recruiting centres in Nepal. Wiry teenagers from the hills continue a long and noble tradition, enlisting — usually for life —

while older generations, now retired, make the long trek each month from the same hills to pick up their pensions. A tough physical examination limits the number of recruits but those who succeed are fitted out with new uniforms and flown abroad for 10 months' basic training, thereafter returning home for their first leave to a hero's welcome from their relatives and neighbours.

The new recruits walk through Dharan smiling proudly and browsing among the **market stalls** in the old town, where vendors peddle oranges, butter, and herbs.

The **orchards** of the Vijaypur Hills are rich and productive, and surplus fruit is preserved in a recently established canning factory. Access is by bus from Biratnagar.

Dharan is also the base for trekking the Makalu region.

Trekking in Makalu

One of the toughest treks in the world takes you from Dharan through the sub-tropical floor of the Arun Valley and over the Shipton Pass to the slopes of the three great peaks of Makalu, Everest, and Lhotse.

The Arun Valley
Close to the ridge on which **Dhankuta** stands lies one of Nepal's most remote and beautiful regions. Nowhere are the country's stunning scenic contrasts more sharply defined than in the Arun valley, in the shadows of the Khumbu Harkna Himal, beneath Makalu's daunting 8,481-metre (27,825-foot) peak, where the wide, lazy Arun River meanders along the valley floor.

The river bestows a mantle of verdant green and nourishes the cool leafy trees which provide shade all along this enchanted valley and its many neighbouring valleys, all as lovely. Its villages have remained unchanged for centuries.

Opposite: Pack beasts carry equipment to the next camp.

Barun Glacier

Makalu Base Camp ▲ MAKALU

BARUNTSE ▲

PEAK 4 ▲ Sherson

PYRAMID PEAK ▲ Mirik ▲ PEAK 3

▲ PEAK 5

CHAMLANG ▲ PEAK 6 Riphuk Kharka Yangle Kharka

Iswa Glacier ▲ PEAK 7

Mumbuk Shipton Pass

Barun Khola

Arun

Kauma

Makalu-Barun National Park Tashigaon

Nabagaon Sedua

Iswa Khola

Mure

Fururu

Arun

Kuwapani

Bhotebas

Panguma

Sabha Khola

Khandbari

Tumlingtar

Khare

Piluwa Khola

Surte Bari Akibunkabeshi

● Bhojpur

Leguwa Ghat

Dhele

Pakribas

Hile

Dhankuta

Tamur

Murughat

Sun Kosi

DHARAN ◉

To Kathmandu

BIRATNAGAR ◉

T I B E T

0   10   20   30   40   50   60 km
0 5   10   15   20   25   30   40 miles

NUPCHU ●

Lhonak Glacier

DROHMO ▲

SHARPU ▲

Kanchenjunga Glacier

YALUNG KANG ▲ KANCHENJUNGA ▲

Khumbakarna Gl.

SOUTH PEAK ▲

JANNU ▲

TALUNG ▲

KABRU ▲

Lapsang La Corner Camp

Ramche

Lapsang

Yalung Bara

Yalung Gl.

RATHONG ▲

KOKTHAN ▲

Torontan Tseram

Lamite Bhanjyang

Yamphudin

Phonpe Mamanke

Meiwa Khola

Tamur

Doban Tambawa

Nesum Taplejung Fun Fun Keswa

Kunjar Bhanjyang

Gupa Pokhari

Chauki

Kabeli Khola

Door Pani

Basantpur

● Phidim

S I K K I M

Mane La

DARJEELING ◉

Eastern Nepal

● Ilam

Mechi

To Siliguri

Birtamodh

Kakar ● Bhitta

Bhadrapur ●

I N D I A

Though only a short distance northward above the tree-clad hills rise the world's mightiest mountains, at its lowest levels the valley could be in Africa. The bare red earth is dotted with stunted, semi-arid, savannah grass. Groves of succulents and stands of banana trees repeat the African image.

The heat of the sun's rays, funnelled into the valley by the rising hills, is merciless. Brickmakers use it to bake their product for the thatched cottages on the hillsides.

In the north, the valley is bounded by the snow-covered 4,100-metre (13,500-foot) Shipton pass — beyond which lie the mountains surrounding the three great peaks of Everest, Makalu and Lhotse.

Anglers delight in the Ishwa valley, its slopes thick with rhododendrons and magnolias and its mountain streams alive with fish. Barun, another valley, its walls a tangled jungle of undergrowth, with rushing streams and plunging waterfalls, forms an amphitheatre, with the distant Makalu centre-stage.

It was in one of the rivers in this area — at a height of almost 5,000 metres (17,000 feet) — that a wildlife expert discovered what may well be the only high-altitude salamander in the world.

Getting there
The initial trek from Dharan follows that of the Kanchenjunga trek to Hile. If you fly from Kathmandu to Tumlingtar you can save at least 10 days. The bus ride from Kathmandu to Dharan takes between 11 and 13 hours and you should reserve a seat well in advance.

Where to stay
You must carry all your supplies, and Sherpa guides are absolutely essential. Mountain sickness is an ever-real threat and, until the monsoons, Shipton Pass is buried in snow.

Trekking (First day)
Outside **Hile**, the Makalu route turns **left** off the one leading to Kanchenjunga, and descends suddenly. A **grove** of **alders**, on the right, serves as a military camp.

To reach Pakeri Bash and its police station, travel on along the **left** of the **ridge** that leads down to the **Arun River**. The **village** sits on top of the ridge and from the opposite slope, in the distance below, you can see the Arun River.

The trail continues down a steep, **rocky path** through **terraced fields** to a small **tea house**, under a bo tree, on top of the narrow ridge.

This is **Dhikure**, with **many houses** and a **school**, and it is there that the trail switches to the **left** side of the ridge and climbs to the **crest**.

Soon it comes to a thick **pine forest** and a **steep hill** where the trail moves again to the **right**, eventually reaching a **rest area**, with two large bo trees, that marks the village of **Dhele**. From Dhele, the path leads down to the **Mangmaya Khola,** a tributary of the Arun River and a **hanging bridge**, about one kilometre (two-thirds of a mile) upstream of its confluence with the **Amur**, where it crosses into the village of **Mongmaya.** Altogether the journey takes about seven hours.

Second day
From there the path along the **right bank** of the **Mangmaya Khola** swings around to the **left bank** of the Arun River which, even during the dry season, is always in spate.

It runs through desolate, almost Africa-like savannah with stunted vegetation and little cultivation. There is a **post office** and a **police station** at **Leguwa Ghat**, just above the **Leguwa Khola**, and slightly upstream a modern **suspension bridge** allows you to cross the river safely, even during the flood and monsoon melt.

If it is the dry season you can cut across the wide **delta** at the confluence by following the **paths** between the **paddy fields** to **Beltal** with its unusual two-storeyed **hotel**.

The path continues through the rice paddies and crosses the **Kyawa Khola** over some **stepping stones**, beneath the village of **Akibunkabeshi** perched on the mountainside above.

There the trail climbs up from the river to a **sandy plateau** of **cornfields**, to return to the banks of the river where its way is blocked by a **cliff** that thrusts into the water.

You have to climb a steep and winding

rocky cliff with only a **steel handrail** for protection. The trail winds down on the other side of the ridge back to the **river-bank** and on to **Surte Bari**, where you camp for the night. Overall, the trek takes from five to six hours.

Third day

On the riverbed, beneath the village, a wide, sandy area stretches to the 20-metre-wide (65-foot) **Piluwa Khola**, which is fordable during the dry season, otherwise there is a **suspension bridge** upstream. A small **ridge** juts out from the left bank of the Arun river and, where the trail crosses the **col**, it goes down again to the riverbed, to travel below cornfields, passing the four-house hamlet of **Domkota**, beneath a sweltering and merciless sun.

From Domkota, where the Arun River forms a large oxbow bend, the path on the **left bank** leaves the river level and leads through neat little **fields** into **Khare** where, among the **thatched-roof houses**, bo trees provide welcome shade.

Leaving the village, the path turns **right** and then immediately **left** through a narrow dry **streambed**. Go up a **hill** of brick-red soil covered with sparse vegetation, and then across some small hills to rest awhile in the shade of the bo trees at **Gande Pani** — after which you cross the **suspension bridge** to the **plateau** of **Tumlingtar**. It is an hour from there to the **airfield** where there is a **hotel**. This trek takes a total of six hours.

Fourth day

From the airfield, climb the hill and walk through level **rice paddies** and scattered **houses** and then across **terraced hills**. To the right, you see the waters of the **Sabha Khola**. In the distance stands Chamlang.

Soon, the path becomes a **ridgeback** with many **tea houses** and shaded **rest areas**. After passing a bubbling **spring**, the trail moves to the **right flank** of the ridge, and after a short climb, you see more **houses** and finally arrive at the **checkpost** at the entrance to **Khandbari**, with its **shop-lined main street** and large open **bazaar**. The walking takes about two-and-a-half hours.

This is the administrative capital of the district, with a **bank**, **hospital** and **school**.

It is a good place to stock up on food and other essentials. A **meadow** outside the village makes an excellent campsite.

From there, the ridge trail continues to **Mani Bhanjyang** where it divides — one trail going left to the ridge route; the other right through the rice paddies. Take the **right** turn for the gentle climb to the village of **Panguma**.

There is not too much to see and you may find the walk somewhat monotonous as you climb to **Bhotebas,** at about 1,707 metres (5,600 feet), where you can camp in one of the fields. The last leg is a brisk three-and-a-half hours.

Fifth day

When you leave Bhotebas, you leave the farmlands and turn **right** to the left of the ridge as it climbs to the pass above. The level path passes through **scrub** and **fields** to **Gogune,** and on into **forest**. After a walk of about two hours, the switchback trail exits at the Gurung village of **Chichira**,

Above: Walking from Lukla towards Mount Everest. The peak at the back is called Diphede.

set on top of a **ridge**, then continues to Kuwapani. At this point, you get impressive but far-distant views of **Makalu**. From the three-house settlement of **Kuwapani,** the path veers to the **right** of the ridge, arriving at **Samurati's lone house** where there are painted *mani* **stones** and a **cave** in which you can sleep. Leaving the village, the path divides into two. Take the **left** fork into the **forest** through **Fururu** to the **rest area** in **Daujia Dhara Deorali**, where the path levels out. Down in the forest on the left, across a small **stream** and over another **ridge**, there is an unusual combination of painted *mani* stones. Eventually, the trail reaches **Mure**, a village at the right of the path, where you can camp in the **fields** or in one of the **house compounds**. The last leg takes about three hours.

Sixth day

Leave the village down a **slope** facing it and the fields of Sedua on the hillside opposite and, beyond them, the **walls** of the **Shipton Pass**. Not long after this, the trail cuts down the ridge, where it veers **left**, at a **single house**, to **Runbaun**. Now the trail becomes extremely steep and rough. Great care must be exercised — and not only on the trail. The **suspension bridge** over the Arun River, which takes about three-and-a-half hours to reach, is narrow and precarious sometimes, with missing footboards. One careless step could be fatal.

After the bridge, the trail climbs steeply along a precarious and crumbling **incline** on the **right bank** up to the **grain fields** and hamlet of **Rumruma**. The trail leaves the hamlet through terraced fields to **Sedua**, set at 1,480 metres (4,855 feet), where you can camp at the **school** near a **spring**. The last leg takes from two-and-a-half to three hours.

Seventh day

From Sedua the trail leaves the Arun River and enters the **watershed** of the **Kashuwa Khola.** Climb a **mountainside** dotted with terraced fields and forested areas. After about two hours' walk, a *chorten* marks the Sherpa village of **Naba Gaon**, with its monastery.

Climb a ridge, lined with *mani* **stones**

on the **right**, and follow the trail along the **right bank** of the **Kashuwa Khola**, through **Kharshing Kharka**, which has **two huts**.

The path cuts through thick **hill forest** where **fallen trees** can make walking difficult. Eventually, it crosses a small **stream** and leads into the remote village of **Tashi Gaon**, set at 2,042 metres (6,700 feet), with its attractive **timber houses** covered with **bamboo roofing**. You can camp in the **fields** near the village. This second leg takes two-and-a-half to three hours.

Eighth day

Leave Tashi Gaon through **forest** up a gentle slope, across a **rocky area** and **stream** to the **meadows** of Uteshe. From the top of the next **ridge** there are striking mountain panoramas where the path veers **right**. It continues gradually upwards, across a **stream** into thick **bamboo**, with no views. Where it leaves the bamboo, the trail enters a **rhododendron forest** and becomes markedly steeper, passing **Dhara Kharka** on the crest of the **ridge**, and on to **Unshisa** on the Ishwa Khola side of

Above: Rhododendron bushes.

the ridge, finally reaching the campsite at **Kauma** at the top of the ridge, after about five hours' walking. About 20 metres (60 feet) down, on the Kashuwa Khola side, there are some **caves** where you can sleep.

Ninth day
From Kauma the trail climbs to the top of a **ridge** that offers the best mountain landscape of the whole trail — a truly dramatic panorama at the far end of the valley of 7,317-metre (24,005-foot) **Chamlang**, 6,739-metre (22,110-foot) **Peak Six**, 6,105-metre (20,030-foot) **Peak Seven**, and the long-awaited 8,481-metre (27,825-foot) **Makalu,** with the outline of the **Kanchenjunga Range** to the east. The trail now begins to climb Shipton Pass.

In fact, there are two passes — **Keke La** and **Tutu La**. Rugged **cliffs** bar the way and the trail traverses **left** to a **small pond**, climbs up to Keke La, at 4,114 metres (13,500 feet), and then down into an S-shaped valley, past a **small tarn**, and up to **Tutu La**. There the trail descends to a level stretch before veering **left**, past a **waterfall** and across a **stream**, and on through **forest** to **Mumbuk,** set at 3,505 metres (11,500 feet) amid pines and rhododendron. This stretch takes about six hours.

10th day
The trail leaves the campsite, following the course of a winding **stream** for about 200 metres (650 feet) before turning **left** down along the side of another rushing **stream**, turning **left** yet again, past a **cave** to the **Barun Khola**.

The path takes the **right bank** with views of Peak Six. Beware of the frequent **rock falls**. Soon Makalu comes into view and the trail exits on to a **terraced hill** and the **meadows** of **Tematan Kharka**.

It continues along a small range of flat hills to **Yangre Kharka** where there are some **caves** and on into **rhododendron forest**. There it leaves the Barun Khola, climbing gently up the side of a wide valley and turns **right**, across a **stream**, to the **single hut** of **Neghe Kharka** 2,670 metres (8,760 feet) — a total walking time of approximately five hours.

11th day
Leave the campsite, pass a **cave** and cross to the **left bank** of the Barun Khola over a **wooden bridge** set on a large boulder in midstream, into **rhododendron forest**. The path now becomes steep as it zigzags up to the **meadows** on the slopes of **Riphuk Kharka**. There, the path leads away from the Barun Khola, on a modest gradient, through **Yak Kharka** to **Ramara** — offering views along the way, one after the other, of 6,830-metre (22,409-foot) Pyramid Peak, 6,720-metre (22,048-foot) Peak Four, 6,477-metre (21,251-foot) Peak Three, 6,431-metre (21,101-foot) Peak Five, Peak Six, and Chamlang.

At Ramara, approaching the Barun Khola, the trail reaches the **snout** of **Lower Barun Glacier** and continues along the glacier's **left bank** to the **headwaters** of the Barun Khola and **Mirik** where there is a **cave** for camping.

12th day
There are no more forests and you must carry enough wood for fuel with you from this point for your energy needs. The trail continues on the **right** across rocky, glacial terrain to **Sherson,** set at 4,572 metres (15,000 feet).

The majestic crest of Makalu dominates the horizon at Sherson as the trail skirts the base of its **south-east ridge** in an easy climb on to lateral moraine. There, glowering down from its massive height, the mountain seems to fill the sky. Take the trail down to the **riverbed,** across the **stream** and up a **terraced hill** to **Makalu base camp,** set in a pastoral meadow at 4,800 metres (15,750 feet), where there is a **stone hut** without a roof.

This is an ideal place from which to explore the area around the foot of this great mountain, including the Barun Glacier.

The trail leads down to the **riverbed** and then along a well-defined **path** that circles **left** to a meadow which is known as **Baruntse base camp,** with stunning views of Everest and Lhotse at the far end of the valley. Climb the **hill** behind for more panoramic views of the world's greatest mountains.

But the best view of all, seen in a full

Above: Trekkers walking to the Everest Base Camp. Following pages: Nepal has some of the most exciting white-water rivers in the world.

360° circle, is from the base of Makalu's south-east ridge, which is reached by cutting across the **riverbed** and climbing for about 90 minutes — when Makalu, Everest and Lhotse seem to encircle you. The return trek to **Tumlingtar** takes about seven days.

Dhankuta

Dhankuta stands on a ridge in the hills above Dharan, pleasantly cool at an elevation of 1,200 metres (4,000 feet), and famous for its orange groves and leafy scenery punctuated by many mountain streams, their crystal-clear waters dancing between grassy banks lined with pine and oak forests. It is also the base for trekking in the Kanchenjunga region. Astride the Sikkim border with eastern Nepal, Kanchenjunga is the world's third-highest mountain, and the 16-day journey depends on absolute fitness and acclimatization, as it takes the trekker from the subtropical lowlands to a height of more than 5,000 metres (16,000 feet) above sea level — around the base of some magnificent satellite peaks — to Yalung glacier.

Getting there

A modern motor road winds its way from Dharan to Dhankuta. On foot, it takes about five hours to climb 32 kilometres (20 miles), via Bijaipur to this ancient Newar town.

Or you can trek off the road. Allow two days and one night to reach Dhankuta, through many small wayside hamlets, with tea houses and bazaars.

Where to stay

You need first-class equipment, including rugged tents and Sherpa guides, together with adequate rations, as food supplies are not easy to obtain in this region.

Trekking (First day)

A wide road dips down to a **riverbed** before climbing steeply to **Shangri-la Pass** at around 1,000 metres (3,280 feet), and then down to the first **campsite** on the banks of the **Leuti Khola River**.

The route continues along the **left bank** of the Leuti Khola, a tributary of the Tamar River, then crosses over a **toll suspension footbridge** to join the **road** that winds its

Above: Wild sheep, the Great Tibetan Sheep at Sagarmatha National Park are diminishing fast through poaching, hunting and encroachment.

way up to **Dhankuta** on the mountain flank on the **opposite bank**. When you cross the **bridge**, report to the **Murughat checkpost,** then walk through the village on to a wide, steep path along a ridge leading to Dhankuta. There is a **tea house** on the **summit** where you can refresh yourself with a cup of sweet Nepali tea before continuing the trek through the twin hamlets of **Teknara** and **Pangure Phedi.**

The next stop after this is **Yuku**, with a wall-shaded **rest area** beneath the lush foliage of its green trees, and then the trail winds along a **ridgeback**, from which Dhankuta comes into view.

Roughly four hours after your walk began, you enter the town. Pitched on the hillside, Dhankuta's paved **main street** climbs steeply up to the **town centre** — with **hospital, hotels, banks** and **government offices** — and then into the **bazaar.**

The streets are lined with myriad **tea houses**, the market town itself serving as a commercial, banking and government centre. One modern wonder for towns-people has been the arrival of electric power.

Dhankuta's gabled **black-and-white houses** and dreamy ways are strikingly reminiscent of a European Alpine village.

At the far end of the town there is a **military post** where the road becomes a mountain trail again.

Lined with many houses, it follows the ridge for 1.5 kilometres (one mile) to **Kakati**, where plenty of **tea houses** offer overnight accommodation. It takes roughly 90 minutes to complete this last leg.

Second day
From Kakati the trail continues to **Mgare**, after which the wayside houses begin to thin out. A **motor road** cuts across the trail, which then continues through many **villages** and **hamlets**, finally arriving at **Hile**, whose Thursday is market day. Tibetan refugees have swollen the town's population. This first leg takes approximately two hours.

From Hile the trail climbs to the **right**, through the green and peaceful **meadows** of the **Milkia foothills**, along a **ridge path**, to the tiny hamlet of **Mure**, which boasts nine timber houses. A notable feature is the many **wooden benches** along the road for the weary traveller — an unusual sight in the Himalaya. From Mure the trail climbs to the summit of a **mountain ridge** and along its crest to the pretty little settlement of **Gurashe**, just six whitewashed houses.

From there to the village of **Jeroboam** it is easy going, all on the level, before the trail winds out of **Jhorbhati** up the **left flank** of the next **ridge** to **Shidua**, at a height of 2,286 metres (7,500 feet), where you can refresh yourself at the **tea house** before making camp in the nearby **meadow**. This second leg takes from three-and-a-half to four hours to complete.

Third day

At Shidua you are on the threshold of the **Makalu** and **Kanchenjunga** ranges — rearing up like a barrier in front of you. From the village, the trail veers **left** as it winds up the left flank of these increasingly steeper foothills to **Chitre**, with stunning views to the north-west, taking in 8,481-metre (27,825-foot) **Makalu** and 7,317-metre (24,005-foot) **Chamlang**.

Leave Chitre by a **path** to the **right** along the **ridgeback**, through more thick **forest** to **Basantpur**, a village of 25 houses. This leg should take about two-and-a-half hours.

From Basantpur, follow the path to **Dobhan**, which splits into two — one continuing along the ridgeback, the other winding up and down the hillside to the right. Stick to the **ridge**: it is shorter and the mountain views are spectacular.

An **irrigation duct** takes water off one of the streams to the nearby fields as the trail climbs a gentle slope through the twin villages of **Tsute**. Beyond them, through the **forest**, the path turns **right**, leaving the ridge to climb through **stands of rhododendron** before emerging in a delightful alpine **meadow** — ideal for camping but without water.

Re-enter the forest, however, and climb gently upwards for about another 15 minutes to the **two houses** of **Door Pani**, at a height of 2,743 metres (9,000 feet), where there is a beautiful **meadow** in which to camp, with plentiful water. This second leg is also around two-and-a-half hours' walk.

Fourth day

From the meadow, forest to another **ridge**, begins to switchback — up true Himalayan fashion. For approximately half-an-hour be scending steeply to the **left** for about metres (650 feet) to the village of **Tinjur Phedi**, with its **tea house**. From there, the trail follows a **ridgeback** through copses of **rhododendron** beneath sprawling alpine **meadows**, and is relatively smooth and even to the hamlet of **Chauki**, with its 11 houses and a **tea house**. It is a walk of about three hours.

There is no cultivation around these parts and the meadows are used for summer pastures. As you walk through these from Chauki, the magnificent peak of Makalu dominates the horizon, but not long after this you get your first glimpse — and what a glimpse it is — of the great **Kanchenjunga**. Soon afterwards, the trail reaches the foot of the **Mongol Bharari Pass**.

Lined with *mani* **stones**, it winds gently up to the **saddle**, through **rhododendron forest**, cresting the ridge at the hamlet of **Ram Pokhari** — two lakes and five small houses.

Now the trail winds along the top of a grassy, undulating ridge, before descending to **Gupha Pokhari** and its enchanting **lake**, at a height of 2,984 metres (9,790 feet). This second leg also takes about three hours.

Fifth day

Take the pass to the **right**, skirting the **ridge** directly in front of you, when you leave Gupha Pokhari. You will get your last glimpse of Makalu and Chamlang before turning **north-east** into the Kanchenjunga massif.

You enter this range on your **right**, along a winding switchback trail, and after an hour's walking, you come to the **crest** of a 3,048-metre (10,000-foot) pass that descends to **Dobhan.** Along the downward trail are many **bunkhouses** for trekkers and porters where it is possible to spend the night if you so wish. After passing these, the trail climbs the second of two small hills before beginning the real descent, through thick **forest**, to the bottom of the **pass** and the

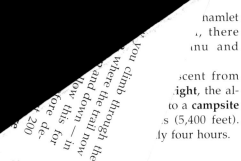

hamlet
ı, there
ınu and

ȿcent from
.ight, the al-
to a campsite
.s (5,400 feet).
.ly four hours.

Sixtu.

Trekking ın   ya is not for those
who seek to clı..   /er upward. Trails
plunge dizzily up and down 3,000 metres
(10,000 feet) or more, and from Nesum the
trail continues its descent through a maze
of **paddy field paths** to Dobhan and the
Tamar Valley.

There are many hamlets, villages, and
tea houses along the way. After about 90
minutes' walk, you reach Dobhan, a picturesque **Newar settlement**, with a **village
store** and many houses. There the trail
crosses the **Meiwa Khola**, a tributary of the
Tamar, on to a level plain with a small
hamlet, after which it reaches the Tamar.
Cross to the **left bank**, via the **suspension
footbridge**, where the road divides — one
a **narrow path** to Ghunsa, the other a long,
climbing **ridgeback trail** to Taplejung.

Now the track climbs steeply as it zig-
zags its way to **Deoringe school** before
easing back into a more gradual climb
through **terraced fields** and scattered
forests, bypassing the hamlet of **Taribun**.
There are many more **houses** along this
well-travelled route. Finally, just above a
public bathhouse, you reach **Taplejung** at
1,768 metres (5,800 feet), the administrative
capital of the district with **post** and **tel-
egraph office, hospital, government offices**
and a **military post**.

Replenish food supplies there but remember that fresh meat and vegetables
are only available at the Saturday market.
This last leg takes around three-and-a-half
hours to complete.

Seventh day
You leave Taplejung and its **cobblestone**

streets, past the **water reservoir**, along the
path to the **airfield** on a really steep climb
that will take you roughly two hours.
There is a **hotel** at the edge of the airfield
on a **level plateau**. Next is a gentle climb
through the flower-filled **meadows** to the
forest, with the mountains to your right,
before descending to **Lali Kharka**.

Across the valley stands **Bhanjyang**,
which you reach the next day, but for now
your descent culminates in the fertile **fields**
around **Tambawa**, at 1,981 metres (6,500
feet), where you can camp in the **fields** or
near the **school**. This second leg takes four
hours.

Eighth day
From Tambawa, it takes about 90 minutes,
first to a **ridgeback trail** and then circui-
tously down the mountain, to **Pa Khola**,
where the trail cuts through terraced **rice
paddies**, then across a **suspension footbridge** to **Kunjari**. Before you reach this
lovely alpine village, surrounded by thick
rainforest, it passes through a few **hamlets**.
The path carries on gently upward out of
Kunjari until you are high above
Tambawa.

Soon it reaches Bhanjyang, with many
tea houses and views of Kanchenjunga
framed by **South Peak, Main Peak** and
Yalung Kang.

The path descends again to the **left** on
an easy slope to the **terraced fields** of
Khesewa, at 1,829 metres (6,000 feet), where
you can camp in the surrounding **fields**.
This second leg takes about three-and-a-
half hours.

Ninth day
From Khesewa, the trail descends through
forest to the **Nandeva Khola** on the **left**
and, crossing the **river**, continues down
along its **banks** before entering the forest
to the **left** to begin the climb up the next
range of hills to **Loppoding**. Next, the path
switchbacks up and down to the **rest area**,
at the delightfully-named hamlet of **Fun
Fun**. After this, follow the **ridgeback** into
the **hills** on the **right bank** of the **Kabeli**

Opposite: Ama Dablam guards the southern approach to Everest.

Khola, before a gradual descent through **rice** and **grain fields** to the village of **Anpan**. This first leg takes around three hours.

From Anpan, the trail follows a ridge-back up an easy slope to **Ponpe Dhara**, which sits on its crest where you can pause to take in the splendid view of distant **Jannu**, before continuing the winding descent through **hamlets** and **farm fields** to the **Khangwa Khola**, which you cross by **suspension bridge**. On the other side, you make the slow climb to the village of **Mamankhe**. This leg takes approximately three hours.

10th day

This starts with an easy climb, which skirts a formidable ridge, to the village of **Dekadin**. After this, the trail follows the **right bank** of the Kabeli Khola, about 200 to 300 metres (650-1000 feet) above its raging waters, winding around various **ridges**, **cliffs** and **streams**.

On the whole, this three-and-a-half-hour walk is an easy up-and-down trek, with constant views of the river below and the little farmsteads and their fields on the hills opposite.

Finally, you descend some **stone steps** to the **river** itself, and then on to another path that takes you on a gradual climb away from the river through **villages** and **fields**.

Eventually, after about two hours' hard climbing, it reaches the remote village of **Yamphudin**, at 2,150 metres (7,050 feet). Report to the **checkpost** and camp in **fields** or **house compounds**.

You may prefer to engage new porters for the hazards of cold, snow and altitude ahead, as those from Dharan are not well-suited to the rugged challenge of the Kanchenjunga range.

11th day

Yamphudin is where the real climbing begins and there are two options for the route to **Lamite Bhanjyang**. The favourite choice is to cross the river and trek through **Dhupi Bhanjyang**. For those who prefer a tougher challenge, however, the second route involves a climb up a **mountain path** from **Yamphudin**, on the **right bank** of **Omje Khola,** which crosses a **stream** early in its

course. It then plunges down through the **fields** and back, after two hours, to the **Omie Khola**, which you must cross again to reach an extremely steep **mountain ridge** that, at first, demands care with every step. But it soon enters the **forest** and there is little or no sense of height.

Gradually, the severity of the gradient eases into an easy climb, still through thick **forest**, until it emerges on a level open **saddle**. Eventually, it reaches the **climbing hut** at **Chitre**, where you can spend the night.

However, in the dry season there is no water, and you will have to walk on another 90 minutes to a little **tarn** beneath Lamite Bhanjyang. Ask if water is available at **Yamphudin** before you set off. The second leg takes around three hours.

12th day

The ridgeback from Chitre is lined with **magnolia** and **bamboo**. Beyond the bamboo belt the trail reaches **Lamite** and its single **shelter** — a simple structure consisting of a roof with supporting posts.

The trail then ascends through thick stands of **rhododendron**, along a **ridge** to **Lamite Bhanjyang**, at 3,430 metres (11,250 feet), with **Jannu** rising up before you above the ridge in all its magnificence, and behind you panoramic views of the foothills around Dharan.

Climb about 150 metres (500 feet) from there on the **right** before descending, through thick forests of **rhododendron**, to the **Simbua Khola**, with Kanchenjunga's majestic snow-clad peak floating above the trees. The gentle descent almost takes the trail to the waters of the river and then climbs along the **left bank** a short distance before crossing over a **wooden bridge** to the **right bank** and a **campsite** at **Torontan**, at 3,078 metres (10,100 feet), where you can sleep in one of the **caves**. This climb takes from three-and-a-half to four hours.

13th day

Follow the path, past the caves, along the **right bank** of the **Simbua Khola**. The forested walls of the valley are thick with **pine** and **rhododendron**. Eventually, after about two hours' walking, it reaches **Whata** with its single **hut**, where it crosses

Above: Women carrying firewood along the Langtang trek.

to the **right bank** of the **stream** in front of the hut and continues through the thick **forest** to the **snowline**.

You will see a **Sherpa shrine** with a huge boulder, shaped like a snake, designed to ward off the demons, for the Sherpas believe that if anyone dies after this point, evil spirits will fall upon the mountains.

The path leads down to the **river bank** and up a difficult **trail** to **Tseram** where you can see your ultimate destination — the terminal moraine of **Yalung Glacier**. Behind it are the 7,352-metre (24,120-foot) **Kabru** and 7,349-metre (24,112-foot) **Talung Peak**. Camp in one of the **caves**. This last leg takes from two-and-a-half to three hours.

14th day

A steep slope, descending from the **left**, bars the way out of Tseram and you have to retrace your trail to the **bank** of the **Simbua Khola**, then around its base, before climbing up through a stony, **terraced field** to **Yalung Bara**, where a single **stone hut** marks the **end of the treeline**. From there, you have to carry enough wood for fuel for the rest of the trek.

Just above, past several small **stone huts**, the trail comes to the **right bank** of the entrance to the Yalung Glacier and **Lapsang**, with Lapsang La Valley at the **left**. This first leg takes about three hours.

Now the trail comes to a tiny **pond** and skirts a protruding **cliff face** — where, suddenly, you see before you the peaks of 7,317-metre (24,005-foot) **Kabru S.**, 6,678-metre (21,910-foot) **Rathong**, and 6,147-metre (20,168-foot) **Kokthan**. Follow the **flat trail** to the **Ramze** at 4,572 metres (15,000 feet), where there is a **hut** in which you can sleep. This second leg takes about one hour.

15th day

The magnificent Yalung Glacier veers **left** at Ramze, and just around the corner next morning you will get your first close-ups of mighty Kanchenjunga. Now it climbs the lateral moraine to a **Buddhist stupa**, from which it descends steeply to the glacier floor and a trail marked by cairns.

Lungs gasp in the rarefied air but eventually, after about four hours of really intense effort, you should reach the **campsite**

Above: Neat Sherpa houses climb the hillside at Namche Bazaar beneath Khumde's icy peak.
Opposite: Intricate detail of a Buddhist religious painting.

atop the glacier, at 4,890 metres (16,000 feet), with magnificent views of 7,710-metre (25,294-foot) **Jannu.**

The vista of the mountains surrounding Yalung glacier opens before you — and at the final camp, **Corner Camp**, at 5,151 metres (16,900 feet), on the **left bank** of the glacier, there is a stupendous mountain panorama, fitting reward for the effort it takes to reach this point — and for the 14-day trek back to Dharan.

Rumjatar
A stiff two- to three-day trek over the western ridge of the Arun Valley takes the fit and the active down into **Rumjatar,** set at 1,371 metres (4,500 feet) in the valley of the **Dudh Kosi River.**

Okhaldunga
Some kilometres west, **Okhaldunga,** a pleasant unspoilt village with an old **fortress,** has given its name to a lyrical essay of hill and valley, river and lake.

Many of the birds that give Nepal one of the most richly varied collections of avifauna in the world are found on the forest-clad 3,000-metre (10,000-foot) **crests** of the **Neche Dahuda Hills,** overlooking the valley floors.

Flocks of birds, some vividly coloured, flit from tree to tree, their dawn chorus in springtime a hosanna to life reborn.

Okhaldunga lies directly at the foot of Everest but few attempt the exhausting trek through these foothills to the roof of the world.

The Terai: East to West

Along Nepal's southern border with India lies a narrow band of fertile plains, the Terai. Flat, and nowhere wider than 40 kilometres (25 miles), the Terai covers 24,600 square kilometres (9,500 square miles). In addition to providing a dramatic contrast to the rest of the terrain of the world's most mountainous nation, the Terai has a charm all its own.

During the monsoon season, tributaries of the Ganges flood the Terai's fields and paddies, depositing soil eroded from the Himalayas.

Often, rivers and streams change course, uprooting stilted huts and villages, washing out roads, and destroying communication links. In the months that follow, crops are planted — rice, wheat, cane, jute, tobacco, beans and lentils — and harvested before the scorching desert winds arrive, preceding the next year's monsoons.

Home to more than half Nepal's people and most of the national industries, this one-sixth of Nepal's land area produces more than 50 per cent of the gross domestic product and is also the last refuge of the country's remaining tigers and rhinoceros.

In October and November, the ideal months for visiting this part of Nepal, the countryside is lush and a hub of activity.

Getting there

The Mahendra (or East-West) Highway links the major towns; footpaths connect everywhere else. Buses travel the main route and can get you to the birthplaces of Buddha and Sita and the jungle wildlife parks, but your feet or a bicycle are the only ways to get off the beaten track.

Sightseeing

On the eastern reaches of the Terai lies **Biratnagar**, Nepal's second-largest city, with over 100,000 people. A major industrial centre with **sugar, rice, textile** and **jute mills**, and small- and medium-scale **factories** for timber products, Biratnagar itself is a town to pass by rather than through, but the attractions of its environs make it worth a stopover.

Around Biratnagar

To the west are the attractions of the area: **green paddies**, **jute fields**, **flood plains** and **marshes**. On the **Indian border**, the massive **Kosi Dam** impounds the **Sun Kosi River**, which is fed by the Tamar River from the slopes of Kanchenjunga and the Arun River from the snows of Makalu.

Built by India, the dam is one of Nepal's major hydroelectric projects. Besides controlling unpredictable floods and generating much of the country's energy, it created new **wetlands** that form the **Kosi Tappu Wildlife Reserve.**

There you can see one of the few remaining herds of **wild water buffalo** and thousands of migratory birds. There is no tourist accommodation in the reserve, the nearest being in Biratnagar.

Janakpur

Of more interest is **Janakpur**, 120 kilometres (74 miles) west of Biratnagar, on the Indian border. With 40,000 Maithili-speaking inhabitants, Janakpur is reputed to have been the ancient capital of Maithili and **birthplace of Sita**, consort of Rama (one of Vishnu's incarnations and hero of the epic *Ramayana*).

It is a major pilgrimage centre for Hindus from all over the subcontinent. An eight-kilometre (five-mile) **brick-paved road** encircles the city and its many sacred Hindu **shrines** and **ponds**, of which Gangasagar and Dhanushsagar are the most outstanding.

Pilgrims to its two famous festivals, commemorating Rama and Sita's wedding and Rama's epic victory over evil, immerse themselves in these sacred waters and flock to **Janaki Temple** to pay homage to Rama and Sita. Built by a Queen of Tikamgarh — in Madhya Pradesh, northern India — in 1900, its delicately carved marble traceries were inspired by the great 17th-century architecture of the Mughals. The delicate **filigrees**, shaped with exquisite beauty, are seen at their best on the elaborate **cupolas, ceilings** and **tiles**. Nearby is the

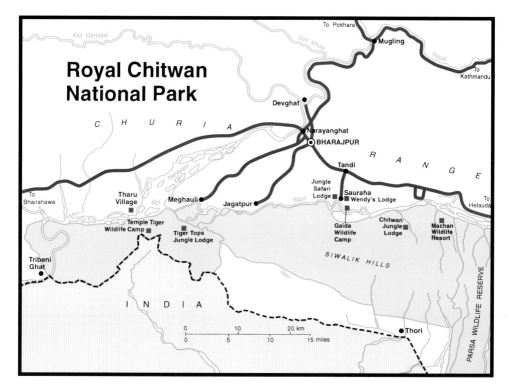

Royal Chitwan National Park

Vivah Mandap, where legend holds Rama and Sita were wed.

The town is also famous as the main stop on one of the world's shortest railways — the 52-kilometre (32-mile) narrow-gauge Nepal Railway that links Nepal with Jayanagar, India. The line is a colourful anachronism that delights inveterate travellers, a time-serving echo of the old British Raj.

Birganj
Eighty kilometres (50 miles) west of Janakpur, the **Mahendra Highway** links up with the **Tribhuvan Rajpath**, for many years the country's main trans-Asia link. To the **south** is the border town of **Birganj**; to the north, through **Amlekhganj** and across the **Mahabharat Lekh hills**, is **Kathmandu Valley**. Along the route is a dramatic view at **Daman**.

Birganj has seen better days. In the 1960s and 1970s, western hippies and mystics queued for clearance into Nepal on the Indian side at Raxaul, and spent the night in one of Birganj's many cheap **lodging houses** before taking the high road to Kathmandu.

It is still a bustling industrial area with **timber yards**, a **sugar mill**, **match factory** and a raucous **bus depot**, where itinerants jostle each other in their eagerness to catch the next, often overcrowded, coach to Kathmandu. It is also a jump-off point for visitors to Royal Chitwan National Park and Parsa Wildlife Reserve.

Royal Chitwan National Park
The highlight for most visitors to the Terai is a visit to Royal Chitwan National Park and Parsa Wildlife Reserve, recreated out of the once-fertile rice and wheat fields that swiftly covered the Rapti Valley after the fall from power of the Rana dynasty in the 1950s. Royal Chitwan, covering 932 square kilometres (360 square miles), was the first of Nepal's extensive network of wildlife sanctuaries which now protect over seven per cent of its territory.

The valley in which it lies forms the flood plains of the Narayari river, joined there by the waters of the Rapti and other streams and feeders to become the second-largest tributary of the sacred Ganges that flows approximately 200 kilometres (125 miles) to the south.

247

Before the park's creation in 1973, Nepal's population explosion had pushed migrants down from the hills, forcing the indigenous Tharu tribes into this area, which was formerly reserved as royal hunting grounds. Using slash-and-burn techniques, they opened up the forests and planted rice and grain. Concerned with the destruction of its traditional hunting grounds, Nepal's royal family planned new strategies for the protection of its wildlife, and King Mahendra established Chitwan in 1973.

The grasslands were rehabilitated, along with the sal *(Shorea robusta)* forests, and slowly the game began to creep back from the uncertain havens it had found outside.

An exemplary model of wildlife management, Royal Chitwan and its denizens have continued to prosper.

Getting there

The park is linked to major centres in Nepal and India by air and road, with scheduled domestic flights to nearby Bharatpur.

When to go

Chitwan is at its best between October and April — and often unbearable during the torrid pre-monsoon heat and the monsoons.

Where to stay

If Tiger Tops pioneered the jungle safari in Chitwan, there are now many lodges, camps, and numerous tea houses in and around the sanctuary that developed in its wake. Best-known are Gaida Wildlife Camp, and its tented Chitwan Jungle Lodge, set in the darkest, deepest jungle, Jungle Safari Lodge, National Park Cottages and Wendy's Lodge.

Outside the park, guests at the Tharu Village Resort can sleep in the traditional Tharu tribal longhouses, see Tharu dances, eat Nepali food and visit local villages. Demand for rooms in and around Chitwan is high. Book well in advance.

Sightseeing

Subsequent extensions, **Parsa Wildlife Reserve**, have given Chitwan a much larger area, embracing smaller **forests** of **khani** *(Acacia catechu)*, **sisso** *(Dalbergia sisso)*, and **simal** *(Bombax malabaricum)* — all valuable indigenous woods. Monsoon fluctuations in the courses of the rivers have created new **ponds** and **lakes** in a park–reserve, which now covers an area of 1,200 square kilometres (470 square miles) of subtropical lowland, bounded by the **Rapti River** in the **north**, the **Reu River** and the **Churia** or **Siwalik Range** in the **south**, and the **Narayani River** in the **west**.

Several **observation blinds** have been constructed next to **water-holes**, where patient visitors might see **tigers** and **leopards** and where most will certainly sight **rhinoceros**, **wild boar**, **deer**, **monkeys** and a multitude of **birds**.

Throughout the park, small fenced **enclosures** contain different kinds of grasses from which agronomists and conservationists hope to regenerate ideal pastures for Chitwan's wild animals.

On clear winter days this jungle has one of the most dramatic backdrops in the world — the stunning ice-clad slopes of **Annapurna**, **Ganesh Himal** and **Himal Chuli** stand out on the horizon in magnificent detail. Needless to say, travel in the park is difficult during the monsoon season (May to September), and the best animal viewing is from February to April.

Any stay shorter than two days is probably not worth the effort, as the key to enjoying the game park is patience.

The elephant has proved the best form of transport in the park. The Royal Nepali Army, which polices the park and enforces conservation laws, makes its patrols by elephant, and park workers move about in similar fashion. It is not uncommon to come across a small workforce resting in the shade of a clump of bombax trees around midday, the elephants relentlessly foraging with their trunks; their handlers, *mahouts*, even sleeping on their backs, many with umbrellas raised as protection against the sun.

Previous pages: Women of the Terai plains relaxing with their babies. Opposite: Tharu farm child on the Terai plains. These families live in airy houses and avoid working during the heat of the day.

Above: Gauguin landscape reflects the rustic pace of the fertile Terai plains as oxen plough a maize field. Previous pages: Tharu farm worker of the Terai plains going home after a hard day's work.

Elephants can usually be hired at the park offices or at one of the lodges. Each beast has its own handler and individual gait. For most, these game rides are the memories that will last longest. The handler, astride the elephant's neck, brushes the **lianas** and the **giant ferns** aside with his steel goad, and the seemingly ungainly three-ton steed steps nimble-footed over fallen logs. In the dark shadows of a thicket, a sudden flash of fawn reveals the flight of a startled **sambar deer**.

Giant butterflies flit from leaf to leaf and beyond the wall of leaves shadows move — perhaps a **tiger**, a **leopard**. However briefly, you can be the last of the Maharajahs.

Out on the plains, the great **Asiatic one-horn rhinos** are moving with steadfast purpose, cropping the grass as a herd of **chital** — timid, fawnlike deer, edge nervously away from the young elephant.

Back in the **forest**, a **jungle fowl** suddenly struts across the trail, and from a low-lying branch, a wild **peacock** takes off in a technicolour cascade of feathers.

It is also possible to travel part-way down the **Rapti River** and its streams by canoe, to view **crocodiles** basking in the sun, as well as a variety of other **riparian flora and fauna**.

Arrangements for a canoe trip can best be made at the **Saura park office**, six-and-a-half kilometres (four miles) **south** of **Tadi bazaar** — on the Mahendra Highway between Marayangarh and Hetauda.

Hiking is allowed in the jungle, but an experienced guide is a must, as trails are not marked and the wildlife can be dangerous.

Rather than being an encumbrance, a guide is an asset who can usually find and identify the wildlife. Many can reel off with computerlike accuracy the names of many of the sanctuary's prolific yet rare bird species.

A more remote wildlife jungle experience in far west Nepal, five hours' drive from **Nepalgunj**, can be found in the **Royal Bardia Reserve**.

Above: Farmers of the Terai plains travel in oxen-driven carriages.

Bharatpur

The twin towns of Bharatpur and Narayanghat are the nearest urban centres to Chitwan. Bharatpur's role in the lowland infrastructure is as an airfield for what the domestc air carrier rashly promises are the daily flights to Kathmandu.

Renowned for the reliability of its international schedules, Royal Nepal Airlines has an equal reputation for the erratic timekeeping of its internal flights — understandable in mountain regions, where weather suddenly closes in, but perplexing to passengers waiting in the balmy and reliable climes of the Terai.

Narayanghat, lying on the **banks** of one of Nepal's three largest rivers, the **Narayani**, and known as the Gateway to Chitwan, is in fact the major junction on the **Mahendra Highway**, with a **spur** climbing up through the **hills** along the **east bank** of the Narayani to **Mugling**, the main junction town between Kathmandu and Pokhara on the Prithvi Highway.

It is also a vital administrative and commercial centre of the Terai and indeed the ethnic capital of the indigenous people of this region, the Tharus.

Bustling Narayanghat with sizeable industries and flourishing markets, is also something of a pilgrimage spot. Each year, in January, tens of thousands flock to the nearby village of **Deoghat** when a **major fair** is held, and immerse themselves at the **confluence** of the **Kali Gandaki** with the waters of the **Trisuli-Marsyangdi**.

Travellers continue their **westward** journey from Narayanghat over the modern **bridge** that spans the river, veering **southwest** along the Narayani's **flood plains** and over the shallow crest of a spur of the **Siwalik Hills** to join the **Siddhartha Highway** — a direct India-Pokhara link — at **Butwal,** on the banks of the **River Tinau**. This market town, with 25,000 to 30,000 inhabitants, is famous for its market gardens and fruit.

Tansen

Northward of Butwal, a small eastward **spur** of the Siddhartha Highway doubles back on itself as it climbs, in just a few

Above: Nepal's only viable population of tigers exists within three sanctuaries – Royal Chitwan National Park, Royal Shukla Phanta Reserve and the Royal Karnali Reserve.

kilometres, to **Tansen** — a town of 15,000 famed for the **erotic carvings** on its **Narayan temple**.

Tansen is also justly renowned — for the sheer beauty of its panoramic vistas of the foothills around it — as a landscape artist's Eldorado.

Craft industries and traditional **Newar houses** also make the town a worthwhile stopover. Its **Bhairavnath temple,** legend says, was carried — lock, stock and timber beams — all the way from the Kathmandu Valley by King Mani Kumarananda Senior: one of history's biggest removal jobs. For anglers, Tansen's leaping streams provide fine sport.

Bhairawa

Hugging the Indian border 40 kilometres (25 miles) southward as the Himalayan crow flies, in sharp contrast to Tansen, **Bhairawa**, the Terai's second-largest industrial centre, turns out the hard stuff of Nepal's liquor trade from a modern **distillery** and also refines sugar, rice and oil.

There is also another **British base**, five kilometres (three miles) outside the town, which signs up more of the stout Gurkha military stock.

Where to stay

Pahupati Lodge, Siddhartha Nagar, Bhairawa. Lumbini Hotel, Bhairawa. Hotel Himalayan Inn, Bhairawa. Hotel Kailash, across from the Post Office. Annapurna Lodge, west of the Post Office on the same road. Mamata Lodge, across from the bus terminal at the border with India. Jai Vijay Lodge restaurant, across the bus terminal.

Lumbini

Nineteen kilometres (12 miles) **south-west** of Bhairahawa is **Lumbini** the birthplace of Siddhartha Gautama Buddha in 540 BC. Since 1958, Lumbini has been in the hands of an international committee established by the Fourth World Buddhist Conference.

At the turn of the century, German archaeologist Dr Feuhrer began excavating

Above: Slender-snouted gharial awaits eventual release from a breeding tank in Royal Chitwan National Park. Following pages: Three generations of Sherpa women in the mountain ranges around Everest.

the **ruins** of the area, including the **Lumbini palace** and **gardens**, several **shrines** and a **monastery**.

He discovered a **sandstone nativity sculpture** depicting Buddha's nativity — now in the **National Museum** — and a soaring **obelisk** erected to honour Buddha by the Mauryan emperor Ashoka when he visited the Lumbini gardens in 249 BC.

The pillar, inscribed in Sanskrit, 'Buddha Sakyamuni, the blessed one was born here,' had been split in two, by a stroke of lightning. Later excavation has revealed a **brick temple, Maya Devi**, said to mark the exact spot where the Buddha was born.

Tilaurokot

When the Buddha was born, his father, King Suddhondhan had as his capital, **Tilaurokot**, 27 kilometres (17 miles) west of Lumbini. Although the **stupas, monasteries** and **palaces** that Chinese travellers wrote about over two millennia ago no longer exist, the Nepalis have preserved the location of the town as a **heritage site**.

Nepalgunj

The westernmost city in Nepal and capital of its region, **Nepalgunj** is an industrial centre on the **Indian border**. It has a population of approximately 40,000 and little to commend it to the tourist.

Royal Bardia Reserve

Few tourists have yet visited the lesser-known trails of western Nepal, in spite of the presence of the **Royal Bardia Reserve**. But the Mahendra Highway, linking east and west, will inevitably encourage more visitors to the region.

Karnali, part of the Royal Bardia Reserve, located on the **eastern bank** of the **Karnali River**, is a sanctuary for the endangered **swamp deer**. There, Tiger Tops runs **Karnali Tented Camp**, with accommodation for 16 guests.

Shukla Phanta, in Kanchanpur district in the westernmost reaches of Nepal, is one of the few places in the country where the endangered **blackbuck** is found.

PART THREE: SPECIAL FEATURES

Above: Tappa dancers from Pokhara region. Opposite: Riotous assembly of revellers carrying burning torches – worked up on a mixture of liquor and stimulants – stagger into the New Year.

Himalaya: Where Men and Mountains Meet

Like the sea from which they rose, the great mountains of Nepal make waves. Aboard the Royal Nepal Airlines daily mountain flight, a pilot explains.

'You can feel already that it's a little bumpy,' he says. 'When the monsoons start, then we get the mountain waves.' These are tremendous thermal breakers in the sky, successive wave upon wave of alternating hot and cold air.

'We can't fly then. The plane pitches up and down just as if you were in a storm-tossed ocean.'

The simile works. You feel you could almost reach out and touch the peaks streaming by on the starboard side. But no words can adequately describe the landscape and its impact — rank upon rank of peaks marching upwards, like a frosty staircase barnacled with icicles, all the way up to the top and down the other side to the Tibetan plateau, which lies at around 4,550 to 5,500 metres (15,000–18,000 feet).

The scenery is cataclysmic. The thrusting jagged spires, knife-edge ridges and glaciers with their surface churned as if by a marching army, deadly pitfalls beneath for the unwary, thrust away into infinity.

Numbur, 6,950 metres (22,800 feet) high, is the pinnacle of a great east-facing amphitheatre, the morning sun scintillating on its snows, a plume of spindrift gusting from the top.

'No matter how many times you fly along here,' says the pilot, 'it's still a surprise. It always takes your breath away.'

From Dhaulagiri and Annapurna in the west to Kanchenjunga in the east is where men measure their mettle midst the most majestic mountains on earth — and sometimes die in the testing. No wonder.

Within a length of 500 kilometres (312 miles), just under two-thirds of the distance between Nepal's east-west borders, and within a breadth of 70 kilometres (44 miles) from south to north, no fewer than 138 peaks rise above 6,100 metres (20,000) feet. Dhaulagiri Himal has 14 major peaks above 6,400 metres (21,000 feet) — six of them on the Dhaulagiri massif alone — of which the lowest is almost 7,318 metres (24,000 feet).

No more than 50 kilometres (32 miles) distant, Annapurna Himal boasts 21 peaks, of which the smallest, Gyaji Kang, has yet to be surveyed. The 20th peak, Pheri Himal, touches 6,171 metres (20,243 feet) and 18 rise above 6,400 metres (21,000 feet).

Beyond this, just 70 kilometres (44 miles) east, lies Manaslu Himal with 12 peaks above 6,400 metres 21,000 feet; 110 kilometres (69 miles) east of that, Langtang Himal's 24 major peaks all rise above 6,100 metres (20,000 feet); and another 70 kilometres (44 miles) on, Rolwaling Himal's 17 peaks all top 6,555 metres (21,500 feet).

Move on now another 50 kilometres (32 miles) and Mahalangur Himal, in the Khumbu region, and Khumbu Himal boast a total of 26 peaks all above 6,400 metres (21,000 feet) between them, including Everest, at 8,848 metres (29,028 feet); and finally, just another 130 kilometres (81 miles) away, at 8,600 metres (28,208 feet), the world's third-highest mountain, Kanchenjunga, dominates 24 sister peaks all above 6,700 metres (22,000 feet).

Not surprisingly, there are few patrols along the Tibet-Nepal and Nepal-India borders. Nor is it any surprise to learn that there are hundreds of mountains in Nepal under 6,100 metres (20,000 feet) — and some above that height — which have yet to be named.

Before 1950, these peaks were shrouded in mystery, virtually unknown except those which could be reached from the Tibetan side, from which all the early assaults on Everest were made.

The Nepalese still rule which peaks may or may not be challenged: only 122 major mountain peaks are open to foreign

Opposite: Clouds begin to wreath the 6,630-metre (21,750-foot) peak of Thamserku.

Above: Snow peaked mountain range.

climbers. The rest, many of them regarded as holy or sacred, remain inviolate. The mystique of mountain-climbing has never been rationalised. The risks are incalculable — an average of one out of every 40 climbers who ascend the major peaks never returns — and success achieves nothing of a scientific or creative nature. George Mallory, who vanished with his companion Andrew Irvine during a 1925 attempt on Everest from the Tibetan side, explained his reason for putting his life on the line simply: 'Because it's there.'

Is that why people take the unforgiving risk? Perhaps so. In 1981, Joe Tasker wrote of climbing in the Himalaya, in his book, *Everest the Cruel Way:*

'. . . the mountains are never conquered; they will always remain and sometimes they will take away our friends if not ourselves. The climbing game is a folly, taken more or less seriously, an indulgence in an activity which is of no demonstrable benefit to anyone. It used to be that mountaineers sought to give credence to their wish to climb mountains by concealing their aims behind a shield of scientific research. But no more. It is now accepted, though not understood, that people are going to climb for its own sake.'

A year later, Tasker was dead, killed with his colleague Peter Boardman on the north-east ridge of Everest — which claimed Mallory and Irvine — in an expedition led by Chris Bonnington.

Later, in a 1985 expedition on the same face, climber Sandy Allan, who was quoted in Andrew Greig's *Kingdoms of Experience,* soliloquised:

'Here, we're here, I'm here, hoping that my ability and the rest of the lads' ability and the gods will see us OK. We're gamblers, we've got no cash; we have lives, we love them, that's the stake.'

He and Tasker were driven by the same passions and dreams as the greatest of all mountaineers, Reinhold Messner, who made his first visit to the Himalaya in 1970: a need to measure himself, a need to be first. If he failed, he was not found wanting.

Like the poles, the greatest heights on earth have always lured the brave and the reckless. Before 1950 no one had been known to reach the summit of a mountain

Above: A serious trekker who has climbed 4,570 metres (15,000 feet). Following pages: Daybreak at trekkers camp on the barren shores of Gokyo's glacial lake, Dudh Pokhari high in the Himalaya.

which stood above the magic 8,000-metres — 26,250-foot-mark, though Mallory and Irvine who vanished on Everest may have actually reached the summit.

It was Frenchman Maurice Herzog and his team who won the first permit to tackle Nepal's giants — Dhaulagiri and Annapurna — and on 3 March 1950, as Shipton and Tilman toiled through the upper reaches of the Langtang Valley, astounded by the size and beauty of its towering peaks and precipices, Herzog and his colleague Louis Lachenal crested the brow of Annapurna's north face and looked down from the peak of the world's 10th highest mountain, the first men ever to stand above 8,000 metres.

At once, Annapurna exacted vengeance. The French pair, descending in appalling weather, lost fingers and toes from frostbite. Unforgiving and vengeful, this 'Goddess of Plenty' has reaped terrible retribution since — by the end of 1984 — it had claimed 31 lives, one for each person who had reached its summit, a figure exceeded only by those lost on Everest.

Though seemingly benign and benevolent when viewed from Pokhara early on a spring day, Annapurna is baleful and malevolent. There is more than just a touch of fancy to the sensations and emotions climbers experience at extremely high altitude. Above 8,000 metres, after all, they are intruding into the 'Abode of the Gods', where mysticism prevails over cynicism.

Reinhold Messner, in solitude on the peaks of major mountains, has experienced this mysticism frequently. During his 1982 solo ascent of Kanchenjunga his perception was profound.

'First, I learned in dreams during the climb and afterwards — and this is true only for climbs of mountains higher than 8,000 metres — the whole dream world changes for a while. . . And second, I found that you see certain things between dreaming and not dreaming because you don't really sleep . . . visions from high altitudes. . . . In the last camp near the summit, I had a very strange vision of all the human parts I am made of . . . not only of my body, but of my whole being.'

When Herzog and Lachenal looked down Annapurna's sheer South Face they judged it unclimbable. Yet 20 years later, a British expedition led by Chris Bonnington, Don Whillans and Dougal Haston achieved the 'impossible'.

During the final leg to the summit, Halston experienced something of the acute awareness which Messner records. Going down the fixed ropes after reaching the peak, Haston suddenly went into a state of total euphoria as he explains very simply in Bonnington's book, *Annapurna, South Face*: 'Everything seemed beautiful. Inside and out.'

The euphoria was short-lived. When Bonnington, who was at the 6,128-metre (20,100ft) Camp III, heard news of the triumph, he wanted to pull everybody off the mountain immediately.

'There was,' he writes, 'a feeling of indefinable menace in the air. It was as if the whole mountain was ready to reject us, as if we were tiny foreign bodies or parasites clinging to a huge, living organism, whose automatic defensive mechanism had at last come to life.'

Whillans shared these feelings. When the two reached Camp III Whillans, a hard-bitten, taciturn Yorkshireman, told Bonnington:

'You want to get everyone off . . . as quickly as possible. It's falling apart. The whole place feels hostile somehow.'

Added Bonnington: 'The strange thing was that the lower one got down the mountain, the more dangerous it felt. . . .' The foreboding was justified. Only hours later, Ian Clough, descending with two other members, was buried under an avalanche and killed instantly.

These avalanches pose as great a threat to climbers as falls. Annapurna with its three other peaks — II, at 7,937 metres (26,041ft); III, at 7,557 metres (24,787ft); and IV, at 7,525 metres (24,688ft) — is particularly hazardous. Avalanches thunder down the slopes almost by the hour just before and during the monsoon season.

Women are as prone to the fascination of mountain climbing as men. Vera Watson and Alison Chadwick Onyszkiewicz fell 457 metres (1,500 feet) to their deaths at a height of around 7,315 metres (24,000 feet), and are among many brave women have met their deaths on the ice-cliffs of the Himalaya.

Since the 1970s, climbing techniques have changed. All these earlier expeditions — Bonnington's 1970 Expedition was on Annapurna for 10 weeks — employed what amounted to siege tactics: establishing a base camp and then a series of camps higher and higher up the mountainside from which to launch an assault on the summit.

The organisation and logistics involved in mounting such an expedition are impressive. Bonnington led a team of 10 world-class climbers to Annapurna — backed up by a small army of porters and Sherpa climbers. The expedition which set off from Pokhara on 22 March 1970 consisted of more than 160 people.

Sponsors had to be found, supplies shipped across the world and then across India and, in addition, Bonnington had to organise liaison and delivery of news film to Britain's Independent Television News service — it was the first expedition ever filmed for television — from his mountain fastness to Pokhara, on to Kathmandu and then London.

Nepal's Ministry of Tourism exercises strict control over the number of expeditions to the mountains which, after Everest, include Kanchenjunga, Lhotse, Makalu, Dhaulagiri, Manaslu, Annapurna and — since 1981 — Cho Oyu.

Permission has to be obtained years in advance. In 1996, for instance, the Ministry knew which expeditions would be climbing Everest in the year 2,000.

There's gold in them thar' hills. Each expedition pays the government a royalty fee. Each expedition must employ a Government liaison officer at base camp and only Nepalese can work as high-altitude guides and porters. The daily rates for such skills and labour remain ridiculously cheap. But the Ministry is clearly aware of the potential of mountain assaults in terms of media coverage and national pride: it keeps a kind of international league table of those national expeditions first to conquer a particular peak.

Of Nepal's 8,000-metre (26,240-foot) or more, summits conquered by 1974, Britain claimed Everest (1953) and Kanchenjunga

Above: Lake and ice field on the way to Gokyo.

(1955); France, Annapurna (1950) and Makalu (1955); Japan, Manaslu (1955), Makalu (S E Summit) (1970) and Kanchenjunga West (1973); Switzerland, Lhotse (1956) and Dhaulagiri (1960); and Spain, Annapurna South (1974).

The first major assault on Everest took place in 1924, when George Mallory and Andrew Irvine disappeared on the mountain close to the summit. Their bodies still lie somewhere beneath Sagarmatha's eternal snows. They took a route along the northeast ridge from Tibet. Mystery still surrounds their disappearance: some believe they might actually have reached the summit and in 1986 the American mountaineer Tom Holze led an expedition to ascertain the truth and launch a search for Mallory's body. Others followed their fatal — and difficult — route. It was only when Nepal opened its borders that the south face, the line taken by Hillary and Tenzing, was approachable. Standing atop the world, Hillary said, profanely: 'We've done the bitch.'

Since it was first surveyed as a climbing challenge by Mallory in 1921, the mountain has punished many of those who challenged

it, claiming more than 60 lives.

Thanks to a revolution in climbing technology it is now possible for much smaller groups than that of 1953 to reach the summit successfully. By 1996 more than 700 people, several of them women, had stood where Hilary and Tenzing first stood — one, a Japanese man called Yuichiro Miura, descending more than 6,000 feet from a height of about 26,000 feet on skis at a speed around 150 kilometres an hour. But this feat cost the lives of six Sherpas accompanying the expedition, who were swept away in an avalanche.

The first woman, Mrs Junko Tabai, also Japanese, conquered Everest on 16 May 1975. Remarkably, in 1995, 40 people reached the peak in a single day. But even after reaching the summit, the euphoria of looking out from the highest point on earth, an exultant moment, is no cause to relax.

The descent is as perilous as the climb upwards. Yasuo Kata, the first person to climb it in three different seasons — in spring, autumn and winter — experienced that exultation for the third time in 1982 but never lived to tell of it. He died in a storm making his way back down the mountain.

For years, it was thought no man could climb to such heights without oxygen but Austrian Peter Habeler and Italian Reinhold Messner achieved the feat in 1978. Two years later, Messner, unquestionably the greatest climber the world has known, repeated the feat in a solo climb, that time from Tibet along the north-east ridge which claimed Mallory and Irvine.

He first established a base camp in mid-July at 6,523 metres (21,400 feet). After weeks of acclimatisation, he set out in the darkness of the Tibetan sky at 0500 hours on 18 August 1980 — reaching the summit above a bank of black storm clouds at 1520 on 20 August, to spend 40 minutes there before returning. Despite the loss of his brother during an assault on Nanga Parbat in 1970 — one of his earliest Himalayan challenges — and most of his toes from frostbite, Messner is driven to climb, as if by some mystical compulsion, in lonely solitude.

During his solo assault on Everest, he experienced wind gusts of more than 80 kilometres an hour. He recalls reaching the summit.

'I sat there like a stone. I had spent every bit of strength to get there . . . I still do not know how I managed to achieve the summit. I only know that I couldn't have gone on any longer . . . I don't think I could handle it again. I was at my limit.'

Yet as long as Sagarmatha stands above the jet streams, so will there be people to challenge her.

Indeed, Messner in 1986 achieved his ambition to climb all 14 of the world's great mountains, including the third highest peak in the world, Kanchenjunga, on Nepal's border with Sikkim, which he saw — 'far to the east . . . protruding above a blanket of clouds, a majestic sight' — from the saddle of the North Col on Everest during the first day of his climb.

Leaving the shadows of the brave and foolish who still lie on Sagarmatha's slopes — including an English religious zealot without any mountain experience who fell to his death in the 1930s after leaving behind in his diary the epitaph: 'Off again. Gorgeous day.' — Messner would have travelled 125 kilometres eastward from Everest as the crow flies to stand atop 8,598-metre (28,208-foot) Kanchenjunga on Nepal's border with India's Sikkim State.

There, too, is a massif of giant peaks — 15 of them above 23,000 feet — and looking westward on a clear day, Nepal in all its diversity stretches out before you to infinity, as if it will never end, from the steamy Terai Plains through its midland mountains and valleys up to the 'Roof of the World'.

Too marvellous by far to be anything but a dream, the astonishing thing is that it exists. If it did not, however, be sure: nobody could ever have invented a country so fabulous. Indeed, alone beneath Kanchenjunga's mighty peak on a moonlit night, the mountain snows soft and luminous, the stars pin-sharp, Kipling might well have written:

> *Still the world is wonderous large —*
> *seven seas from marge to marge —*
> *and it holds a vast of various kind of man*
> *And the greatest wonders of this world*
> *are by nature here unfurled.*

Left: Sir Edmund Hillary. Opposite: Mount Everest, the highest point on earth.

Wildlife

Nepal has a splendid collection of rare and beautiful animals. You will find tropical giants like the elephant and rhinoceros, ancient crocodiles and alligators, the elusive snow leopard and the awesome tiger.

The Terai has the widest variety of wildlife. In the past, hunting was a popular sport in the royal game reserves. That, coupled with the demand for trophies of certain animals, severely denuded the animal population until they were protected by the government.

The royal Bengal tiger and the great Indian one-horned rhinoceros are among the endangered animals. Most of the rhinos live in Royal Chitwan National Park.

About 50 Asiatic elephants migrate from one wildlife reserve to the other, following ancient migratory routes. Today, much of the same land along the routes is covered with farms.

Other rare animals are the *arnua*, a powerful and aggressive water buffalo ensconced in the tiny island reserve of Kosi Tappu in southeast Nepal.

The *gahr*, a huge wild bovine growing to 1.8 metres (5 foot 7inches) tall, weighs almost a ton.

On the middle hills, wildlife is more elusive, owing to the density of human settlements. In some parts, the local people still hunt wild boar and pheasants.

There are frequent encounters with leopards, which have managed to survive well in the midlands, preying on livestock and pye-dogs. Some have even been sighted in the hills around Kathmandu.

In addition to the many wild animals, legendary ones also abound in Nepal — the Hindu mythological Garuda, the powerful bird mount of Vishnu; the Nagas, snake people, who inhabited Kathmandu when it was a lake; and the Cheppu, a creature so peculiar-looking that no one really knows what it looks like. But of all the legends, the one still fuelled by recent sightings, evidence, and rumours is that of the Yeti, known by many cultures and by myriad names: the Bhutanese and Tibetans call it the *yeh teh* (man of rocky places), *kang mi* (snow man) and *dzu teh* (cattle lifter). Although no one has actually seen the Yeti, large footprints found in the snow have defied classification. Unusual droppings, a tuft of hair and an ear-splitting shriek were other possible Yeti clues.

The famous Yeti scalp of Thangboche monastery was sent abroad for analysis, only to be diagnosed as the 200-year-old scalp of a Himalayan mountain goat.

You might hear that someone reportedly has seen a Yeti, but finding them in person is a challenge. The Yeti remains elusive, if only to suggest possibilities we may only imagine.

Wildlife refuges

For a very long time the Terai was an impenetrable wilderness, plagued with malaria, from which only the indigenous Tharu people had immunity.

It served as the perfect barrier against invasions from the south. Under the reign of the Ranas, the Terai received special protection against poaching, settlements, and wood-cutting.

During the winter months, the forests reverberated with the sound of gunshots, as the Ranas and their guests hunted tigers, elephants, deer and wild boar. Even so there was no real harm done to the wildlife population of the jungles.

In 1955, a massive malaria-eradication drive cleared the area for settlement and by 1960 had practically wiped out the disease. With foreign aid, large tracts of land were resettled and lowland hill groups began making a living from the fertile soil. In a few years, almost two-thirds of the forests had disappeared.

In 1962, the Royal Chitwan National Park was created to protect the dwindling numbers of rhinos in the region, and some 20,000 villagers who had made their homes there were resettled. Within the

Opposite: Blackbuck in Kathmandu's Royal Shukla Phanta Wildlife Reserve.

Above: 376 elephants were lined up to salute her when Queen Elizabeth II visited Nepal in 1961.
Opposite: Royal Bengal tigers are found in the Royal Chitwan National Park.
Following pages: Tourists ride Maharajah-style through Royal Chitwan National Park.

decade, more national parks were created to preserve the endangered habitat and its animals. Some other parks are the Royal Shukla Phanta Wildlife Reserve, Royal Bardia National Park and Kosi Tappu Wildlife Reserve.

The constant struggle between the pressure of human population and preserving dwindling numbers of wildlife continues. The Terai has proven the industrial and agricultural rice-bowl of Nepal; its fertile lands sustain the country's growing population.

Although there are still incidents of poaching and encroaching, the most effective use of the wildlife preserves is the efficient management of its resources and its animal population. During the harvest season, villagers are allowed to enter the lower reaches of the Royal Chitwan National Park to cut the tall elephant grasses that are used for thatch.

The future of the rich fauna of Nepal depends on efficient and creative management of the national parks. The Royal Chitwan National Park has leased lands to several tourist safari camps. Best known among the luxury lodges are Tiger Tops, Island Jungle Resort, Temple Tiger, Chitwan Jungle Lodge, Machan Wildlife Resort and Gaida Wildlife Camp.

These lodges offer comfortable living quarters; some have tented camps. Common activities are elephant-riding, canoeing and jungle walks. Food is excellent, with Nepalese, Chinese and Continental cuisine.

A cluster of lodges and guide services has sprung up on the outskirts of the park in the town of Sauraha. Accommodation is much cheaper than at the lodges. You can hire a guide, book an elephant ride or arrange for a dugout trip down the river.

If you venture into the park on foot, you must hire a guide: the jungle is fraught with danger and the animals are not tame. The dense jungles of Chitwan hide the animals well and you might miss sighting even a rhino if it is not pointed out to you. Royal Bardia National Park is the only other park with a safari camp. Tiger Tops Karnali Lodge is one of the most isolated safari experiences.

Bird Life

Nepal is rich in birdlife, being endowed with nearly 25 per cent of the world's bird species. In addition, the country's diversity of habitat and altitude, from the cultivated, lowland wetlands to the mixed forest and alpine peak regions, provides stunning backdrops and appropriate conditions for an unusual range of over 840 species of resident and migratory birds.

Nepal stands at the ornithological centre of Asia, where two diverse geographical regions meet and overlap — the Palaearctic region to the north and the Oriental region to the south. The country is thus an important stopping-off point for bird migrants; at different times of the year, it provides a temporary home for hundreds of different species on their journeys across the Himalaya and between east and west.

Among all the birds to be found in Nepal, only the spiny babbler is considered unique to the country. This shy, dark-olive-brown bird inhabits semi-cultivated scrubland. It is not always easy to see in the tangled thickets but it may be glimpsed scratching on the ground for small insects, or in awkward flight from one bush to another, or sitting atop a small tree singing its pleasant song or mimicking other birds.

The tropical lowlands

One of the best birding areas of Nepal is the Terai, the alluvial plains that form the country's breadbasket. Watered by mountain run-off, the Terai is extensively cultivated with rice and wheat. Despite the resulting disruptions to the habitat, mainly due to physical changes in the forest structure, any of nearly 600 lowland species of bird may be spotted here, especially along the Terai's watercourses and in its ponds and small lakes.

There are two important birdlife sanctuaries in the Terai — in the east with Kosi Tappu Wildlife Reserve, along the Kosi River to the extreme south-east, near Biratnagar; Shukla Phanta in the far south-west, near Mahendranagar and the lesser-known

Bardia Wildlife Reserve is also a good place to see western lowland varieties of bird, with 250 recorded species. Specials to be seen in Shukla Phanta are the swamp partridge, Eurasian lapwing, black-necked stork, spoonbill, brown fish owl, the blue-eared barbet and the great slaty woodpecker.

It is the Kosi River area that provides what is probably Nepal's best areas for bird-watching, however. More than 280 different species have been recorded in the Kosi Tappu reserve, and the area is particularly interesting during migration periods. Easily seen are a number of species of waders and shorebirds — terns, gulls, storks, snipes, waterfowl, gallinules, ibis, egrets, cranes, cormorants, ducks, as well as hawks and eagles — birds of prey common throughout Nepal. The lucky enthusiast might also spot the rarer black-necked stork or the purple heron. The mallard duck is uncommon, unlike the pintail, and the shoveler can be seen swimming in the Kosi River around March, its bill pointing down.

The rare vagrant falcated teal might be sighted, with its handsome green-and-bronze head and long nape of feathers, and the black and white cotton teal is common. The migratory greylag goose might be seen sitting on the banks of the river in February or March, a trans-Himalayan migrant bar-headed goose in November. Many snipe species are common, including pintail, wood and jack snipe.

The area around the Kosi Barrage, about 10 hours from Kathmandu by bus or one hour by flight, is reckoned to be the very best of the birding venues despite the threats posed by human encroachment. The lesser teal, tan-coloured and stretching its neck when alarmed, is common there, as is the Brahminy duck (ruddy shelduck), also a reddish tan, with a white wing patch. White-eyed and common pochard are to be found around all the Terai ponds in the spring, February-March, when many species are present in their hundreds.

The barrage area is an important resting

Above: The Indian Roller, seen very rarely in Nepal.

point for trans-Himalaya migrants, and the watershed environment of marshland, wooded valley, flood plain and reedbed supports a huge number of species. Particularly interesting birds in this area are the Bengal florican, swamp partridge and the red-necked falcon.

Common barrage area birds include the red-vented bulbul, red-whiskered bulbul, collared bush chat, large and little cormorants, garganey, Eurasian kestrel, grey-headed flycatcher, night heron, bronze-winged jacana, small pied king-fisher, white-breasted kingfisher, black-shouldered kite, dark kite, honey kite, red-wattle lapwing, spurred-wing lapwing, white-throated munia, paddyfield pipit, Hodgson tree pipit, spotted redshank, common sandpiper, brown shrike, grey shrike, black-headed shrike, white stork, black stork, open-billed stork, black-bellied tern, Indian river tern, little tern, whiskered tern, great thick-knees (great stone plover), Tickell's leaf warbler and several species of myna and parakeet.

Throughout the lowland areas, crested finch larks and chestnut-breasted bee-eaters can be seen. A more unusual sight is the Indian roller. In the south-east low-lands of the Churia and Shivalik hills, little spiderhunters and fairy bluebirds, minivets, pittas, leafbirds, forktails and cuckoo-shrikes might be sighted.

Situated between the two sanctuaries of Shukla Phanta and Kosi Tappu, along the southern border of Nepal in the central lowlands, are the Royal Chitwan National Park and the Parsa Wildlife Reserve. Royal Chitwan offers a number of unusual species, including the yellow-bellied prinia and the rufous-necked laughing thrush. Look out also for hornbills, ospreys, parakeets, kingfishers, crakes, wood pigeons, white-eyes, paradise flycatchers, sunbirds and bitterns, as well as the incongruous-looking great hornbill. More than 450 different species have been recorded in this park, making it an outstanding venue for bird-spotters.

The midlands
Midland Nepal, which includes the Kathmandu Valley, ranges upwards from cultivated terraces through scrub growth

and dense oak forests. Low cloud keeps the region perpetually damp, so many of the subtropical trees are covered in lichen and moss and surrounded by ferns, attractively frosted in winter. The distant hills rise like a fairytale backdrop beyond the shadowed valleys.

In the Kathmandu Valley, several rare birds might on occasion be seen, including the black-capped oriole, the emerald cuckoo, the blue-throated flycatcher, the pygmy blue flycatcher and the white-gorgetted flycatcher.

The most common birds in the midland areas are the black drongo, golden oriole, bush chat, partridge, black-capped sibia, mistle thrush, nuthatch, red-tailed munia and spot-winged black tit. In the forests on the hillsides, treecreepers can be sighted. The spiny babbler is at home there.

In the eastern Mai Valley, in Ilam district, are the rarer tailed wren babbler, black-spotted yellow titmouse, purple cochoa, blue-eared barbet and little spiderhunter. The red-headed babbler is typical in this area.

About 12 kilometres (7.5 miles) north of Kathmandu lies the Sheopari Wildlife Reserve, where common forest birds such as flycatchers, barbets, thrushes and eagles can be seen. In the Langtang National Park and on the Gosainkund and Langtang treks, also north of Kathmandu, high-altitude birds can be seen. One of the most important and rare birds of Nepal, the Ibisbill, breeds near the Kyanjin monastery in the Langtang Valley. To the south, in the montane forests of Phulchowki, at 2,758 metres (9,050 feet), look out for the cutia and the Mrs Gould's sunbird.

The Himalaya
The harsh character of the alpine environment in the peak region supports relatively little wildlife; nevertheless, more than 200 avian species appear there. An amazing 77 species have been recorded among the snow and ice of the extreme altitudes above the treeline at 4,267 metres (14,000 feet). The red-headed babbler ventures to surprising heights, and the yellow-billed chough, the grosbeak and the lammergeier (bearded vulture), ravens and eagles can be seen soaring in the skies. Look out for

the snowcock and the snow partridge, bar-headed goose, spotted nuthatch, buntings and vultures. Some of these birds reach heights of over 7,500 metres (24,600 feet). The Himalayan honey guide can sometimes be seen suspended upside-down on honey-combs hanging from rocky cliffs near high-altitude watersheds.

Sagarmatha National Park in the Khumbu region of Mount Everest offers spectacular scenery and fascinating bird-viewing of more than 130 species, including pheasants, snow partridges and Himalayan griffon vultures.

Trans-Himalayan zone
A few birds are true to this area, north of the Himalaya, in the near-arid districts of Dolpo, Manang and Mustang, where the drier climate favours some Tibetan species. These include the Tibetan snow finch, Tibetan serin and the Tibetan partridge. Also to be seen are the Eurasian griffon vulture, golden eagle and pied magpie.

The Danphe Monal Pheasant
Widely distributed in all Nepal's high mountain national parks is the Danphe (Impeyan) pheasant, the national bird of Nepal, celebrated in Nepalese folk songs and culture. The large, striking, electric-blue cock has a wirelike crest tipped with metallic green feathers, and metallic bronze wings and purple rump. Its display dances during mating are particularly colourful. The Danphe favours oak-rhododendron forests mixed with open glades, as well as hillsides with low grass cover. The birds live singly or in pairs, mainly on a diet of alpine plants, and can be seen digging around with strong bills in the alpine pastures. The Danphe is protected by Nepalese law but the bird's appeal to hunters has depleted its numbers.

Easily seen are the common quail and partridge. Look out for the Kalij pheasant, the Common Koklas pheasant and sand-grouse. The Himalayan Blood pheasant can be found near the snowline. The female Himalayan bustard quail is unusually brightly coloured compared with her drab partner; she takes the initiative during courtship, fighting with other females over desirable males — but not staying long with one partner even after he is won.

Much of Nepal's fabulous pheasant life has been painted by Timothy Greenwood, SWLA, the official artist and founder-member of the World Pheasant Association who, for more than two decades travelled extensively all over the world painting rare pheasants, including those of Nepal, Bhutan and Pakistan.

For Nepal, his exquisite bird, flower and animal paintings, seen in many exhibitions and some of which, in 1984, were reproduced in the English glossy magazine *Country Life*, have included the Himalayan Monal (Impeyan) *Lophophorus impeyanus;* the Himalayan Blood pheasant *Ithaginis cruentus cruentus;* the Common Koklass *Pucrasia macrolopha macrolopha;* the Cheer pheasant *Catreus wallichi;* the Nepal Kalij *Lophura leucomelana leucomelana;* the Satyr pheasant (Crimson-horned) Tragopan *satyra;* the Himalayan snowcock and the colourful Western tragopan.

With all Nepal's avifauna to choose from, it was pheasants which were selected to illustrate the dust cover of the third (1984) edition of *Birds of Nepal*, everyone's bird guide to the country.

Bird zonation
The Kali Gandaki River, running through central Nepal, effectively divides the country's birdlife into distinct eastern and western zones. Particular to the eastern side are birds such as the rufous-bellied shrike babbler, golden-breasted tit babbler, brown parrotbill and Blood pheasant. Particular to western areas are, for example, the spot-winged black tit, white-throated tit, mistle thrush and white-cheeked nuthatch.

Migration
A number of birds have been noted to use Nepal's rivers as 'signposts' on their migratory routes and, each season, hundreds of thousands of birds make a stopover. They come from the Central Asian highlands through the high Himalayan passes along the Arun, Kali Gandaki, Karnali and Mahakali rivers.

The demoiselle crane arrives in midland Nepal in October from its southward flight.

The wagtails arrive in September. Also seen arriving in the Kathmandu Valley are the Himalayan piedwood-pecker, pochard, teal and grebe.

The bar-headed goose, lammegeier, golden eagle, cranes and many other migrants can be seen at amazing heights on their trans-Himalaya journeys. Many are altitudinal migrants along the Himalayan foothill regions, moving northwards in the summer after wintering in India.

The most numerous regular winter migrants occur in the lower wetlands — ducks, geese, swallows, flycatchers, warblers, pipits and finches.

Above: The Himalayan Blood Pheasant.

Flora

Nepal is considered by some to have one of the richest national treasures of wild plants and flowers, with some 6,500 species of trees, shrubs and wild flowers identified.

The country's wide diversity of climates and altitudes ranges from the tropical, flat Terai, at up to 300 metres (1,000 feet), through the sub-tropical wooded mid hill valleys at 1,000-2,000 metres (3,300-6,600 feet); the lower temperate zone, at 1,700-2,700 metres (5,600-8,900 feet); the upper temperate zone, at 2,400-4,000 metres (7,900-13,100 feet); the sub-alpine zone, at 3,000-3,500 metres (9,900-11,500 feet) and the alpine zone, 4,000 metres (13,100 feet) to the snowline and trans-Himalayan arid zone. The rapid changes in altitude during many journeys in Nepal offer an astonishing range of vegetation species within very small areas; spectacular evolutions can be seen within as short a distance as just two kilometres (a mile).

The largest area of dense forest is in the Terai, and is predominated by the broad-leafed, semi-deciduous, hardwood sal tree *(shorea robusta)*, which dominates the landscape, rising to heights of 30 metres (100 feet). The wood is used for building houses, temples and bridges. The pillars and beams of the temples in Kathmandu stand testimony to its enduring quality. Other main trees in the forests of the Terai are the khair *(Acacia catechu)*, whose yellow flowers enliven the spring, and the sisso *(Dalbergia sissoo)*.

The forests are interspersed with grasslands and riverine ecosystems. Elephant grass grows to six metres tall and is used for building walls and thatching roofs. Acacia, rosewood and the silk cotton tree, which grow in deciduous moist forests; kapok-like material from the latter is used for stuffing mattresses and cushions.

In the sub-tropical wooded hills grow horse-chestnut and the chir pine, while the wild flowers include the luculia, the osbeckia and the St John's wort. In the Kathmandu Valley grow silky oak, eucalyptus and bottlebrush trees, among flowering cherry and stunning blue-mauve jacaranda, imported from South America along with bougainvillea, poinsettia and hibiscus.

In the lower temperate zone are found the evergreen oak, horse-chestnut, maple, walnut, blue pine, chir pine, poplar, alder, birch and larch — including the notable Larix potaminii.

The upper temperate zone is home to more oak forests, and wet forests of the national tree, rhododendron (laligurans), which grows interspersed with hemlock, birch and conifers to heights of 18 metres (60 feet). In March and April, the hills are ablaze with fiery-red rhododendron flowers. Blue pines also grow in these high forests, with spruce and firs, and in some parts of the east with yew and hemlock.

Eastwards of Jumla, the ground is carpeted with flowers in summer — edelweiss, forget-me-nots, corydalis, campanulas, roses, impatiens and anemones. Orchids of many varieties can be found in the cooler, mist-covered woodlands, which also foster geraniums, larkspur, poppies, saxifrage and sedums, as well as ferns among the damp, moss-covered trees.

In the sub-alpine zone, the vast forested areas have valuable spruce, fir, cypress, juniper and birch extending to the treeline at 4,270 metres (14,000 feet). Dwarf rhododendron, ephedra, cotoneaster, primula and saxifrage decorate the alpine region, but only true alpine vegetation — hardy conifers, scant grasses and robust wild flowers such as the stellara — can survive in areas above 4,000 metres (13,120 feet). Grassy pastures border the snowline, but beyond that only lichens thrive.

The Royal Chitwan National Park is outstanding in Nepal, and even in Asia, for its rich and diverse ecosystem — primeval forest, grasslands *(phanta)*, floodplains,

Opposite: Painting by Timothy Greenwood, of Himalayan Snow Cocks.

Above: In spring, the hills are ablaze with firery red rhododendron flowers.

rivers, marshes and lakes, supporting a wide spectrum of botanical and biological interest. Vine-draped trees, often decorated with pretty flowering parasites, form the roof canopy in the forested areas, over a deep-litter forest floor that conceals a wealth of insect and eco system.

The endemic flora zone is in the north-east region of the country, and hosts a fair number of indicator plants, such as gentian, primula (any of 67 species) and impatiens.

In eastern Nepal, magnolia (*magnolia campbelli*) are to be seen in abundance. The habitat there supports many endangered wild plants and the rich diversity of plants is partly a result of natural hybridisation in the past.

Flowers are important in the culture of Nepal. Women use red rhododendron blossoms to adorn their hair; a garland of marigold might be wrapped around a chignon. Individual blossoms are used as offerings to the gods, along with grain and vermilion.

Above and Opposite: Thick forests and flowering plants are found around the National Parks.

Kingdom of the Gods

The world's only Hindu kingdom, birthplace of the Lord Buddha, modern Nepal is ruled by a modern monarch, King Birendra Bir Bikram Shah Dev. The country is known as the 'Abode of the Gods', for not only was the Lord Buddha born there, but the most eminent of Hindu deities, Lord Shiva, together with his consort, Parvati, is believed to live among the world's greatest mountains. The north summit of sacred Gaurisankar, 7,144 metres (23,438 feet), represents Shiva, the south Parvati.

Gaurisankar is also sacred to Buddhists, especially to the Sherpa people of this region, who call it 'Jomo Tsheringma'.

Gaurisankar did not yield easily. As recently as 1979, an American and a Sherpa born in the mountain's shadow were the first to reach the summit and gaze upon this haven of the gods. Many other gods and goddesses make their home among the Himalaya: Sagarmatha atop Everest, and Annapurna, 'Goddess of Plenty', atop the 8,092-metre (26,545-foot) peak of Annapurna I, while Ganesh, the elephant-headed God, resides on top of 7,406-metre (24,298-foot) Ganesh Himal I.

All are living deities to most Nepalis, who worship their gods and goddesses in temples that pepper the land from end to end. More than 98 per cent of the people are Hindu or Buddhist. New deities are constantly discovered or created. The *Mahabharata* says that there are more than 33,000 Hindu deities. Other, later sources number 15 more than 30 million! At most times, the dividing line between the Buddhists, Tantrics and Hindus is thin enough to make them indivisible.

Hinduism, in fact, is an entire way of life. Cushioned against life's hardships by their philosophy, the seemingly happy-go-lucky Nepali has not evolved by chance but through a carefully developed acceptance of destiny. This sustains the people so well that, in the midst of dire poverty, the poorest often display the most amazing cheerfulness.

Hinduism seeks no converts, nor does it attempt to impose its tenets on non-Hindus. 'Live and let live' is the Hindu credo — and all living creatures are sacred. By the same standard, it abhors proselytism — the act of seeking converts to another faith. Evangelism is a criminal offence in Nepal, with stiff jail sentences for both preacher and listener.

Worshippers belong to six main sects: Vaishnavas, Shivas, Shaktas, Ganpatyas, Saurapatyas and Smrathas; the last worship all Hindu deities.

In Nepal, the Shiva cult is the most popular, above all in his most gentle manifestation as Pashupati, the shepherd, or literally 'Lord of the Animals'.

He is most often represented by the lingam, a stone symbol of his sexual organ. Most often, the lingam is set inside a representation of the female sex organ, yoni, of Parvati, Shiva's consort. One particular lingam in one of Kathmandu's oldest temples, at Pashupatinah, has five faces — one on each side and an amorphous one on top — and is said to be endowed with cosmic power.

It is well-guarded and only priests are allowed to enter the precinct where it is kept, perhaps because Pashupati is believed to be an alchemist who can turn base metal into gold.

Shivaists — worshippers of Shiva — regard the lingam as the fountain of life and the source of pleasure, according to Nepali religious authorities.

Swami Hariharananda Saraswati, in the 1941 treatise *Karaparati*, says, 'The symbol of the Supreme Being (*Purusha*), the formless, the changeless, the all-seeing eye, is the symbol of masculinity, the phallus or

Opposite: Intricate bronze-worked Buddhist Sambara in a Patan shop window depicts the union of male and female.

Above: Shrine of Dakshin Kali where male birds and small goats are sacrificed.

lingam.' He adds: 'The symbol of the power that is Nature, the source of all that exists, is the organ or the yoni.' Only under the shape of a lingam, could Shiva, the giver of seeds, be enveloped in the yoni and be manifested. 'Pleasure dwells in the sex organ,' writes Saraswati, 'in the cosmic lingam and yoni whose union is the essence of enjoyment. In the world also, all love, all lust, all desire is a search for enjoyment. . . . Divinity is the object of love because it is pure enjoyment. . . . The whole universe springs forth from enjoyment; pleasure is found at the root of everything.

'Perfect love itself is the transcendent joy of being.'

Hindus have many phallic symbols — one shaped like an egg, one that is a formless mass, one as an altar fire, one as an arrow and another as a light. The Shiva lingam is always represented in erect form.

Divided into three parts, the lowest part is square and concealed in the pedestal, the second is octagonal and set in the yoni, and the third is cylindrical and rises above the yoni.

The divine cow
Sacred to all Hindus is the domestic cow, also Nepal's national animal. It plays a significant role in the country's religious rites.

It is used to exorcise evil spirits and to turn an unlucky horoscope into one of good augury. Devout Hindus often touch a cow's tail in the belief that it will help them cross the river Vaitarani on their way to paradise.

As in India, these animals are left to wander freely in both town and country. *Mahabharata*, the great Hindu religious epic, avers that those who kill, eat or allow any cow to be slaughtered are condemned to hell.

When someone dies, families donate a cow to one of the Brahmans in the belief that the cow will reach their dead kin in heaven.

Shamanism
In the isolated communities of the Nepal Himalaya, the creed of the Shaman — spirit-possessed holy men — is still as strong as it was 15 centuries ago. In Shamanism, all illnesses are believed to

Above: Nepalese traditionally carry the bride to the temple for the wedding ceremony.

be caused by the wrath of gods or the mischievous soul of a dead ancestor.

Thus, spirits with names like 'Warrior King of the Black Crag' and 'Great Lord of the Soil God' and 'Fierce Red Spirit' are invoked from the shadows of eternity. These take hold of the Shaman and then exorcise evil and sickness from the patient.

Convulsive shaking during a ceremony known as *puja is* the key sign of possession. If the Shaman cannot find the lost soul of the patient, then the victim will die.

Minor illnesses, however, are less traumatic, for both patient and witch-doctor. Then the *jhankri* invokes a magic formula called *phukne*, and caresses away the pain of the affliction with a broom, while reciting sacred prayers, mantras.

Rituals

Superstition and religion are indivisible, and are deep-rooted, in Nepali society.

Never step over someone's feet or body when you can walk around them, and never offer 'polluted' food — food that you have tasted or bitten into.

In Nepal, the left hand is tainted and it is impolite to pass on things or offer something with the left hand. It is just as impolite to receive anything with the left hand. Always use the right hand — or both hands together. This will signify that you honour the offering and the recipient or donor.

Most Nepalis take off their shoes before they enter a house or a room, so avoid entering any house unless you wish to spend some time in it — for instance, to eat or to drink tea.

The cooking and eating areas must be especially respected. Never enter these when wearing shoes — and remember that the fireplace in any home is regarded as sacred. Most Nepalis squat cross-legged on the ground to eat, so take care not to stand in front of them because your feet will point directly at their food.

In the Terai, witch-doctors, *jhankri*, invoke the timeless arts of voodoo — beating drums and sacrificing black chickens to drive evil spirits out of the sick. In some places, the placenta of newborn babies is preserved in an earthen pot for a few days — a potent omen for good.

289

Above: Nepalese celebrate marriages during a special season. Clad in an elegant sari the bride sits amongst her relatives.

Astrologers cast horoscopes, and traditional taboos are still honoured. Some people will not eat garlic, onions and chives. Others refuse beef but will eat buffalo meat, which is not considered sacred — hence the many cafés serving 'buffburgers'. Rituals are particularly in evidence during births, marriages and funerals. Special ceremonies are held six days after birth, for the christening, the first rice-feeding, the first hair cutting, and the coming of age.

Six days after a child is born, the door of the house is opened and lamps are lit — inviting God to enter and write the child's destiny. Marriage is celebrated early in Nepal — an unborn child is sometimes pledged to another in an arranged marriage.

'The Enlightened One'

Lumbini, in the Terai of southern Nepal, is the birthplace of Siddhartha Gautama Buddha. It is as sacred to the world's 400 million Buddhists as Makkah (Mecca) is to the Muslims and Bethlehem to the Christians.

The Buddha was born in 540 BC in a garden, under a grove of cool, leafy trees. His mother, Maya Devi, had been on her way to her mother's home in Devadaha, when she went into labour and sought sanctuary in the garden. It was hot and humid and the grove of trees was welcome shade.

Son of King Suddhodhan, the Buddha wanted for nothing as he grew up at his palace home at Taulihawa, about 24 kilometres (15 miles) from Lumbini. When he played in the garden within the palace walls, his eyes often turned northward to the distant Himalayan peaks, then already an inspiration for the founder of what would become one of the world's major religious forces.

At the time of the Buddha's birth, there was great poverty and hardship among the people, but Siddhartha Gautama, sheltered by privilege, knew nothing of this.

He was 29 before he set foot outside the palace, persuading his charioteer to drive him around the nearby countryside. So overwrought was the prince by what he saw that he quit the palace and became an ascetic, wandering around the countryside, close to death most of the time from self-deprivation.

Finally, he abandoned his wandering way of life and became a recluse. He spent his days meditating on life until, under a pipal tree at Gaya near Benares, India, he evolved the philosophy which would sustain millions through the next 2,500 years. Out of this came his name — 'The Enlightened One' — the Buddha.

He reasoned that the way to enjoy life to the full was to reject extremes of pleasure or pain and follow an 'Eightfold Path' based on 'Four Noble Truths'. Mankind suffered, pronounced the Buddha, because of its attachment to people and possessions, in a world where nothing is perManint. Desire and suffering could be banished by an attachment to rightfulness. The individual, he theorized, was simply an illusion created by the chain of cause and effect, *karma*, trapped in the cycle of incarnation and re-incarnation. Nirvana, the highest point of pure thought, could only be attained by the extinction of self — and the abolition of *karma*.

The Buddha preached his doctrine for 45 years before attaining nirvana with his death at the age of 80. In the centuries that have followed the Buddha's death, sectarian differences have caused schisms in Buddhism, so that in India there is the Mayahana school of Buddhism and in Southeast Asia and Sri Lanka the Hinayana school. The latter more closely follows the Buddha's original teachings.

Another unique form of the faith is Tibetan Buddhism. It believes that the religion's leading figure, the Dalai Lama, is the reincarnation of his predecessor. In Nepal the predominant form of the faith is the Mayahana school, subtly interwoven with Tibetan and Tantric influence.

Tantra is a Sanskrit word for weaving. Tantrism literally reiterates the Buddhist thought — all things and actions are part of a living, constantly changing tapestry — but is opposed to meditation. Devotees express themselves in actual experience and direct action. One Tantric cult, the *shakti*, praises the female counterpart of a god. Some Tantric texts suggest all sin is removed through wine, flesh, fish, women and sexual congress — and some suggest that sex is not only the ultimate form of bliss and tranquillity but also wisdom.

At his coronation on 24 February 1975, King Birendra declared Nepal 'an international zone of peace' — in keeping with the first tenet of the Buddhist religion — and 10 years later, this zone had been endorsed by 75 of the world's nations.

Both the motif and the heart of this international zone is the Lumbini garden, which was visited in 1967 by U Thant, then secretary-general of the United Nations. Many Buddhist nations have built their own commemorative shrines to the 'Enlightened One' in Lumbini.

Treasury of Religious Art

Nepal is perhaps the world's greatest treasury of Buddhist and Hindu art, and most art in Nepal is of a religious nature. More than 2,500 years of the Hindu and Buddhist faith have given Nepal an unrivalled collection of religious architecture and art, from the simple Buddhist stupas to the ornate Hindu pagoda temples.

The Indian Emperor Ashoka was one of the earliest-known contributors to Nepal's artistic heritage. Not only did he construct stupas in Patan and Lumbini, and numerous monasteries, or *gompa*, but he also established trade, cultural and religious ties between the two areas.

Ashoka's priests probably originally brought their own Indian artists — wood and stone cutters, carvers, architects and painters. Eventually, a professional artist class developed in Nepal, with its own style.

The development of a wholly Nepali form of artistic expression seems to have begun between the fourth and seventh centuries AD. Five centuries later, Tibetan influences began to appear in the native art forms: Tantric and Lamaist themes filled with sinister and demoniac images such as Bhairav, the God of Terror.

In the 13th century, Chinese influences became apparent, but the admiration for each other's art proved mutual. The Nepali

architect Araniko was so highly venerated for his style that the mandarins of China invited him to Beijing to work for them.

The richest periods of Nepali expression were during the early Lichhavi dynasty, between the 4th and 9th centuries, and in the Malla epoch, from the 13th to the 18th centuries. These royal houses were great patrons of the arts, as the ruling house of Nepal is still. Many of the art treasures from these periods were destroyed, not only in the recurrent earthquakes but also by the Muslim invader Shams-ud-din Ilyas of Bengal, who swept with his armies through the Valley in the 14th century, and desecrated virtually every temple and piece of religious art in Patan, Kathmandu and Bhaktapur. But those that have survived are considered so priceless that, in 1970, Germany undertook to finance their renovation and preservation, and also to make an inventory of the major works, especially the temples.

It is said that there are more temples in Kathmandu than houses, but the same seems to hold true outside the Valley. And although much of this heritage from the Malla dynasty and that of other eras was destroyed in the great earthquakes of 1833, 1934, and 1988, an incomprehensible amount remains.

Students of religion, art or architecture need many months to absorb the wonders of Nepal.

The pagoda
Of the many architectural styles in Nepal, one of the most striking is the pagoda. The pagoda temple originated there and is said to have its origin in the practice of animal sacrifice.

One theory on the evolution of the pagoda argues that worshippers found it necessary to have an altar that was sheltered to keep the rain from extinguishing the fire. It was also necessary, however, to cut a hole in the roof in order to let out the smoke. To keep the rain from entering the hole, a second roof was added on top of the first.

Most pagodas stand on a square base, or plinth, of brick or wood, and have two to five roofs, each smaller than the one below. The uppermost roof is usually made of metal and gilded, as are frequently the lower ones. The buildings are richly adorned with carved pillars, struts, doors, and other woodwork.

Most decorative carvings are of various deities of all sizes and shapes, such as gods with many arms, or deified, humanized animals, often in erotic poses. The deity to whom the temple is dedicated is usually housed on the ground floor; the upper levels are more decorative than functional. Some art historians believe that the receding upper tiers are intended to represent the umbrellas that protect the deity from the elements. Above the main entrance is a semicircular tympanum, or *torana*, usually with the enshrined deity as the central figure.

The Nyatapola temple in Bhaktapur is considered the most impressive pagoda in the country.

The shikara
Although the shikara is of northern Indian, rather than Nepali, origin, many of Nepal's temples follow its architectural form: a simple square tower of bricks or stones and mortar, with a small room at the base that houses the god or goddess. Variations on *shikara* have pillars, balconies and surrounding interconnected towers, and may also house deities. The Krishna Mandir in Patan is an excellent example of a stone shikara, but the most interesting shikara in Nepal is the Mahabuddha, Temple of One Thousand Buddhas, also in Patan. This shikara is built with each brick containing an image of the Buddha.

The gompa
The *gompas* are another architectural form indigenous to Nepal and neighbouring Tibet, the Buddhist monasteries of the high mountains. Although they follow a fairly simple floor plan, all are delicately

Opposite: Black stone sculpture of Chatya, sitting in four different positions, outside the Buddhist temple in Patan.

Above: Colourful and detailed illustrations found outside Thyangboche Monastery.
Opposite: Newar artist at work on a Thangka, in the ancient town of Bhaktapur.

adorned and embellished. Many date back to the time of Ashoka.

The most striking example of this architecture in Nepal is the Thyangboche Monastery, at Khumbu, near Mount Everest. There are about 400 Buddhist monasteries in the Kathmandu Valley; those near the stupa at Bodhnath are open to visitors.

In more intricate style are the Hindu monasteries, 30 of which are located in the Valley. These serve as centres of Hindu study and learning. The most beautiful is probably the Pujahari Math in Bhadgaon.

The Buddhist stupa is the oldest and simplest of the Nepali art forms. On its base, usually a stepped pyramidal platform, is a solid hemispherical mound in white, adorned by a spire. The mound represents the universe, and the pairs of eyes on the four sides of the spire symbolize the four elements of earth, fire, air and water. The 13 steps between the dome and the spire represent the 13 degrees of knowledge needed to attain nirvana; the canopy that surmounts the top of the spire represents nirvana. Each stupa is usually ringed by

prayer wheels, each of which is given a twirl by devotees as they circle the shrine clockwise.

The oldest known stupas in Nepal are those erected by Ashoka in Patan, but the most famous are those of Swayambunath and Bodhnath.

Delicate workmanship

Most Nepali art is worked in stone, metal, wood or terracotta. Compared with other art forms, there is very little painting in the history of the country's art but the fine, filigree detail of Nepali sculptures in these four materials is very delicate. The earliest expression is Buddhist, from about the 3rd century BC. Its surviving examples are four stupas in Patan, Kathmandu, and the Ashoka pillar at Lumbini.

Nepali art reached a zenith in the Lichhavis dynasty. Working in stone, local artists learned all that they could from India's Gupta, Deccan and Pala schools of art. These they refined and presented in indigenous creations with distinctive Nepali features.

Above: Patan's 16th-century terracotta Mahabuddha Temple built by the scholar, Abhayraj and his descendants. Every brick carries the image of Buddha.

They also began to work various metals, producing intricately wrought bronzes of mythical and religious figures. Some of their 1,500-year-old works, exquisite in their detail and imagery, still survive in the Kathmandu Valley.

The metallic sculptures of Tara, Vajrapani, Maitreya, Umamaheshwara and the Buddha are among the most illustrious, for both their style and their antiquity.

More latter-day examples of Nepali metal-work exist in the hollow-cast statues of kings and queens, in the gilded sculpted doors, and in other artefacts of the art cities of Patan, Bhaktapur and Kathmandu. Tibetan bronzes are notable for the holes set in them for paper prayers, mantras, votive offerings of grain and precious stones, or for religious icons.

Dating some of these masterpieces defies the art historian. Inscribed with the images of a pantheon of gods, both Buddhist and Hindu, most are believed to be from the Pala or an earlier era. Even more detailed and expressive than stone and metal are the wood carvings which grace the buildings of Nepal, on struts, pillars, beams, doors, windows, cornices, brackets and lintels, inside and outside temples and private homes.

The ivory windows of the Royal Palace in Kathmandu's Durbar Square are a well-known example of this art form, but count-less others can be found in varying stages of repair and disrepair in the once-elegant Rana palaces and villas in Kathmandu.

On a walk through the back streets of Kathmandu's Old Town, you can find windows peeking through the tail of a peacock, others grotesquely circled by skulls, and a variety of suggestive and erotic motifs.

Developed from the 12th century as an integral part of Nepali traditional architec-ture, wood art has always been the purview of the Newaris.

The Newaris established a large vocabulary that included every component part and exact detail of traditional carving. These medieval texts have passed down through the generations and still serve as the instruc-tional handbooks for wood carvers.

The skill of the Newar craftsman is seen

in the absence of either nails or glue in his works. And the erotica that adorn the temples throughout the country leave no doubt about the vividness of their artistic imaginations. Given the Hindu philosophy that worships Shiva's lingam, the religious of old considered the sexual nature of such art and temple decoration profoundly significant.

Nepal's history of terracotta art goes back to the 3rd century BC, but in Kathmandu it reached its peak during the 16th and 18th centuries. Outstanding examples of friezes and mouldings decorate the buildings from this era in Kathmandu Valley and can also be found in the museums.

Notable are the bands of male and female figures, *nagbhands,* that stretch around some temples, depicting Hindu narratives and epics. The gateway to the Taleju temple in Hanuman Dhoka, Bhaktapur, and Patan's Mahabuddha and Maya Devi temples are outstanding examples of this art form. Pottery has been practised for over a thousand years in Nepal, and some fine examples survive. The pottery centre of Kathmandu Valley is Thimi, where potters make figurines, smoking pipes, lampstands and flowerpots.

Religious paintings

Most Nepali painting is of a religious nature and has existed since the ascendancy of the Lichhavi dynasty in the 4th century.

The earliest surviving specimens, however, in the form of illustrated manuscripts, date back only to the 11th century. These manuscripts were produced in Buddhist monasteries and, together with *thangka* — a style of painting that features favourite gods and lesser deities and are inevitably subdued in form and colour — represent the major style of painting in Nepal.

In recent years, the government has asked donor nations and Unesco to help in the restoration and preservation of Nepal's artworks.

It has been estimated that at least half of Kathmandu's most priceless works from the last 2,000 years have been lost in the 50 years since Nepal opened its borders to the rest of the world, much of it spirited away in a vacuum of control by ruthless middlemen and art dealers acting on behalf of wealthy art collectors and museums in the West, thus robbing Nepal of its art.

Of the country's 200 most valuable paintings — all more than a thousand years old — only three remain.

Above: Detail of a Buddhist religious painting, *thangka*, from the Tibetan *thang* for sacred writing and *ka* for record.

Tastes of Nepal

Basic fare

If you are eating out country-style in Nepal, remember that most of the country is rural. Don't expect too much in the way of culinary adventure. It is basically vegetarian.

Home cooking keeps to simple essentials. The staple is rice, *bhat,* soaked in a gravy of pulse, *dhal,* with vegetable side dishes. You can spice these meals up with some of the country's tangy herbs and chutneys.

This basic fare varies according to the region and available seasonal fruits and vegetables. Some particular forms of Tibetan and Sherpa food, for instance a gluey barley flour and potatoes, or rancid tea, salted with yak butter and churned Tibetan-style with globs of grease floating on the surface, might be hard for the first-time visitor to swallow. The national drink is *chiya,* tea brewed with milk, sugar, and sometimes spices. It is served in glasses, scalding hot.

During festivals the standard vegetarian diet is relieved with dishes of chicken and goat meat. Arrange your trip to coincide with a festival, when the communities join hands to serve a greater variety of food.

Outside Kathmandu, travellers on day outings should carry their own food, either snacks from the Annapurna or Nanglo bakeries, or fresh fruit for a picnic. More cosmopolitan menus are available in Kathmandu.

The metropolitan Nepalis have acquired the culinary taste of their Indian neighbours so, in the capital, you can expect to enjoy a wide range of curries.

If you have never been to India, you should try Indian yoghurt, *lassi,* either salted or sweet, and confections like halva and Indian ice cream, *kulfi.*

Tea served in the lowland and midland regions is sweet and stimulating, but whatever you do, wherever you go, avoid drinking unboiled water. Nepal's Star and Golden Eagle lager beers are excellent and there is a stronger, mountain brew — the Nepali equivalent of kill-me-quick — *chhang,* made from fermented barley, maize, rye or millet. *Arak* (potato alcohol) and *rakshi* (wheat or rice alcohol) also have their adherents.

The local brewers also produce strong spirits — whisky, rum, and gin — but there is no wine industry. Imported beers, spirits and wines are available in most major tourist centres — at a price.

Opposite: Vendor selling fresh fruits and vegetables in Bhaktapur. Right: Some restaurants offer traditional floor seating.

Top: Crocodiles basking in the sun on river banks are a common sight in the tropical jungles of Nepal. Above: Thundering rivers cascading down from the Himalaya are a rafter's delight.

Sports clubs

Jungle Safari

While the high Himalaya makes up Nepal's northern region, the southern lowland, known as the Terai, is covered with dense tropical jungles teeming with diverse wildlife and exotic birds. There, in some of the world's most exciting safari destinations, you will be able to go deep into the jungle on an elephant's back or in a four-wheel drive vehicle to view wild animals in their natural habitat. Other thrills available to the visitor are canoe rides on the jungle rivers, nature walks, bird-watching excursions, and village tours.

Among the 14 national parks and wildlife reserves in the Kingdom, the Royal Chitwan National Park (932 sq km) is the most popular safari destination. More than 43 species of animals are found in Chitwan. The endangered one-horned rhino, Royal Bengal tiger, Gharial crocodile, four-horned antelope, striped hyena, and the Gangetic dolphin are the main attractions there. The best part is that it is close to Kathmandu and easily accessible, only 165 km (103 miles) overland, and Bharatpur airport, adjoining the park, is a mere 25-minute flight away (there are daily flights from Kathmandu). Many adventurers also choose to go down by raft. However you go, a jungle safari is an experience you will remember for a long time.

Rafting and Kayaking

Nepal has earned a reputation as one of the best destinations in the world for white water rafting. Nepal's thundering waters, coming from the glaciers of the mighty Himalaya, provide not only unmatched thrills for rafting but also the opportunity of immersing oneself in the landscape. A rafting trip will be a never-to-be-forgotten highlight of your stay in the country.

Rivers are graded on a scale of one to six, with one being a swimming pool and six a one-way ticket to your Maker. Four is considered to be quite challenging, without being excessively dangerous to the novice rafter. Five requires some previous river experience. Some of the popular rafting trips are: The Trisuli River (grade 3+) one of the favorites of Nepal's raftable rivers. Due to its proximity to Kathmandu and its easy road access, most rafting companies offer trips on the Trisuli. For first-time rafters it offers plenty of excitement. Many choose to incorporate a ride down the Trisuli with either a trip to Pokhara or to the Royal Chitwan National Park.

The Kali Gandaki (4 – 4+) winds through remote canyons and deep gorges for five days of intense rapids among gorgeous wilderness and ·mountain views. The run flows 120 km and its challenges are continuous. Trips on the Kali Gandaki begin and end in Pokhara and offer an exciting alternative to the Trisuli.

The Bhote Kosi (4 – 5) is worth special mention. It is a two-day run of pure adrenaline located only three hours from Kathmandu. Twenty-six kilometres (16 miles) of continuous white water soaks rafters as they shoot through a veritable maze of canyons and boulders. Little more than a swimsuit is needed for this one. The raging Marshyangdi (4 – 5) is a relative newcomer in this group. The Marshyangdi run is four days of uninterrupted white water. Flowing through the gorges of the Annapurnas, it offers 52 km (32 miles) of boiling foam between towering peaks. Trips on the Marshyangdi start from Pokhara.

The Karnali River (4 – 5) in the far west is the longest and largest river in Nepal. To arrive at its banks requires a two-day trek from Suikhet in the Terai. The next 90 km (56 miles) are spent flying through spectacular landscapes and narrow gorges and down some of the most challenging rapids in the world. For the remaining 90 km (56 miles), the scenery and wildlife are the main attraction, as is the abundance of fish. During most of this trip the wilderness is unspoiled by human habitation.

The Sun Kosi (4 – 5) is Nepal's second offering for expedition rafting. With a put-in only three hours from Kathmandu it is more easily accessible than the Karnali while nevertheless offering an incredible stretch of exhilarating white water. The run is 270 km (168 miles) and requires 8-10 days to complete with road access only at the beginning and end. On the third day rapids reach the upper 4 classifications and the remainder of the trip is consistently intense — the white water stays white until the very end.

Mountain flight

Few other experiences come close to matching the feeling of going on a mountain flight to encounter the tallest mountains of this earth. No wonder mountain fly-bys have become a popular tourist attraction in Nepal. Four airlines offer regular forays into the snow-capped peaks of the Himalaya.

Mountain flights appeal to all types of traveller. For those restricted by time or other considerations from going trekking, these flights offer a panoramic view of the Himalaya in just one hour. Even those visitors who like the rigours of a trek still don't miss the opportunity to "conquer" the mountains in one fell swoop.

Travellers take off from Kathmandu in the early morning for an hour's-worth of spectacular mountain scenery. As the aircraft lifts up and heads toward the east, passengers don't have to wait long to find out what's in store for them. There they are: the mountains, forbidding and majestic, as they have been since time began.

First, to their far left, visitors see Gosaithan — also called Shisha Pangma — standing at the majestic height of 8,013 metres (26,290 feet). Immediately to the right of Gosaithan there appears Dorje Lakpa 6,966 metres (22,854 feet), a mountain that looks like a number 8 lying down and covered with snow. To the right of Dorje Lakpa is Phurbi-Ghyachu, which looms over the Kathmandu Valley.

As the plane moves along the mountains come closer and closer. Next in vision is Choba-Bhamare, the smallest of the lot at a 'mere' 5,933 metres (19,465 feet) but singularly stubborn as it has never been climbed. Then appears the mountain that is not only prominent in sight but also in spirituality: Gauri-Shanker. Lord Shiva and his consort, Gauri, are said to protect this mountain. At the proud height of 7,134 metres (23,405 feet), its summit resisted all attempts to climb it until 1979. Gauri-Shanker is sharp and very conspicuous during the mountain flight.

As the plane moves towards the land of the rising sun, the eastern Himalaya, a succession of glorious mountains follow. Melungtse, a plateau-like mountain, stretches up to 7,180 metres (23,557 feet). Chugimago at 6,297 metres (20,659 feet) is still a virgin, waiting to be conquered. At 6,956 metres (22,821 feet), Numbur mountain resembles a breast, the maternal source in the sky providing pure milk to the Sherpas of the Solukhumbu. Next is Karyolung, an intensely white mountain that, at 6,511 metres (21,361 feet), gleams with the rising sun. Cho-Oyu is the eighth highest mountain in the world, reaching up to 8,153 metres (26,750 feet); it appears stunningly beautiful from the aircraft.

Next on the menu is Gyachungkang 7,952 metres (26,089 feet), considered extremely difficult climb. To the right of Gyachungkang is Pumori 7,855 metres (25,771 feet), which means West Peak, signifying its direction from Everest. Finally, there's Everest itself 8,848 metres (29,028 feet), known as Sagarmatha by the Nepalese and Chomolungma by the Tibetans. Much has been written about Everest, but nothing can quite prepare you for the moment when you actually witness it face to face during a mountain flight. Yet even while it looms in front of one's eyes it remains an enigma, this highest spot on earth.

Hot Air Ballooning

To look up into the sky and see the towers of the Himalaya is awe-inspiring and certainly a valid and popular reason to visit to Nepal. To walk in those mountains is more wonderful still. But to glide silently among them: this is perhaps the most thrilling of all. The adventure of hot air ballooning is now available in Kathmandu.

The principles governing hot air balloons are very simple. Propane gas is fired into the balloon (or envelope as it is called) which heats the air and causes it to rise.

Above: A helicopter hovers in front of Mount Ama Dablam in the Everest region.

Once the balloon fills with enough hot air it takes to the skies. From then on it is the wind which decides where the balloon goes. Altitude is controlled by adding more or less hot air to the envelope and, in this way, air currents can be ridden to reach a desired destination.

Usually flights begin shortly after dawn, when winds are their calmest. Once the balloon is full and all systems double checked, the lines are let loose and the passengers' basket is carried up over the morning fog and into the sun-lit skies. The balloon will float at about 1,200 to 1,500 metres (3,937-4,921 feet) above the Valley, which will bring passengers close to 3,000 metres (9,842 feet). From this altitude the entire Himalayan range will be in sight: 360 degrees of visibility is what the balloon affords, as well as fantastic downward views of the Kathmandu Valley itself.

After 15 minutes or so at this altitude, enough time for people to take their photos and persuade their jaws to close again, the balloon will descend for a gentle flight over the sights of the Kathmandu Valley. By the time the basket sets down again,

roughly one hour after take-off, the balloonists will have experienced Kathmandu and the mighty Himalaya from an entirely new perspective.

Mountain Biking

Mountain biking is a fast-growing and practical way to see rural Nepal. The villages are quaint and you will see the Nepalese people as they are. You can ride through rice fields, bike to the Terai towns or test your mountain biking skills by travelling to Mount Mera with your bike. The mountain biking possibilities are virtually endless in Nepal for there are many mountain mud tracks that offer a paradise for the action biker.

Nightlife

It's evening, and you are just back from a sightseeing tour or a delightful shopping binge. So what do you do? Go back to your hotel room? No, Kathmandu is not going to let you off so easily. There are plenty of wonderful places to dine, and a range of food available to suit every taste. But for the night owl there are other attractions, too.

Casinos

Kathmandu offers visitors an array of action-packed casinos where you can enjoy 24 hours of fun and games. There are four casinos in Kathmandu, all located in the premises of the city's top hotels, which offer poker, flush, baccarat, roulette, pontoon, blackjack, as well as card games and slot machines. All the games are played with 'chips' which can be purchased with US dollars or Indian rupees.

Getting there is no problem. You can hop on the hourly casino bus at one of the city's major hotels for free transport from 8 to 11pm. Check with the hotel reception desk for pick-up times. The bus also returns customers to their hotels every hour from 11pm to 3am, again free of charge.

Casino Anna is located at Hotel De L'Annapuna on Durbar Marg, Kathmandu's most fashionable address. Casino Everest is at The Everest Hotel, New Baneswar, a fast-rising ritzy neighbourhood on the highway to the airport. Casino Nepal, Kathmandu's oldest casino and a legend in its own time, is located at the Soaltee Holiday Inn Crowne Plaza, Tahachal, on the western side of town. Casino Royale is housed in the enchanting old palace wing of the Hotel Yak & Yeti on posh Durbar Marg.

Culture

Cultural programmes offer a fascinating glimpse of Nepal's diverse ethnic and cultural traditions. There are several places in Kathmandu where folk dances and musical performances are held every evening. Nepalese folk dances are an expression of joy. They celebrate the changing of the seasons or youthful romances. Evening time in rural Nepal is often filled with the sound of village song festivals and spontaneous gatherings.

If you want to enjoy Nepalese folk dances, but don't feel like going on a mountain trek, you can take in one of the cultural programmes in Kathmandu for a lively evening of cultural enlightenment. Performances are given nightly by the Everest Cultural Society at the Hotel De L'Annapurna, Durbar Marg, and the New Himalchuli Cultural Group. Call for information and performance schedules. Your hotel can also arrange tickets and transportation. Enjoy the evening.

Movies

There are several cinema halls in Kathmandu where you can sit back and experience the celluloid offerings of Kathmandu and Bombay. Nepalese films and Hindi movies from India are the most popular cinematic fare around there. You can know it's a cinema hall by the huge colourful posters outside of the hero thrashing the villain. Tickets are not very expensive (Rs 2 to 21.25), and there are three shows every day: 11.30am, 2:30pm and 5:30pm (four shows on Saturday). Call to find out what's showing.

Above: Hot air ballooning is the latest adventure sport in Nepal.

PART FOUR: BUSINESS NEPAL

The Economy

Nepal is a sovereign independent kingdom, landlocked and bounded to the north by the Tibetan Autonomous Region of the People's Republic of China, and to the east, south and west by India. The country is 885 kilometres (553 miles) from east to west and its breadth varies from 145 to 241 kilometres (90 to 150 miles) from north to south. Its total area is 147,181 square kilometres (56,827 square miles).

The major thrust of the economic policies introduced with the adoption of the new Constitution in 1990 was a liberal, open-door policy favouring increased private-sector participation in trade, investment and tourism and related commercial activities.

Infrastructure

The country is divided into five development regions comprising 14 zones and 75 districts. Road access is limited; roads are expensive to build, particularly in terrain such as characterises Nepal, and some that have been built have not been able to withstand the weather, particularly the monsoon. Roads do continue to be extended, however, ever further into rural areas.

Rural electrification is scanty, and the service is anyway too expensive for most Nepalis, especially compared with fuelwood, which is apparently "free".

The telephone system is spreading and, more efficient than it once was, now serves a good segment of the population.

Agriculture

The economy is mainly agricultural. Ninety per cent of the population lives in rural areas and more than 81 per cent of the labour force is employed in the agricultural sector, which contributes more than 50 per cent (including forestry, hunting and fishing) of the gross domestic product (GDP).

The inhospitable terrain — remote valleys and high mountains — means that output is low and mainly at subsistence level. Even then, large areas of the country cannot produce enough food to feed their sections of the population. There is only a modest production of cash crops, the main ones being rice, wheat, maize, barley, millet, potatoes, sugarcane, tobacco, cardamom, fruits and oil seeds.

Irrigation is vital, to allow a second crop during the dry season, but government efforts in this regard have not really trickled down effectively to the small farmer.

The use of fuelwood for most energy needs has contributed extensively to deforestation, which in turn has led to soil erosion and depleted land productivity. Silt carried by rivers to the Bay of Bengal has led to flooding.

Industry and trade

Nepal has few natural resources and consequently little industry, although there is a large pool of available labour. Sixty per cent of industrial output comes from traditional cottage industries and 40 per cent from modern industries. The latter include Tibetan carpets. Though made largely from imported wool, Tibetan carpets provide a labour-intensive industry that now earns about 50 per cent of Nepal's foreign exchange, producing more than 1.5 million square metres of carpet and employing more than 300,000 people. It is almost wholly based in Kathmandu Valley, as is the ready-made garments industry, which is also a significant export industry. Bricks and tiles are also made.

Industries that have been developed are aimed more at import substitution than at exports, but the huge resources of India to the south and the vast range of products it supplies not only drain foreign exchange but have made it difficult for local industries to become established and profitable. The long-term aim is to establish industries in Nepal which can export goods to northern India, and the government is trying to woo foreign investors for this, but at present the country has a large foreign exchange deficit.

Corruption and smuggling are rife in trade, which is dominated by India, with goods reportedly moving between India and Nepal in a circle which allows profits to be skimmed off at each juncture. A large segment of the business concerns in Nepal are Indian-owned.

Mining

Mica is mined to the east of Kathmandu, and there are small deposits of cobalt, copper, iron ore and lignite.

Tourism

Tourism is an important source of foreign exchange, with nearly 400,000 tourists per year visiting Nepal. Receipts from tourism amount to nearly 16 per cent of foreign exchange earnings at approximately US$12 million but a significant proportion of this goes out of the country to pay for imports to meet tourists' needs.

Energy

Energy is derived mainly from traditional sources, mainly wood, with mineral fuel and lubricants being imported. Use of fuelwood and resulting deforestation has become a major problem.

The country has one of the world's highest potential for hydro-power. The country's rivers are exploited for hydroelectric power, but this is still not enough. Nepal still needs to "import" electricity from India. The inhospitable terrain makes the development of hydroelectricity difficult as a realistically cheap alternative to fuelwood for domestic use. Each dam-site requires an expensive road network to connect the project. The Government has encouraged many joint ventures in the mini- and small-hydro project; some are under construction. Several private sector power projects are due for completion by year 2002/2003.

Five-Year Plan

The Ninth Five-Year Plan was launched in 1997, under which agro-based industries would be the main feature of support by the Government. Besides agriculture; forestry, livestock, fish farm, sericulture and fruit plantation get soft and easy loans. Human resource development is also an important area that will receive substantial inputs. Joint venture colleges for medicine and management are encouraged. The promotion of joint ventures in the banking sector, finance companies, aviation and tourism are top priorities. Technical and finance resources are actively sought from multinational organisations that are willing to invest in the country. Nepal has signed the M.I.T.I.G. recognised by the W.T.O. to protect the interest of foreign investors from nationalisation. Repatriation of earnings in foreign exchange is also guaranteed.

The Government started a privatisation drive in 1992 and is pursuing its policy of disinvestment of loss-making industries in the public sector. The Finance Ministry has a high level Privatization Committee that decides on the performance of industries that need to be privatized. There are proposals in the near future to privatize the Nepal Tea Development Corporation, Himal Cement, Udayapur Cement, Hetauda Cement, Royal Nepal Airline Corporation, the National Transport Corporation, Rastriya Banijya Bank, Nepal Orind & Magmesite and the Janakpur Cigarette Factory.

Nepal is one of the world's poorest countries, still struggling to overcome the legacy of its former feudal lifestyle and, in recent times, has relied on international aid to survive. The country comes to the end in the year 2000 of a 15-year Basic Needs Programme launched in 1985, one of whose aims was to double agricultural production by the end of the century. Under this programme development of agro based industries has flourished. Vegetable seed farms, poultry and fish farming have seen a big growth. The Government will continue to increase its support to this sector. Its poorly performing public sector which has drained the national resources will be gradually privatized. A vigorous decentralised administrative policy is being persued.

Education

Nepal has 22,455 primary schools — one close to most villages, 5,407 lower secondary schools, 2,886 secondary schools and four universities; Tribhuvan, Mahendra Sanskrit, Kathmandu and Eastern.

Primary education begins at the age of six and is free up to secondary level schooling. Secondary education, from age 11, lasts another five years. Officially, educational enrolment is high, at more than 70 per cent, but only about a third of this number actually attends or completes primary schooling.

Secondary education enrolment is little over a third, and only just over 10 per cent of boys and three per cent of girls completes secondary school. Illiteracy remains at more than 55 per cent.

Population

Population growth is frighteningly high, doubling every 27 years through the addition of half a million people a year at the rate of 2.4 per cent, and poverty is a major problem, particularly in the midland hills region but also spreading to the lowlands as a result of the increasing cultivation of the Terai. Nepal's population is now estimated to stand at a little over 21 million, nearly a million of them in the capital, Kathmandu.

Overpopulation has caused a high degree of environmental damage in Nepal's fragile ecology, particularly through deforestation and the over-intensive use of land exploited to unsustainable levels.

Forested areas were "nationalised" by the Nepal government in the 1950s. This programme had a deleterious effect, with the local communities who had formerly sustained the forests concerned only to exploit them. These are slowly being handed over to communities and organisations.

Moves towards land reform have proved largely ineffectual, with fewer than 20 per cent of the population still owning more than 60 per cent of arable land. Sizes of smallholdings have continued to fall, the average being only half a hectare in the midland hilly region and not much more than one hectare in the Terai. Many people remain tenant farmers and there is significant unemployment.

The gap between rich and poor in both urban and rural areas is extreme, and the Government is hard pressed to bring development to the grassroots.

Government family planning efforts are not very effective, and the isolated nature of many villages and hamlets makes education and services difficult to administer. Tradition places high value on children, especially illiterate farming communities, the more so as infant and child mortality is high. More than two-fifths of all children are undernourished.

The status of women remains low and programmes to counter this have had limited success. Women provide nearly 60 per cent of all agricultural labour in Nepal.

Foreign aid

Foreign aid to Nepal is high, and falls into three basic categories:

(i) bilateral and multilateral aid, with foreign governments funding infrastructural development projects and so-called Integrated Rural Development Projects. This kind of aid comes mostly from Japan, USA, Germany, Australia, Holland, Britain, France, China and India.

(ii) projects co-ordinated by non-governmental organisations (NGOs);

(iii) loans provided through the World Bank, the International Monetary Fund, the Asian Development Bank and various United Nations agencies, for major projects, including irrigation and hydroelectric energy projects.

Foreign aid accounts for 50% of the Nepali budget, which has caused problems of aid dependency.

The philosophy of foreign aid is also deeply questioned by some Nepalis, as is the appropriateness of some of the projects funded. Too often, it seems, the only ones to benefit have been the foreign companies involved in construction and the supply of materials for huge programmes, and their Nepali counterparts.

Most of the projects that have seen some benefit for the local people have been those that are less ambitious and more locally appropriate.

Bureaucracy

The stifling bureaucracy that hinders much third world development is no less in evidence in Nepal. For most would-be entrepreneurs, getting licences is a laborious business, and corruption has taken its toll. It is only possible to negotiate endless bureaucratic details with an appropiate sum of money. Low salaries and a tendency to promote the connected few contribute to a never-ending spiral in this regard.

Demographic and Social Indicators

Population: 21 million (1998)
Population growth rate: 2.08%
Life expectancy at birth: Males — 56.5 years; females 57 years (1996)

Physicians to population: 1 per 16,110 persons
Hospital beds/population: 1 per 3,894 persons
Infant mortality rate: 84 per 1,000 live births
Literacy rate: Males – 39.6%; Females – 54.5% (1991)
Radio: Radio Nepal – with five regional stations. FM transmission in Kathmandu Valley. Ninety per cent of the population has access to medium wave transmission.
Television: 40% of the population has access to Nepal Television.
Newspapers: Daily 148; bi-weekly 6; weekly 761, bi-monthly 134; monthly 489 (1997)

Economic indicators

Gross Domestic Product: US$ 4,232 million (1995)
Per capita GNP: US$ 200 (1996)
Foreign exchange reserve: US$814.53 million (1997)
Major imports: Petroleum products, chemicals and drugs, food and live animals, machinery and transport equipment.
Total imports: US$ 1,351.53 million (1996)
Major exports: Woollen carpets, ready-made garments, pulses, handicrafts, hides and skins, cardamom, jute, tea.
Total exports: US$ 349.67 million (1996) Trade balance: US$ 1,001.86 million deficit (1996)
Major trading partners:
Export: (in % of total trade 1994/95) Germany 37%; USA 29%; India 19%; Switzerland 3%; Italy 2%; United Kingdom 2%; Belgium 2%.
Import: India 32%; Hong Kong 17%; Singapore 17%; Japan 5%; China 4%; Germany 3%; New Zealand 2%.
Staple food: Rice, wheat, maize, potatoes
Total arable land: 25%
Major cash crops: Jute, sugar cane, tobacco, oil seeds
Major industries: Rice and flour mills, cigarettes, sugar, cement, beverages, jute, handicrafts, carpets, ready-made garments, tourism.
Distribution of manufacturing value added:
Textiles and clothing 39%
Food, beverages and tobacco 31%
Chemicals 4%
Machinery, transport equipment 1%
Others (including tourism) 25%
Roads: 11,456 km, of which 3,613 km are tarred. (1997)
Railway: 52 km
Airports: Total 44 (international 1; domestic 43)
Helipads: Approximately 97 .
Electricity: Total generating capacity: 83,000 MW
Total installed capacity: 261,538 MW
Tourist arrivals: 390,000, of whom 118,032 were from India.

PART FIVE: FACTS AT YOUR FINGERTIPS

Nepal is a sovereign independent kingdom situated between 80° 4' and 88° 12' east longitude, and 26° 22' and 30° 27' north latitude. It is bounded to the north by the Tibetan Autonomous Region of the People's Republic of China, and to the east, south and west by India. The country is 885 kilometres (553 miles) from east to west and its breadth varies from 145 to 241 kilometres (90 to 150 miles) from north to south. Its total area is 147,181 square kilometres (56,827 square miles).

Nepal can be divided into three main geographical regions:
(a) Terai region — the southern lowland Terai covers 17 per cent of Nepal;
(b) hilly Midland region — 68 per cent of the country;
(c) Himalayan region — the altitude here ranges from 4,900 metres to 8,850 metres (16,000 feet to 29,000 feet) and includes eight of the highest 14 summits in the world. The Himalaya covers 15 per cent of the total land area of Nepal.

Visa and immigration requirements
Passports are required except for nationals of India and Nepal holding proof of nationality and coming from India.

Visas are required except for nationals of India or Nepal. Visas obtained from Nepalese embassies abroad are valid for up to 60 days; visas issued upon arrival are valid for a maximum of 30 days. Double and multiple entry visas can also be obtained. Visa extensions are from the Central Immigration Office and up to a total of 120 days. After 30 days, a fee of one US dollar per day is levied for extensions.

All tourist visas are valid for Kathmandu Valley, Pokhara and Chitwan.

Visa fees:
a) Single entry: US$30 for up to 60 days.
b) Double re-entry: US$40.
c) Multiple re-entry: US$60.

Tourists are required to pay in dollars at the airport and may also be required to do so at border posts; cash dollars should therefore be carried for this purpose. One passport-sized photo will also be required.

Tourists are required to complete disembarkation and embarkation cards upon arrival and departure.

Your visa is valid for Kathmandu Valley, Pokhara Valley, Royal Chitwan National Park and motorable roads throughout the country except restricted areas.

For trekking, a separate permit must be acquired from the Immigration Office in Kathmandu, or in Pokhara, and can only be extended at these two places. (See Trekking, below)

It is always advisable to obtain any kind of visa in advance, as dealing with immigration usually involves time-consuming long waits, and possibly having to return later to collect visas and permits.

Health requirements
Nepal does not require any specific immunisations for visitors. However, immunisation against cholera, meningitis, tetanus, diphtheria, typhoid, malaria and hepatitis should be considered. (See below and page 33 for more details on health.) Seek the advice of your doctor before travelling.

International flights
Tribhuvan International Airport is the major airport, situated near Kathmandu. This is served by Royal Nepal Airlines and a number of other international carriers, with direct flights to many parts of the world.

An Airport Taxi Service is available to shuttle passengers between the airport and downtown Kathmandu. Private or metered taxis are also available, at between Rs150-200. Private taxis may charge slightly more than the ordinary taxi.

Departure tax
International departures: Passengers departing from Tribhuvan Airport (Kathmandu) must pay a departure tax of Rs 600. Domestic departures Rs 100.

Entry points
Entry points all by land route except Kathmandu.
i.   Tribhuvan International Airport, Kathmandu.
ii.   Karkavita, Jhapa (eastern Nepal).
iii. Birganj, Parsa (central Nepal) also by rail.
iv.   Kodari (northern border, central Nepal)
v.   Belhia, Bhairahwa (Rupandehi, western Nepal)
vi.   Jamunaha, Nepalgunj (Banke, mid-western Nepal)
vii. Mohana, Dhangadhi (Kailali, far-western Nepal)
viii. Gadda Chauki, Mahendranagar (Kanchanpur, far-western Nepal)

ix. Purang — Muchu, at the Tibet China- Nepal border (Simikot, far-western Nepal) special permit required, only trekking cross border land route to Mount Kailash in Tibet.

Customs

Visitors are permitted to import the following for their personal use: 200 cigarettes, 50 cigars, 1.15 litres alcoholic liquor, 12 cans of beer, one pair of binoculars, one movie camera or one video camera with 12 rolls of film, one still camera with 15 rolls of film, one tape-recorder with 15 tape reels or cassettes, one perambulator, one laptop computer. It is advisable on arrival to have the customs enter electronic items in the passport to facilitate easy departure formalities.

Objects of archaeological or historic value may not be exported and should not be purchased. All metal statues and antique paintings, carpets and other objects must be checked by the Department of Archaeology before being sent or carried out. Travel agents and craft dealers can assist in this process. For further information, contact the Customs Department, Tripureshwar (tel. 215525, 221781).

Domestic air services

Royal Nepal Airlines, Necon Air, Nepal Airways, Everest Air, Buddha Air, Lumbini Airways, Yeti Airways, Gorkha Airline and Cosmic Air provide services between the 25 regional airports in Nepal. Some of the major destinations are served by as many as 10 flights per day. Helicopter charter services are provided by Asian Airlines, Karnali Airlines, Cosmic Air and Gorkha Air.

Road services

Kathmandu is connected with India through the fertile plains of the Terai by picturesque highways. Visitors are permitted to drive their own cars but their vehicles must possess an international carnet.

Long-distance day or night bus services are available from Kathmandu to the border and to other towns and cities in Nepal. These start from the Gongabu bus terminal on the Ring Road near Balaju.

Only about one-third of Nepal's 11,714 km road network has a tarred surface.

Taxis and local bus services

There are many buses and minibuses available at Ratna Park (old bus station) which serve various destinations in the Kathmandu Valley. There is also a trolley bus service which starts at Tripureshwar (near the Dasharath Stadium), runs along the Araniko Highway, and ends at Surya Vinayak (Bhaktapur). The bus service operates from 0500 or 0600 until 2000 or 2100 on popular routes.

Metered taxis are available — look for the black licence-plate with white lettering. A trip inside the city should cost between Rs80 and Rs250, depending on the distance. No tip is expected. There are also private taxis, which charge slightly more than the ordinary taxis, and the black, three-wheeled auto rickshaws which charge slightly less. Cycle rickshaws cost about Rs. 20 for a journey of a few blocks — but negotiate the fare before setting off.

Car hire

Cars can be hired through a travel agent or car rental company. Normal charge is around Rs 800 for a half-day and Rs 2,000 for a full day. An international driving licence is required.

Cycle hire

Mountain bikes and other bicycles are cheap and probably the best form of transportation for economy tourists. Mountain bikes can be hired for around Rs 100 per day and ordinary bikes for around Rs 35 per day.

The Kathmandu Valley has a vast network of tracks, trails and back roads, some of them the most rugged in Nepal. Other destinations from Kathmandu are Dhulikhel, Kodari, Hetauda, Narayanghat or Pokhara, from where one can also bike to Sarangkot, Naudanda, Baglung and Lumbini.

Kathmandu's air is heavily polluted, so cyclists in the city are advised to wear masks.

Trekking

There are many long treks in Nepal, some of which still see only a handful of Western walkers each year. As per the latest trek permit regulations, no trek permit is required for Everest, Langtang, Helambu, Annapurna and Rara. Recently opened routes — in the Central region around Manaslu, Mustang in the upper Kali Gandaki valley; in the far western region, Shey Gompa in the Dolpo area, Simikot trek and furthest east, Kanchenjunga trek require special permits, fees and a Government Environment Officer.

The six popular longer treks are the Everest Base Camp Trek (three weeks, maximum altitude 5,545 metres, 18,200 feet), Helambu (one week, 2,800 metres, 9,200 feet), Langtang (10 to 12 days, 3,800 metres, 12,470 feet) and Jomsom (one week, 3,700 metres, 12,140 feet) treks, the Annapurna Circuit (three weeks, 5,400 metres, 17,700 feet) and the Annapurna Sanctuary Trek (10 to 14 days, 3,000 metres, 9,850 feet).

A trekking permit is required to visit Nepal's interior; this is available from the Department of Immigration offices in Kathmandu and Pokhara, and can only be extended at these offices. Two passport photos are required for each permit. Fees, payable in rupees, vary from US$5 – 70 per week, depending on the trekking area. Different areas required different permits, and application forms are colour-coded accordingly, so be sure you get the correct one. Leave ample time for the bureaucratic delays involved in getting permits. There are regular permit-checking points along trails, so do not attempt to trek without a permit.

Rafting and kayaking
Nepal is earning a reputation as one of the world's best places for white-water rafting and kayaking. There is a list of rivers where the sports are permitted.

The longer river trips offer the best range of scenery and rapids and allow participants enough time to develop skills and friendships. Most long trips take from 8 to 12 days, with a long period spent rafting in wilderness. The Karnali, the Sun Kosi and the Tamur are all classic rivers with exciting white water and excellent beaches.

Rivers that lend themselves to medium-length trips are the Trisuli, the Kali Gandaki, the Seti and the Marsyangdi.

Day trips are run mainly on the Trisuli, close to Kathmandu, but the Upper Sun Kosi and Bhote Kosi are also possible.

The best time for rafting is March to early June. Rafting in September to early November requires more expertise, as rivers are high and fast after the monsoon. Rivers are graded 1-6, with 6 being very difficult.

Rafters and kayakers need permits, obtainable from the Ministry of Tourism, at the Exhibition Ground in Kathmandu, at US$5. A passport photo and a photocopy of passport is required.

White Water Nepal, by Peter Knowles and David Allardice, is an excellent reference book.

Mountain flights
Mountain flights are organised by several air companies and take about one hour, flying along the great Himalayan range to Everest or west to Dhaulagiri past such giants as Annapurna. There is also a 'complete Himalayan panorama' flight which covers the entire Nepal Himalayan range.

Hot-air ballooning and hang-gliding
Hot-air ballooning is picking up fast in Nepal and the views are spectacular once up over Kathmandu Valley. Hang-gliding is also enjoyed and encouraged.

People have tried ballooning over Mount Everest or other major peaks, landing in Tibet. Such expeditions require lenghty and special permission from the governments of Nepal and China.

Mountaineering
Expeditions must have prior approval from the Ministry of Tourism, Mountaineering Division, Kathmandu, which will issue a permit for the climb, with fees payable at least two months in advance. There are strict rules for climbing groups. Foreign expeditions must contain at least three Nepalese members

Nightlife
Wining and dining is a serious sport in Kathmandu, which has more than a thousand pubs and restaurants — from five-star hotels to down-to-earth trekkers' joints, and from discos to casinos. Kathmandu offers an extensive variety of cuisine, both local and international, whilst drinks range from imported brands to the local rice beer and high-altitude punch.

Conference facilities
Kathmandu offers a choice of conference centres. The recently-built Birendra International Convention Centre of Nepal is a state-of-the-art facility with seven meeting areas. Other venues include the Royal Nepal Academy, Rastriya Sabha Griha, the Russian Cultural Centre and the Bhrikuti Mandap Exhibition Hall. Conference facilities are also available at larger hotels.

Climate
There is a wide range of climatic conditions in Nepal, from the tropical rain forests in the south to the snowcapped mountains and glaciers in the north. The main rainy season is between late June and September, when temperatures are at their hottest. The remainder of the year experiences warm and settled weather. Rainfall decreases from east to west.

Kathmandu is cold from early November to mid March. Mornings can be cold and foggy and temperatures can go below freezing in January and February.

It is hot through May to mid-June, with temperatures rising to over 33°C (91°F) in Kathmandu. Showers heralding the monsoon begin in May, and the monsoon itself starts at the end of June, when nights are warm and sticky. Even in summer, Kathmandu's night time temperature difference of 8°C makes it bearable.

Temperature
	Jan	Feb	Mar	Apr	May	Jun	Jul	Aug	Sep	Oct	Nov	Dec
Max°C	18	19	25	28	30	29	29	28	28	27	23	19
Min°C	2	4	7	12	16	19	20	20	19	13	7	3

Humidity
am %	89	90	73	68	72	79	86	87	86	88	90	89
pm %	70	68	53	54	61	72	82	84	83	81	78	74

Rainfall
mm		15	40	22	58	122	245	373	345	155	38	8	3

Clothing
There are vast temperature changes from the Terai to the Himalaya, so it is advisable to take both light and warm clothing in casual, comfort-

able styles. In the mountain areas, warm clothes in wool or down materials are vital.

At lower altitudes, in the Terai, the temperature drops considerably after dark, but the days are comfortably warm throughout the year, so cotton clothing is ideal.

Good walking shoes with emphasis on good sturdy soles, are a must for trekkers. Mini-shorts and other revealing clothes are not appropriate.

Most kinds of clothing are available at fairly cheap prices in Kathmandu.

What to take with you

Protection from the sun is needed on treks, so sunglasses, a hat and a good sunscreen are advisable. Calamine lotion is good for sunburn, along with proprietary preparations. Protection from the rain is needed during the wet season – ponchos or umbrellas are cheaply available.

In the summer months, insect repellent is a good investment. Toilet paper is available, as are most pharmaceutical goods including female tampons. A flashlight and a padlock and key could prove useful.

Currency

Non-Indian visitors are not allowed to import or export Nepali or Indian currency.

All other travellers must fill in a currency form giving their name, nationality, and passport number but not the amount of currency imported. All your foreign exchange transactions are recorded on this form and stamped by the bank or other authorized dealer. The official exchange rate is published daily in *The Rising Nepal* newspaper and broadcast by Radio Nepal in the Nepali language.

Excess Nepali rupees can be converted back into hard currency as long as they do not exceed 10 per cent of the total amount changed.

There is an exchange counter at Tribhuvan Airport open throughout the day, every day. The New Road Gate exchange counter of Rastriya Banijya Bank is open daily from 0800 to 2000. The Nepal Bank on New Road is open from 0010 am to 1500, Sunday to Thursday, and from 0010 am to 1200 on Fridays.

The official rate of exchange fluctuates against all currencies. Dollars are in high demand, but black market dealings are illegal.

There are 100 paisa to one Nepali Rupee. Banknotes are in denominations of 1,000, 500,100, 50, 20,10, 5, 2 and 1 rupee. Coins are in denominations of 1.00 Rupee and 50, 25,10 and 5 paisa. Half a rupee (50 paisa) is called a *mohar*, while 25 paisa is referred to as *asukaa*.

Currency regulations

Foreign visitors, other than Indian nationals, are required to pay their hotel bills and for their air tickets in foreign currency. Other payments must be made in Nepalese currency, which can be bought at the foreign currency exchange counter at the airport, or at banks or authorised foreign exchange dealers.

Tourists, other than Indian, are not allowed to import or export Indian currency. The rates of exchange for foreign currencies are determined by the Nepal Rastra Bank and are announced in the press daily. Banks and hotels charge commission for money changing. It is advisable to keep all the encashment receipts. On the day of departure upto 10% of the total value of foreign exchange changed can be reverted in case there are leftover rupees.

Banks

There is a wide choice of banks and authorised moneychangers, particularly in Kathmandu and Pokhara. Bank opening hours are 1000 to 1400 from Sunday to Thursday and 1000 to 1200 on Fridays. They are closed on Saturdays and other holidays.

The Nepali rupee is tied to the Indian rupee at the rate of IRs 100 to NRs 160. Other official exchange rates are set by the Nepal Rastra Bank.

It is advisable to carry a mix of cash, travellers cheques and credit cards in order to have a number of options.

Credit cards

International credit cards are accepted at major establishments.

Shopping

Nepal has many fine handicrafts, including hand-knotted woollen carpets, jewellery, pashmina shawls, woollen knitwear, embroidery, thangka paintings, wood carvings, metalwork, ceramics and pottery, rice paper and stationery.

The Supermarket, New Road, Kathmandu, and numerous department stores offer a good selection of imported products. Thamel Treks shops have the best bargains for outdoor clothing and gear. Bargains can also be had on imported designer goods from trainers to perfumes.

The traditional khukri, the curved metal knife synonymous with the valour of Gurkha soldiers, is a popular memento for many visitors.

Kathmandu's spice market at Ason is well worth a look, and tea shops offer a wide selection of Nepalese tea, attractively packaged to make useful gifts to take home. Ready-to-cook spices for curries are available as well.

People

Nepal has a population of more than 21 million (1998), with a number of races living in different regions, with diverse cultures, languages and dialects. The majority live in rural areas and have a life that is simple and traditional. They are delighted to meet foreigners, but they and their culture should be treated with respect in return.

Be decently clad (sun and beach wear is not ideal for exploring the city or villages). Public displays of affection between men and women are frowned upon.

Ask permission before taking people's photographs, and remember to pay due respect to Nepalese modesty, as well as to anything connected with religion. Drug use and trafficking are regarded as serious offences by the authorities. Visitors are also asked not to encourage begging, since this will only promote a culture of dependence. Reliable societies and organisations exist and donations given would be put to use for the community.

History and government

In 1990, Nepal adopted a democratic form of government based on multi-party elections within a constitutional monarchy. The Constitution affirms that Nepal is a multi-ethnic, multi-lingual, democratic, independent, indivisible, sovereign, Hindu and constitutional monarchical kingdom. The Constitution guarantees the safeguarding of basic human rights, freedom and equality.

Following the adoption of the new Constitution, multi-party elections were held in 1991 and a new government sworn into power on a clear mandate to improve the economic and social well-being of the Nepalese people.

The major thrust of the new economic policies introduced at that time was a liberal open-door policy favouring increased private sector participation in trade, investment, tourism and related commercial activities.

The first election saw a clear majority for the Nepali Congress. However this fell to inter-party disputes and a subsequent election in 1995. Nepal has a bicameral legislature. The lower house, the House of Representatives, consists of 205 members. Members to the lower house are elected every five years. The upper house, the National Assembly, is made up of 60 members who have a six-year tenure in office. Fifteen members are elected by the local government, 35 members by proportional representation, and 10 members are nominated by the King.

Nepal has a long and distinguished history, covering more than 20 centuries. The stupas of Patan and Swayambhunath are believed to be more than 2000 years old. The country is an amalgamation of a number of medieval principalities. Before the campaign of national integration launched by King Prithivi Narayan Shah, the Kathmandu Valley was ruled by the Malla Kings, who made great contributions to art and culture. In 1768AD, the Shah dynasty ascended the throne of the unified kingdom. The current monarch, His Majesty King Birendra Bir Bikram Shah Dev, is the 10th King in the Shah dynasty.

Nepal is one of the founder members of the South Asian Association for Regional Cooperation (SAARC).

Language

Nepali is the kingdom's lingua franca, spoken by about 60 per cent of the population. Educated people speak and understand English. Hindi, Maithali, Bhojpuri, Tharu, Tamang, Newari, Sherpa, Tibetan and a number of other regional dialects are also spoken.

Religion

Hinduism is the main religion, observed by 86.5 per cent of the population. Buddhism accounts for 7.8 per cent, Islam 3.5 per cent and others 2.2 per cent. The exquisite medieval art and architecture of the Kathmandu Valley vividly reflect the artistic ingenuity and the religious traditions of the people.

Visitors to Hindu temples or Buddhist shrines are expected to remove their shoes. Entry to some temples may be prohibited to non-Hindus. Leather articles are not allowed in the temple precinct. It is better not to touch offerings or persons when they are on their way to shrines. Walking around a temple or stupa is traditionally done in a clockwise direction.

As a general rule, temples, stupas and monuments may be photographed but it is best to obtain approval from authorised persons beforehand. Modest contributions are also welcome for this as donation boxes are discreetly in place.

Time

Nepal is 5hrs 45 mins ahead of London (GMT), 10 hrs 45 mins ahead of New York and 3 hrs 15 mins behind Tokyo.

Business hours

Government offices are open from 1000 to 1700 in the summer and until 1600 in the winter. On Fridays, these offices are open until 1500 only. Offices are closed on Saturdays and public holidays.

Communications

Telephone, telex, fax, email and internet services connect Nepal to all parts of the world. International direct dialling is available from major centres and even in remote hilly district headquarters. Nepal has one of the most reliable and extensive communication facilities in South Asia.

Media

The major newspapers in Kathmandu are:
The Rising Nepal (government English daily)
The Kathmandu Post (English daily)
Gorkhapatra (government Nepali daily)
Kantipur (Nepali daily).

A limited number of International newspapers and magazines are also available.

Radio Nepal broadcasts programmes on both short wave and medium wave in three sessions between 0600 and 1100. FM programmes are also broadcast for entertainment. English news bulletins are broadcast daily at 0800, 1305 and 2000.

Nepal Television transmits from 0630 to 0900 and from 1730 to 2230. On Saturdays, special entertainment programmes are transmitted from 1200 to 1700.

Electricity
220 volts/50 cycles

Health
If you are trekking, rafting, etc, it is wise to carry a simple medical kit (containing, for example, painkillers, antiseptic cream or spray, antihistamine, anti-diarrhoea preparation, rehydration mixture, calamine lotion, insect repellent, eye-drops, water purifying tablets, bandages and Band-Aid, scissors, etc.).

Care in what you eat and drink is the most important health rule. Do not consume water from taps, streams, etc., and this includes ice in bars. Reputable brands of bottled water or soft drinks are generally fine. Take care with fruit juices, particularly if water may have been added. Milk should be treated with suspicion, as it is often unpasteurised. Boiled milk is fine if kept hygienically, and yoghurt is usually good. Tea or coffee is usually fine, since the water will have been boiled. Salads and fruit should be washed with purified water, or peeled where possible. Beware of ice cream that has melted and been refrozen. Thoroughly cooked food is best, but not if it has been left to cool.

Stomach upsets are the most likely travel health problem, but the majority of these will be relatively minor. Wash your hands frequently. Clean your teeth with purified water — not from the tap. Avoid climatic extremes: keep out of the sun when it is hot; dress warmly when it is cold. Day and night temperatures fluctuate and one can easily catch a cold. Dress sensibly: you can get worm infections through bare feet. Try to avoid insect bites by covering bare skin when insects are around, by screening windows and by using insect repellents.

Medical services
Private Clinics: The CIWEC clinic (tel. 01-410983) in Durbar Marg is used by many foreign residents in Kathmandu. It has operated since 1982 and has an international reputation. It is open from 0900 to 1300 and from 1400 to 1600 and is staffed by Westerners. A single visit will cost around US$30.

The Nepal International Clinic (tel. 01-412842), located near the Jaya Nepal Cinema, close to Durbar Marg, also has a good reputation. It is open from 0930 to 1300 and from 1400 to 1700. A consultation costs around US$25.

Hospitals: The Patan Hospital (tel. 522295 or 521048), in the Lagankhel district of Patan, close to the last stop of the Lagankhel bus, is partly staffed by Western missionaries and is recommended.

The Teaching Hospital (tel. 01-412303) is also satisfactory.

The centrally located government-operated Bir Hospital is not recommended. Private clinics are available for cardiac problems, the Apollo and Norvic are well equipped. Others for general hospitalisation are the Om Nursing Home, Model Hospital and B & B. There are also many diagnostic centres.

Pharmacies
Pharmacies are widely available in most towns and are usually associated with a doctor's clinic nearby. A prescription is not required to purchase drugs in Nepal and almost anything, provided you know the generic and proprietary name, is available.

Medical insurance
A travel insurance policy that covers medical treatment and evacuation by air is advised. Make sure the policy covers the activities you will be undertaking in Nepal, e.g. trekking or river-rafting. Check that your policy includes emergency flights out — if seriously ill or injured, you would probably need to be flown at least to Bangkok.

Clubs/sports activities
Golf, tennis, football, squash, cricket, mountain biking, rafting and athletics (including marathons and triathlon competitions) all feature in Nepal's sporting calendar. The Everest Marathon and the Rickshaw Rally are annual events attracting competitors from all over the world.

The Royal Nepal Golf Club is situated on the airport road. A highly rated international standard course has been put in place at the Le Meridian in Gorkarna forest beyond Bodhnath.

Security
There is a special Tourist Police Unit in Nepal to deal with tourists' problems. Contact the Tourist Information Centre, Basantapur (tel. 220818) or the Department of Tourism, Babar Mahal (tel. 247041).

Theft is not particularly common, but things can and do disappear, so ensure you know what is happening to your bag or pack, particularly on public transport. Be more alert in crowded areas. It is unlikely that anything lost can be recovered and getting a police report for an insurance claim is difficult and time-consuming.

Customs

Travellers are allowed to carry 200 cigarettes, 20 cigars, one bottle of spirits, and two bottles or 12 cans of beer free of duty. Personal effects exempt from duty include binoculars, cameras, film stock, record player, tape recorder, transistor radio, and fishing rod and accessories.

Forbidden imports

Firearms and ammunition (unless you hold an import license obtained in advance), radio transmitters walkie-talkies, and drugs.

Video and 8 mm and 16 mm movie cameras require special permits.

Souvenirs

On departure, souvenirs can be exported freely but antiques and art objects need special clearance from the Department of Archaeology, National Archives Building, Ram Shah Path, Kathmandu, which takes at least two days. Nepal is concerned to preserve its priceless art treasures and it is forbidden to export any object more than 100 years old. If in doubt, consult the Department of Archaeology.

Forbidden exports

Precious stones, gold, silver, weapons, drugs, animal hides, trophies, wild animals. Pets such as Tibetan dogs, may be exported.

Buses

In Kathmandu the main bus station is opposite Kanti Path, next to Tundikhel parade-ground. Minibuses depart from near the post office. For Pokhara, they leave from the Madras Coffee House (near Bhimsen Tower). In Pokhara, the bus terminal is close to the post office.

BUS SERVICES

To: **Patan Gate:** 7 am to 7 pm FROM Ratna Park (in front of Indian Airlines office).

To: **Jawalkhel, Lagankhel:** 7 pm FROM National Stadium.

To Bhaktapur 7 am to 8 pm FROM National Stadium (trolley bus) and Baghbazar (local bus).

To: **Pashupatinath, Bodhnath:** 6 am to 6 pm FROM Ratna Park.

To: **Dhulikhel:** 6 am to 6 pm FROM Main Bus Station.

To: **Barabise** (Chinese Road): 5:40 am to 4:45 pm FROM Main Bus Station.

To: **Kodari** (mail bus): 6 am FROM near Post Office.

To: **Balaju:** 7 am to 7 pm FROM near Post Office and Rani Pokhari.

To **Trisuli** 7 am and 12:30 pm FROM Pakanajol.

To: **Pokhara and Jomosom** (trekking) 6:30 am to 9 am FROM near Post Office Main Bus Station.

To: **Birganj** (connections to Raxaul, India): 6:30 am to 9 am from near Post Office Main Bus Station.

To: **Janakpur** (connections to Indian border at Jaleshwar): 5am FROM Main Bus Station

To: **Biratnagar** (connections with **Jogbani,** India): 5 am FROM near Post Office.

To: **Kakar Bhitta** (connections to **Siliguri and Darjeeling):** 5 am from Main Bus Station.

To: **Pokhara to Bhairawa** (connections to **Nautanwa,** India) 6 am to 9 am FROM near Post Office in Pokhara Town.

In Brief

Trekking Advisory

Those who climb have many reasons, some inexplicable to people who suffer from vertigo and other neuroses, but among the major delights must be the views.

To stand at these heights and survey the cloud-wreathed panorama of fluted ice walls, glaciers, hanging ice-cliffs, sheer rock walls and the almost sheer scree approaches, the dangers faced, the hazards overcome, must surely be triumph indeed.

For the great majority, however, the closest they will come to this ultimate conquest is on foot around the base of the mountains.

Thousands spend their Nepal holiday trekking through this tangle of mountains, delighting in the crisp mountain air and camping in alpine meadows, the challenge of negotiating dizzying mountain footpaths with a giddy drop at their feet and crossing over lung-sapping, snow-covered passes at between 4,570-5,790 metres (15,000-19,000ft): victory enough for those without the skills, time, money or equipment to cling to one of the monstrous walls, traverses or the ridges higher-up, simply 'because they're there'.

A risk which the trekker shares with the climber is that of mountain sickness: a combination of nausea, sleeplessness, headaches and potentially lethal oedemas, both cerebral and pulmonary.

Sudden ascents to heights of 3,660 metres (12,000 feet) and more, without acclimatization, lead to accumulations of water on the lungs or brain. Swift descent and prompt medical treatment is the only answer.

Around Dhaulagiri and Annapurna there are dozens of trekking options from which to choose. But around Manaslu Himal there are not so many. All the more delightful perhaps because they're still not beaten tracks and take you to the feet of such giants as 8,158 – metre (26,766 – foot) Manaslu and its sister peaks, including sacred 7,406 – metre (24,298 – foot) Ganesh Himal and its seven lesser peaks and forbidding 7,893 – metre (25,895 – foot) Himal Chuli. All Nepal is geared up to cater for the high-altitude trekker. In summer — between April and October — the major blemish is the number of leeches. These persistent and loathsome creatures infest the muddy trails and infiltrate everything.

The best time to trek is late September and early October when the mountain views are incredible (and continue to be so throughout crisp winter), or in the first quarter of the year when haze tends to cover the peaks.

There are literally hundreds of treks to choose from in the major trekking regions. Your choice will depend upon the time you have and the time of year.

The regions are **Kanchenjunga, Makalu, Khumbu Himal, Rolwaling Himal, Langtang Himal-Jugal Himal, Ganesh Himal, Manaslu, Annapurna Himal,** and **Dhaulagiri Himal.**

Trekking is one of the best experiences for those fortunate enough to participate in one. Whether it is the gentle kindliness of the people you meet on the way or the unparalleled beauty of rolling green hills is debatable, but what is surely the one constant is that you will leave with a great respect for the country and its people.

Depending on the season you trek you could either find the forest drenched with flaming red rhododendrons in the spring or watch a snow-capped mountain change in a spectacular sunset in the winter.

Since much of Nepal's northern regions are still unreachable by road, the beauty of the mountains are accessible only on foot. You could get a bird's eye view of a mountain by taking the mountain flight but nothing can bring you as close to the world's giants as a trek.

There is a certain progression to trekking which is a function of its activities. The initial days of a trek can be hard except for the very physically fit; your muscles will be sore. You should establish your own pace instead of trying to keep up with the leaders of the trek. Once your body has acclimated to the physical demands of the trek, the moments you have to yourself are a real treat. Many trekkers have very insightful experiences by virtue of being able to think through things while they walk.

On the trail you will meet many people; some curious, some intrusive, others fellow travellers. This is part of the trekking experience; try not to be impatient. It is much more pleasant to play along instead of being confrontational. If you wish to be left alone do not engage your little followers; they will soon leave you in search of other amusement.

This section will give you some guidelines regarding general preparations for a trek, and some survival tips. Listed are some of the ways you could go trekking:

• **Trekking with a guide**
• **Trekking without a guide**
• **Joining an organized trek with a trekking agency**

Trekking in Nepal is for the most part very safe. But there are still the occasional instances when articles have disappeared from camp sites. We recommend at least hiring a guide for treks off the beaten path or in remote areas where it is not easy to buy food as you go along. Most villagers grow vegetables only enough for their family consumption in areas where the land is hard to cultivate.

Trekking without a guide is an option in popular routes where you can stop for food and board in the tea-houses. These tend to be more crowded but you will be able to interact with the local people more.

Trekking with a Guide
If you are trekking with a guide and staying in tea-houses, you will be insulated from most problems. A guide will provide you with accurate trails, arrange for porters, negotiate prices, and have a good idea of what to avoid so that your trek will be trouble-free.

Depending on the route you want to take, you can alternate between camping and staying in lodges. Your equipment should include tents and cooking items.

It may not be worth your time to bring these with you; your guide can hire this in Kathmandu. Remote treks require more preparation and luggage so it may take a few days to have everything you need. You will have to carry food and supplies for your group and the guide. The porters take care of their own food but it must be carried from the starting point.

The challenge of this kind of trek is that you will have to spend more time in Kathmandu to locate a guide, arrange for all your supplies and equipment, and storage for the luggage you will not take on the trek.

Although you will probably have luck with a knowledgeable and interesting guide, you won't be able to know this until you are on the trek.

It is advisable to be patient and flexible in case things do not go at the same pace you are used to. The beauty of the entire experience is that you will be given a crash course in the culture of the Nepalese people since you will be interacting with them closely.

Trekking without a Guide

Trekking without a guide will limit you to popular routes unless you plan to carry with you enough food and fuel for two weeks.

There are numerous tea-houses or the more upscale lodges that provide both food and accommodation. Although you will find Western food listed in the menus, eating Nepalese food is more ecological and less of a drain on the limited supply of fire-wood.

Take a good map with you or have a good idea of how long a day's trek will take before you start every morning. You should reach your campsite or night's lodging before it gets dark to avoid running off the mountainside.

Some trail suggestions are: Annapurna Circuit, Jomsom, Everest Base Camp

With a Trekking Agency

If you want a luxurious and structured trek go with a trekking agency. When Nepal initially opened to tourists, Mountain Travel was the pioneer treks organizer.

Retired British Gurkha officer Lt-Col Jimmy Roberts started Mountain Travel and catered to tourists in the best colonial-style. Porters will carry everything from tables, chairs, tents, sleeping bags and anything else you need for a trek. There are now more travel agencies with trekking sub-divisions than there are mountains to name them after. Besides arranging for all the needs of a group, treks can be customized to suit a small group or if you choose you can trek with a group put together by the company. On such a trip your liaison is the *sirdar* (head guide) who takes care of all details. If you need anything, he is the one you should talk to.

Also with the group will be a cook, his kitchen boys and a retinue of porters to carry all the equipment. Luxuries such as a dining tent and accompanying table and chairs have to be carried as do a substantial amount of non-perishable foods.

These trips are usually planned before you arrive in Kathmandu and you will not have to spend precious time on the details. The price you pay is that the route is pre-determined and less likely to diverge to more interesting sites.

Trekkers will also have less interaction with the local people. The advantage of this kind of trek is that security in the campsite is less of an issue and, if there is an injury, the group is better equipped to handle the emergency.

Comforts

Naturally you will be paying more for these. A typical day begins with your wake-up call and morning tea. Outside your tent a basin of hot water is ready for your morning wash. You will need to be packed and ready to leave before you sit down for breakfast.

In the meantime the sherpas will be busy taking down tents and packing your luggage into the porter *dhokos*. The morning trek is usually shorter than the post-lunch trek. At the lunch stop the cooks and kitchen boys are ready and waiting with a simple meal.

By the time you leave, the porters and sherpas are already making their way for the campsite. Dinner is an elaborate sit-down affair; it is amazing what cuisines a few pots and pans can produce. Cooks alternate Nepali, Chinese, and Continental meals. Depending on what you like these treks can be extremely enjoyable. The comforts and time saved on preparations are worthwhile if you don't have the time to arrange your own trek in Kathmandu.

Season

The best months for trekking are the dry fall to spring of October to March. The clear skies after the rains reveal spectacular views of majestic peaks and the rolling green mountainsides verdant after the heavy rains.

The leeches, rampant in the wet months, disappear from the trails. But being the peak season, the trails are usually packed with fellow trekkers of the same mind.

Trekking in the monsoon is most likely to be quite uncomfortable: The trails are wet and slippery, and bridge conditions (you will be crossing bridges on your trip) are unstable, if they have not been washed away.

Views are obscured by the clouds, but if they do clear, the views are far better than any other time in the year. This alone is worth risking a trek in the monsoon. The trails are usually empty with trekkers being at a minimum; you will only have to contend with the leeches. If you are interested in local flora and fauna this is probably the best time to explore the backroads of the country.

Preparations

To travel to Nepal you will need a visa. (See page 308, for more details.) If you are only trekking in Kathmandu and Pokhara valleys and Royal Chitwan National Park you won't need a trekking permit.

All other areas require a permit issued at the Central Immigration Office and at the office of the Home and Panchayat Ministry in Kathmandu. There are some restricted areas closed to trekkers which should be observed.

One helpful hint is to carry several passport photographs which can be used for trekking permits, visa extensions or other official documents.

There are many instant passport photograph services at camera stores just in case you forget. Usually most of these services can be taken care of for you by the trekking agencies, but should you choose to do it on your own here are a few pointers to help you survive the sometimes difficult ordeal.

Allow for a two-working-day turnaround time for your trekking permit to come through; Saturdays are public holidays and there are many festivals which are also government holidays. When you deal with immigration officials do so with tact.

The activities by many foreigners to outwit the system has led to a generally wary attitude toward all trekkers. Be patient and offer all the information they ask for.

What to wear

Layers and natural fibres are basics for trekkers. Loose-fitting trousers for men and long skirts for women are the most comfortable clothes. For outerwear, wool is a good choice in the winter; a water-proof light jacket over the sweater will keep you both warm and dry.

Highly specialized manmade fabric such as polypropylene and fibre-insulated outer garments are also a good bet as they dry quickly. In the dry winter, down garments are an excellent one-piece protection.

Down jackets and down pants are good for lounging in at night at the campsite. A cap will keep you warm for the night since a lot of heat escapes from your head.

Baseball caps or hats are also great for shielding the intense sunlight. Plan to take sunglasses for high-altitude treks within the snowline; they should cover all sides of your eyes.

In the rains you could get by with the classic Nepali black umbrella and a poncho-styled raincoat. Most rain gear will keep you dry but if humidity is constantly at 100 per cent, the unbreathability of the fabric will get you drenched on the inside. Carry several pairs of socks so that you will have dry ones to change into at camp.

In the lower altitudes shorts are a comfortable basic. In order to be sensitive to the sensibilities of the native people the shorts should be long and not too revealing. Skirts made of light material are favoured for women.

Food

Unless you trek with the commercial trekking agencies, the food you will find in the hills will depend on the remoteness of your route, the season and what the villagers can spare.

Some items can be purchased in most villages or individual households. You can supplement local items with dehydrated foods and canned goods from Kathmandu; good buys are powdered milk, tea, coffee, spices.

The selection of trekking foods in specialized stores is amazing and fun as you discover all sorts of knick-knacks for your trip.

The rule of thumb on buying supplies for a trek is that most luxury items — anything besides what is grown in the hills — should be bought in Kathmandu.

On the road you will be able to buy rice; lentils (dal); seasonal vegetables such as spinach, gourds and beans; barley, corn and millet flour; eggs; and chickens.

The most basic foods eaten by Nepalis are rice and lentils (dal-bhaat). There may be a vegetable curry (tarkari) and condiments to accompany the dal-bhaat.

Meat is only eaten on special occasions as it is expensive for most rural Nepalis. If you are doing a tea-house trek, you can buy meat dishes if available in addition to the usual fare.

The same precautions for food should be applied to food while trekking. If trekking with a guide, one of the first things he will look for at a campsite is a water source. Water is boiled in most of the tea-houses.

It may be impossible to be as careful as you want but most trekkers are able to manage with only a few run-ins with the 'Kathmandu Belly'.

The Guides

Although the word Sherpa is synonymous with guide, it actually denotes the group who migrated from Tibet and settled in the Solu-Khumbu region.

Their culture and traditions are closer to that of Tibetans, but they have their own dialect and customs. Today in trekking and mountaineering circles the term Sherpa classifies the job functions of the position.

Sherpas traditionally act as the guides and operations staff. The head Sherpa is known as *sirdar*. Sherpas-in-training have frequently doubled up as cooks, kitchen boys and porters. There are a good percentage of Tamangs, Gurungs and Rais ??? who work in the trekking industry.

A good sirdar is the key to a do-it-yourself trek. He will take care of hiring porters, dealing with day-to-day problems, purchase food on the road and keeping the group on the road. An established Sherpa will not carry equipment or cook.

Most sirdars speak English. Others speak Japanese, German, French or other languages depending on what projects they worked in previously.

Unless you have a particular cook in mind, perhaps one who was referred to you, the sirdar may recommend one who has worked with him. Likewise he will pick his group of Sherpas.

Porters are hired to carry your luggage, food, and equipment. In addition they also carry their own food. The limit is 30 kgs a porter. If you hire your porters earlier in the trip you are responsible for their transport to the starting point of your hike.

Your sirdar should be aware if the porters are lowland people: They will not have the clothes, shoes, bedding or shelter for the high altitude. If you are forewarned it will not come as a shock in the middle of your journey.

Some trekkers have felt embarrassed hiring porters for no better reason than to carry their luggage while they walk with only a small day pack.

You should not be embarrassed to use porters since portering is one of the few migrant jobs that put money back into the economy of the mountains.

In the northern regions such as Khumbu there is an option to use pack animals. Yaks and zopkio (sterile male offspring of a cow and a yak) can carry up to 50 kilos (Ibs 110).

In the course of the journey you will come to know your guides and porters. Although you do not need to share everything with them, a token of appreciation every so often goes a long way to building goodwill and morale. A soda in the middle of the day, or a good meal with a special dish are some suggestions. You will be the best judge of what your staff would consider a treat.

Trekking in the Monsoon

A few precautions and luck should prepare you for a rainy season trek in the mountains. Luck figures prominently if you want to see the rare but spectacular views of the mountains when the clouds break.

Remember that if you choose to trek in the rains you will get wet no matter how you pre-pare yourself and your equipment. The objective is to have enough to minimize your discomfort.

Raingear, the light and breathable kind, is necessary as is protection for your backpack. You can buy plastic sheets or bags in trekking stores to cover your equipment.

Wear light cotton shirts or T-shirts and have a light jacket for the odd cold days. You should have at least two pairs of shoes because they are bound to get wet.

If you have leather shoes be warned that they will be destroyed after getting soaked for a few times. Strapped rubber sandals are a good alter-native for walking short distances. You can get cheap footwear in Kathmandu but the sizes above 10 are few and far between.

Healthwise you have to be on guard. The rains are indiscriminate about sweeping refuse into the rivers. Drink only boiled or bottled water to prevent parasitic infections, hepatitis and typhoid. The trails abound with leeches so tuck the bottoms of your trousers into your socks or make frequent checks and carry salt to sprinkle on ones that latch on.

Finally, choose a drier region such as the upper Kali Gandaki, Manang, Khumbu, and allow for delays and cancellations of flights. Other deterrents include flooded rivers, and washed out bridges and roads.

Khumbu is only for the serious, hardy trekker — a 25 to 30 day trip walking between Sherpa villages. Though the scenery is sensa-tional, it's extremely cold. If you fly in and out, expect some delays.

Lukla flights are inextricably tied to the weather — and if you miss your flight you drop back to the bottom of the list which, on one occasion, meant an extended stay of some three weeks for one unlucky person.

By plane it is only 40 minutes from Kathmandu to **Lukla,** more than 2,700 metres (9,000 ft) above sea level. Its landing strip is on an uphill gradient, one side of which drops precipitously thousands of metres to the floor of the Dudh Kosi valley.

Namche Bazaar is well above Lukla. There is also a 4,000-metre (13,000-ft) airfield nearby — at **Syangboche** where guests of the Everest View Hotel alight. Each bedroom in this hotel is equipped with oxygen.

But Nepal's main trekking area is around **Annapurna Himal** and **Dhaulagiri Himal** from Pokhara with dozens of medium- and high-altitude walks to choose from, including the 'Royal Trek' which follows in the footsteps of the Prince of Wales and gives you three to five days in the Gurung and Gurkha country, east of the Pokhara valley.

Highlights of the six- to 10-day trek from Ghandrung to Ghorapani are outstanding pano-ramas of Machhapuchhare, Annapurna, and Dhaulagiri. The 17- to 19-day Kali Gandaki to Muktinath route is in excellent condition in the winter, although some snow is possible at Ghorapani.

In contrast with the dozens of trekking options around Dhaulagiri and Annapurna, there are few around **Manaslu.**

In the far west, trekking from Jumla always poses problems — simply because it's so difficult to reach this remote region.

It is the spectacular scenery which makes the effort worthwhile. The trekking 'high season' is between October and December, the classic time for high-altitude climbing treks when the more popular routes — Khumbu, Pokhara, Ghandrung, Ghorapani and Annapurna — are congested.

Trekking Gear

Trekking along these rough, rocky trails de-mands that you wear strong, comfortable boots with good soles. At low altitude, tennis shoes or running shoes provide adequate cushioning for the feet .

But good boots are essential at higher eleva-tions, and in snow, large enough to allow one or two layers of heavy woollen or cotton —

never nylon — socks, of which you will need plenty. Wearing light casuals or sneakers after the day's work will help relax your feet. For women, wraparound skirts are preferable to slacks. Shorts offend many mountain communities. Men should wear loose fitting trousers or hiking shorts. For clothing, two light layers are better than a single thick one. If you get too hot, you can peel the top layer off. At really high altitudes wear thermal underwear. It's best to carry too many clothes than not enough. Drip-dry fabrics are best.

Your pack should be as small as possible, light, and easy to open. The following gear is recommended: Two pairs of woollen or corduroy trousers or skirts; two warm sweaters; three drip-dry shirts or T-shirts; ski or thermal underwear (especially from November to February); at least half-a-dozen pairs of woollen socks; one pair of walking shoes; one extra pair of sandals; light casual shoes or sneakers; woollen hat; gloves or mittens; strong, warm sleeping bag with hood; a thin sheet of foam rubber for a mattress; padded anorak or parka; plastic raincoat; sunglasses and sun lotion; toilet gear; towels; medical kit; water bottle; and a light day pack. Your medical kit should include pain killers (for high-altitude headaches); mild sleeping pills (for high-altitude insomnia); strepto-magna (for diarrhoea); septram (for bacilliary dysentery); tinidozole (for amoebic dysentery); throat lozenges and cough drops; ophthalmic ointment or drops; one broad spectrum antibiotic; alcohol (for massaging feet to prevent blisters); blister pads; bandages and elastic plasters; antiseptic and cotton-wool; a good sun block; and a transparent lip salve.

In addition to these, you should carry a torch, candles, lighter, pocket knife, scissors, spare shoelaces, string, safety pins, toilet paper, and plastic bags to protect food and wrap up wet or dirty clothes and carry your litter, plus food, tents, and photographic equipment. Much of this can be bought in Kathmandu. Cooking and eating utensils are normally provided by the trekking agency and carried by the porters.

Always carry your trekking permit in a plastic bag where you can get to it easily. Lock your bag against theft or accidental loss. Make sure you have plenty of small currency for minor expenses along the way. Carry a good supply of high-energy food such as chocolate, dried fruits, nuts, and whisky, brandy, or vodka for a warming nightcap.

Water is contaminated so do not drink from streams no matter how clear or sparkling they look. Chlorine is not effective against amoebic cysts.

All water should be well boiled or treated with iodine: four drops a litre and left for 20 minutes before drinking.

But note that at high altitude water boils at temperatures below 100°C (212°F) — not warm enough to kill bacteria. A pressure cooker solves the problem and also cooks food faster.

Normally the day starts with early morning tea at around six o'clock. Break camp and pack, followed by a breakfast of hot porridge and biscuits, ready to be on the trail by around seven o'clock. Lunch is taken around noon, the cook having gone ahead to select the site and prepare the meal. By late afternoon, the day's trek is ended and camp pitched, followed by dinner. At these high altitudes, after a hard day's walking, there's little dallying over the camp fire. Though sleep is fitful and shallow, most are ready to hit the sack by 2000. Speed is not essential.

Pause frequently to enjoy the beauty of a particular spot, talk to the passing locals, photograph, or sip tea in one of the rustic wayside tea shops. Walk at your own pace. Drink as much liquid as possible to combat high altitude and heat dehydration. Never wait for blisters to develop but pamper tender feet with an alcohol massage.

Altitude sickness

There are three main types of altitude sickness. Early mountain sickness is the first, and acts as a warning. It can develop into pulmonary oedema (waterlogged lungs) or cerebral oedema (waterlogged brain).

The symptoms are headache, nausea, loss of appetite, sleeplessness, fluid retention, and swelling of the body. Altitude sickness develops slowly, manifesting itself two or three days after reaching high altitude. The cure is to climb no higher until the symptoms have disappeared.

Pulmonary oedema is characterized, even when resting, by breathlessness and a persistent cough, accompanied by congestion of the chest. If these symptoms appear, descend at once.

Cerebral oedema is less common. Its symptoms are extreme tiredness, vomiting, severe headache, staggering when walking, abnormal speech and behaviour, drowsiness, even coma. Victims must return at once to a lower altitude and abandon all thoughts of their trek.

If left untreated mountain sickness can lead to death. It's endemic in the high Himalaya where even experienced mountaineers sometimes forget that the mountains begin where other mountain ranges end. For instance, the Everest base camp is some 1,000 metres (more than 3,000 ft) higher than the summit of the Matterhorn. Above 3,000 metres (10,000 ft) the air becomes noticeably thinner. Youth, strength and fitness make no difference. Those who climb too high, too fast, expose themselves to the risk of Acute Altitude Sickness. At 4,300 metres

(14,108 ft), for example, the body requires three to four litres of liquid a day. At low altitude try to drink at least a litre a day.

You should plan frequent rest days between the 3,700- and 4,300-metres (12,000 and 14,000-ft) contours, sleeping at the same altitude for at least two nights. Climb higher during the day but always descend to the same level to sleep. Never pitch camp more than 450 metres (1,500 ft) higher in any one day, even if you feel fit enough for a climb twice that height.

If you begin to suffer early mountain sickness, go no higher until the symptoms have disappeared. If more serious symptoms appear, descend immediately to a lower elevation. Mild symptoms should clear within between one and two days.

If the victim is unable to walk he should be carried down on a porter's back or by yak. No matter what the reason, never delay, even at night.

Some victims are incapable of making correct decisions and you may have to force them to go down against their will. The victim must be accompanied. Treatment is no substitute for descent. If a doctor is available, he can treat the victim but the patient must descend.

Because of a lack of radio communications and helicopters, emergency evacuations are difficult to organize. Such rescue operations take time and cost a great deal of money. Some agencies may be able to arrange helicopter rescues for trekkers but individuals stand no chance.

A risk that the trekker shares with the climber is that of altitude sickness: a combination of nausea, sleeplessness, headaches, and potentially lethal oedema, both cerebral and pulmonary. Sudden ascents to heights of 3,650 metres (12,000 ft) and more, without acclimatization, can lead to an accumulation of water, either on the lungs or brain. Swift descent for prompt medical treatment is the only answer.

National Parks and National Reserves

Royal Chitwan National Park
Size: 932 sq km (360 sq miles).
Geographical location: The oldest national park in Nepal is situated in the subtropical inner Terai lowlands of south-central Nepal. The park was designated as a World Heritage Site in 1984.
Vegetation: 70 per cent of the park vegetation is sal forest. The remaining vegetation types include grassland and riverine forest.
Fauna: The are more than 43 species of mammals in the park. Wildlife includes wild elephants, tigers, leopards, the endangered one-horned rhinoceros, wild boar, deer, four-horned antelope, striped hyena, pangolin, Gangetic dolphin, monitor lizard and python. Other animals found in the park include the sambar, chital, hog deer, barking deer, sloth bear, palm civet, langur and rhesus monkey. There are over 450 species of birds in the park. Among the endangered birds are the Bengal florican, giant hornbill, lesser florican, black stork and white stork. Common birds seen in the park include peafowl, red jungle fowl and different species of egrets, herons, kingfishers, flycatchers and woodpeckers.

Lake Rara National Park
Size: 104 sq km (41 sq miles).
Geographical location: North-west Nepal with most of it lying in Mugu District. A small area is within Jumla District of Karnali Zone. This is Nepal's smallest park containing the country's largest lake.
Vegetation: The park contains mainly of high-altitude conifers, oak and rhododendron forests.
Fauna: Wildlife includes Himalayan black bear, leopard, goral, Himalayan tahr and wild boar. Resident Gallinaceous birds and migrant waterfowl are found. The great-crested grebe, black-necked grebe, and red-crested pochard are seen during winter. Other common birds are the snowcock, chukor partridge, Impeyan pheasant, kalij pheasant and blood pheasant.

Langtang National Park
Size: 1,243 sq km (480 sq miles).
Geographical location: Situated in the Central Himalayas.
Vegetation: The complex topography and geography, together with varied climatic patterns, have enabled a wide spectrum of vegetation type to be established. This include small areas of subtropical forest, temperate oak and pine forests at mid-elevation, with alpine scrub and grasses giving way to bare rocks and snow. Oaks, chirpine, maple fir, bluepine, hemlock, spruce and various species of rhododendron make up the main forest species.

Fauna: This is haven for the endangered snow leopard, leopard, Himalayan black bear, red panda, and wild dog. The Trisuli-Bhote Kosi forms an important route for birds on spring and autumn migration between India and Tibet.

Sagarmatha National Park .
Size: 1,243 sq km (487 sq miles).
Geographical location: North-east of Kathmandu in the Khumbu region of Nepal. The park includes the highest peak in the world, Mount Sagarmatha (Everest) and several other well-known peaks.
Vegetation: Includes pine and hemlock forests and at lower altitudes, fir, juniper, birch and rhododendron woods, scrub and alpine plant communities, bare rock and snow.
Fauna: Wild animals most likely to be seen in the park are wolf, bear, musk deer, feral goat species. The snow leopard and Himalayan black bear are present but rarely sighted. Other mammals rarely seen are the weasel, marten, Himalayan mouse hare (pika), jackal and langur monkey. The brilliantly coloured crimson-horned or Impeyan pheasants are found.

Shey-Phoksondo National Park.
Size: 3,540 sq km (1,367 sq miles).
Geograhical location: The mountain region of western Nepal, covering parts of Dolpa and Mugu Districts. It is the country's largest national park.
Vegetation: Luxurious forests, mainly comprised of blue pine, spruce, cypress, poplar, deodar, fir and birch.
Fauna: The park provides prime habitat for the blue sheep and snow leopard. Other common mammals found are yak, wilddog, brown bear, muntjak, goral, thar and jackal, Himalayan weasel, Himalayan mouse hare, yellow throated marten, langur and rhesus monkeys. The park is equally rich in many species of birds, such as the Impeyan pheasant, blood pheasant, cheer pheasant, red and yellow billed chough, raven, jungle crow and snow partridge.

Royal Bardia National Park and Reserve
Size: 968 sq km (374 sq miles).
Geographical location: The mid-far western Terai, east of the Karnali River, the largest and least disturbed wilderness in the area.
Vegetation: About 70 per cent of the park is covered with dominantly sal forest with the balance a mixture of grassland, savannah and riverine forest.
Fauna: An excellent habitat for endangered animals such as the rhinoceros, wild elephant, tiger, swamp deer, black buck, gharial crocodile, marsh mugger crocodile and Gangetic dolphin. Endangered birds include the Bengal florican , lesser florican, silver eared mesia and Sarun

crane. 200 species of birds, and many snakes, lizards and fish have been recorded in the park's forest, grassland and river habitats.

Makalu-Barun National Park and Conservation Area.
Size: 2,330 sq kms (900 sq miles).
Geographical location: The Park and Conservation area are situated in the Sankhuwasbha and Solukhumbu Districts, bordered by the Arun River on the east, Sagarmatha (Mt Everest) National Park and on the west, the Nepal-China border on the north and the Saune Danda (ridge) to the south. This is the only protected area in Nepal with a strict nature reserve.
Vegetation: The park has some of the country's richest and unique pockets of plants and animals. There are 47 varieties of orchids, 67 species of valuable aromatic plants, 25 of Nepal's 30 varieties of rhododendron, 19 species of bamboo, 15 oaks including Arkhoulo, 86 species of fodder trees and 48 species of primrose.
Fauna: Over 400 species of birds have been sighted in the Makalu-Barun area, including two species never before seen in Nepal, the spotted wren babbler and the olive ground warbler. Wildlife includes the endangered red panda, musk deer, Himalayan black deer, clouded leopard and possibly the snow leopard, in addition to more substantial populations of ghora, Himalayan tahr, wild boar, barking deer, Himalayan marmot and weasel, common langur monkey and the serow.

Kosi Tappu Wildlife Reserve.
Size: 305 sq kms (118 sq miles).
Geographical location: On the flood plains of the Sapta-Kosi in Saptari and Sunsari Districts of Nepal. The reserve is defined by the eastern and western embarkments of the river.
Vegetation: Mainly sand with a few patches of scrub forest and deciduous mixed riverine forest.
Fauna: The reserve offers important habitat for a variety of wildlife. The last surviving wild buffalo are found there. Hog deer, wild boar, spotted deer and blue bull and 280 different species of birds have been recorded. These include 20 species of duck, two species of ibis, many storks, egrets and herons. The Kosi Barrage is extremely important as a resting place for migratory birds. Many species recorded there are not seen elsewhere in Nepal. Also seen are the endangered gharial crocodile and Gangetic dolphin in the Kosi River.

Parsa Wildlife Reserve
Size: 1,200 sq km (470 sq miles).
Geographical location: Bounded by the Rapti River in the north, the Rewu River and the Churia or Siwalik Range in the south and the Narayani River in the west.
Vegetation: Small forests of Khani, sisso and

simal — all valuable indigenous woods.

Fauna: Elephants are the best form of transport. Samta deer, tiger and leopard. Giant butterflies flit from leaf to leaf. On the plains the great Asiatic one-horn rhinos, chital and deer are sighted, peacocks and jungle fowl and crocodiles in the Rapti River.

Royal Shukla Phanta Wildlife Reserve.
Size: 305 sq kms (118 sq miles).
Geographical location: In the southern part of far-western Nepal in Kanchanpur District.
Vegetation: Predominant sal associated with asna, simal, karma, khair and sissoo are found along the riverside.
Fauna: The reserve provides prime habitat for the endangered swamp deer. Other wild animals in the reserve are the wild elephant, tiger, hispid hare, blue bull, leopard, chital, hog deer and the wild boar. A total of 200 species of birds have been recorded in the reserve. Many grassland birds along with the rare Bengal florican can be seen in the phantas. Marsh mugger, Indian python, monitor lizard and snakes such as cobra, krait, and rat snakes are also found.

Sheopari Wildlife Reserve
Geographical location: About 12 kms (7.5 miles) north of Kathmandu.
Vegetation: Ranges upwards from cultivated terraces through the scrubland dense oak forests. Most of the subtropical trees are covered in lichen and moss and surrounded by ferns.
Fauna: Common forest birds such as flycatchers, barbets, thrushes and eagles.

Hunting Reserves

Dhorpatan Hunting Reserve.
Size: 1325 sq km (511 sq miles).
Geographical location: In the Dhaulagiri Himal in western Nepal.
Fauna: The prime habitat for the blue sheep. Other mammals include ghoral, serow, Himalayan tahr and Himalayan black bear. Pheasant and partridges are also found.

Demographic profile

Location
Nepal is a sovereign independent kingdom situated between 80° 4' and 88° 12' East longitude, and 26° 22' and 30° 27' North latitude. It is bounded to the north by the Tibetan Autonomous Region of the People's Republic of China, and to the east, south and west by India.

Area
The country is 885 kilometres (553 miles) from east to west with a non-uniform mean width of 193km (120 miles)from north to south. Its total area is 147,181 square kilometres (91,930 square miles).

Population
Population of Nepal increased from 15,022,839 in 1981 to 18,491,097 in 1991 with an annual growth rate of 2.0 per cent. In 1991, 7.8 per cent of the population was found in the mountains, hills and Terai region. Urban areas covered 9.2 per cent of the total population in 1991.

The population for 1998 is estimated to be 21,843,068 with an annual growth rate of 2.39 per cent. The current population in urban areas is expected to be about 12 per cent of the total population.

Sex, age and marital status
In the census females outnumbered males. For the 1998 estimate females were 10,939,621 and males were 10,903,447.

The life expectancy at birth is 53 for men and 51 for women. The improvement over previous years is due to better infant care, with greater attention being paid to immunisation of pregnant women against tetanus, and children below two years of age against infectious diseases.

Legally, men and women can marry at the respective ages of 21 and 18. However, tradition still determines the age of marriage, particularly of women, and many marry well below the legal age.

Age Structure
About 1.1 million (Approximately 5 per cent of Nepal's total population) are elderly, i.e aged 60 and above.

Literacy
For the purpose of commutation, it is assumed that the age group zero to six years is illiterate. Therefore, seven years or above is the yardstick used to determine the nation's literacy status. In the last 20 years a number of new schools have come up in villages. Official figures show that there are 22,372 schools and the literacy rate nearing 38 per cent, or about six million persons. Men are, on average, better educated.

Educational attainment

Though education is free in government-aided schools few children study beyond the primary school level.

From primary school, progress is made through middle and high school. Beyond high school, there is a period of intermediate studies which determines whether an individual will proceed to tertiary education or pursue vocational training. University students graduate with either a BA or Bsc degree in the general category.

Health service

Private Clinics: The CIWEC clinic (tel. 01-410983) in Durbar Marg is used by many foreign residents in Kathmandu. The Nepal International Clinic (tel. 01-412842) , located near the Jaya Nepal Cinema, close to Durbar Marg, also has a good reputation.

Hospitals: The Patan Hospital (tel. 01-521034 or 522266), in the Lagankhel district of Patan, close to the last stop of the Lagankhel bus, is partly staffed by Western missionaries and is recommended.

Festivals

December -January
Seto Machhendranath Snan

This is when all the gods (Machhendra idols) are given a bath with holy water and their robes and jewellery are changed. Lord Machhendra's week-long bathing festival is celebrated every year in the courtyard of the temple in Kathmandu. Crowds come each day to leave offerings and watch Machhendra being rubbed, anointed and transformed by the priests.

The holy month of Magh

During this month all religious ceremonies are forbidden, no weddings or celebrations take place. Magh Sankranti is the end of the coldest months and is marked with ritual bathing. Many pilgrimage to the shrines around Pashupatinath and bathe in the sacred Bagmati, where women form miniature Shiva lingams of sand, which are worshipped by lights and offerings.

Bhimsen Puja

Bhimsen is one of the few Nepalese gods whose idol is always found in the second level of the temple. This is an occasion of merrymaking. Bhimsen is taken from his silver-encrusted temple near the old palace square, placed in a temple-like litter and carried through the streets with a parade of musicians and devotees.

A thousand and one lights

Trekkers pass through streets of Kathmandu swathed in heavy layers of clothing, huge leather fur-lined boots, thick ornate head-gear, the women in traditional multi-coloured woollen aprons. They wear heavy coral and turquoise necklaces, earrings, trinkets and amulets against evil spirits. They all come for the celebration of Tibetan New Year, and the annual Festival of Lights commemorating the completion of the Bodhanath shrine.

February-March
Shiva Ratri

Festivities take place at all Shiva temples and particularly at the great Pashupatinath Temple, and devotees come from all over Nepal and India. People dress up in their best clothes and walk in and out of the temple. In the evening the King and the royal family pay homage to Lord Pashupatinath and offer him gifts. The temple yard is lit with oil lamps. The saddus entertain the crowds by rolling in the ashes, performing impossible feats of yoga or sticking thorns through their tongues. The surrounding slopes, lit by camp-fires, echo with singing and chanting of Shiva's many names. Devotees remain awake throughout the night, many taking a bath in the holy waters. Bonfires are lit and families stay awake to glorify the Supreme Lord of Creation.

Holi

Named after the mythical demons of Holika is when men, women and children may find themselves covered with red powder or red liquid. Splashing of colour on passers by is accepted. Holi is also known as the Festival of Colours and people wear old clothes because of colour stains. The festival is said to be inspired by the exploits of Krishna, when he caught his milkmaids sporting in the Jamuna River. An umbrella is set up in the centre of Kathmandu and on the final day the umbrella is taken down. Other activities such as Guru Mapa also take place during this time. Singing and dancing continues until late at night.

Chakandeo Jatra

Travelling traders in Nepal are affluent citizens. On this occasion they worship Chakandeo whose towering idol stands in a side porch of the Bhagwan Bahal shine in Thamal. Each year on Holi Purnima, Chakandeo's image is carried up and down from Thamal Bahal. The parade is led by men and musicians clashing cymbals and thumping drums. Gifts and offerings are given by low-caste garbage women and are accepted.

Pisach Chaturdast, Pahachare and Ghora Jatra

In Nepal there are many *ajima* or 'grandmother' goddesses and the Goddess Kali controls witchcraft, black magic and casting of spells. Lord Shiva, who is depicted as husband of Goddess Kali, is taken from Pashupatinath Temple and carried on a ceremonial palanquin through the streets of Kathmandu with a loud fanfare of music. Ghora Jatra, the Festival of Horses, is now an official sports day. Legend has it that the horse festival was held to celebrate a victory over a demon named Tundi.

Balaju Jatra or Lhuti Punhi
Hundreds of people make the pilgrimage into the Valley to keep an all-night vigil at the famous Buddhist shrine. As a special punishment to gain religious merit, some pilgrims attempt to thread their bodies through the narrow valleys through the mouth of lahan cave. Most of the crowd goes to Balaju Park for holy baths at Baisdhara, the pool into which water flows from twenty-two carved dragons' mouths. These bathers worship at Narayan's feet, burying his image with offerings of rice, flowers, coins and red powder.

Sapna Tirtha Mela
Hundreds climb through the night to the northern slope of near-by Shivapuri mountain, where the source of the holy Bagmati River flows from the open mouth of a bronze tiger mask. They take prasad from the gods with sprinkling of the sacred water and bathe in an adjacent pond. They collect leaves and flowers from the holy site and tie them in a bouquet at the tip of a long stick.

April-May
Nawabarsa and Bisket (Nepalese New Year)
New Year's Day, which always falls in the middle of April, is observed throughout Nepal as the first day of the official Nepalese solar calendar. The most important New Year festival in the Valley is held at Bhadgaon town, and this festival is called Bisket in reference to the Newari words *bi* for 'snake', and *syako* for 'slaughter', a celebration to commemorate the death of two serpent demons.

Mata Tirtha Puja
The term applies to a formal duty when affection and respect are displayed. Evident everywhere is a demonstrated reverence, respect and affection for parents, senior kinsfolk, ancestors, brothers and sisters, sons and daughters and always little children. This festival is celebrated on the last day of the dark fortnight of April or early May when every Nepali must 'look upon his mother's face'. For those whose mother is living, the household bustles on this day with preparation of special foods and gifts.

Rato Machhendranath Rath Jatra
One of the most famous and spectacular of all Kathmandu Valley festivals takes place in April or early May, when Lord Machhendra's towering, massive chariot is hauled through the narrow streets of Patan town, just across the river from Kathmandu. For this occasion Kumari of Patan, a living goddess, is carried to Jawalakhel to witness the exhibition of the *ghoto*, where she is surrounded by admirers to make offerings. During this holy day some rain must fall as a sign of Machhendra and brings roars of joy from ecstatic crowds.

May-June
Sithinakha or Kumar Sasthi
Sithinakha is known as *Kumar Sasthi*, Kumar's Sixth Day, marking the occasion of his birth in the lunar fortnight of May. It is also the beginning of the rice-planting season, the day for cleaning wells, the conclusion of the Newar people's *Dewali* worship and time for stone-throwing fights. The idol of Kumar is at last removed from the temple and placed in an ornate, gilt-roofed palanquin litter. The long poles are hoisted upon men's shoulders and a joyful procession moves around the winding city streets.

July-August
Ghanta Karna
This is the Night of the Devil, when Nepalese celebrate their victory over the most dreaded of all demons to terrorise the county-side in ancient times. Ghanta Karna is often known as *Thathemus* or *Gathemanagal*. A vividly painted, glowering demon's face is affixed to an effigy, and a pumpkin marked with evil sexual organs is placed at its feet. People come to hang tiny cloth devil dolls on the effigy, and toss coins to it, hoping to avoid the ravages of disease and the wrath of evil forces. Finally, with the ending of the Ghanta Karna rituals, Nepalese families gather to celebrate in great, convivial feasts of thanks-giving, usually in the home of the senior clan member.

Gunla
During these auspicious thirty days Buddhists devote themselves with great enthusiasm to fasting, penance, pilgrimages and holy ceremonies, with a typically Nepalese climax of feasting, merrymaking and rejoicing. The focal point for Gunla Activities in Kathmandu is the massive, white-domed stupa called Swayambhunath, dedicated over 2,000 years to Adi Buddha. Fasting, singing and praying, the devotees climb the 365 steps that lead to the stupa where they slowly circle the sacred shrine. Gunla Buddhist housewives fashion tiny images — figures of Buddha, various deities, and toy chaitya shrines — from special clay pressed into moulds, each image 'given life' by the insertion of a grain of unpolished rice. With the completion of the rituals the idols are immersed in the sacred waters.

Naga Panchami

Nepalese respect, fear and worship snakes, believing there are Serpent Gods who for six months inhabit the face of the earth and the remainder of the year dwell far underground as a pantheon of Nagas or Snake Deities. Naga Panchami is the annual day set aside for the worship of snakes, many people perform small *pujas* throughout the year in places where Snake Gods are said to dwell, in the corners of gardens and courtyards, in drains and near water spouts, pools and springs and streams. Snake Gods are widely worshipped as controllers of rainfall and the day of the Snake Gods falls during the monsoon rains.

August-September
Gai Jatra

On this day every recently bereaved family must honour the soul of their dead by sending a religious procession through the streets. The Gai Jara, or cow procession, consists for each family of a live, decorated cow or a young boy gorgeously costumed to represent one, together with family priest, a troupe of musicians and a small boy in the guise of a *yogi* or holy man. People give food and coins to members of each procession, including the cow and all must pass the Royal Palaces. When the cow procession returns to the bereaved households, religious ceremonies are again performed and cloth 'tails' of the cow-costume cut into strips and tied about the necks of family members to protect them from misfortune.

Krishan Jayanti

In Nepal the great Lord Krishna is one of the most adored of all deities. Krishna is their ideal of manhood, his doctrine of *bhakti* promising salvation to all who devote themselves completely to him while dedicating themselves to the unselfish fulfilment of earthly duties. On this day of Krishna's birth, worshippers carry his garlanded and ornately clothed idols in procession through the streets in their arms, on platforms on their shoulders, or in open trucks crowded with revellers. Troupes of musicians follow, while groups carry tall banners proclaiming that 'Krishna is God'.

Gokarna Aunsi

In the Nepalese religion, tradition and culture is a reverence for one's father both in life and after his death. No man relaxes until he has produced a son, for it is the responsibility of male offspring, the eldest to perform the purification rites necessary to bring peace to the father's soul after his body is cremated. The most auspicious day for honouring fathers is Gokarna Aunsi, when all who can go to Gokarna village, where one of the most sacrosanct of all the countless

Shiva lingams in the Valley is enshrined. This carved stone phallic symbol of Lord Shiva is worshipped, renowned for his close communion with the souls of the dead.

Tij Brata

Every year, in August or early September, there is a three-day festival claimed by Nepalese women for themselves alone. Nepalese women strive for what is desired by women everywhere — a happy and productive marriage, good fortune and long life for her husband, and the purification of her own body and soul. Women fast for three days. All through this day and evening, groups of women flock the roads and pathways leading to the great temple of Lord Shiva. Those unable to travel to the holy waters must bathe in their homes in accordance with the same ceremony.

Ganesh Chata

An idol of Ganesh is worshipped in every home regardless of caste, creed or status. Each neighbourhood, village, city or region has its own Ganesh temple and holds an annual festival in his honour. Women fast every Tuesday, the day set aside to honour Ganesh. Thus each year in September, Ganesh is honoured with offerings of sesame, sugar and radishes, and sighting of the moon is avoided. After sunset people close themselves in their homes.

Indra Jatra and Kumari Jatra

This starts with the raising of the flag of Indra before the old palace at Hanuman Dhoka in Kathmandu. This flag signifies that Lord Indra has come to the Valley, and when it flies, peace, prosperity and unity are assured in the land. For this ceremony hundreds of spectators crowd into the palace square and on to the surrounding temples. Each night the shrines and ancient palace buildings crowding the Hanuman Dhoka square are aglow with oil wicks. Nepalese folk dramas are presented around the city and ancient dances are performed in the streets by the light of flaming torches. In the afternoon of the day before full moon, ecstatic mobs gather near Hanuman Dhoka to have a glimpse of the beautiful Newari girl, Kumari, worshipped as goddess of peasants and kings alike. This festival lasts for eight days.

September-October
Sorah Sraddha

In Nepal, the most important duty is worshipping the souls of departed relatives and ancestors, for their spirits remain very much alive and require endless attention. This is part of daily life and Nepalese perform specific religious ceremonies periodically and offer gifts to the souls. During Sorah Sraddha, hundreds of worshippers at temples and holy places perform Sraddha rites. *Sraddha* means 'gifts offered with faith'.

Dasain or Durga Puja
This is the longest and most joyous time of year, celebrated countrywide by all. Families reunite; blessings, gifts and glad tidings are exchanged, public parades, ancient processions and traditional pageants are held; and the powerful Goddess Durga is worshipped everywhere with *pujas*, ritual holy bathing, offerings, animal sacrifices, so that her idols are drenched for days in blood. During this festival most Government institutions and schools are closed for ten to fifteen days.

Pachali Bhairab Jatra
On Pachali Bhairab night the ponderous Bailab *kalash* is carried in triumphant procession from his home to his shrine near the river, where he is worshipped throughout the night with music, religious ceremonies and gifts. Sacrifices of animals are given and the blood is made to spurt high over the *Kalash*.

Tihar or Diwali
The five days of Tihar are celebrated in October. Tihar means a row of lamps and lighting displays are seen in every home especially during Laxmi Puja. Nepalese adore the Goddess Laxmi and make gifts and offerings to her. Children run through the streets with glittering sparklers, and fireworks are heard all around. The festival honours certain animals on successive days. Cows are offered rice, dogs are garlanded, cows have one horn painted in silver and bulls are also honoured. Deepvali is the most important day when the Goddess Laxmi comes to visit every home which has been lit for her. On the last day of Tihar, every boy and man is worshipped by his sisters and receives their blessings. They receive a tikka mark from their sisters.

Haribodhini Ekadasi
This day is observed by fasting especially by those who look upon Lord Vishnu as the Supreme God. No meat is eaten by the orthodox; the law does not allow butchers to sell meat on Ekadasi days. Activities take place at Vishnu temples and devotees make a circuit of the important ones from Ichangu Narayan to Changu Narayan, Bishanku Barayan and Sekh Narayan.

Mahalaxmi Village Puja
Mahalaxmi is the great Goddess of wealth, wife of Lord Vishnu. This is a festival of harvest because to farmers wealth is rice. Musicians, singers, dancers and actors stage amazing programmes. A lot of outdoor feasting goes on, food is cooked and served by men. At the end of the festival it is believed that Mahalaxmi will watch over the next year's harvest.

November-December
Gujeswari Jatra
Hundreds come daily to this goddess for the blessing of fertility, relief from sickness, the fulfilment of needs and desires, and for power. Gujeswari is a form of Kali, Durga and Taleju who represents Shakti. Water always stands in the *kunda* at a Gujeshwari shrine, indicating that this sacred pit opens onto a spring. Devotees in hundreds come to give offerings and scoop out water for blessings.

Indriani Puja and Nhaya Gaya Jatra
The worship of Shakti is Supreme Energy, represented in Devi goddesses. Each community, city and village is protected by its own patron goddess. Dignitaries, relatives, friends and neighbours come from miles around for this celebration. The festival is held at the temple of the Goddess Indriani near the Vishnumati River. The palanquin of Indriani is carried to the village square. When Indriani is installed in her temple the whole country celebrates with family feasts.

Bala Chaturdasi
Nepalese believe that for one year after death the wandering soul hovers about before entering the underworld. Relatives provide comfort and peace by performing *puja* ceremonies and lamp-lighting rituals; pilgrimages and offerings are given in the name of the dead. During the night the lamps and flaming ceremonial torches are carried down to the river and cast into the sacred waters. Devotees take a holy bath and pay respect to the Lord Shiva and start the pilgrimage by foot over and around the sacred hills.

Sita Bibaha Panchami
Most Nepalese know the story of Rama. On this day his idol is dressed as the bridegroom, and placed under a lavishly decorated *khat* on the back of an elephant. A fringed gold-tipped ceremonial umbrella is made to whirl over his head while musicians play and the mob swarms along to Sita's temple.

Yomarhi Punhi or Dhanya
Yomarhi Punhi is a celebration related to Newari farmers and is observed in every home. Yomarhi cakes are made and a simple religious ceremony blesses the cakes and give thanks to the gods of harvest. Cakes are distributed amongst family members. People come from all around to the tiny village of Thecho to see the dancers and musicians. This day can be compared with Halloween.

Public holidays

All Festivals (page 323) are not normally Public holidays but celebrated by different communities and actual holidays are not declared more than a year in advance as dates vary from year to year. The department of Tourism in Kathmandu publishes an annual brochure indicating the specific dates of each festival during the coming year. All Saturdays are Public and Government Holidays. Check in Nepal for exact dates.

Lunar Calendar

The Nepalese Lunar Calendar

Magh	(January-February)
Falgun	(February-March)
Chaitra	(March-April)
Baisakh	(April-May)
Jeth	(May-June)
Asaar	(June-July)
Saaun	(July-August)
Bhadra	(August-September)
Ashwin	(September-October)
Kartic	(October-November)
Mangsir	(November-December)
Pus	(December-January)

Museums of Nepal

Nepal - a land of many wonders - is often called an open air natural and cultural museum. Some of the important museums worth visiting are as listed:

The National Museum
Located at the western end of Kathmandu and a few minutes walk from the famous Swayambhu stupa. It has a large collection of weapons, art and antiquities of historic and cultural importance. It was initially built as a collection house for war trophies and weapons. The museum has an extraordinary collections of weapons, locally made firearms captured from the various wars, leather cannons and relics of natural calamities like the Great Earthquake. Other artefacts include ancient statues, paintings, and murals.

The Natural History Museum
Located on the southern slope of Swayambhu hill, the museum has a collection of different species of animals, butterflies and plants. The special feature of this museum is a serial display of diverse life species from prehistoric shells to stuffed animals, birds, crocodiles and other exhibits. Amid the stuffed cats, goats and guinea pigs are some exotic creatures of Nepal, the Danphe pheasant, the gharial crocodile, the Himalayan black bear and the barking deer.

Kaiser Library
Located near Thamek, the main tourist centre of Nepal containing a collection of 30,000 books of Kaiser Shumsher Jung Bahadur Rana. Many of the books are romances and adventure-writings from Europe. It is said that Kaiser Shumsher knew many of the books by heart and took pride in the diversity of the collection.

The National Bronze Art Museum
This has a collection of some of the finest pieces of bronze created by Valley artisans and the number of items is about 900. The art work ranges from Malla to the later period. The oldest work of art there is believed to be from the 11th century AD.

The National Art Gallery
Located in the Palace of Fifty-five Windows in Bhaktapur which is believed to be the first in the Kathmandu Valley to use glass, much coveted by the ancient rulers. Within the palace are beautiful paintings of erotic motifs and animals. The stonework is worth seeing and a room outlines the life and times of the Shah kings of Nepal. Also on display are items used by famous people and scriptures that are among the most valuable in the kingdom.

The National Woodworking Museum
Located in Dattatreya Square, Bhaktapur this museum often surprises visitors as it contains very finely carved pillars, windows, doors, and struts. Also, there are wood carving samples that go back to the 15th century. The building was constructed in the 15th century by King Yaksha Malla.

The Tribhuvan Memorial Museum
Located inside the palace complex, the museum displays all the events, personal belongings and mementos of the late King Tribhuvan who re-established the Shah's dynasty.

The Mahendra Museum
Exhibits the cabinet room, office chamber, the personal belongings and the creations of the late King Mahendra.

The Birendra Museum
Located inside the palace complex, the personal possessions of the present monarch, His Majesty King Birendra Bir Bikram Shah Dev, are displayed including the royal attires donned during various state and historic occasions. Also there are gifts, medals and honorary titles received from heads of state and others.

Patan Museum
Located in the residential palace compound of the Keshv Narayan Chowk inside the Royal Palace Complex at Paan Durbar Square. There you can see exhibits dating back to the 11th century or

even earlier. Some 200 objects of more than 1,500 in the national sacred art collection have been selected for permanent display. They are mostly cast in bronzes and gilt copper with work that covers both Hindu and Buddhist iconolgy.

The National Woodworking Museum
Located in the 15th-century restored building known as Pujarimath in Bhaktapur, excellent examples of master wood workmanship are exhibited of the Newari artisans of the Kathmandu Valley. The building itself is worth looking at as it is adorned with carved wooden windows, including the famous peacock and other latticed windows.

The Bronze and Brass Museum
Located opposite the National Woodworking Museum, and containing typical Newari bronze and brass utensils, ritual posts, lamp stands and jars used in medieval times.

Asa Archives
Located on the western fringe of the old part of Kathmandu, the archives possess an exceptional collection of over 6,000 loose-leaf handwritten books and 1,000 palm-leaf documents. The rare collection is an insight into the library tradition of medieval Kathmandu. The oldest manuscript here dates back to AD 1464, Most of the manuscripts are in Sanskrit and Nepalbhasa languages.

Kapilvastu Museum
Located in Tilaurakot about 26 km (16miles) from Lumbini, the place of Buddha, this museum contains an interesting collection of coins, pottery, toys and other artefacts dating to the 7th century AD. Also displayed are some unique jewellery pieces from the same period.

The Pokhara Museum
Located between the bus stop and Mahendra Pul in Pokhara, exhibits reflect the ethnic mosaic of western Nepal. The lifestyles and history of ethnic groups such as the Gurung, Thakali and the Tharu are attractively displayed through models, photographs and artefacts. One major attraction is a display highlighting the newly-discovered remains of the 8000-year-old settlement in Mustang.

Bibliography

Peisssel, Michel *Tiger for Breakfast*, Hodder and Stoughton, 1966
Shaha, Rishikesh *An Introduction to Nepal*, George Allen & Unwin, 1971
Flemming, Flemming and Bangdel Singh *Nature Himalayas*, 1976
Smith, Pye Charlie *Travels in Nepal*, Aurum Press Limited, 1988
Shrestha, Tej Kumar *Wildlife of Nepal*, Curriculum Development Center, 1979
Prakashan, Sahayogi *The Art of Nepal*, Sahayodk Prakashan, 1978
Muni, S D Nepal an *Assertive Monarch*, Chetna Publications , 1977
Bernier, Ronald *The Nepalese Pagoda*, S Chand & Company, 1979
Ali, Salim *The Book of Indian Birds,* Natural History Society, Mumbai, 1979
Chaudhari, N C *Hinduism,* Chatto and Windus, London, 1979
Davies, Philip *The Splendours of the Raj*, John Murray, London, 1984
Prater, S H *The Book of Indian Animals*, Natural History Society, Mumbai, 1948
Woodcock, Martin *Guide to the Birds of the Subcontinent*, Collins, London, 1980
Harle, J C *The Art and Architecture of the Indian Subcontinent*, Penguin India reprint, New Delhi, 1986

Wildlife Checklist

Mammals

BUSHBABIES, BABOONS, & MONKEYS
(Primates)
Rhesus Monkey
Langur Monkey
Common Langur
    Monkey

RODENTS
(Rodentia)
Himalayan Marmot

HERMITRAGUS
Himalayan Tahr
Tahr

PANGOLINS
(Pholidota)
Pangolins

HARES & RABBITS
(Lagomorpha)
Mouse Hare
Hispid Hare
Mouse Hare (Pika)
    Himalayan

CARNIVORES
(Carnivora)
Leopard
Snow Leopard
Clouded Leopard
Striped Hyena
Wild Dog
Wolf
Jackal
Palm Civet
Bear
Himalayan Black Bear
Sloth Bear
Brown Bear
Weasel
Himalayan Weasel
Tigers

WHALES AND DOLPHINS
(Cetacea)
Gangetic Dolphin

ELEPHANT
(Proboscidea)
Wild Elephant

ODD-TOED UNGULATES
(Perissodactyla)
Rhinoceros
One-horned Rhinoceros

EVEN-TOED UNGULATES
(Artiodactyla)
Hog Deer
Barking Deer
Music Deer
Spotted Deer
Swamp Deer
Sambar Deer
Chital Deer
Wild Boar
Red Panda
Yak
Feral Goat
Goral
Blue Bull
Serow Antelope
Four Horned Antelope

Reptiles and Amphibians

Lizard
Python
Gharial Crocodile
Marsh Mugger
    Crocodile

Birds

FLORICANS
Bengal Florican
Lesser Florican

STORKS
(Ciconiidae)
Black Stork
White Stork
Open-billed Stork

PHEASANTS
Impeyan Pheasant
Cheer Pheasant
Blood Pheasant
Mallard Pheasant
Crimson-horned
    Pheasant
Danphe (impeyan)
    Pheasant
Golden Pheasant
Kalij Pheasant
Koklas Pheasant

HERONS, EGRETS, & BITTERNS
(Ardeidae)
Night Heron
Purple Heron
Egrets
Bittern

WOODPECKERS
(Picidae)
Woodpecker

FLYCATCHERS
(Muscicapinae)
Flycatcher
Blue-throated
    Flycatcher
Grey-headed Flycatcher
Paradise Flycatcher
Pygmy Flycatcher
White-gorgetted
    Flycatcher

WARBLERS
(Sylviidae)
Olive ground Warbler
Large bush Warbler
Pallas's grasshopper
    Warbler
Tickell's leaf Warbler
Yellow-bellied Quail
Himalyan Bustard
Prinia

BABBLERS & CHATTERERS
(Timaliidae)
Spotten wren Babbler
Golden-breasted tit
    Babbler
Red-headed Babbler
Red-headed shrike
    Babbler
Rufous-bellied shrike
    Babbler
Scimitar Babbler
Spiny Babbler
Tailed Wren Babbler

BIRDS OF PREY
(Accipitridae)
Eagles
Golden Eagle
Steppe Eagle
Dark Kite
Honey Kite

SHRIKES
(Laniidae)
Black-headed Shrike
Brown Shrike

Chestnut-throated
    Shrike
Cuckoo Shrike
Grey Shrike

THRUSHES, WHEATEARS & CHATS
(Turdinae)
Rufous-necked
    laughing
    Thrush
Mistle Thrush
Bush Chat
Collared-bush Chat

TITS
(Paridae)
Simla black Tit
Spot-winged black Tit
White-throated Tit

BARBETS
(Capitonidae)
Blue-eared Barbet

HORNBILLS
(Indicatoridae)
Hornbill
Great (ground) Hornbill

BEE-EATERS
(Metropidae)
Chestnut-breasted
    Bee-eater

BLUEBIRD
Fairy Bluebird

BULBULS
(Pycnonotidae)
Red-vented Bulbul
Red-whiskered Bulbul

BUNTING, CANARIES & FINCHES
(Fringillidae)
Bunting
Tibetan snow Finch

CROWS
(Corvidae)
Red-billed Himalayan
    Chough
Yellow-billed Chough

COCHOA
Purple Cochoa

CORMORANTS
(Phalacrocoracidae)
Large Cormorants
Little Cormorants

CRAKES, GALLINULES, & RAILS
(Rallidae)
Crakes

CUCKOOS & COUCALS
(Cuculidae)
Emerald Cuckoo

DRONGOS
(Dicruridae)
Black Drongo
Raquet-tailed Drongo

DUCKS & GEESE
(Anatidae)
Brahminy Duck
Golden-eye Duck
Mallard Duck
Pink-headed Duck
Pintail Duck
Shoveler Duck
Bar-headed Goose
Grey-headed Goose
Common Pochard
White-eye Pochard

FORKTAIL
Forktail

GARGANEY
Garganey

GODWIT
Godwit

GRIFFON
Himalayan Griffon

GROSBEAK
Grosbeak

GROUND-PECKER
Hume's Ground-pecker

HONEYGUIDES
(Indicatoridae)
Himalayan Honey
 guide

JACANA
(Jacanidae)
Bronze-winged Jacana

JUNGLE
Red Jungle-fowl

KESTREL
Eurasian Kestrel

KINGFISHERS
(Alcedinidae)
Small pied Kingfisher
White-breasted
 Kingfisher

LAMMERGEIER
Lammergeier

LAPWINGS
Lapwing
Red-wattle Lapwing
Spurred-wing Lapwing
Eurasian Lapwing

LARKS
(Alandidae)
Crested Lark
Finch-bill Lark
Short-toed Lark

LEAFBIRD
Leafbird

MAGPIE
Pied Magpie

MINIA
Red-tailed Minia

MINIVET
Minivet

MUNIA
White-throated Munia

MYNA
Myna

NUTHATCHES
Nuthatch
Eurasian Nuthatch
Spotted Nuthatch
White-cheeked
 Nuthatch

ORIOLES
(Oriolidae)
Black-capped Oriole
Golden Oriole

OSPREY
(Pandionidae)
Osprey

OWLS
(Tytonidae)
Dusky horned Owl
Tibetan Owl

PARAKEET
Parakeet

PARROTBILL
Brown Parrotbill

GAME BIRDS
(Phasianidae)
Common Partridge
Snow Partridge
Swamp Partridge
Tibetan Partridge

PEAFOWLS
Common Peafowl
Mallard Peafowl

DOVES & PIGEONS
(Columbidae)
Blue rock Pigeon
Rock Pigeon
Snow Pigeon
Turkestan hill Pigeon
Wood Pigeon

PIPIL
Hodgson tree Pipil

PITTAS
(Pittidae)
Pitta

PLOVERS & TURNSTONES
(Charadriidae)
Plover

RAVENS
(Corvidae)
Raven
Tibetan Raven

REDSHANK
Spotted Redshank

ROLLER
(Coraciidae)
Indian Roller

SANDGROUSE
(Pteroclididae)
Red Sandgrouse
Tibetan Sandgrouse

SANDPIPER
(Tringa Hypoleucos)
Common Sandpiper

SIBIA
Black-capped Sibia

SNIPES
(Scolopacidae)
Fantail Snipe
Jack Snipe
Solitary Snipe
Wood Snipe

SNOWCOCK
Snowcock

STONE-CURLEW
Stone-curlew

SPIDERHUNTER
Little Spiderhunter

SUNBIRD
(Nectariniidae)
Sunbird

SWALLOWS & MARTINS
(Hirundinidae)
Martin
Yellow throated Martin

TEALS
(Anas)
Cotton Teal
Flacated Teal
Lesser Teal

GULLS & TERNS
(Laridae)
Black-billed Tern
Caspian Tern
Indian river Tern
Little Tern
Whiskered Tern
Herring Gull

THICK-KNEE
Great (great stone
 plover) Thick-knee

TITMOUSE
Spotted yellow
 Titmouse

TREECREEPER
Treecreeper

TWITE
Tibetan Twite

VULTURES
(Accipitridae)
Vulture
Eurasian griffon
 Vulture

WAGTAILS, PIPITS, & LONGCLAWS
(Motacillidae)
Wagtail
Blyth's Pipit
Paddyfield Pipit

WALLCREEPER
Wallcreeper

WHITE-EYE
(Zosteropidae)
White-eye

WOODCOCK
Woodcock

WOODPECKERS
(Picidae)
Great slaty Woodpecker

Listings

Airlines

Aeroflot
Kamaladi
Tel: 226161/
227399 (Resv)

Air Canada
Durbar Marg
Tel: 222838/224854
Resv: 222838
Fax: 227289

Air France
PO Box 256
Durbar Marg
Tel: 223339/248059
Fax: 226642

Air India
PO Box 314
Hattisar
Kamalpokhari
Tel: 416721/
415637 (Resv)

Air Mauritius
PO Box 5519
Kamaladi
Tel: 410208/
413734 (Resv)
Fax: 410576

Alitalia
PO Box 6156
Naxal
Tel: 222290/
418911
Fax: 410171/
418615

American West
Airlines
Windrost Travel
PO Box 10607
Durbar Marg
Tel: 220155/
225181 (Resv)
Fax: 225275

Asian Airlines
Helicopter
PO Box 4695
Tridevi Marg
Tel: 423273/
416116
Fax: 423315

Bangladesh
Biman
Marcopolo
Business Hotel
Kamal Pokhari
Tel: 442269/
416582 (Resv)

British Airways
Durbar Marg
Tel: 222266/
226611 (Resv)
Fax: 225241

Buddha Air
Naya Baneshwor
Tel: 474459

CAAC Airlines
Kamaladi
Tel: 411302/
411770 (Resv)
Fax: 419778/
416541

Cathay Pacific
PO Box 535
Kamaladi
Tel: 411725-6

China Airlines
PO Box 827
Hattisar
Tel: 412778/
419573 (Resv)
Fax: 412687

Delta Airlines
Durbar Marg
Tel: 220759 (Resv)
Fax: 226795

Dragon Air
PO Box 4163
Durbar Marg
Tel: 227064/
223162/223502
Fax: 227132

Druk Airlines
PO Box 4797
Durbar Marg
Tel: 225166/231890
Fax: 227229

Dynasty Aviation
Ka-3-78, New
Baneshwor
Tel: 225602
Fax: 522958

East West Airlines
Kamaladi
Tel: 225875/223219
Fax: 225875

Emirates
PO Box 939
Kantipath
Tel: 212080/
220579 (Resv)
Fax: 220267

Eva Airways
Lazimpat
Tel: 414318
Fax: 415381

Everest Air
PO Box 10760
Tel: 479094-5/
480431-3/475733/
222290/241016
(Resv)/471068
(Airport)
Fax: 470255/
226941/228932

Gorkha Airlines
PO Box 9451
New Baeshwor
Tel: 475855/
423137 (Resv)
Fax: 471136

Himalayan
Helicopters
Durbar Marg
Kathmandu
Tel: 217226/244381
Fax: 225150

Indian Airlines
Hattisar
Tel: 227289/
419649/414596
(Resv)/272647
(Airport)

Japan Airlines
Durbar Marg
Tel: 222838/
224854 (Resv)
Fax: 227289

Korean Air
PO Box 939
Kantipath
Tel: 212080
(Resv)/227563/
220579/214192/
216080
Fax: 220267

Kuwait Airlines
PO Box 3226
Kantipath
Tel: 222884/
227387 (Resv)
Fax: 227392

Lufthansa
PO Box 214
Durbar Marg
Tel: 222121/
223052/224341
(Resv)/472254
(Airport)
Fax: 221900

Lumbini Airways
PO Box 6215
Kantipath
Tel: 230148/
482725/230631
(Resv)
Fax: 414182

Modilufts
Durbar Marg
Tel: 223045/47357
(Cargo)

Necon Air
Tel: 473860/
480565/474933/
242507/472542
(Resv)/480473
(Airport)

Nepal Airways
Hattisar
Tel: 418494/
416575/410091
(Resv)

North West
Airlines
Lainchaur
Tel: 418387/
423143/4 (Resv)
Fax: 423145/
418382

Pakistan
International
Airlines
Durbar Marg
Kathmandu
Tel: 223102/
227429/472256/
472257-8 (Airport)
Fax: 220106

Philippines
Airlines
Kantipath
Tel: 226262
Fax: 224436

Qantas Airways
Durbar Marg
Tel: 228288
Fax: 221180

Qatar Airways
Hattisar
Tel: 422961/
422963 (Resv)/
470311 (Airport)

Royal Brunei
PO Box 5519
Kamaladi
Tel: 410208/
413734 (Resv)
Fax: 410576

Royal Dutch
Airlines (KLM)
PO Box 629
Durbar Marg
Tel: 224895
Fax: 224797

Royal Nepal
Airlines
New Road
Tel: 220757/
244055 (Resv)/
470311 (Airport)
Fax: 225348

Saudi Arabian
Airlines
Kantipath
Tel: 222787/
222387 (Resv)
Fax: 227392

Scandianavian
Airlines System
(SAS)
Shahid Sukra
Mark
Kupondole
Lalitpur
Tel: 524732/
524232 (Resv)
Fax: 521880

Singapore Airlines
Durbar Marg
Tel: 220759/
472294 (Airport)
Fax: 226795

Swissair
PO Box 170, Naxal
Tel: 413017
Fax: 420970

Thai Airways
International
Durbar Marg
Tel: 223565/
221247/224917/
225084 (Resv)
Fax: 221130

Trans World
Airlines
PO Box 5351
Kamaladi
Tel: 473440/
411725-6
Fax: 470287/272201

Royal Nepal Airlines offices & Agents Abroad

Australia
South Pacific
Express
Level 13
257 Collins Street
Melbourne VIC
3000
Tel: 61-3-6545185
Fax: 61-3-6504650

South Pacific
Express, Level 7
207 Murray Street
Perth WA 6000
Tel 61-9-3213751
Fax: 61-9-3215210

South Pacific
Express
Level 17
456 Kent Street
Sydney 200
Tel 61-2-2647346
Fax: 61-2-2647046

Bangladesh
Bengal Airlift Ltd.
Elite House
54 Motijheel
Commercial Area
Dhaka 1000
Tel: 880-2-259594
Fax: 880-2-833048

China
RNAC
Room 315
1558 Dingxi Road
Shanghai

China Eastern
Airlines
Hong Qiao
International
Airport
Shanghai 200335
Tel: 86-21-2558899/
2557829
Fax: 86-21-2557929

Germany
Poststrasse 2-4
60329
Frankfurt Main
Tel: 49-69-259345
Fax: 49-69-259344

Hong Kong
RNAC
Room 704
Lippo Sun Plaza
Building
28 Canton Road
Trsimshatsui
Kowloon
Tel: 852-3759151/
3753152
Fax: 852-3757069

India
RNAC
222 Maker
Chamber V
Nariman Point
Bombay 400 021
Tel: 91-22- 2835489/
2836197-9

RNAC
41 Chowringhee
Road
Calcutta 700 071
Tel: 91-33-298534/
298549

RNAC
44 Janapath
New Delhi 100 001
Tel: 91-11-
3321572/3323437

RNAC
Maurya Shopping
Arcade
South Gandhi
Maidan
Patna 800001
Tel: 91-612-235659

Japan
RNAC
Matsuzaki Bldg.
No. 902
3-1-21 Kitahama
Chuo-ku
Osaka 541
Tel: 81-6-2292545
Fax: 81-6-2292544

Himal World
Service
Shinjuku Daikan
Plaza
Business No. 905
7-9-15
Nishishinjuku
Shinjuku-ku
Tokyo 160
Tel: 81-3-33693797
Fax: 81-3-
33699822

Oman
Elsa Travels
Rowi Street
PO Box 36, Muscat
Tel: 968-795118/9

New Zealand
South Pacific
Aviation
199 Ponsonby Rd
Auckland
Tel: 64-9-3601747
Fax: 64-9-3761737

Pakistan
Crown Travels
No. 7, 1st Floor
Services Club
Extension Bldg
Mereweather
Road, Karachi
Tel: 92-21-525128
Fax: 92-21-514522

Saudi Arabia
Yusuf Bin Ahmed
Kanoo
PO Box 37
Dammam 31411
Tel: 966-3-8348880
Fax: 966-3-
8345369

Singapore
03-07/08
Peninsula
Shopping Centre
3 Coleman Street
Singapore 0617
Tel: 65-3395535

Taiwan
Overseas Travel
Service
3F No. 156 Fu
Shin Road, Taipei
Tel: 886-2-5144600
Fax: 866-2-7191556

Thailand
10/12-13, 2nd Floor
Sivadon Building
1/4 Convent, Road
Bangkok 10500
Tel: 66-2-333921/4
Fax: 66-2-335937

United Arab Emirates
Eisa Travels
Airport Road
PO Box 11266,
Dubai
Tel: 971-4237348
Fax: 971-4284200

United Kingdom
Brightsun Travel
UK Ltd
1st Floor, 13 New
Burlington St.
London W1X1FE
Tel: 44-171- 4940974
Fax: 44-171-4941767

USA
Travel
Promotion Inc.
767 5th Avenue
NY 10153,
New York
Tel: 1-818-7671833
Fax: 1-212-7600434

Travel
Promotion Inc.
8129 San
Fernando Road
Sun Valley
CA 91352
Tel: 1-818-7671833

Travel
Promotion Ltd
3050 Rost Oak
Blvd.
1320 Houston
Texas 77056
Tel: 1-713-6238740

Airports

Tribhuwan
International
Airport
Tel: (Int.) 470311
(Domestic)
470668

Banks

Kathmandu
Agricultural
Development Bank
Tel: 211744/
211802/211806
Fax: 416306

American
Express Bank
Tel: 229053/214926
Fax: 228837

Bank of
Kathmandu
PO Box 9044
Tel: 421552
Fax: 418990

Citibank
Hotel Yak & Yeti
Durbar Marg
Tel: 227884
Fax: 227884

Everest Bank
Tel: 482578
Fax: 482263

Himalayan Bank
PO Box 3810
Tel: 227745
Fax: 222800

Nepal Arab Bank
PO Box 3729
Tel: 227181/
226785-6
Fax: 226905

Nepal -
Bangladesh Bank
Putali Sadak
Tel: 421569/418707

Nepal Bank
New Road
Tel: 224337/224808

Nepal
Grindlays Bank
New Baneshwor
Tel: 228474
Fax: 228692

Nepal
Indo-Suez Bank
PO Box 3412
Durbar Marg
Tel: 228927
Fax: 226349

Nepal Rastra Bank
PO Box 73
Tel: 410201/
419804-5
Fax: 416306/
414553

Nepal SBI Bank
PO Box 6049
Tel: 225326/
230808/413102/
422879
Fax: 221268

Rastriya Banijya
Bank
Tangal
Tel: 419821/410852

Standard
Chartered Bank
PO Box 1526
Tel: 220129
Fax: 220129

Business Associations

Kathmandu
Trade Promotion
Centre
PO Box 825
Tel: 478144/5
Fax: 478143

Carpet & Wool
Development
Board
Lazimpat
Tel/Fax: 411286

Central Carpet
Industry
Association
PO Box 2419
Tel: 413135/422729
Fax: 422891

Federation of
Nepalese
Chambers of
Commerce &
Industry
PO Box 269
Tel: 230407
Fax: 227322

Garment
Association of
Nepal
Sangkhamul Rd
New Baneswor
Tel: 223173/233692

Handicraft
Association of
Nepal
PO Box 784
Thapathali
Tel: 212567
Fax: 222940

Hotel Association
of Nepal
G.A.A. Building
Thamel
Tel: 412705
Fax: 417133

National
Productivity &
Economic
Development
Centre
PO Box 1318
Tel: 272522
Fax: 272530

Nepal
Association of
Rafting Agents
Ghantaghar
Tel: 221197

Nepal
Association of
Travel Agents
Garidhara Road
Goma Ganesh
Naxal
Tel: 220759
Fax: 411764

Nepal Chamber
of Commerce
PO Box 198
Kanti Path
Tel: 222890/230210
Fax: 229998

Nepal Foreign
Trade Association
PO Box 541
Basantpur
Tel: 223784
Fax: 224094

Nepal Incentive
Convention
Association
Sanepa, Patan
Tel: 535036
Fax: 527724

Nepal Leather
Industry & Trade
Association
PO Box 8006
Tel: 214603

Nepal
Mountaineering
Association
Naxal
Tel: 411525
Fax: 416278

Tourists Guide
Association of
Nepal, Kamalkshi
Tel: 225102
Fax: 247076

Trekking Agents
Association of
Nepal, Naxal
Tel/Fax: 419245

Car Rental

Goodwill Vehicle
Service
Kamal Pokhari
Nr. Kamal
Pokhari Sports
Club
Tel: 410704
Fax: 226472

Highway Star
PO Box 4404
Naxal
Narayan Chaur
Tel: 413928/411562

Lama
Transportation
Management
Service
Kamaladi
(near Ganesthan)
Tel: 222594

New Buddha
Vehicle
PO Box 897
EPC No. 5134
Hattisar
Tel: 413685

Trans
International
Nagpokhari
Naxal
PO Box 5160
Tel: 416891

Mt. Everest
Transportation
Service
Kasturi Arcade
Durbar Marg
Tel: 423779
Fax: 228816

Prajapati
Transport Service
PO Box 8975
EPC: 5262
Bhagwan Bahal
Thamel
Tel: 424692/524078

Transportation
Mediator Service
PO Box 4616
Kamaladi
Tel: 410981
Fax: 524078

Credit Cards

Kathmandu
American
Express Bank
Kantipath
Tel: 226635/214926
Fax: 228837

Himalayan Card
PO Box 3810
Karmachari
Sanchaya Kosh
Building
Tridevi Marg
Thamel
Tel: 225399/227756
Fax: 222800

Visa & Master
Card
PO Box 3729
Nabil Bank
Kantipath Branch
Tel: 227181/228538
Fax: 226905

JCB, Visa &
Master Card
Nepal
Grindlays Bank
Kantipath
Tel: 527659
Fax: 228692

Foreign Diplomatic Missions

Kathmandu
Australia
Bansbari
Tel: 411578/
413076/417566
Fax: 417533

Austria
PO Box 146
Hattisar
Tel: 410891
Fax: 226820

Bangladesh
PO Box 789
Naxal
Tel: 411958/414943

Belgium
PO Box 3328
Laldurbar
Tel: 228925/214760

Canada
Lazimpat
Kathmandu
Tel: 415193/389

China
Baluwater
Tel: 411740/416485
Fax: 411388

Denmark
PO Box 5598
Baluwater
Tel: 413010/20
Fax: 411409

Egypt
Pulchowk
Lalitpur
PO Box 792
Tel: 524418
Fax: 522975

Finland
PO Box 2126
Lazimpat
Tel: 417221/416636
Fax: 416703

France
Lazimpat
Tel: 412332/414734

Maldives
PO Box 324
Durbar Marg
Tel: 223045
Fax: 224001

Netherlands
Kumaripati
Lalitpur
PO Box 1966
Tel: 523444/522915

New Zealand
PO Box 224
Dillibazar
Tel: 412436
Fax: 414750

Norway
Jawalakhel
Lalitpur
PO Box 1045
Tel: 521646
Fax: 521720

Phillippines
PO Box 2640
Toyota House
Sinamangal
Tel: 478301-5
Fax: 471195

Poland
Ganabahal
Tel: 221101
Fax: 224823

Spain
PO Box 459
Battisputali
Tel: 472328/473724
Fax: 47139

Sweden
Khichapokari
Tel: 220939
Fax: 221826

Switzerland
Jawalakhel
Lalitpur
Tel: 523168/468
Fax: 525358

Turkey
Bijulibazar
Tel: 221158/
523596/524596
Fax: 523520

United Kingdom
PO Box 106
Lainchour
Tel: 410583/414588

USA
Paniphokhari
Tel: 411179/
411613/413980
Fax: 417533

Government Departments

Civil Aviation
Babar Mahal
Tel: 211828/213226
Fax: 225347/8

Commerce
Naya Baneswor
Tel: 227364/227404
and:

Babar Maha
Tel: 217672/223489

Epidemiology
Teku
Tel: 215050/227268

Foreign Affairs
Sital Niwas
Tel: 416010/5

Home Affairs
Singh Durba
Tel: 224849/
228024

Hydrology &
Meterology
Babar Mahal
Tel: 212151/ 213425

Immigration
Tridevi Marg
Thamel
Tel: 418573
and:
Airport Road
Pokhara
Tel: 21167

Industry
Tripureshwor
Tel: 212357/
213838/215030/
226686

Information
Bagbazar
Tel: 222317/716

National Parks
& Wild Life
Conservation
Babar Mahal
Tel: 220850/912

Postal Services
Dillibazar
Tel: 411353

Roads
Babar Mahal
Tel: 211109/377

Survey
Min Bhawan
Tel: 226813

Tourism
Babar Mahal
Tel: 247037/39/
41
Fax: 227281

Hot Air Ballooning

Kathmandu
Balloon Sunrise
Nepal
PO Box 11
Hattisar
Tel: 418214/
424131/2
Fax: 424157

Hotels

(2-Star)
Bhaktapur
Club Himalayan
Nagarkot Resort
Nagarkot
Windy Hills
Tel: 290883/227767
Fax: 290868

Chitwan
Chitwan Key
Man Hotel
Bharatpur Height
Chitwan
Tel: 056-20200
Fax: 419798

Hermitage Hotel
Sauraha
Tel: 424390
Fax: 424390

Jungle Camp
Hotel
Royal Chitwan
National Park
Tel: 240669/222132
Fax: 222132

Lovely River
Resort
Thimura
Tel: 056-29401
Fax: 425042

Riverside Spring
Resort
Kurintar
(PO Box 4384
Kathmandu)
Tel: 233727
Fax: 232163

Safari
Narayani Hotel
Bharatpur
Tel: 056-20634
(Resv): 525015-18
Fax: 056-21058

Daman
Everest Panorama
Resort
(PO Box 3035
Kathmandu)
Tel: 415372-3/
415057/Daman
40382
Fax: 416028/
Daman 40380

(3-Star)
Dhanding
New Hotel
Crystal
Nagdhunga
Tel: 20035-6 /22427
Fax: 20234

Jhapa
Airport Rest
House
Bhadrapur 15
Tel: 023-20329
Fax: (Resv) (01)
227073/226655

Kathmandu
(5-Star)
Annapurna
(Hotel de l')
PO Box 140
Durbar Marg
Tel: 221711
Fax: 225236

Everest Hotel
PO Box 659
Baneswor
Tel: 220567/226081
Fax: 226088/
224421

Mercure Hotel
Kathmandu
PO Box 324
Lazimpat
Tel: 419358
Fax: 416071

Soaltee Holiday
Inn Crown Plaza
Tahachal
Kathmandu
Tel: 272555
Fax: 272205

Yak & Yeti Hotel
PO Box 1016
Durbar Marg
Tel: 248999/
240520
Fax: 227781/2

(4-Star)
Bluestar Hotel
PO Box 983
Tripureswar
Tel: 228833
Fax: 226820

Dynasty Plaza
Hotel
Woodlands
PO Box 760
Durbar Marg
Tel: 220123/
222683
Fax: 225650/
223083

Himalaya Hotel
PO Box 2141
Kupondole
Lalitpur
Tel: 523900
Fax: 523909

Kathmandu
Hotel
PO Box 4504
Maharajgunj
Tel: 410786/
418494
Fax: 414091

Malla Hotel
Lekhnath Marg
PO Box 787
Tel: 410620/966
Fax: 418382

Narayani Hotel
PO Box 1357
Pulchowk
Lalitpur
Tel: 525015-18/
527442
Fax: 521312

Shangri-La Hotel
PO Box 655
Lazimpat
Tel: 412999
Fax: 414184

Shanker Hotel
PO Box 350
Lazimpat
Tel: 410151/2
Fax: 412691

Sherpa Hotel
PO Box 901
Durbar Marg
Tel: 227000/102/
402/602
Fax: 222026

Woodlands
Dynasty Plaza
PO Box 760
Durbar Marg
Tel: 222683/
220123
Fax: 225650/
245691

(3-Star)
Garden Hotel
PO Box 5954
Naya Bazar
Thamel
Tel: 411951/415690
Fax: 418072

Harati Hotel
PO Box 289
Chhetrapati
Tel: 221969/226527
Fax: 223329

Hotel Manang
PO Box 5608
Thamel
Tel: 410993/419247
Fax: 415821

Marcopolo
Business Hotel
Kamalpokhari
Tel: 415432/416432
Fax: 418832

Marsyangdi
Hotel
PO Box 5206
Thamel
Tel: 412129/414105
Fax: 410008

Mountain Hotel
PO Box 900
Kantipath
Tel: 220481/
224498/224086
Fax: 227736

Summit Hotel
PO Box 1406
Tel: 521810/524694
Fax: 523737

(2-Star)
Ambassador
Hotel
PO Box 2769
Lazimpat
Tel: 410432/414432
Fax: 413641

Blue
Diamond Hotel
PO Box 2134
Jyatha
Tel: 226320/907
Fax: 226392

Eden Hotel
Tel: 213863

Excelsior Hotel
PO Box 4583
Thamel
Tel: 411566/220285
Fax: 410853

Gautam Hotel
Jyatha
Kantipath
Tel: 244515-7
Fax: 245232/222602

Greenwich
Village Hotel
Kupandol
Lalitpur
PO Box 837
Tel: 521780/522399
Fax: 526683

Karnali Hotel
PO Box 5537
Maharajgunj
Tel: 418634/414925
Fax: 414906

Kathmandu
Guest House
PO Box 2769
Thamel
Tel: 413632/418733
Fax: 417133

Manaslu Hotel
Lazimpat
Tel: 410071/413470
Fax: 416516

Mandap Hotel
PO Box 3756
Thamel
Tel: 413321/419735
Fax: 419734

M. M.
International
Hotel
PO Box 147
Thamel
Tel: 411847/423595
Fax: 418578/423442

Norbhu
Lankha Hotel
PO Box 8246
Thamel
Tel: 414799/410630
Fax: 229080

Nuptse Hotel
Naya Bazar
Thamel
Tel: 278833/416956
Fax: 411582

Orchid Hotel
Tripureshwor
Tel: 240437/
240472/242777
Fax: 229080

Paradise Hotel
PO Box 1011
Kantipath
Tel: 212746/214983

Rara Hotel
PO Box 3295
Kantipath
Tel: 226969/222436
Fax: 229158

Ratna Hotel
PO Box 6267
Bagbazar
Tel: 224809/220001

Sangam Hotel
Baghbazar
PO Box 9110
Tel: 220219/240555
Fax: 228496

Stupa Hotel
PO Box 1922
Boudha
Tel: 470400/
470385/480311/2
Fax: 478386

Tayoma Hotel
Chhetrapati
Thamel
PO Box 5703
Tel: 244149/
244291/222617
Fax: 222037

Thamel Hotel
PO Box 11767
Thamel
Tel: 417643/
414693/423968
Fax: 418547

Tilkho Hotel
Thamel
Tel: 410132/416820
Fax: 418538

Tridevi Ltd.
Thamel
Tel: 411566/220285
Fax: 412822

Trivedi Hotel
Trivedi Marg
Thamel
Tel: 412261
Fax: 412261

Tushita Rest
House
Kantipath
PO Box 3004
Tel: 216913/242943
Fax: 228066

Utse Hotel
Thamel
Tel: 226946
Fax: 226945

Vaishali Hotel
Thamel
Tel: 413968/423934
Fax: 414510

Vajra Hotel
Bijeswari
Tel: 271545/
272719/271824
Fax: 271695

(1-Star)
Aloha Inn
Jawalakhel
Lalitpur
PO Box 7348
Tel: 522796/
526414/527831
Fax: 524571

Aquamarine Hotel
Shantinagar
New Baneswor
Tel: 478753/4
Fax: 472810

Blue Ocean Hotel
PO Box 10894
Thamel
Tel: 412577/418499
Fax: 425325

Buddha Hotel
PO Box 5439
Thamel
Tel: 413194

Budget Hotel
Sundhara
Tel: 218712

Central Hotel
PO Box 1756
Durbar Marg
Tel: 220730/222997
Fax: 227431

Chitwan
Jungle Lodge
Durbar Marg
Tel: 228458/
222679/228918
Fax: 228349

City Center
New Road
Tel: 223336

Clarion Hotel
PO Box 676
Man Bhawan
Tel: 524512
Fax: 224464

Dhulikhel
Lodge Resort
PO Box 6020
Tel: 212988/11-
61114/61494
Fax: 222926

Dhulikhel
Mountain Resort
PO Box 3203
Lazimpat
Tel: 420774
Fax: 420778

Durbar Hotel
PO Box 9700
Durbar Marg
Tel: 243170
Fax: 242573

Dwarika's
Kathmandu
Village Hotel
PO Box 459
Battisputali
Tel: 470770/473724
Fax: 471379/225131

Fort Resort Hotel
Naldum Nagarkot
Tel: 290869/232829
Fax: 228066

Four
Seasons Hotel
PO Box 4790, Teku
Tel: 243938/244767
Fax: 220494

Gaida Wildlife
Jungle Lodge
& Jungle Camp
Durbar Marg
Tel: 220940
Fax: 227292

Ganesh
Himal Hotel
PO Box 3854
Chhetrapati
Tel: 223216
Fax: 227049

Garuda Hotel
Thamel
Tel: 414766/
416776/416340
Fax: 413614/472390

Gauri Shankar
Thamel
Sallaghari
PO Box 3022
Tel: 411718/605
Fax: 411605

Godavari Village
Resort Hotel
Amarabati
Godavari Lalitpur
Tel: 228253
Fax: 526683

Hill Side Hotel
Teku
Tel: 213839

Himalayan
Shangri-La Resort
Dhulikhel Ward 1
Tel: 423939
Fax: 423939

Himalayan
View Hotel
PO Box 218
Kantipath
Tel: 216531
Fax: 419317/411055

Holy Castle Hotel
PO Box 3211
Bhotebahal
Tel: 228364
Fax: 220178

Iceland
View Hotel
PO Box 5881
Thamel
Tel: 420678/416686
Fax: 420678

Island Jungle
Resort
Durbar Marg
Tel: 220162/229116
Fax: 225615

Khumbila Hotel
Gausala
Battishputali
Tel: 472561

Machan Wildlife
Resort
PO Box 3140
Durbar Marg
Tel: 225001/
245401-2
Fax: 240681/231957

Marsyangdi
Mandala Hotel
Chhetrapati
Dhobichowr
Tel: 242411/220275
Fax: 220275

Mayalu Hotel
PO Box 1276
Durbar Marg
Tel: 223596

Moonlight Hotel
Pakanajole
Thamel
Tel: 425188/420636
Fax: 419452

Mt. Makalu Hotel
Dharmapath
Tel: 224616/223955
Fax: 524571

Mustang Holiday
Inn Hotel
PO Box 3352
Jyatha
Thamel
Tel: 226538/244241
Fax: 228216

My Home Hotel
Thamel
Kwapurnoo
House No. 4
Tel: 232188
Fax: 224466

Norling Hotel
PO Box 9192
Jyatha
Thamel
Tel: 240734
Fax: 226735

Shakti Hotel
Thamel
Tel: 410121/423328
Fax: 418897

Shambala Hotel
PO Box 3039
Chhetrapati
Tel: 225986
Fax: 414024

Shikhar Hotel
Satgumati
Thamel
Tel: 415588
Fax: 220143

Sita Hotel
Thapathali
Tel: 245965/231712
Fax: 229407

Sky Hotel
Lagantole
Tel: 220530

Space Mountain
Hotel, Nagarkot
Bhaktapur
Tel: 290871
Fax: 241812

Sunset View Hotel
Shankhamul
Tel: 482172
Fax: 482219

Tibet Guest House
PO Box 1132
Chhetrapati
Tel: 214383/241556
Fax: 220518

Tiger Tops
Karnali Lodge
PO Box 242
Tel: 411225
Fax: 414075/419126

Tiger Tops Tharu
Safari Resort
PO Box 242
Tel: 411225
Fax: 414075

Valley View Hotel
Teku
Tel: 213681/242571
Fax: 242571

Victoria Hotel
Bagh Durbar
Sundhara
Tel: 231954/224278

Yellow
Pagoda Hotel
PO Box 373
Kantipath
Tel: 220337/8
Fax: 228914/225002

Lumbini
Nirvana Hotel
PO Box 24
Siddharthanagar
Tel: 20516/20837/
(Resv): 1-225370/
247422
Fax: 21262

**Pokhara
(2-Star)**
Fish Tail Lodge
Tel: 20071
Fax: 225236

Saino Inn Hotel
Santpatan
Lake Side
Tel: 22868
Fax: 1-418578

(1-Star)
Base Camp Resort
Lake Side
PO Box 182
Tel: 21226/
22949/23653
Fax: 20903
(Resv) 1-226367

Bed Rock Hotel
Lake Side
Tel: 1-425304
Fax: 1-413118

Dhaulagiri View
Hotel
Dhampus VDC
Ward No. 6
Tel: 20218

Dumori Hotel
Lake Side
Tel: 21462
Fax: 1-419796

Kantipur Hotel
Greater Lake Side
Baidam
Tel: 20886/7
Fax: 20886/1-
423232

Nature's Grace
Lodge
Baidam-6
Lake Side
Tel/Fax: 20793/
27220

Shangrila
Village Resort
Gairi Patan
Tel: 22122/
23700/23676
Fax: 20958

Shikhar Hotel
Lake Side
Tel: 21966
Fax: 22201

Silent Peak Hotel
Lake Side
Baidam 6
Tel: 21237

Snow Land Hotel
Lake Side
Tel: 20384
Fax: 20958

Sunrise Hotel
Mahendra Pool
Tel: 21714

Thoungla Hotel
Lake Side
Tel: 21157
(Resv): 1-241211

Tragopan Ltd.
Rastra Bank Chok
Tel: 21708

Vision
Himalayan Hotel
Lake Side
Tel: 23201
Fax: 1-418578

Hospitals

Kathmandu
Apanga Bal
Hospital
Jorpati
Tel: 470874

Ayurved Hospital
Nardevi
Tel: 220764

Bankali Mental
Hospital
Gausala
Tel: 470302

Bhaktapur
Hospital
Doodh Pati
Bhaktapur
Tel: 610676/798

Bir Hospital
Tudikhel
Ratnapark
Tel: 221119/988
(Emergency):
223807

Birendra Police
Hospital
Maharajgunj
Tel: 225344

Birendra Army
Hospital
Chhauni
Tel: 271940/1

Blood Bank
Bhikruti Mandap
Tel: 225344

CIWEC Clinic
Durbar Marg
Tel: 410983

Eye Hospital
Tripureshwor
Tel: 215466/
213317/213765

Homeopathic
Hospital
Pulchowk
Lalitpur
Tel: 522092

Infectious Disease
Hospital
Teku
Tel: 211112/344

Jana
Chikistsalaya
Nhyokha
Tel: 228456

Kanti Children's
Hospital
Maharajgunj
Tel: 414798/
413398/411550

Khagendra Nava
Jeevan Kendra
Jorpati
Tel: 471678

Kathmandu
Model Hospital
Bagh Baza
Tel: 232752

Leprosy Hospital
Tika Bhairab
Lalitpur
Tel: 290545

Maternity Hospital
Thapathali
Tel: 211243

Mental Hospital
Lagankhel
Lalitpur
Tel: 521612

Nepal Anti TB
Hospital
Kalimati
Tel: 270483

Nepal Anti TB
Hospital
Thimi
Bhaktapur
Tel: 610706

Nepal
International
Clinic
Durbar Marg
Tel: 412842

Patan Hospital
Lagankhel
Tel: 522295/
521048/521034

Singh Durbar
Vaidhyakhana
Singh Durbar
Tel: 228326

Teku Hospital
Teku
Tel: 211112

Tilganga Eye
Centre
Gausala
Tel: 475927/476575

T.U. Teaching
Hospital
Maharajgunj
Tel: 412303/404/
505/808

Mountain Biking Agencies

Bhrikuti
Himalayan Treks
PO Box 2267
Nagh Pokhari
Naya Bato
Tel: 417459
Fax: 413612

First Nepali
Mountain Bikers
PO Box 2247
Thamel
Tel: 279062/
272212/416596
Fax: 411055

Himalayan
Mountain Bike
PO Box 2247
Tel: 416596
Fax: 411724

Tibet Travel
& Tours
Trivedi Marg
Thamel
PO Box 7246
Tel: 231130
Fax: 228986

Police

Emergency Police
Tel: 100

Bhaktapur
District Police
Office
Tel: 610106

Kathmandu
Police
Headquarters
Naxal
Tel: 410088/
411210/659/705

District Police
Office
Tel: 228989

Lalitpur
District Police
Office
Tel: 521115

Post Offices

Kathmandu
Foreign Post
Office
Sundhara
Tel: 211760

General Post
Office
Singh Durbar
Tel: 223512

Royal Nepalese Embassies Abroad

Bangladesh
United Nation
Road
2, Baridhara
Diplomatic
Enclave
Dhaka
Tel: 880-2-
601790/601890/
602091
Fax: 880-2-886401

Belgium
Avenue Franklin
Roosevelt, 24
1050 Brussels
Tel: 32-2-
6494048/
6498133/6491865
Fax: 32-2-6498454

China
No. 1, Sanilitun
Xiluijie-Lu
Beijing
Tel: 86-10-5321795
Fax: 86-10-5323251

Egypt
9 Tiba Street
Dokki
Cairo
Tel: 20-2-361590/
360426
Fax: 20-2-704447

France
45, Bis rue des
Acacias
75017 Paris
Tel: 33-1-46224867
Fax: 33-1-42270865

Germany
Im Hag 15,
D-5300 Bonn
Tel: 49-228-
343097/343099
Fax: 49-228 -
856747

India
Barakhamba
Road
New Delhi
110001
Tel: 91-11 3329969/
3327361/3329218
Fax: 91-11-
3326857

Japan
14-9 Tokokoki
7-chome
Setagaya-Ku
Tojyo 158
Tel: 81-3- 37055558/
9
Fax: 81-3 - 37058264

Mayanmar
16, Natmauk
Yeiktha
PO Box 84
Yangon
Tel: 951-550633/
553168
Fax: 951-549803

Pakistan
506, Street No.84,
Attaturk Avenue
Ramna G-6/4
Islamabad
Tel: 92-51-210642
/212754
Fax: 92-51-217875

Russia
2nd
Neopalimovsky
Pereulok 14/7
Moscow
Tel: 7-95-2447356
/2419311
Fax: 7-95-2440000

Saudi Arabia
Khazan Street
nr. Prince
Musaed Palace
PO Box 94384
Riyadh 11693
Tel: 966-4024758/
4036433/4039482
Fax: 966-4036488

Thailand
189 Sukhumvit 71
Road
Bangkok 10110
Tel: 66-2-3917240 /
3902280
Fax: 66-2-3812406

United Kingdom
12A Kensington
Palace Gardens
London W8 4QU
Tel: 44-171-
2291594/2296231
Fax: 44-171-7929861

USA
2131 Leroy Place,
NW
Washington DC
20008
Tel: 1-202 -
6674550/2
Fax: 1-202 6675534

United Nations
Suite 202
820 Second Ave
New York, USA
Tel: 1-212-
3704188/9
Fax: 1-212- 9532038

and:
1, rue Frederic-
Amiel
1203 Geneva
Switzerland
Tel: 41-22-3444441
/3452934
Fax: 41-22-3444093

Rafting Agencies

Kathmandu
Action Adventure
PO Box 5278
Balaju
Tel/Fax: 271967

All Nepal
River Trek
PO Box 7140
Trivedi Marg
Tel: 225392
Fax: 220143

Alpine Trekking
& Expedition
Jyatha
Thamel
Tel/Fax: 226980

Arun River
Adventure
Thamel
Tel: 421732
Fax: 414742

Canyon
Expeditions
Jyatha
Thamel
Tel: 224430
Fax: 220143

Dragon River
Rafting
PO Box 5211
Trivedi Marg
Tel: 223758
Fax: 423427

Equator
Expeditions
Thamel
PO Box 8404
Tel: 424344/425800
Fax: 425801

Everest River
Adventure
PO Box 8622
Thamel
Tel: 416951
Fax: 419870

GST River Rafting
PO Box 5184
Thamel
Tel: 412116/423416
Fax: 418578

Gorkha's River
Expedition
PO Box 6526

Great Himalayan
Rivers
PO Box 4931
Lazimpat
Tel: 410937
Fax: 412757

Greenways River
Adventures
PO Box 8160
Thamel
Tel: 411216
Fax: 424051

Hillary Rafting
Hotel Garuda
Building
PO Box 1771
Thamel
Tel: 426551/525354
Fax: 413614

Himalayan
Adventure
Rafting
PO Box 1946
Maharajgunj
Tel: 411866/420637
Fax: 410858

Himalayan
Encounters
PO Box 2769
Thamel
Tel: 417426
Fax: 417133

Himalayan
Experience
PO Box 824
Gairidhara
Tel: 412013

Himalayan Magic
Adventure
PO Box 7112
Thamel
Tel: 225897/247922
Fax: 224466

Himalayan River
Exploration
PO Box 170
Lazimpat
Tel: 411225
Fax: 414075/
419126

Himalayan
River Rider
PO Box 2384
Lazimpat
Tel: 419233
Fax: 414390

Himalayan
River Runner
PO Box 7533
Durbar Marg
Tel: 230896
Fax: 226912

Himalayan
Thrills
PO Box 2743
Nagpokhari
Tel: 413323
Fax: 420905

Himalayan
Water Ways
PO Box 5802
Jyatha
Tel: 226790
Fax: 419419

Himalayan
White Water
PO Box 3725
Lazimpath
Tel: 419819
Fax: 415401

Himalayan White
Water Thrills
PO Box 8049
Nagpokhari
Tel: 413323
Fax: 412897

Himalayan
Wonders
PO Box 2446
Thamel
Tel: 414049/426720
Fax: 419317

Holiday
Adventure
PO Box 5514
Thamel
Fax: 417045

Kailash Export
Narsingh Camp
Thamel
Tel: 229222/
223610/472114
Fax: 224785/473791

Manakamana
River Adventure
PO Box 2913
Jyatha
Tel: 224217
Fax: 229459

Mountain River
Adventure
PO Box 1173
Kantipath
Tel: 221585
Fax: 220178

Mountain
River Rafting
PO Box 10115
Thamel
Tel: 425770/418633
Fax: 425769

NK's River
Experience
PO Box 1914
Jholhhen
Tel: 223170/240318
Fax: 241945

Nepal Outdoor
Centre
PO Box 3917
Jyatha
Tel: 226464
Fax: 226945

Nepal River
Excursion
PO Box 2455
Jyatha
Tel: 220097
Fax: 220059

Nepal River
Exploration
PO Box 3203
Lazimpat
Tel: 420774/420776
Fax: 420778

Outdoor
Adventure Club
PO Box 5101
Gairidhara
Tel: 412038
Fax: 227567

Peace Zone White
Water Rafting
PO Box 2841
Thamel
Tel: 423428/
245501
Fax: 226521

Racing River
Adventure
PO Box 4396
Jyatha
Tel: 227238
Fax: 226945

Raft'n Nepal
River
PO Box 6615
Maharajgunj
Tel: 220474
Fax: 473956

Rafting Rivers
PO Box 6615
Kantipath
Tel: 220474
Fax: 227600

Rafting Team
PO Box 6401
Thamel
Tel: 227506
Fax: 228163

Raging River
Runner
PO Box 5184
Jyatha
Tel: 214712
Fax: 229983

Rapid Action
Nepal
PO Box 3022
Keshar Mahal
Thamel
Tel: 415506
Fax: 411878

Rapid Adventure
Nepal
PO Box 3863
Maharajgunj
Tel: 416751
Fax: 410407

River Tour
Dhobighat
Tel: 521057
Fax: 411277

Shiva's River
Adventure
PO Box 5514
Thamel
Tel: 414167/417685
Fax: 419361

Speed River
Rafting Nepal
PO Box 6651
Durbar Marg
Tel: 231039/222399
Fax: 222422

Splash River
Adventure
Thamel
Tel: 215959

Sunkoshi River
Adventure
PO Box 2735
Tel: 416963

Sunny River
Adventure
PO Box 5630
Jyatha
Tel: 215221
Fax: 229459

Surprise River
Adventure
PO Box 7263
Thamel
Tel: 425932/
412636

Ultimate
Descent Nepal
PO Box 6720
Thamel
Tel/Fax: 229389

Victoria
River Tours
PO Box 536
Tel: 226130
Fax: 224237

Viking
Adventures
Thamel
Tel: 423363
Fax: 424360

West Himalayan
Outdoor
PO Box 6955
Ganeshwor
Tel: 411790
Fax: 416417

White Water
Experience
PO Box 3973
Jyatha, Thamel
Tel: 225667
Fax: 220143

White Water
Rafting
PO Box 2118
Jyatha
Tel/Fax: 226885

Wild River
Adventure
PO Box 2525
Thamel
Tel: 229288

Wilderness
River Treks
PO Box 4834
Tel: 225683
Fax: 224785

Yeti White
Water Rafting
PO Box 2488
Kantipath
Tel: 225982
Fax: 223590

Zenith Rafting
PO Box 4163
Durbar Marg
Tel: 223162
Fax: 227132

Taxis

Kathmandu
Night Taxi Service
New Road
Tel: 224374

Kathmandu
Yellow Cab (KYC)
Tel: 420987
Sun Cab
Tel: 417978/414018

Tourist Information Centres

Kathmandu
Tribhuvan
International
Airport
Tel: 470537

Basantpur
Kathmandu
Tel: 220818

Pokhara Airport
Tel 061-20028

Bhairahawa
Tel: 071-20304

Birgunj,
Parsa
Tel: 051-22083

Janakpur
Tel: 041-20755

Kakarvitta
Jhapa
Tel: 023-20208

Visit Nepal
Secretariat
Singh Durbar
Tel: 228847

Travel Agencies & Tour Operators

Kathmandu
Adventure Travel
Nepal Ltd.
PO Box 3989
Tel: 411225
Fax: 414075/419126

Air Link
Kamaladi
Tel: 224114/
247074/246375
Fax: 221111

Akash Travels
& Tours
Jamal
Tel: 221592/220829
Fax: 230352

Akush Travel
& Tours
Tel: 423130/410652
Fax: 415775

Aloha Travels
International
Jawalakhel
Lalitpur
Tel: 527381/526414
Fax: 524571

Alpine Travel
Service
PO Box 1787
Durbar Marg
Tel: 223814/
225020/225362
Fax: 223814

Amadablam
Adventure Group
PO Box 3035
Lazimpat
Tel: 415372/415573
Fax: 416029/421882

Ankur Tours
International
Chhetrapati
Thamel
PO Box 4782
Tel: 214532/
246901/248521
Fax: 227058

Annapurna
Travel & Tours
PO Box 7145
Durbar Marg
Tel: 223530/
223763/223940
Fax: 222966/
220215

Arniko Travel
Bhatbhateni
Tel: 421861/414594
Fax: 411878/
423315

Asian Adventure
Travel & Tours
Tridevi Marg
Thamel
Tel: 424249/415506
Fax: 411878

Asuka Travel
& Tours
PO Box 1633
Hattisar
Tel: 410652/423130
Fax: 415779

Atlantic Tours
& Travel
PO Box 9006
Lal Durbar
Tel: 231525
Fax: 232573

Atlas Travel
& Tours
PO Box 1851
Durbar Marg
Tel: 224254/
221402/226606
Fax: 220082

Bagmati Tours
& Travel
PO Box 2291
Durbar Marg
Tel: 226607/221814
Fax: 229416

Broadway Travel
PO Box 5328
Fax: 481174

Buddha Travels
& Tours
PO Box 9568
New Baneshwor
Tel: 214905
Fax: 220191

Caravan
International
PO Box 3904
Durbar Marg
Tel: 243233/227434
Fax: 241177

Chino Travel
& Tours
Thamel
Tel: 415318/420647
Fax: 420050

Continental
Travel & Tours
PO Box 1278
Durbar Marg
Tel: 224299/223912

Creative Travel
& Tours
Kamladi
Tel: 424946
Fax: 412946

Culture Tours
PO Box 1147
Kantipath
Tel: 226603/
217756/226489
Fax: 227538

Danfe Travel
Center
PO Box 4429
Kamalpokhari
Tel: 420457
Fax: 415719

Deewa Travel
Service
Khichapokhari
Tel: 230944
Fax: 415719

Devi International
Travel & Tours
PO Box 8961
Thamel
Tel: 425924
Fax: 410079

Dhaulagiri Travel
& Tours
Mitra Park
Chabahil
Tel: 473308/477093
Fax: 473234

Dream Holidays
Travel & Tours
Thahity
Kwabahal
Tel: 221755
Fax: 221755

Dream Travels
PO Box 4096
Jyatha
Tel: 227236
Fax: 223515

Emery Express
Travels
Kha-1-508,
Nagashtan
Sundhara
Tel: 221726
Fax: 225277

Enjoy Nepal
Travel & Tours
PO Box 2527
Nag Pokhari
Tel: 224123/
418179/413147
Fax: 228904/222609

Everest Express
Tours & Travel
PO Box 482
Durbar Marg
Tel: 220759
Fax: 226795

Everest Travel
Service
Pratap Bhawan
PO Box 223
Kantipath
Tel: 221216/
225263/227291
Fax: 225019

Evergreen Tours
International
PO Box 11266
Thamel
Tel: 423752/3
Fax: 420274

Experience Nepal
Tours & Travels
PO Box 2811
Thamel
Tel: 411772/
414348

Explore Nepal
Richa Tours
& Travel
1st Floor, Namche
Bazaar Building
Thamel
Tel: 420710/
423064
Fax: 229304

Express Travel
& Tours
PO Box 1918
New Road
Tel: 224448
Fax: 230083

Fewa Travel
& Tours
PO Box 2949
Basantapur
Tel: 216948/
216227/213976
Fax: 222976

Fishtail Sight
Seeing Tours
& Travel
Thamel
Tel: 419673

Foothill Trekking
Lazimpat
Tel: 420505
Fax: 417347

Four Seasons
Travel & Tours
Patan Dhoka
Lalitpur
PO Box 1357
Tel: 526894
Fax: 521291

Friendly Travel
& Tours
PO Box 3921
Thamel
Tel: 212874/220171
Fax: 220171

Fuji Tour Nepal
PO Box 7350
Tripureshwor
Tel: 214452
Fax: 224431

Gaida
Wildlife Camp
PO Box 2056
Burbar Marg
Tel: 220940/227425
Fax: 227292

Gandaki Tours
and Travel
Pako New Road
Tel: 228092/
240392/241092
Fax: 221112

General Travel
& Tours
PO Box 3245
Gyaneshwor
Tel: 422754
Fax: 417979

Global Travel
Lal Durbar
Durbar Marg
Tel: 244356
Fax: 228032
Telex: 2671

Gorkha Travels
PO Box 629
Durbar Marg
Tel: 224895
Fax: 224797
Telex: 2255

Great Himalayan
Adventures
PO Box 1033
Kantipath
Tel: 216144/216913
Fax: 228066

Green Hill Tours
PO Box 5072
Thamel
Tel: 414803/416596
Fax: 424066

Gulliver's Travels
PO Box 1618
Kamaladi
Tel: 229096
Fax: 229096

Gurans Travels
& Tours
Kupondole
Lalitpur
PO Box 2727
Tel: 524232/
524732/524773
Fax: 521880
Telex: 2660

Harati Travel
& Tours
PO Box 1238
Thapathali
Tel: 222859
Fax: 229002

Hariyali Travel
& Tours
Thapathali
Tel: 233447/
233038/211689
Fax: 472208

High
Mountain Tours
PO Box 1027
Hattisar
Tel: 424386/422964
Fax: 413394
Telex: 2638

Hill's Queen
Travel & Tours
PO Box 7669
Durbar Marg
Tel: 229429
Fax: 220118

Hillary Travels
& Tours
PO Box 1771
Thamel
Tel: 416443
Fax: 472390

Him Skikhar
Travels & Tours
Thamel
Tel: 222234
Fax: 228030

Him-Hans
Travels
PO Box 9640
Tel: 417710/420985
Fax: 414779

Himalayan
Holidays Travel
Gairidhara
Naxal
Tel: 410482
Fax: 415669

Himalayan Land
Travel & Tours
PO Box 7254
Thamel
Tel: 221168/481955
Fax: 221168

Himalayan Silk
Road Travel
PO Box 9591
Tel: 416225
Fax: 416225

Himalayan
Travels & Tours
Durbar Marg
Tel: 223045
Fax: 224001
Telex: 2273 HTT
NP

Himgiri Travel
Agency
Thamel
Tel: 226048
Fax: 242325

Indra Travels
& Tours
PO Box 1145
Thamel
Tel: 220971/
223605/213837
Fax: 229967

International
Travel Bureau
PO Box 1273
Dhumbarahi
Ring Road
Tel: 418594
Fax: 418561

Intertours Nepal
PO Box 3896
Pratap Bhawan
Kantipath
Tel: 225619/
223966/214959/
476460/476461
Fax: 226610
Telex: 2620

Intourist Tours
& Travels
PO Box 207
Lake Side
Pokhara
Tel: 21213/21944
Fax: 21944

Jet Express Tours
& World
Transportation
PO Box 3269
Kamaladi
Tukucha
Tel: 413870/416871
Fax: 416870

Karthak Travels
PO Box 4963
Durbar Marg
Tel: 227555/227733
Fax: 227919

Kathmandu
Experience
Travels & Tours
PO Box 5576
Maitighar
Tel: 215998
Fax: 227521

Kathmandu
Travels & Tours
PO Box 459
Tel: 471577/472556
Fax: 225131/472379

Kathmandu-
Lhasa Tours
& Travel
PO Box 9179
Jyatha
Thamel
Tel: 240220/231060
Fax: 240220

Khetan Travel
Agency
PO Box 6156
Naxal
Tel: 222290/418911
Fax: 410171/418615

Krishna
International
Travel & Tours
Tripureshwor
Tel: 215236/212195
Fax: 229980

Kumari Tours
& Travels
PO Box 2884
Durbar Marg
Tel: 220725/
222519/225670
Fax: 225679

Lalima Travels
PO Box 3639
Kamaladi
Tel: 221111/
224114/217715
Fax: 229025/
223050

Lalitpur Tours
& Travels
Kupondole
Shahid Sukra
Marg, Lalitpur
Tel: 522508
Fax: 527013

Last Minute
Travel & Tours
PO Box 7814
Tel: 535138
Fax: 526123

Link Travels
& Tours
PO Box 6122
Tel: 230318/242359
Fax: 248214

Lotus Travel
& Tours
PO Box 2281
Kamaladi
Tel: 230570/
240106/220493
Fax: 245552

Lovely Travel
& Tours
PO Box 10352
Bagbazar
Tel: 241427/246424
Fax: 221979

Lukla Travels
PO Box 2025
Lazimpat
Tel: 417190/416503
Fax: 415346

Lumbini Travels
& Tours
PO Box 720
Kantipath
Tel: 225234/967

Mahakala Travels
& Tours
Lazimpat
Tel: 414318
Fax: 415381

Maitri Travels
& Tours
Thamel
Tel: 226655/227073
Fax: 227073/227564

Malla Travel
& Tours
PO Box 2036
Lekhnath Marg
Tel: 410635/415502
Fax: 418382

Mandap Travels
PO Box 3756
Thamel
Tel: 413859/
413321/419735
Fax: 419734

Manjushree
Travel & Tours
New Road Gate
Tel: 223574/
224922/227162
Fax: 227644

Marcopolo
Travels Nepal
PO Box 2769
Gyaneswor
Tel: 414192/
411780/420752
Fax: 418479/413641

Mayura Travels
& Tours
PO Box 7307
Thapathali
Tel: 226978/217647
Fax: 226978

Memoire Tours
& Travels
PO Box 4007
Thamel
Tel: 414270/471293
Fax: 220040

Mendo Travel
& Tours
Tridevi Marg
Tel/Fax: 423757

Mercantile
Travels & Tours
PO Box 876
Durbar Marg
Tel: 223499/
220773/223616
Fax: 225407/224839

Monal Travel
& Tours
PO Box 5002
Putalisadak
Tel: 418950/418791
Fax: 418551

Mountain
Travel Nepal
PO Box 170
Tel: 411225
Fax: 414075/419126

Mountain
Voyages Nepal
PO Box 3357
Thamel
Tel: 224049/223100

Muktinath Travel
& Tours
PO Box 2004
New Road
Tel: 221385/223539
Fax: 220543

Namaste Travels
PO Box 2566
& 3313
Maitighar
Tel: 225405/
227484/212918
Fax: 226590

Natraj Tours
& Travel
PO Box 495
Ghantaghar
Kamaladi
Tel: 222906/
222532/222014
Fax: 227372

Nepal Cultural
Experience
Special Interest
Tours
Kupondole
Lalitpur
PO Box 9082
Tel: 522494/536704
Fax: 524944

Nepal Express
Travel Service
PO Box 2987
Durbar Marg
Tel: 221277/
223348/227432
Fax: 227983

Nepal Holidays
International
Travel & Tours
PO Box 10925
Thamel
Tel: 413367/425140
Fax: 224621/425140

Nepal Phoenix
Travels
PO Box 759
Nagpokhari
Tel: 415617
Fax: 417542

Nepal Travel
Agency
PO Box 1501
Ramshah Path
Tel: 413188/421013
Fax: 420861

Newa Travel
Thamel
Tel: 226790/228404
Fax: 419419

Nilgiri Tours
& Travels
PO Box 151
Damside
Pokhara
Tel/Fax: 61-20969

Nuptse Travels
PO Box 4848
Thamel
Tel: 412833/
416686/416956
Fax: 411682

Nyatpolo
Travel & Tours
PO Box 3811
Hattisar
Tel: 416224
Fax: 229967

Om Travels
& Tours
PO Box 5355
Thamel
Tel: 419019/417369
Fax: 419858

One World Travel
Kamaladi
Tel: 422783
Fax: 474627

Orchid Tours
& Travel
PO Box 4730
Kamal Pokhari
Tel: 416167
Fax: 414904

Osho World
Travel
PO Box 5211
Karmachari
Sanchaya Kosh
Building
Thamel
Tel: 423426/
223758/224258
Fax: 423427

Overseas
Travels Nepal
PO Box 4890
Ravi Bhawan
Tel: 272060/80
Fax: 271443

Pacific Travel
& Tours
PO Box 6138
Gairi Dhara
Tel/Fax: 418444

Pagoda Travel
& Tours
PO Box 4666
Basantapur
Tel: 231501/225266
Fax: 227881

Panas Travel
Agency
PO Box 709, Naxal
Tel: 423735
Fax: 227795

Panorama Tours
& Travel
PO Box 3507
Nagasthan
Sundhara
Tel: 214290

Paradise Tours
& Travels
PO Box 2388
Kantipath
Tel: 225898
Fax: 419250

Parbat Tours
& Travels
PO Box 3634
Durbar Marg
Tel: 410207

Pashupati Tours
& Travels
PO Box 2292
Kantipath
Tel: 217682/224695
Fax: 229082

Pawas Travel
& Tours
PO Box 709
Thamel
Tel: 220541
Fax: 227333/227795

Peace & Happy
Travels & Tours
Lakeside
Baidam-6
Pokhara
Tel: 61-21827
Fax: 61-20879

Peace Travel
& Tours
PO Box 2075
Kantipath
Tel: 225638/
226567/226069
Fax: 227569

Pokhara Tours
& Travels
PO Box 827
New Road
Tel: 222038/
224613/412778
Fax: 412687

Poon Adventure
& Travel
PO Box 10695
New Baneshwor
Tel: 23068
Fax: 220143

Prashant Travel
& Tours
PO Box 2442
Durbar Marg
Tel: 226151/
224798/222566
Fax: 224408

President Travel
& Tours
PO Box 1307
Durbar Marg
Tel: 220245/
221774/228288
Fax: 221180

Princess Travels
& Tours
PO Box 2488
Kantipath
Tel: 225982/217098
Fax: 223590

Puja Travels
& Tours
Pulchowk
Harihar Bhawan
Lalitpur
Tel: 523659
Fax: 522477

Pumori Travel
& Tours
PO Box 8630
Durbar Marg
Tel: 214697

Rainbow Travels
& Tours
Kantipath
Tel: 216153/
214463/212266
Fax: 227431

Rath Nepal Tours
& Travels
PO Box 10691
Nagpokhari
Naxal
Tel/Fax: 419320

Ravis
Adventure Nepal
PO Box 4476
Maharajgunj
Tel: 410688/419523
Fax: 411567

Reed Travels
Thamel
Tel: 243471/226585
Fax: 243564

Rhino Travel
Agency
PO Box 5026
Thamel
Tel: 420316/416918
Fax: 417146

Royal Himalaya
Tours & Travel
PO Box 10102
Boudha
Tel: 471548/
478566/472588
Fax: 480856

Saathi Nepal
Travel & Tours
Kamaladi
Tel: 424070
Fax: 418919

Sagarmatha
Travels & Tours
New Baneshwor
Tel: 217116/
217418/232232
Fax: 526467

Saiyu Travel
PO Box 3017
Durbar Marg
Tel: 224248/221707
Fax: 226430

Savana Travel
& Tours
Kashmiri Takiya
Durbar Marg
Tel: 220714/
227341/231748
Fax: 221351

Sayambhu
Travels & Tours
Maitighar
Tel: 213018/454
Fax: 231454

Sema
International
Tours & Travels
Lazimpat
Tel: 415374
Fax: 412746

Seva Travels
& Tours
PO Box 2325
Thamel
Tel: 230412
Fax: 419317

Shakti Travel
& Tours
PO Box 913
Lazimpat
Tel: 415083/457
Fax: 415083

Shambhala
Travels & Tours
PO Box 4794
Durbar Marg
Tel: 225166/
231890
Fax: 227229

Shangri-La Tours
PO Box 989
Kantipath
Tel: 226138-9/
225552
Fax: 227068

Shanker Travels
& Tours
PO Box 529
Lazimpat
Tel: 411465/
412465/413479
Fax: 419614

Shashi's Holidays
International
Travel & Tours
PO Box 4588
Ranipokhari
Kantipath
Tel: 227018/
216208
Fax: 228868

Sherpa Society
Travel Co.
Jyatha
Thamel
Tel: 227233
Fax: 470153

Sherpa Travel
Service
PO Box 500
Kamaladi
Tel: 222489/
220243/227312
Fax: 227243

Shikhar Nepal
Tours & Travels
PO Box 3893
Thamel
Tel: 228955/
228163/217255
Fax: 229967

Shiva Travel
PO Box 3545
Thamel
Tel: 215650/212256
Fax: 220969

Sierra Travels
& Tours
Durbar Marg
Tel: 222985/228194
Fax: 228194

Siris Travels
PO Box 4176
Putalisadak
Tel: 412877/
412790/421587
Fax: 419250

Sita World
Travel Nepal
Tridevi Marg
Thamel
Tel: 418363/
418738/423418
Fax: 227557/423422

Sitara Travels
PO Box 6841
Kamalpokhari
Tel: 411008/419570
Fax: 220549

Sky Line Tours
& Travel
Basantapur
Durbar Square
Tel: 212191/216567
Fax: 223217

Span Travel
& Tours
PO Box 1109
Kamalpokhari
Fax: 1-415410

Sport & Nature
Hattisar
Tel: 414890
Fax: 416873

Star Tours
& Travels
Thahity
Kwabahal
Thamel
Tel: 241573/244091

Student Travels
& Tours
Air House
Maitighar
PO Box 4701
Tel: 225452/224730
Fax: 226248

Sukunda Travel
& Tours
PO Box 4376
Thamel
Tel: 412399/213546
Fax: 417555

Sungava
International
Tours & Travel
PO Box 12337
Thamel
Tel: 225293/243714

Suruchi Travel
& Tours
PO Box 5029
Jamal
Tel: 226654
Fax: 226314

Surya Travel
& Tours
PO Box 2786
Kantipath
Tel: 414259/410402

Swiss Travels
& Tours
PO Box 3856
& 4753
Khichapokhari
Tel: 222318/224395
Fax: 227707

Takura Travels
PO Box 5053
Tel: 422250/422911
Fax: 418245

Tibet Travels
& Tours
PO Box 7246
Tel: 231130
Fax: 228986

Tika Travel
& Tours
Kantipath
Tel: 217279

Times Travel
& Tours
Aeroflot Bldg.
Kamaladi
Tel: 223219/247058
Fax: 225875

Tiny Tours
& Travels
PO Box 1348
Shiva Arcade
Basantapur
Tel: 213416

Tour D'Heritage
Nepal
Kupondole
Tel: 536090/521348
Fax: 535090

Tourist Service
PO Box 1855
Dharma Path
Tel: 220745/
220851/247844
Fax: 220040

Trans Globe
Travel & Tours
PO Box 8070
Naxal
Tel: 413294
Fax: 419385

Trans
Himalayan Tour
PO Box 283
Durbar Marg
Tel: 223871/224854
Fax: 227289

Travel
Connection
PO Box 4268
Tel/Fax: 429023

Travel
International
PO Box 4431
Kantipath
Tel: 415222

Travel Lines
Tours & Travels
PO Box 4849
Hattisar
Tel: 419018
Fax: 415145

Travel Link
Service
PO Box 9057
Ikhapokhari
Chhetrapati
Tel: 212849/231618

Travel Market
PO Box 9649
Hattisar
Tel: 423266/
418526/421716
Fax: 423267

Travel Team
Durbar Marg
Tel: 225678/223643
Fax: 223737

Trimurti Travels
& Tours
Naxal
Tel: 410854/
270229/278458
Fax: 278913

Universal Tours
& Travels
PO Box 939
Kantipath
Tel: 212080/
216080/214192
Fax: 220267

Vardhan Travel
& Tours
PO Box 469
Durbar Marg
Tel: 216880/224238
Fax: 225415

Victoria Travel
& Tours
PO Box 536
Kamaladi
Tel: 226130
Fax: 224237

Village Travel
& Tours
Trivedi Marg
Thamel
Tel: 423502/3
Fax: 421440

Vision Tours
& Travels
PO Box 10666
Thapathali
Tel: 244116
Fax: 244114/229407

Visit Nepal
Travel & Tours
PO Box 7150
Dharmapath
Tel: 244700/
245700/228385
Fax: 220210/423456

Welcome Travel
& Tours
PO Box 9167
Jyatha
Tel: 226146
Fax: 229982

Windrose Travel
Service
PO Box 1544
Durbar Marg
Tel: 220155/
225181/220794
Fax: 225275

Wonderland
Holidays Tours
& Travel
Hotel Yak &
Yeti Road
Laldurbar
Tel: 226469
Fax: 226479

World Travels
Nepal
PO Box 2155
Durbar Marg
Tel: 226275/227810
Fax: 226088

Yak Adventure
Travel Ways
Kamaladi
Tel: 422758/410411
Fax: 419778

Yangrima Tours
& Travels
PO Box 2951
Kantipath
Tel: 226062/225608
Fax: 227628

Yatri Tours
PO Box 5912
Kantipath
Tel: 228933/214715
Fax: 227600

Yeti Travel
& Tours
PO Box 76
Durbar Marg
Tel: 221234/
221739/221754
Fax: 226152/3

Ying Yang
Travels
PO Box 10410
Thamel
Tel: 423358/9
Fax: 421701/414653

Zen Travels
& Tours
PO Box 4441
Tel: 424146/415260
Fax: 412945

Zenith Travel
PO Box 4163
Durbar Marg
Tel: 223162/
223502/227064
Fax: 227132

Trekking/ Mountain- eering

Kathmandu
Above the Clouds
Trekking &
Mountaineering
PO Box 2230
Thamel
Tel: 416909
Fax: 416923

Adventure
Himalayan
Trekking
PO Box 3028
Tel: 416402
Fax: 227945

Adventure
Tenzin Trekking
PO Box 3647
Tel: 414405
Fax: 415289

All Nepal
Trekking
PO Box 4048
Thamel
Tel: 229445
Fax: 220143

Amadablam
Trekking
PO Box 3035
Lazimpat
Tel: 415372/3
Fax: 416029

Annapurna
Mountaineering
& Trekking
PO Box 795
Durbar Marg
Tel: 226299
Fax: 226153

Apisaipal Treks
& Expedition
Centre
PO Box 5966
Tel: 413873
Fax: 416850

Asian Trekking
PO Box 3022
Trivedi Marg
Tel: 413732/415506
Fax: 411878

Atlas Trekking &
Mountaineering
PO Box 5767 &
10119
Samakhusi
Tel: 230458
Fax: 410845

Back Track
Adventures
Sifal
Tel: 471504
Fax: 471322

Barun Adventure
Trekking
PO Box 5123
Chhetrapati
Tel: 212928
Fax: 228179

Bhrikuti
Himalayan
Treks/Asian
Encounters
PO Box 2267
Tel: 417459
Fax: 413612

Blue Mountain
Treks &
Expedition
PO Box 6846
Trivedi Marg
Tel: 412985
Fax: 229234

Chomolhari
Trekking Agency
Durbar Marg
Tel: 231039
Fax: 222422

Circuit Treks
PO Box 1273
Maharajgunj
Tel: 418594/413397
Fax: 418561

Cosmo Trekking
Lazimpat
Tel: 416226
Fax: 415275

Crystal
Mountain Treks
PO Box 5437
Naxal
Tel: 412656
Fax: 412647

Culture Trekking
Chamber Bhawan
Kantipath
Tel: 226603/
226489/241436
Fax: 227538/227392

Dhaulagiri
Trek House
PO Box 2583
Chuchepati
Chabahil
Tel: 470495
Fax: 227919

Discover
Himalaya Sherpa
Trekking &
Mountaineering
PO Box 3597
Jyatha
Tel: 226487
Fax: 222026

Eco Trek
PO Box 2455
Thamel
Tel: 417420
Fax: 271570

Equator
Expeditions
PO Box 8404
Thamel
Tel: 425800
Fax: 424944

Everest
Adventure
PO Box 647
Dilli Bazar
Tel: 412516
Fax: 415126

Everest Express
Trekking
Durbar Marg
Tel: 220759
Fax: 226795

Everest Express
Trekking
PO Box 482
Durbar Marg
Tel: 223233
Fax: 226759

Everest Trekking
Kamaladi
Tel: 226358/220558
Fax: 224031

First
Environmental
Trekking
PO Box 8056
Thamel
Tel: 417343/424346
Fax: 423855

Foothills
Trekking
PO Box 3966
Lazimpat
Tel: 420505
Fax: 417347

Four Season
Trekking
PO Box 2369
Jyatha
Tel: 214237/222637
Fax: 226952

Ganesh Himal
Trekking
PO Box 3834
Thamel
Tel: 414185/416282
Fax: 417121

Glacier Safari
Treks
PO Box 2238
Thamel
Tel: 412116
Fax: 418578

Gorkha Treks
PO Box 4509
Lainchour
Tel: 413806
Fax: 229380

Great Himalayan
Adventure
PO Box 1033
Kantipath
Tel: 216144/216913
Fax: 228066

Green Lotus
Trekking
PO Box 1091
Tel: 419138
Fax: 227919

Guides For
All Season
PO Box 3776
Gairidhara
Tel: 419035
Fax: 416047/412647

Guiding &
Trekking
Expedition
Service
PO Box 2081
Tel: 413645
Fax: 414184

Happy
Adventure Trek
PO Box 5708
Thamel
Tel: 418811
Fax: 220161

Hard Rock Treks
& Expedition
PO Box 10220
Thamel
Tel: 228067
Fax: 229967

Hari's Tara
Trekking
PO Box 708
Thamel
Tel: 418685/420064
Fax: 414099

Highlander
PO Box 3005
Thamel
Tel: 217613/416896
Fax: 419317

Highlander
Trekking &
Expedition
PO Box 10987
Thamel
Tel: 243158/
424563/424066
Fax: 419317

Him Treks
PO Box 2383
Sano Gaucharan
Tel: 419233
Fax: 414390

Himalayan
Adventures
PO Box 1946
Maharajgunj
Tel: 411866
Fax: 410858

Himalayan
Excursion
PO Box 1221
Thamel
Tel: 418407
Fax: 418913

Himalayan
Expeditions
PO Box 105
Thamel
Tel: 213229/229031
Fax: 226622

Himalayan
Explorers
PO Box 1737
Sano Gaucharan
Tel: 419858
Fax: 411069

Himalayan Hill
Treks
PO Box 1066
Tel: 521057
Fax: 411277

Himalayan
Holidays
PO Box 5513
Gairidhara
Tel: 410482
Fax: 272866

Himalayan
Journeys
PO Box 989
Tel: 226139/8
Fax: 227068

Himalayan
Nature Treks
PO Box 3879
Tel: 416704/422746
Fax: 229380

Himalayan
Pathfinder Treks
PO Box 6569
Thamel
Tel: 425700/
426700/2418055
Fax: 220210/423456

Himalayan
Waves Trekking
Thamel
Tel: 416831
Fax: 420637

Iceland Trekking
& Expedition
PO Box 3385
Thamel
Tel: 217509
Fax: 414440

In Wilderness
Trekking
PO Box 3043
Boudhanath
Tel: 473700/478109
Fax: 470760

Inner Nepal Trek
PO Box 536
Kamaladi
Tel: 226130
Fax: 224237

Kailash
Himalayan Trek
PO Box 4781
Bagh Bazar
Tel: 229249/412049
Fax: 223171

Karyang Kurung
Treks &
Expedition
PO Box 3890
Thamel
Tel: 412663
Fax: 227795/229459

Ker and Downey
Nepal
Maharajgunj
Tel: 416751/410355
Fax: 410407

Khumbila
Mountaineering
& Trekking
PO Box 731
Kamalpokhari
Tel: 413166
Fax: 416559

Kohinoor Trek
Service
PO Box 2782
Nazal
Hattisar
Tel: 410558/412506
Fax: 422441

Lama Excursions
PO Box 2485
Durbar Marg
Tel: 220186/226706
Fax: 227292

LamjungTrekking
& Expeditions
PO Box 1436
Kupondole
Tel: 522964
Fax: 226820

Langtan Ri
Trekking
PO Box 7103
Thamel
Tel: 423586/360
Fax: 424267

Last Frontiers
Trekking
PO Box 881
Lainchour
Tel: 416146
Fax: 414512

Lotus Treks &
Expedition
Kamaladi
Ganeshthan
PO Box 2282
Tel: 230570/
240106/220493
Fax: 220495

Malla Treks
PO Box 5227
Lekanath Marg
Tel: 418387/410089
Fax: 423143

Mandala
Trekking
PO Box 4573
Kantipath
Tel: 228600
Fax: 227600

Marcopolo Treks
& Expeditions
PO Box 2769
Tel: 414192/418832
Fax: 418479/413641

Maya Trekking
PO Box 1178
Boudha
Tel: 470266
Fax: 470261

Mendo Trek &
Expedition
Tridevi Marg
Thamel
Tel/Fax: 423757

Monal Trekking
PO Box 5002
Kamaladi
Tel: 418950
Fax: 418551

Mount Makalu
Trekking
PO Box 3039
Jyatha
Tel: 417116
Fax: 414024

Mountain Cougar
Trekking
PO Box 1889
Jyatha
Thamel
Tel: 225630
Fax: 227919

Mountain
Adventure
Trekking
PO Box 3440
Thamel
Tel: 227040
Fax: 525126

Mountain
Travel Nepal
PO Box 170
Lazimpat
Tel: 414508
Fax: 414075

Mountain Way
Trekking
PO Box 59
Rastra Bank
Chowk, Pokhara
Tel: 61-20316/
21171/23317
Fax: 21240

Natraj Trekking
Kantipath
Tel: 226644
Fax: 227372

Natural Explorer
Treks &
Expedition
Tridevi Marg
Thamel
Tel: 226613
Fax: 224247

Nepal Hanuman
Trekking
PO Box 2926
Thamel
Tel: 417157
Fax: 227919

Nepal Himal
Treks
PO Box 4528
Baluwatar
Tel/Fax: 419796

Nepal Insight
Trekking
PO Box 3851
Tel: 470299
Fax: 226820

Nepal
Panorama Trek
PO Box 4529
Thamel
Tel: 228033
Fax: 413056

Nepal Trekhouse
PO Box 1357
Tel: 528838/535181
Fax: 526990

Nepal Trekking
& Expedition
PO Box 4564
Kamaladi
Tel: 217715/224189
Fax: 221111/229025

Nepal Valley
Trekking
PO Box 5535
Thamel
Tel/Fax: 1-413707

Nepal Wildlife
Adventure
PO Box 1985
Maitidevi
Tel: 413303
Fax: 472529

Nilgiri Treks &
Mountaineering
PO Box 6911
Thamel
Tel: 414059/424544
Fax: 414050/222026

Overseas
Adventure
Trekking
PO Box 1017
Thamel
Tel: 229145
Fax: 418758

Pabil Treks
PO Box 2607
Kamalpokhari
Tel: 418532
Fax: 414184

Pariwar Trekking
PO Box 2414
Thamel
Jyatha
Tel: 232825/248813
Fax: 222835

Peake Trekking
Chhetrapati
Thamel
Tel: 243296
Fax: 245137

Pleasure Trekking
PO Box 303
Tel: 226499
Fax: 220143

Poon Hill
Trekking
PO Box 2994
Jyatha
Thamel
Tel/Fax: 229122

Potala Trekking
PO Box 7008
Thamel
Tel: 410303
Fax: 220143

President Treks
& Expedition
PO Box 1307
Durbar Marg
Tel: 220245/226744
Fax: 221180

Rai International
Trekking
PO Box 4627
Durbar Marg
Tel: 222726
Fax: 226820

Regal Excursions
PO Box 4325
Tel: 421738
Fax: 412546

Rowling Trek
& Expedition
PO Box 3870
Hotel Yak &
Yeti Plaza
Tel: 228823
Fax: 525919

Royal
Mt.Trekking
PO Box 10798
Durbar Marg
Tel: 217780/241452
Fax: 229380/245318

Sagarmatha
Trekking
PO Box 2236
Kantipath
Tel: 411110
Fax: 415284

Shangri-La
Holidays
PO Box 771
Lazimpath
Tel: 415283/
415754/ 420252
Fax: 420239

Sherpa & Swiss
Adventures
PO Box 1805
Tel: 416218
Fax: 415567

Sherpa Alpine
Trekking Service
PO Box 2390
Thamel
Tel: 227239
Fax: 220143

Sherpa
Cooperative
Trekking
PO Box 1388
Durbar Marg
Tel: 224068
Fax: 227982

Sherpa
Excursions
PO Box 1556
Maharajgunj
Tel: 411510
Fax: 415577

Sherpa Nippon
Trejks
PO Box 7132
Thamel
Tel/Fax: 412744

Shiva Trek &
Expedition
PO Box 5385
Baluwatar
Tel: 412334/420789
Fax: 419704

Snow Leopard
Trekking
PO Box 1811
Naxal
Tel/Fax: 414719

Sports & Nature
PO Box 3048
Hattisar
Tel: 414890
Fax: 416873

Star Treks &
Expedition
PO Box 6566
Thamel
Tel: 410418
Fax: 226763

Summit Nepal
Trekking
PO Box 1406
Kupondole
Height
Lalitpur
Tel: 525408/521810
Fax: 523737

Tai Himal
Trekking
PO Box 3017
Durbar Marg
Tel: 221707
Fax: 226430

Tawache
Trekking
PO Box 2924
Jyatha, Thamel
Tel/Fax: 227295

Thamserku
Trekking
PO Box 3124
Naxal
Narayanchour
Tel: 414644
Fax: 227042

Third Pole
Trekking
PO Box 5503
Thamel
Tel: 410834
Fax: 414387

Tibet Travel Tour
Tridevi Marg
Tel: 231130/228986
Fax: 415126

Tip & Top
Trekking
PO Box 1760
Kesharmahal
Thamel
Tel: 419973
Fax: 220143

Trans Himalayan
Trekking
PO Box 283
Durbar Marg
Tel: 224854
Fax: 227289

Trekking Team
PO Box 6401
Thamel
Tel: 227506
Fax: 228163

Universal
Alpine Service
PO Box 939
Kantipath
Tel: 216080
Fax: 220267

Venture Treks &
Expeditions
PO Box 3968
Kantipath
Tel: 221585/
244651/225780
Fax: 220178

Vision Himalayan
Trekking &
Expedition
PO Box 8546
Chhetrapati
Tel: 213588
Fax: 223315

White Magic
Unlimited
Trekking
PO Box 2118
Thamel
Tel: 227885
Fax: 226885

Wilderness
Experience
PO Box 4065
Tel: 417832/
410518
Fax: 222026

Wonderland
Trekking
PO Box 3056
Thamel
Tel: 225293
Fax: 414184

World Peace
Trekking
PO Box 550
Thamel
Tel: 417170
Fax: 220143

Yeti
Mountaineering
& Trekking
PO Box 1034
Ramshahpath
Tel/Fax: 410899

Yeti Trekking
PO Box 2488
Kantipath
Tel: 225982/
217098
Fax: 223590

Youth & Student
Trek &
Expedition
PO Box 4701
Air House
Maitighar
Tel: 240463
Fax: 226348

Zenith Trekking
PO Box 4163
Durbar Marg
Tel: 223162
Fax: 227132

Restaurants

American
Ground Round
Jyatha
Thamel
Tel: 229294

Chinese
Arniko Room
Hotel De
L'Annapurna
Durbar Marg
Tel: 221711

The China Town
Lazimpat
Tel: 410298

Gompa
The Bluestar
Hotel
Tripureswor
Tel: 228833

Imperial Pavilion
The Malla Hotel
Lekhnath Marg
Tel: 410620

Nanglo Chinese
Room
Durbar Marg
Tel: 222636
New Road
Tel: 240138

Omei
Jyatha
Thamel
Tel: 226412

Rice and Bowl
Saket Complex
Tripureswar
Tel: 246409

Tian Rui
Thapathali
Tel: 243078

Tien Shan
Hotel Shangri-La
Lazimpat
Tel: 412999

Continental
Base Camp
Coffee Shop
Hotel Himalaya
Kupondole
Tel: 523900

Coffee Shop
Hotel De
L'Annapurna
Durbar Marg
Tel: 221711

Garden
Summit Hotel
Kupondole, Patan
Tel: 521894

The Lotus Cafe
Hotel Manang
Thamel
Tel: 410933

Lumbini
Coffee Shop
The Bluestar Hotel
Tripureswar
Tel: 228833

Rum Doodle
Thamel
Tel: 414336

Nanglo Cafe
and Pub
Durbar Marg
Tel: 222636

Fastfood
The Bakery Cafe
Durbar Marg
Tel: 224707

Jawalakhel
Tel: 522949
New Road
Tel: 240138

Hot Breads
Durbar Marg
Tripureswar
Jawalakhel
Tel: 221331

French
The Gurkha
Grill Soaltee
Holiday Inn
Crowne Plaza
Tahachal
Tel: 272550

The Kokonor
Hotel Shangri-La
Lazimpat
Tel: 412999

Everest Steak
House
Chhetrapati
Thamel
Tel: 217471

Rendezvous
The Malla Hotel
Lekhanath Marg
Tel: 410620

Health Food
New Orleans
Cafe and Blue
Note Jazz Bar
Thamel
Tel: 4257367

Tibet Canteena
Chhetrapati
Thamel
Tel: 216741

Indian
Soaltee Holiday
Inn Crowne Plaza
Tahachal
Tel: 272550

Far Pavilion
The Everest Hotel
New Baneswar
Tel: 220567

Ghar-E-Kabab
Hotel De
L'Annapurna
Durbar Marg
Tel: 221711

Jewels of Manang
Hotel Manang
Thamel
Tel: 420314

The Himalchuli
Soaltee Holiday
Inn Crowne Plaza
Tahachal
Tel: 272550

Moghlai Handi
Tripureswar
Tel: 243338

Moghul Mahal
Tripureswar
Tel: 245776/232227

Tansen
Durbar Marg
Tel: 224707

Third Eye
Thamel
Tel: 227478/229187

Vaishali
The Bluestar Hotel
Tripureswar
Tel: 228833

Italian
The Alfresco
Soaltee Holiday
Inn Crowne Plaza
Tahachal
Tel: 272550

Fire and Ice
Thamel
Tel: 225390
Ext: 342

Laxmi Narayan
Steak House
Thamel
Chhetrapati
Tel: 227188

Pizzeria
Panorama
Thamel
Tel: 216863

Tara
The Malla Hotel
Lekhnath Marg
Tel: 410620

Cafe Wintergarden
Durbar Hotel
Durbar Marg
Tel: 243170

La Dolce Vita
Thamel
Tel: 419612

Les Yeux
Thamel Chowk
Tel: 213722

Mamma Mia
Pizzeria
Thamel

Japanese
Maki
Durbar Hotel
Durbar Marg
Tel: 243170

Fuji
Kantipath
Tel: 225272

Koto
Durbar Marg
Tel: 226025

Kushi-Fuji
Durbar Marg
Tel: 220545

Sunset View
Hotel Sunset View
New Baneswar
Tel: 229172

Aji-No Silk Road
Thamel
Tel: 423681

Korean
Seoul Ari-Rang
Durbar Marg
Tel: 232105

Nepali
Bhanchha Ghar
Kamaladi
Tel: 225172

Krishnarpan
Dwarika's
Kathmandu
Village Hotel
Batisputali
Tel: 470770

The Chalet
Hotel Himalaya
Lalitpur
Tel: 523900

Kathmandu
Kitchen
Durbar Marg
Tel: 223850

Thamel House
Thamel
Tel: 410388

Royal Kasturi
Kantipath
Jyatha
Tel: 212082

Newari
Murxana
Kamaladi
Tel: 416731

Bhoe Chhen
Lal Durbar
Kathmandu
Tel: 221811

Russian
The Chimney
Hotel Yak & Yeti
Durbar Marg
Tel: 413999

Thai
Baan Thai
Durbar Marg
Tel: 243271

Tibetan
Sherpaland
The Everest Hotel
New Baneswar
Tel: 220567

Mountain View
Mountain View
Guest House
Kumaripati
Lalitpur
Tel: 524168

Utse
Jyatha, Thamel
Tel: 228952

Vegetarian
The Naachgar
Hotel Yak & Yeti
Durbar Marg
Tel: 413999

Chandi-Ki-Thali
Ghar-e-Kabab
Hotel De
L'Annapurna
Durbar Marg
Tel: 221711

Mithai Sweets &
Snacks
Tripureswar
Tel: 243338

All pictures by **Mohamed Amin** and **Duncan Willetts** except the following:

Fredrik Arvidsson: Pages 1, 2-3, 90, 101, 102 (Bottom), 114, 115, 144, 147, 149, 165, 190 (Top), 220, 225, 274.

Tim Greenwood: Pages 190 (Bottom), 227, 279, 281, 282.

Index

(Illustrations are indicated in bold)